THE ABYDOS TRIAL
FROM THE FILES OF THE
OFFICE OF PARANORMAL RESEARCH
BOOK 2

Terence West

THE ABYDOS TRIAL
FROM THE FILES OF THE
OFFICE OF PARANORMAL RESEARCH
BOOK 2

DOUBLE DRAGON

Chapter One

It was cold and dreary, but what was new? The dark, gray clouds had been threatening rain all day, but had just let loose a light sprinkling. Such was life in Seattle during the winter. He pulled his collar up around his neck to fight against the biting wind. Picking up his pace, he began to move briskly along the old, paved road. Dark streaks of asphalt cut across the faded gray surface of the road, signs that at least the county had tried to patch it. Tall weeds and grass had begun to reclaim what was originally theirs by jutting up through cracks and old potholes. Nature had a way of doing that.

He tilted his head back and stared at the clouds. They were a cocktail of black, various shades of gray and a few stray tendrils of white. The storm was fast approaching. The crack of thunder echoed in the distance causing his skin to crawl. Thrusting his hands into the deep pockets of his black, wool coat, he wrapped it tightly around his chest. The cold was penetrating his bones, making him feel perpetually damp.

He was late for work, which in itself wasn't that unusual. He had been on several occasions lately. Warnings had been issued, of course, but this time, it was different. This time, he would be fired. There were no other options in his mind. His supervisor would check the time cards just before lunch, as he always did, then haul out the chopping block.

He was going to have to drag his sorry carcass home after lunch and tell his girlfriend he lost his job. It wasn't bad enough that the bank had repossessed his car two weeks ago, but they were also falling behind on their mortgage payments. He felt a knot begin to form in his stomach, while acid threatened to backwash into his throat. He hated bills. They were the very bane of his existence. Such was the life of an artist.

Jax was a writer. From the moment he came home from the processing plant, that was all he did. When he was in college, he had at least had a computer to use, but now he sat at the dining room table in the center of his small singlewide trailer and wrote with pencil and paper. It was maddening to a certain degree, living hand to mouth, but that was his life now. No more depending on Mommy and Daddy for his weekly cash stipend, no more tooling around in the Lexus before class, no more mansion on the lake. It was all up to him now, and it was all because of a woman. His woman.

How he hated her for it.

It wasn't entirely her fault, he knew, but she was convenient, and he needed someone to blame. Jax had, at least, been a willing accomplice. During their junior year of college, he and Sara had met and fallen in love. They were both English majors with a passion for the written word. He couldn't count the nights they had spent just reciting their favorite poems to each other, her favorite was Yeats, his— Shakespeare. They knew they were perfect for each other, but his parents had thought differently.

He pushed the thoughts away. That was the last thing he needed right now. Reaching into his jacket pocket, he pulled out a red and white soft-pack of cigarettes and peered inside. Two smokes left. He considered his options for a minute, then decided to go ahead. He was already late as is. Grabbing the butt of the cigarette with his lips, he pulled it free of the pack. Depositing the pack back in his pocket, he produced a small silver lighter and lit the cigarette. Jax ran his hand through his short, messy dark hair. The rain was making it worse, but by this point, he didn't care. He took a long drag off the cigarette and slowly exhaled the smoke.

Jax felt the rain begin to swell. The drops were growing in size and frequency. He quickened his pace as a cold shiver ran down his spine. Twisting his head around, he glimpsed a dark form standing amidst the tall weeds just off the road.

It wasn't moving.

Jax stopped. Turning his body ever so slightly, he focused his attention on the form. He couldn't tell what it was through the rain. Focusing his eyes, he began to make out the vague outline of a woman. A feeling of dread passed over him. Something wasn't right here... He couldn't quite put his finger on it, but there was a definite twinge of danger. Jax's senses were buzzing. Every nerve in his body was screaming for him to run, but curiosity overrode them. He stood firm in his spot, waiting, watching.

He suddenly felt a presence to the rear. Spinning around, he came face to face with another large black form. Stumbling back, he stifled a gasp in his throat. She was wearing a long, black, form-fitting robe with dark lace trimming. A hood was pulled up, while a thin veil of black lace fell over her face. All he could make out was the hint of her lips. He took another step back as they curved into a sultry smile.

"What do you want?" Jax stammered.

7

"To release you," the woman replied. Her voice was unnatural. It had an almost metallic tone to it, as if a machine were reproducing it. "I can give you everything you ever wanted."

"I don't know who the hell you are, lady, but I've got to get to work. I don't have time to screw around."

The woman raised her arm and extended her hand in one fluid motion. "I think you will make time for this."

Jax felt compelled to take the woman's hand. He raised his hand slowly toward hers, but yanked it back at the last moment as if he had been burned. "Who are you?" he asked pleadingly.

"I am the way. Take my hand, Jax. Everything will be fine."

Jax took a deep breath. A tingle of electricity washed over his body as an overwhelming, peaceful sensation set in. He wasn't afraid anymore. Reaching up, he took the woman's hand.

***

Lexy Weiss watched a bolt of lightning arc across the dark sky. The stream of pure electricity flashed for an instant sending a blanket of seething white light down upon the city. The light permeated every corner, every alley and every haven of the night, but only for an instant. The familiar rumble of thunder followed its bright counterpart, announcing their power and glory.

She lifted her hand and pressed it against the glass feeling the cool air outside. Storms usually had a rejuvenating effect on her, but this night, it

8

was different. There was too much on her mind to find any ease in the Earth's majesty. She watched the rain hit the window and run down as it made its way back to the ground, where it would re-join the water table and start the process again.

Touching her forehead to the glass, she let the coolness soothe her throbbing headache. Turning slightly, she glanced over at the small kitchenette in her apartment. She wondered quickly if she should take another aspirin this late at night. It would probably interrupt her sleep, but then what didn't lately? Lexy looked out the window across the Emerald City—Seattle, Washington—through the haze of rain. It was strikingly beautiful, as all major cities are when seen from this high up. The lights twinkled on and off across the city as brownouts affected them and as people arrived home or went to sleep. She wondered for a moment if the storm had anything to do with the twinkling lights and if she should fish out the emergency candles from her hall closet.

Lexy pulled herself away from her seventeenth-floor window and looked around her small apartment. The floor plan, which was roughly rectangular, had a small living room situated in the middle, with a kitchen to the left and bedroom and bathroom, the right. It was sparsely decorated, but then again, it was all she could afford on her teaching salary. An old green couch (she found it at Goodwill one afternoon fresh out of college) sat in the middle of the room flanked on both sides by two large bookcases, while a small coffee table lived in front of the couch amidst the sea of tan carpet. A battered television was situated on a faux wood entertainment center in front of her.

On the far back wall there was a large, wooden desk her parents had given her during her freshman year of college. On it, her one luxury, a state-of-the-art computer she claimed was an "educational tool", but in reality, she spent more time in chat rooms and message boards than researching lesson plans.

She loved the Internet. It was the one place where she could go and leave herself behind. On occasion, she had logged into a chat room as a man, just to see what kind of response she would get. She had a set of "cyber friends" she had never met in real life, but she knew the deepest, darkest secrets of their lives. The Internet was strange that way. She found that people had no problem speaking their minds there, saying things she couldn't even begin to explain the rationale of. It was anonymity at its finest. That's probably why she liked it so much. She could leave her mundane existence behind for an hour or two and become the person she wished to be in real life—charming, sexy, but at the same time, friendly and wise. She thought about logging on, but reconsidered.

A stack of ungraded papers sat in the middle of her coffee table she had assured the students would be corrected by tomorrow. Her workload wasn't heavy and she'd had ample time to get the job done, she'd just been procrastinating. Fresh out of college, she'd accepted the first position that had come down the pipe. She was a young, headstrong history teacher with a mind to change the system. Now, five years later, she had slipped into the routines of her work: read a chapter, take a test, read a chapter, take a test. Gone were the inspired lectures of her first two years, now replaced by "reading time". The students were still learning the subject matter, of that she was certain, but she wasn't instilling the wonder and awe she had felt sitting in her high school history class as she listened to true tales of great battles, heroes and the evolution of our society.

She couldn't pinpoint the exact moment when she lost her lust for educating, but she knew what the culprit was, or rather "who". She had bonded with several teachers on the staff who had been at this same job for what seemed to Lexy, like eons. They had grown cynical of their profession, and some, even fearful of the students. She had listened to these old crows sit around the teacher's lounge and rattle on about how they needed raises, that their classrooms needed better equipment and their general dismay with the state of the education system in America. At first, Lexy found herself arguing with her colleagues, but now, she found herself sitting in on these discussions, sipping a cold cup of coffee and dreaming of how her life could've been much different. They had "infected" her with their cynicism, but she knew no one was to blame but herself. She could've easily taken her lunch somewhere else, or used her free period to grade papers, but instead, she found herself day after day in the teacher's lounge, listening to the same old tired rhetoric.

But that wasn't what was really bothering her, was it?

She moved through the living room and sank down into the couch. She watched a small cloud of dust rise from the cushions, then slowly settle back down. Focusing on the large window in front of her, she watched another bolt of lightning tear through the heavens on its suicidal path toward the ground. Every night, the dreams came. She was so exhausted, but she didn't want to go to sleep, unwilling to face the horrible images again.

Those women…those poor women…but they weren't real, right? They were just figments of her overactive imagination, right? They couldn't be real. She had been watching the news religiously lately and no word of their fate had been uttered. The police couldn't keep something like that bottled up, could they? Or perhaps they just hadn't found the bodies yet. Lexy shook her head. It was all a dream, she convinced herself; something stress related. That's all it could be.

She gave the clock on the wall a quick glance. It was closing in on two in the morning, and she had to be to work in five hours. Her first class was at seven-thirty and she needed at least half an hour of prep time beforehand. She needed to sleep. Her body needed time to recharge. She could feel the heaviness in her limbs. They were already beginning to succumb to sleep.

Sitting forward on the couch, she ran her hands slowly over her knees and then leaned her head back. Tightening the muscles in her neck, she twisted her head to the right, then to the left. It popped several times in both directions. She felt the usual twinge of numbness, but it returned to normal. She knew she would have to stop that nasty habit if she didn't want to end up with arthritis in her neck. She smiled at the thought. It was an old wife's tale. Popping your neck or knuckles didn't result in arthritis, she told herself, but it probably didn't do much to prevent it either. Arching her back, she felt her tired muscles stretch out.

Standing up, she looked one last time out the window at the rain, then closed the drapes. She had to go to bed. It was Monday tomorrow, and she didn't want to face the week with a lack of sleep. Reaching down, she grabbed the tests off her table and stacked them neatly together. She slid a small silver paperclip over them and deposited them on her computer desk as she headed for her bedroom. Looking back into her living room before she clicked off the lights, an odd thought crossed her mind. *Maybe I need a pet to keep me company...* Flipping off the light switch, she adjourned to her cramped bedroom.

This room, much like her computer, was something she splurged on. She loved to lie in bed Sunday mornings, smoke cigarettes and read magazines. It was her private time. Her own little slice of the week when she could just retreat and relax. She didn't allow herself to think about work, bills, or anything else that caused stress in her life. This was *her* time. Because this was the room she found herself in the most, she outfitted it accordingly. A large, four-poster bed was pressed against the back wall with a round, wooden nightstand accompanying it. A beautiful lamp sat in the middle of the stand, along with several books and magazines she had been perusing. Long, lush drapes hung over the window and a matching rug took up most of the floor in the room.

She moved toward a tall mirror that hung on the opposite wall and stared at the reflection. She was wearing a simple pair of gray sweats and a white t-shirt that showed off her midriff. Her curly brown hair was held up messily behind her head by a tortoise-shell barrette, while a slim pair of reading glasses perched on her nose. She was twenty-nine years old, on the very verge of thirty, an age she had always associated with "old".

She was slim, but not quite in the best shape of her life. She was beginning to see the results of her inactive lifestyle on her body. She glanced down at her breasts. She had always secretly wished they were bigger. Maybe her life would've been better if they had been... She let out an uncomfortable laugh. She didn't want to believe that, but somewhere, back in the deep, dank, recesses of her mind, she did. She stared at the dark bags beneath her brown eyes. Along with her lips, her eyes had always been her favorite feature. A boy in high school had told her that she had "the most beautiful bedroom eyes". That had been a defining moment in her life. She had gone from awkward teenager to a woman at that instant. She wondered for a moment whatever happened to that boy, but quickly let the thought slip away. It wasn't worth dwelling on.

Moving to the side of her bed, she removed her glasses and set them carefully on the nightstand. Reaching into her hair, she pulled out the clip and deposited it next to her glasses. Running her hands through her shoulder length hair, she let her head fall back as a yawn escaped her lips. She slipped comfortably into her unmade bed and pulled the blankets up to her chin. Snapping off the light, she watched a blue-white crackle of light fill her room and fade away.

She closed her eyes. Luckily, Spring Break was only a week away and then she could finally catch up. Rolling onto her side, she adjusted the pillows beneath her head and let go. She needed to sleep....

***

Sara was sitting alone. She had chewed her nails down to stubs on her fingers and had been chain-smoking ever since. Flipping her dirty brown hair out of her eyes, she leaned back in her seat at the kitchen table. She took a long, deep breath, then returned her attention to the papers scattered before her. All of them bills.

She grabbed a small, blue wallet off the edge of the table and flipped it open. Thumbing through the check register, her mood worsened. They were several thousand dollars in debt, and she had no way of paying that money. Jax was their only source of income. She glanced at her small butane lighter. *It would be easy to burn this place to the ground*, she thought.

"Where is that son of a bitch?" she yelled angrily. It was no secret between the two that their love had drowned some time ago in a sea of debt. She had encountered the phrase, "living on love" in her studies. She scoffed, mildly amused. *Love* doesn't pay the bills.

Sara heard a loud knock at the door. Quickly pulling the bills into a pile and crushing out her cigarette, she moved toward the front door. Leaning to her right, she lifted two of the blinds and peeked through the window. There was nothing there. Sara furrowed her eyebrows and turned away from the door. That was when she heard another knock at the back door.

Sara jumped. Pressing her hand against her chest, she walked quickly through a small hallway toward the back door. She gently placed her hands on the cool, metal door and listened. "Who is it?" she asked. There was no reply. After a moment, she slid her hand down the door to the handle. Sara slowly pushed open the door. Taking a step outside onto the small, rickety porch, she glanced around the house. It was raining and a fog had set in killing visibility. Their house was at least a mile in every direction from neighbors, leaving her all alone. She squinted her eyes and peered into the dense fog trying to make out shapes and forms. There was nothing.

"This isn't very funny!" Sara yelled to no one and everyone at the same time. "Knock it off!"

Taking a step back into the house, she pulled the door closed behind her. It was some neighbor's kid, she assured herself, playing a prank on her. She muttered several profanities under her breath as she twisted the small silver lock. Turning to her right, she stopped and fell back to the floor.

"Jax?" she asked softly.

It was Jax. She could easily tell. He was still wearing the clothes he had left in two days ago, but something wasn't quite right. He was motionless. Sara couldn't even see his chest rising and falling with breath. She leaned slowly forward and rolled

16

onto the balls of her feet. Standing up, she reached for the hallway light switch. She laid her fingers gently on the rocker switch and clicked on the light and gasped. "What in God's…?"

Before she had even finished her question, Jax was upon her with animal fury, ripping and tearing at her flesh. Sara screamed out, but her voice was drowned in a gurgle deep in her lungs.

***

Lurching straight up in bed, Lexy felt a trickle of sweat run down her forehead and over her lips. Her mind was frantic with the images she had just seen. They were so vivid and detailed, as if she was actually there, but that couldn't be. She glanced over at her small alarm clock. Two hours had gone by. Her chest heaved as she tried to catch her breath. Reaching over to her nightstand, she clicked on her lamp.

A cold shudder passed over her body, then nausea gripped her stomach. Leaping out of bed, she looked at the red mess she had been sleeping in. It was splattered haphazardly on the walls around the bed, while small droplets were scattered about the floor. Tears welled up in her eyes. Her mind had gone into a state of shock at the sight. Looking down, she saw her body was also covered with blood.

Was it hers?

She hysterically ripped off her shirt and sweats and began to examine her body. There were no signs of cuts or wounds, but the blood was everywhere. It had permeated her clothes and was

17

still wet on her skin. She didn't know what to do, then a single thought erupted in her brain.

Running naked through her apartment, she snatched her telephone off the stand in the kitchen. Lifting the white receiver to her mouth, she dialed 911.

"911 operator. Please state the nature of your emergency," the calm female voice answered over the phone.

"Please help me!" Lexy shouted. "Everything's covered in blood! I don't know what to do!"

"What's your address?" the voice asked quickly. "Ma'am?"

Lexy strained her mind, but couldn't come up with the information. Looking at her phone, she could see her own bloody fingerprints on its white surface. She gasped and dropped the phone to the floor feeling revulsion at the sight. Lifting her hands, she stared in horror at the red substance covering her fingers and the darker areas where clotting had begun to take place. She had to get the blood off. She had to get clean. Charging back down the hall, she turned into the bathroom and jumped into the shower. Twisting the knobs on the shower all the way on, she sank down into the corner as the water began to wash over her. She was shaking as she watched the blood mix with the water and swirl down the drain.

***

Thomas Weiss sat down at the kitchen table in his luxurious home and opened his morning newspaper. Lifting a dark blue coffee mug from the table, he took a long sip of the hot liquid inside. He looked out the kitchen window at the beautiful morning dawning over Washington D.C. It was going to be a beautiful spring day. A small smile passed over his lips. Turning away from the window, he dug into the paper.

The telephone rang.

Setting the paper aside, he moved swiftly toward the phone hanging on the wall. He had to grab it before it woke up his wife. He had always been an early riser, while his wife liked to sleep in. He was just glad he could afford the lifestyle that allowed her to do that. Grabbing the phone off the base, he cleared his throat once, then pressed the talk button.

"Chairman Thomas Weiss," he answered confidently. "Dad?" he heard a weak, sobbing voice ask.

"Lexy? Is that you, honey?" he asked, the confidence quickly fading from his voice. "What's wrong?"

A pause.

"I'm in jail," Lexy replied hesitantly. "What in God's name happened, Lexy?" Another pause.

"I murdered someone," Lexy said through her tears.

Thomas felt the phone slip from his grasp as he stumbled back. His legs were weak rubber beneath him. Not thinking, he fell back toward his chair, but missed, hitting the floor. Pulling himself up off the floor, he quickly reached down and retrieved the phone. "Everything's going to be all right," he assured her. Without another word, he hung up the phone.

19

Chapter Two

Nick Bishop sat quietly in the back of a bookstore, slowly paging through a thick volume on his lap, mainly looking at the pictures. Stopping, he glanced around the small store. It was no more than one hundred feet wide with three rows of bookshelves occupying the center. On the far walls there were various displays featuring crystals, incense and small colorful statues of various gods. A lone female shopkeeper stood quietly behind the register near the front of the store watching over the few patrons she had. Behind her stood a large artificial waterfall built into the wall surrounded by several homemade dreamcatchers and other various trinkets. She was tall and fairly attractive, but not Bishop's type.

The first time she asked him to meditate around a crystal, he knew he would scream.

This was "Ancient Ways", a bookstore that specialized in hard-to-find occult books. It always had the smell of rose petals, despite some of the older books' best efforts to fill the store with their musty scent. If Bishop was looking for a specific book that, for some reason, was not contained within the Office of Paranormal Research's vast library, this is where he came. It was comfortable here. He knew the owner and generally felt accepted. This was a place where you could discuss anything from politics to black magic and not catch an odd look.

Bishop stood and replaced the book back into its space on the shelf. Adjusting his knee-length, black leather jacket, he dug into the pocket and produced his wallet. Stopping in front of the shopkeeper, he smiled. "How's business, Sandy?"

Sandy Weich looked up from her register and returned Bishop's smile. "Same old, Bish. What's new down at the Office of Paranormal Research?"

"Buried knee deep in paperwork, that's what," Bishop admitted. "Lately, we've just been visiting various cranks along the eastern seaboard listening to them spin tales of their own encounters with the paranormal. Not very exciting."

"Sorry to hear that," Sandy admitted as she adjusted her glasses. She was just a hair shorter than Bishop with medium length blonde hair and blue eyes.

She usually had her hair tied up and wore loose fitting clothes, even though her figure could handle anything she threw at it. "I hear there are several fine openings in the fast-food industry."

Bishop laughed. Lifting his hand, he rubbed it quickly through his short, messy brown hair. "Can I take a look at that crystal necklace behind you?"

"This one?" Sandy asked.

"No," Bishop pointed to a small white crystal hanging from a black leather band. "That one."

"Someone special in your life?" Sandy asked with a grin as she plucked the necklace from the rack.

"No, but that doesn't mean I can't keep trying," Bishop replied with a smirk and a twinkle in his blue eyes. Holding the crystal in the palm of his hand, he gave it a quick, cursory glance, then nodded. "I'll take it. How much?"

"Ten dollars," Sandy replied as she punched the keys on her tired register. Bishop dropped a twenty-dollar bill on the counter, then slipped the necklace into his pocket. Waiting for his change, he returned his attention to Sandy.

"What were you reading over there?" she asked as she handed him his change and receipt.

"Oh," Bishop said with a laugh, "a book on monsters. I have this fascination with the Loch Ness Monster."

"Couldn't you get the OPR to fund a research trip to Scotland?" Sandy asked.

"I don't know. I never thought of that," Bishop admitted. "I've always wanted to see what was actually in the Loch." He looked at the blonde woman seriously and lowered his voice, "If it's not a damned monster, then what the hell is it?"

Sandy reached over the counter and pinched Bishop's cheek between her thumb and forefinger. "You're so cute," she said mockingly.

Bishop brushed her hand away from his face with a laugh. "Thanks, Sandy."

"Anytime, Bish," Sandy said with a soft smile.

Bishop turned away from the counter and started to walk toward the door. Reaching down to his shirt collar, he lifted his black sunglasses and slipped them on. Stepping out into the bright spring morning sunlight, he glanced around the streets of Washington D.C. He turned and gave Sandy one final wave as he moved away from the large glass windows of her shop. His next stop was breakfast. He glanced down at his watch and smiled. He still had two hours before he had to be at work and he intended to make full use of them. On most days, he had to clock in by nine, but Chairman Weiss had given his team half the day off today. Bishop couldn't figure out why he had given them the morning instead of the afternoon, or why Weiss just hadn't given them the full day off.

Turning the corner, he noticed two young women crossing the street in his direction. Looking up ahead, he saw a car barreling down the street toward them. They weren't jaywalking and had the light, but it didn't look like the car was going to stop.

"Look out!" Bishop shouted. Springing off his toes, he charged toward the women. Catching the car, a late model sedan, in his peripheral vision, he could see that it had no intention of stopping. Focusing on the women, he could see them talking obliviously amongst themselves. Diving forward, he wrapped his arms around their waists and through pure adrenaline alone, pushed them out of the way just as the sedan sped past. Quickly rolling onto his back, he tried to catch a glimpse of the driver, but could only see a mass of black hair. She looked somehow familiar, though....

"Oh, my God, what the hell are you doing?" one of the women asked angrily.

Bishop stood up and dusted off his jacket with a smile. "I'm sorry, I had to...."

"Get away from us, you pervert!" the woman shouted. "I have a can of mace in my purse," she admitted boldly.

"Didn't you see the car?" Bishop asked confused. The woman started to dig into her purse.

"But I...."

"We'll call the cops if you don't leave us alone."

Bishop turned to his left and pointed up the street. "Didn't you two see the car that was about to hit you?" He looked down the street. "It was a dark blue sedan…." he let his words trail off. There was nothing there. The connecting street had no intersection for several blocks, and the car was gone.

"I didn't see anything," the first woman said angrily. "You better get out of here." She had her white can of mace firmly in her hand and pointing at Bishop. "I know how to use this," she threatened.

Bishop shook his head. "I'm sorry. I don't understand." Holding up his hands in surrender, he quickly moved away from the two women. "I'm sorry," he reiterated. He watched as the two women turned away and start to run in the opposite direction. Making it back to the sidewalk, Bishop turned and looked down the street again. "What the hell is going on here?"

The sudden chirp of his cellular phone startled him. Reaching into his pocket, he felt something sharp prick his finger. Lifting it out, he saw the broken chards of the crystal necklace. "Great." Grabbing his phone, he begrudgingly hit the talk button. "Bishop here." He listened quietly to the voice on the other end for a moment, then nodded. "I'm on my way."

So much for my morning off, he thought as he stepped into the street to hail a cab.

***

Zachary Cane was the oldest member of his OPR team. An import from Britain, he had lived in

24

the United States for close to thirty years now. He hated to admit it, but this country had rubbed off on him. He had always been proud of his heritage, but it was hard to maintain in a country that views things a little differently than he did. He would never outright claim that he was American, but this place was now more his home than England.

He stood in front of the bathroom mirror in his apartment staring at himself. He was in his late fifties. His neatly trimmed goatee had gone gray and his temples were beginning to follow suit. He lifted a brush off the sink and pulled it through his brown hair. Setting it back down, he switched to his blue electric razor. Clicking it on, he began to run it over his neck and cheeks, careful not to hit his goatee and sideburns.

Pulling the razor away, he looked at the salt-and-pepper hairs caught in the blades. He hated getting older. He had always thought that men aged gracefully, but his face was a roadmap of crow's feet and small scars that chronicled his life. He wasn't bad looking by any means; he just realized that all the buxom twenty-year old women were finally out of his league…unless he had money. Pulling on a dark gray t-shirt, he moved out of his bathroom and looked around his apartment. He didn't have money.

It was a tiny apartment with only a small living room, an equally sized kitchen, one bathroom and one bedroom. The living room was scattered with research books and papers from his work. Several old pizza boxes and an occasional Chinese food carton rounded out the mess. A large television stood in the middle of the room in front of a dark blue recliner. An image of Bigfoot was paused on the screen from a documentary he had been watching earlier that morning.

Turning away from the living room, he moved into the kitchen. Reaching up into a cabinet, he removed a short, plastic glass and turned toward the refrigerator. Setting the glass down, he pulled open the door and peered inside. The fridge was essentially empty. A carton of milk was perched in the door with its two neighbors, the molding slices of cheese. A lonely jug of orange juice sat on the bottom shelf with an old carton of eggs and a brown head of lettuce still in the plastic wrap. Sighing, he retrieved the orange juice and set it next to his glass, then he closed the refrigerator. He twisted off the lid and started to pour the pulpy liquid into the glass, but stopped.

"Why dirty a glass?" he asked himself. "I'll just have to wash it later." He turned and looked at his sink. It was piled high with dishes and glasses, and what looked like a half-eaten bag of cookies. Lifting the jug of juice to his lips, he took three large swallows before dropping it down to the counter. Ignoring the jug, the glass and his dishes, he moved back into his bedroom.

Cane immediately began to sift through the various piles of clothing that dominated the floor of his bedroom. Finding what he was looking for, he instinctively lifted it to his nose. With a grunt, Cane pulled his face away from the rank garment and tossed it back. Skirting around the piles as if they were landmines, he headed for his closet. Sliding the door open, he was greeted by dozens of empty hangars and several pairs of shoes tossed loosely on

26

the floor. Shaking his head, he glanced down at his attire. He was wearing a pair of black Dockers with his gray t-shirt and a pair of shoes. He usually liked to wear at least a collared shirt to work, but laundry day wasn't until the end of the week, so he would have to make do.

Cane remembered that he had half a day off as he glanced at the digital clock by his bed. It was just after nine o'clock. Walking back out into the living room, he glanced around the disaster area, then headed for the coat closet. Reaching inside, he removed his favorite black leather jacket and pulled it on. It hung just above his knees and had several tears and bruises. In Cane's opinion, this was the mark of a good leather jacket. Grabbing his keys off the table next to his chair, he started to head toward the door when he heard his phone ring. He stopped momentarily and listened. It was probably the office, and since he was headed there anyway, he decided to ignore it. He knew the machine would get it. Locking the door behind him, he headed down the hallway toward his elevator.

The answering machine beeped once and Cane's greeting message played: "This is Cane. Leave a message."

"Cane, this is Dawn. Are you there?" She paused. "If you're there, please pick up. We have an emergency." She waited for an answer, after a moment, she decided to continue. "Chairman Weiss' daughter is in jail on suspicion of murder.

He's called an emergency meeting at ten this morning. If you get this message, please call me."

***

Kelley Windel strode through the halls of the Office of Paranormal Research wearing a long black skirt, a tight, white t-shirt and a light jacket. Her blonde hair was in a ponytail, except for two small wisps that hung down on the left side of her face. She was considered by many to be exceptionally beautiful.

Kelley, a nurse by training, had an unfortunate encounter with shadowlike beings in her hometown of Stone Brook, Florida before joining the OPR. There, she was rescued by Cane and Bishop, and in the end, even helped defeat the phantom menace. It was then the invitation to join the team was issued. She hadn't walked out of the ordeal unscathed though. Her chest and arms were a patchwork of scars, courtesy of the shadows that had attacked and tortured her. She had even lost the love of her life in the attack. She thought about Joanne almost every day, but her thoughts always turned morbid when she remembered the lifeless look on Joanne's face after the shadows had finished with her.

Taking a deep breath, she listened to the click of her high heels on the polished hallway floors of the building. Glancing left, she looked at the numerous pictures that adorned the walls. Some were supposed photos of ghosts, UFOs and other paranormal hallmarks. There was even a blurry picture of the woods that supposedly showed the dark outline of the Mothman. Kelley snickered at the thought. What a preposterous tale, and that anyone could believe it was beyond her comprehension.

Returning her attention in front of her, she saw her office door looming ahead. The door was closed. Either that meant she was the first one in this morning, or whoever was in there just didn't want to be disturbed. She hoped for the former. She wanted to catch up on some paperwork and take advantage of a quiet office. Reaching down for the door handle, she twisted it once to check if it was locked. To her dismay, the door opened. Pushing the door open, she saw Dawn sitting at her desk with phone in hand.

She and Dawn Lassiter didn't get along at first. Kelley was never really sure why. Perhaps she enjoyed being the token woman on the team, or maybe it was that Dawn just didn't like her. Whatever the case may have been, things were different now. In the months that Kelley had been on the team, she and Dawn had grown very close. They often spent their off hours together, which was more than she could say for the rest of the team. Kelley had spent a few rare evenings with Cane, but they just seemed like they were from different worlds. Bishop, on the other hand, was charming and always fun, yet he was so focused on the paranormal, he often didn't talk about anything else for hours. There was nothing wrong with that—in small doses.

Kelley glanced around the office. The wall to her left was entirely composed of glass, giving them a beautiful view of Washington D.C. To her right was a long corkboard littered with newspaper clippings and a large map of the United States with various colored pins sticking into what seemed like random locations. At the far end of the office was a row of tall, black filing cabinets they used to store some of their research and case files. She never understood why Dawn and Cane kept the cabinets in the office. Five floors below them, the OPR had a massive records library located in the basement. Every file or clipping even remotely pertaining to anything paranormal was stored there and available at a moment's notice.

"Good morning," Kelley said as she walked into the office.

Dawn looked up at her partner and smiled. "Morning," she whispered, her attention still on the phone.

Kelley envied Dawn. In her opinion, Dawn was the perfect woman: she was gorgeous with long curly brown hair and deep green eyes. She always appeared immaculately kept, and was knowledgeable on many subjects. Dawn, much like Cane and Bishop, favored long black leather jackets, but she wore them with more *style*.

"Why are you in so early?" Kelley wondered as she moved across the office the four shared. Walking around Dawn, she pulled out the chair to her desk and sat down. She immediately kicked off her shoes and placed them neatly beneath her chair. It was a bad habit.

"Chairman Weiss called me in this morning at seven," Dawn replied, the phone still firmly attached to her ear. "Yes, I'm still holding," she said.

Kelley looked at her quizzically.

Dawn slipped her hand over the phone. "I'm on hold with the Seattle Police Department."

"What's going on?" Kelley asked.

30

"I'll tell you when everyone gets here." She looked at Kelley seriously. "This isn't good."

Chapter Three

Two men walked briskly into the Seattle Police Department's lobby and moved directly toward the reception desk. Both were dressed in dark trench coats with dark suits beneath. Each man looked as if he was in his late thirties and they were both exceptionally groomed. Not a hair on their heads seemed to be out of place, despite the constant rain outside, and no trace of facial hair could be seen.

The officer behind the desk looked up at the two men. His glance showed only passing interest as he continued to work on the newspaper's latest crossword. "Can I help you?"

The two men dug into their pockets and produced small billfolds. Flipping them open, they dropped them on the desk in front of the young officer. The first man leaned an elbow onto the desk. "I'm Special Agent John Fowler, and this is my partner, Greg Allen. We're with the Federal Bureau of Investigation," he added, purposely overenunciating the words.

The young officer looked up from his crossword with a continued lack of interest. "What can I do for you, Agents?"

"We're here to see Captain Hart," Fowler replied coolly. "We're expected," he added.

The officer nodded as he reached for the black telephone on his desk. Punching in a three-digit number with the eraser end of his pencil, he waited for an answer. "Yeah," he said slowly after a moment, "I have two FBI agents waiting up here for you. They say you're expecting them." He listened briefly, then nodded. Returning the phone to its cradle, he pointed his thumb over his shoulder. "Captain will see you now."

Fowler smiled and shook his head. "Thanks. You've been a great help." Fowler grabbed their badges off the desk.

The officer looked down at his crossword quickly. "Five letter word synonymous with the FBI," he tapped his pencil once and smiled. "I got it, D-I-C-K-S."

Motioning to Allen, Fowler moved past the officer into the heart of the police station. It was much cleaner than he expected. Being a New York native, Fowler had seen his share of police precincts while working as a cop and then with the FBI. The floors were never this clean, nor were the desks. Each was arranged in a similar manner: a desk blotter in the center with a lamp off to one side and a cup of pencils on the other. Some had a few personal effects, such as picture frames or small trinkets, but for the most part, they were all very sanitized.

John Fowler was a ten-year veteran of the FBI. He had spent time as part of the New York Police Department before moving to the Bureau. Trained as a criminal profiler, both he and his partner were attached to the Violent Crimes Division. They worked on mass murderers, serial killers and homicides of particular brutality. He was a just a little over six feet tall, thin, but built wide at the shoulders. He had sandy blond hair neatly parted down one side, and a pair of deep-set blue eyes. He wore a perpetual scowl. Even in the brightest conditions, it appeared as if his eyes were in

33

shadow. Something, he had confessed to Allen, he had picked up as a beat cop in New York.

Greg Allen, on the other hand, was much younger than Fowler. He had been accepted to the academy right out of college with his shiny new degree in criminology. He was slightly taller than Fowler, and thinner. He had almost the same style haircut as his partner, but it was a little more modern in design. His brown hair matched his dark-colored eyes perfectly, adding to his "baby face" appearance. Allen had been assigned to Fowler and the Violent Crimes Division fresh out of Quantico. Getting assigned to the Violent Crimes Division was a sure-fire way to get noticed by superiors and climb the ladder of success. He hoped one day to have his own plush office on the fourth floor of the J. Edgar Hoover Building and a gold nameplate that read "Deputy Director".

Fowler and Allen stopped in front of a translucent door with the captain's name stenciled on it. Reaching forward, Fowler tapped heavily on the glass twice.

"Come," they heard a gruff voice say from inside.

Reaching down to the handle, Fowler pushed the door open and stepped inside. Captain Hart's office was decorated with dozens of pictures of him shaking hands with celebrities he had met over the course of his career. There were a few that Fowler didn't recognize, but they were probably local celebrities and politicians. Captain Hart, a heavy-set man roughly the same age as Fowler, was stuffed behind his thick wooden desk, fiddling with a pair of silver handcuffs. Two chairs sat facing his desk with a third in the corner occupied by another man.

Fowler strode into the office like he owned the place. He had a confidence in his stride. He was good at his job, and he wanted everyone to know it. Stopping, he extended his hand to Hart. "Agent John Fowler."

"Good to meet you, Agent," Hart replied in the same rugged voice they had heard outside the door. "Have a seat."

"Thank you," Fowler said politely as he sat down. "This is my partner, Agent Greg Allen."

Allen shook Hart's hand as he sat down.

Hart looked the two men over, then pointed to the man at the rear. "Agents, I would like you to meet Detective Jim Spenser. He's in charge of this case."

Spenser nodded at the two agents. He was a well-built man in his forties with short cropped dark hair. His face was hard and gaunt, looking as if it had been sculpted with a chainsaw. He was wearing a dark gray pin-striped suit with a black tie. If anything, he looked more like a mobster than an officer of the law.

"I don't know why they sent you out here," Hart admitted as he locked and then unlocked the cuffs. "We have the killer in hand."

"We think, as the Bureau does," Fowler started, "that you have the wrong person."

Hart started to argue, but Fowler held up a hand to silence him.

"Please, let me finish." He waited for a moment to see if Hart would reply. Once satisfied, he continued. "We've done an extensive profile using the information available to us on the previous four deaths and came to the same conclusion: a woman could not have committed this crime. The sheer strength alone required to strangle the victims, then mutilate them would almost instantly rule out a woman."

"I think that's a sexist statement," Hart shot back. "You're making a general accusation based on gender. How do you know what this woman's strength is?"

"Our research also shows women are generally not serial killers," Allen added without missing a beat. "Statistically, most mass murderers and serial killers are men."

"Now you're quoting statistics to me?" Hart asked insulted. "We have the girl in lock-up right now. She came in last night with the latest victim's blood all over her, and she knew intimate details of the crime scene. We haven't released any information to the press, how could she know that?" Hart didn't wait for an answer. "With the blood alone, any jury in the country would convict her."

"I tend to agree," Fowler said, "but you would be leaving the real killer on the street. Do you want to be the department known for sending an innocent woman to prison?"

"That's not for me to decide," Hart said, slamming the cuffs on his desk. "My men merely collect the evidence. We don't make assumptions of innocence or guilt."

"Let's cool off here," Spenser said from the back of the room. He had a low and gravelly voice that commanded attention. It wasn't the tone or inflection, but rather the volume. Spenser spoke quietly, forcing everyone to remain quiet to hear him. "Captain, I think we need to hear what these federal boys have to say."

Hart looked at Spenser, then back to the Agents. "All right," he said after a deep breath, "what does your profile say?"

"We're looking for a white male between the ages of thirty-five and forty. As with most serial killers, this man may have suffered some trauma as a child to warp his psyche. He may have had abusive parents, or been molested as a child, maybe even taken advantage of by an authority female figure in his life and that's why he strikes out at women. His motives are still unclear, but he seems to only strike at women. No male bodies have been found that match his MO.

"From the position of the bodies and the pooling of the blood inside them, we think he strangled his victims from behind, then lowered them to the ground. He didn't drop them, because we would have found tell-tale bruising on their backs."

"Why does *he* mutilate them after they're dead and take organs?" Hart asked, emphasizing the gender of the subject.

"To take their power away," Allen speculated, "or to remove their gender. In two of the murders, the women's breasts were cut off and in another, the uterus was removed. This man not only hates the female gender, but everything that makes them women as well. It's not enough for him to just kill them, he must destroy what they are.

"This man is probably between five foot nine and six feet tall," Fowler continued. "He's more than likely built well with good upper body strength."

"Are we looking for someone with medical training?" Spenser asked. "Not necessarily," Allen replied. "From what we understand, the organs were not removed, rather, hastily hacked out. Anyone with a fifth-grade level of intelligence could identify most of the major internal organs. He may have studied to be a doctor, but never completed the schooling."

"So basically, we're hunting Jack the Ripper." Hart asked after a brief pause.

"We think we understand his pattern," Fowler added, ignoring Hart's comments. "If we're right, he will strike again within the next few days."

"And if you're wrong?" Hart asked.

"Then by all means, prosecute the woman you have in lock-up," Fowler said with a smirk, "if you want that on your conscience."

Hart shot up from his desk and moved swiftly toward the agents, despite his size. "Listen here, you smug son of a bitch, I don't have to sit here and be bullied in my own office. I want you two out of here, right now."

Fowler and Allen stood and started toward the door. Grabbing the handle, Fowler turned around and looked back at Hart. "As of right now, the FBI is taking over this case."

Both Hart and Spenser started moving toward the two agents angrily. "The government expects your full cooperation," Fowler added as he and Allen exited the office.

"That rat bastard," Hart muttered to himself.

Spenser looked over at his friend questioningly, "Do they have jurisdiction?"

Hart nodded. "'Fraid so." He slumped down on the edge of his desk. "Looks like you'll be working with a couple of G-men on this one, Jim."

Spenser nodded slowly. "I can't help but wonder if they were right. What do you make of their profile?"

"It's garbage," Hart answered cynically. "I still think we're on the right track with this Weiss woman. She's the key to all this." Hart stopped to think for a moment. "Get out on the street, Jim. Kick over every stone and find out what the fuck is really going on out there."

Spenser stood and moved toward the door. Stopping, he turned back to his captain. "I've got a bad feeling about this one."

Hart stood up and patted Spenser on the back. "Me too, Jim. Me too."

***

Bishop, Dawn, Cane and Kelley were seated at their desks when Chairman Weiss entered the room. He was dressed impeccably in a suit and tie, and despite the horrible news earlier this morning, seemed relatively well composed. He was carrying a small folder of papers under his arm as he moved around to the front of the office. Dropping the papers on Dawn's desk, he stood with his back to the windows facing his team.

"My daughter Lexy is being accused of murder," he stated without hesitation. "She was arrested in her apartment at four this morning,

39

Pacific Standard Time. They found her babbling incoherently in the shower, completely naked and covered with someone else's blood. Upon questioning this morning, she admitted to knowing crime scene details that have not been made available to the press or public regarding at least seven previous murders. This, along with the blood found on her and in her apartment, places her at the scene of the latest murder. I want you to use all your resources and find out what happened to my daughter." Weiss turned and started out of the office. Stopping just short of the door, he placed his hand on the doorframe. "I would consider this a personal favor, Cane." Letting his hand fall, Weiss walked briskly out of the office without looking back.

Cane leaned back in his chair. "What do you make of that?"

"He waved the truce flag," Dawn said as she started to rifle through the pages in the folder Weiss had left. "No egos on this one."

"Have you guys ever worked a straight murder case before?" Bishop asked. His hands were folded in front of him as he leaned on his desk.

"Counting the 'Phantoms' case last year?" Dawn thought for a moment, "No."

Cane leaned forward and looked at Kelley. "What did you pick up off Chairman Weiss?"

Kelley shook her head. "He's broken inside. He usually has a wall up around his thoughts, but today, I think any of you could've read them. He's genuinely concerned about the safety and well-being of his daughter."

Cane turned to Dawn. "What's in the file?"

40

"Plane tickets to Seattle, Washington," Dawn said as she flipped through the contents, "a contact's name—one Captain Tyrrell Hart of the local P.D., crime scene reports from the previous four murders, and the statement taken from Lexy Weiss this morning."

"How the hell did he get that?" Bishop asked in amazement. "Weiss has connections," Cane said dryly.

"Four murders?" Kelley wondered. "She's the suspect in a serial killer murder case?"

"It appears so," Dawn said while perusing the reports. "What time does our plane leave?" Cane asked.

Dawn quickly read the tickets. "Four o'clock this afternoon." She handed the tickets to Cane, "And we're traveling first class."

"A welcome surprise," Cane said with a grunt. "Looks like we don't have time for details right now," he said to his team. "We'll brief once we land in Seattle."

"Cane," Bishop said slowly, "what are we going to do? We're paranormal investigators and this case is obviously rooted in the normal. We may not even be able to see Lexy. The police probably have her locked up tight."

Cane looked at Bishop, then at Kelley and Dawn. "We'll just have to do our best." Slipping the tickets into his jacket pocket, he stood. "Let's meet back here at two in the afternoon, then we'll all head to the airport together. Agreed?"

The other three members of the team nodded.

"I don't usually make speeches," Cane conceded, "but this is a member of our family that's in trouble. Let's do this one right."

Chapter Four

Lexy was alone with her thoughts. Curled up in the corner of the main interrogation room, she awaited the return of the police. Anything, even more interrogation, would be better than the dreams and the blood. She began rummaging through childhood memories buried deep within her subconscious trying to find even a moment of release, but there was none to be had. She couldn't escape the gravity of the situation. It was slowly crushing her beneath its weight.

She had been in this same room, with the exception of being forced to change into the standard orange jail clothes, all morning. She wondered briefly if the police had bothered calling her school's principal to let him know she wouldn't be in today, or for that matter, for the rest of her life. She couldn't help but sound grim. Yesterday, she had been a high school teacher grading papers and looking forward to Spring Break, now she was being accused of a crime she may or may not have committed. She couldn't be sure.

She shook her head. How could she not be sure? Either she did it, or she didn't. There was no gray area here. You couldn't *almost* kill someone and end up in pool of blood. She knew vital crime scene details, from where the bodies were found, to how the killer mutilated them. That alone could convict her, but the kicker was most definitely the blood. How had the last victim's blood ended up in her apartment if she had not been at the scene of the crime? One of the officers had informed her earlier they were still running tests on the blood to make an

43

exact match with the victim, but early indications were positive.

Lexy leaned her head back against the cool concrete wall behind her and slowly turned her attention to the large mirror in the front of the room. She had read enough books and watched enough cop movies to know it was a two-way mirror, and they were probably watching her right now. If not watching, at least videotaping to review later. She scanned the interrogation room. The walls were concrete painted white with a gray floor. A thick, red line ran down the center of the room, what purpose it served was unclear to Lexy. A metal table sat in the middle of the room, accompanied by four chairs securely bolted to the floor. She wondered how many officers were hit with chairs before they instituted that safety feature? There was something missing, though. She couldn't quite put her finger on it at first, but after a long morning spent there, it dawned on her. There was no cliché hanging light that would slowly sway back and forth through the darkened, smoke-filled room. Instead, two long strips of fluorescent lights were firmly attached to the ceiling spilling down hard, white light. A solitary surveillance camera whirred back and forth from its position in the corner, its dark, unblinking eye seeing all. It was slightly unnerving thinking who might be watching at the other end.

The click of the doorknob interrupted her thoughts. Looking up, she watched two well-dressed men enter. Both men dug into their jacket pockets and produced their badges.

"I'm Special Agent Fowler, and this is my partner, Agent Allen," Fowler said gruffly. "Let's talk." Fowler and Allen sat down at the metal table and began to pull out several papers from a yellow folder.

Allen looked over at Lexy. "Could you take a seat, Ms. Weiss?"

Lexy slowly lifted herself off the floor and moved toward one of the chairs opposite the two men. Sliding down into it, she placed her elbows on the table to prop herself up. She was exhausted. "So they called in the FBI?" Lexy asked as if trying to make small talk.

Fowler and Allen glanced at her, then at each other, and finally back to their notes. Allen smiled politely. "Most people in your situation don't try and make chit-chat with the Feds."

Lexy nodded. "Sorry. I'm new at this."

Fowler lifted a stack of papers and tapped them on the desk. Laying them neatly down in front of him, he laced his fingers together. "Do you understand why you're here?" he asked slowly.

"Yes."

Fowler took a slow breath. "Then you know what kind of trouble you're in, right?"

"I have a pretty good idea," Lexy admitted.

Fowler's face darkened. "I don't think you want to be fucking with us." Lexy dropped her head. She found herself suddenly wishing to be alone again. "Sorry."

"Let's start from the beginning," Allen said after a moment. "State your name and occupation please."

"Virginia Alexis Weiss," Lexy said still looking at the floor. "I teach tenth grade history."

"Okay," Allen said as he quickly jotted down several notes on a small pad of paper. "Can you tell us where you were last night?"

"Home," Lexy said quickly. "All night."

"Was there anyone with you?" Fowler asked. Lexy shook her head.

"So you have no way to verify your whereabouts last night?"

"No," Lexy said slowly. "I don't."

Fowler lifted the stack of papers in front of him and began to flip through them. Stopping, he pulled out a photo and set it in front of Lexy. "Do you recognize this woman?"

Lexy looked at the black and white image of a woman's face. She knew this photo had to have been taken at the crime scene. There was a small smattering of blood on her right cheek and Lexy could just make out the slit in her throat. "I do."

"How do you know this woman?" Fowler asked.

"I saw her in my dream last night. She was the woman who was murdered," Lexy stated matter-of-factly.

"You saw this woman in your dream?" Fowler asked slowly. "That's right."

Fowler leaned back in his chair and rubbed his chin. He was a master tactician and he was baiting the hook, hoping to catch Lexy in a lie. His voice was calm and level. "Can you explain to me," he paused again, "why this woman's blood was found in your apartment, and on your person, if you merely *dreamed* about her?"

"I don't know," Lexy admitted. "All I remember is going to bed, and then having the dream. It was horrible. Every detail was so clear, so frighteningly vivid. Then I woke up covered in blood."

Fowler leapt up from his seat and slammed his fist against the table, "Do I look like Agent fucking Mulder to you?" He pointed to Allen. "Does he look like Agent Scully? No, and do you know why? Because you and I live in the real world and in the real world, we don't have dream killers with razors on their fingertips, or fluke monsters that live in the sewers. You killed that woman," he shouted. "You followed her into the alley," he moved around the table quickly behind Lexy, "then you gutted her. Isn't that right?" Leaning down, he began to whisper angrily in her ear. "You strangled her with your bare hands, and then cut her open like a pumpkin. What did she do, fuck your boyfriend? Or," Fowler paused, "she was your lesbian lover and you caught her with a man. That must've drove you out of your fucking mind."

"I don't even know that woman," Lexy shouted. "I have no idea who she was!" She felt her lower lip begin to quiver.

"You're lying," Fowler growled. He moved back around the table and produced another photo of the woman, this time, a full image of her naked, mutilated corpse. Slapping the image down in front of Lexy, he leaned over on the table. "This was Mary Glass, single mother of three." He let the words sink in for a moment. "She had three children, Lexy, and you diced her up like a pig for Christmas dinner."

"I didn't do it," Lexy whispered as a tear fell down her cheek. She couldn't take her eyes from the image. She had hoped, in some small way, that the whole thing had been a figment of her imagination, but now, looking at the photo, it suddenly became real, horribly real. Lexy's body began to shiver.

Fowler sat back down in his chair and looked over the trembling woman in front of him. She was about to break. That was exactly where he wanted her. "Do you realize if you lie to us, you are committing perjury? That's a serious crime."

"I know what it fucking is. I'm not an idiot," Lexy shouted. "Why did you do it, Lexy?" Fowler asked calmly.

"I didn't do any—"

"You left those three kids without a mother, Lexy," Fowler stated without changing his inflection. "Why did you do it?"

Tears were falling freely from Lexy's eyes. "I didn't kill her," she whispered. "I would never do something that horrible."

"That's not what the courts are going to see. They're going to see a woman who was found with the victim's blood all over her, and a woman who, in her statement, had intimate knowledge of a crime scene."

"There's no motive," Lexy said slowly.

"Motive?" Fowler asked. "Are you serious? Motive is shit to me," he slammed his fist on the table. "Do you understand? Shit." He watched the young woman in front of him teetering on the verge of a breakdown. He had her. "From the evidence I have in my hand right now, any jury would send

48

you away for a very long time. You may as well 'fess up and save us all a lot of trouble. This isn't going to end well for you, Lexy. I promise you that."

Lexy took a deep breath and wiped the tears from her face with the back of her hand. "I want to see my lawyer right now."

Fowler slammed his fist against the table again. "Just admit it! You killed that woman! You snuck up on her, strangled her and then gutted her! Admit it!"

Lexy stood and swept all of Fowler's papers onto the floor. "I want my lawyer right fucking now!"

Fowler stood and walked briskly toward the door while Allen knelt down to scoop up the papers. "I'm going to find out what happened, Lexy." Fowler threw open the door and marched out of the room, followed closely by his partner.

Lexy quickly moved around the table to the two-way mirror. She began to beat on the mirror with the palms of her hands. "Did you get all that?" she screamed. "You son of a bitches!" Turning away from the mirror, she slowly sank down to the floor and sobbed.

***

"Why did you do that?" Allen asked. "You didn't need to grill her like that." Fowler stopped just outside the door to the interrogation room and turned back to his younger partner. "For God's sake, Greg, the woman was covered with the

49

victim's blood when the ambulance found her this morning. How do you explain that?"

"I can't," Allen said slowly, "but she doesn't fit the profile."

"Profiles aren't always right, Greg. You have to learn that. And just because she's a woman, doesn't mean we have to go light on her. That's the number one mistake made by investigators. Never underestimate a woman," Fowler advised.

Allen nodded. "What's the plan?"

"Let's start working the previous crime scenes. Maybe we can find something the local PD missed." Fowler shook his head. "There's something here we're not seeing."

"What do you mean?" Allen asked as he tried to arrange the mess of papers in his arms.

"I'm not sure," Fowler replied, "but something's out of place. This all feels very familiar to me. I can't explain why."

***

The flight from D.C. to Seattle was a turbulent one. The plane, on several occasions, had encountered thick pockets of wind and rain causing it to be jolted around the sky. The "fasten seatbelts" sign had gone off shortly after take-off from Dulles, then had been relit about ten minutes outside Cincinnati. Upon landing, Bishop actually watched a mother of two fall to her knees and kiss the ground. He thought that only happened in the movies.

Moving through the Seattle terminal, Cane had taken the lead with Dawn closely behind. Bishop and Kelley had fallen slightly behind their partners, but kept a careful eye on the two. It was closing in on nine o'clock Seattle time and all were eager to get to the hotel and rest. They were all understandably anxious to get caught up on the details of the case.

"Ever been to Seattle before?" Bishop asked.

Kelley nodded. "I spent one summer here with an aunt of mine. My parents decided they needed time to work on their marital problems, so they shipped me off to live with Aunt Lilly."

"Auntie Lilly doesn't sound so bad," Bishop said with a smile.

"Except for the fact Aunt Lilly was a total shut-in," Kelley added. "Her only company was her eleven cats—which I had to clean up after. I never even had the chance to get out and see the city. I spent two months locked in a small apartment. The only contact I had with the outside world was through the television, or the rare occasion when I convinced Aunt Lilly to order pizza."

"I take it back," Bishop chuckled. "Isn't it funny?"

"What?" Kelley asked.

"About your aunt," Bishop explained.

"I don't think that's funny at all," Kelley shot back. "That was probably the worst summer of my life."

"No, not that," Bishop corrected her, "it's interesting that everyone has someone in their family just like that. Mine was Grandpa Bishop. After Grandma died, he became a hermit. He lived on a big ranch just outside Fort Worth, Texas. A few months after he lost Grandma, he sold off every

51

head of cattle and just lived in the farmhouse. No one even knew he had passed on until the grocery boy arrived three weeks later."

"That's awful."

"No," Bishop said slowly, "it really wasn't that bad. Most of the family had already made their peace with him. They were all relieved he was finally joining his wife."

"How long were they married?"

"Well, if you believe in past lives like they did, most of eternity," Bishop said. "They both knew they had been married to each other in all their previous lives."

"Soul mates," Kelley said with a sigh. "What a beautiful concept."

"So you believe in reincarnation?"

"Let's just say that my mind is very open to all possibilities," Kelley smiled. "You should've been a politician with the way you danced around that answer," Bishop joked.

Kelley reached over and slapped Bishop's shoulder. "I'm serious."

"I know," Bishop conceded. "I was just teasing."

Kelley nodded. "I can read minds, remember?" The two fell silent for a moment as they walked. "Have you ever met Lexy Weiss?" Kelley asked.

"Haven't," Bishop admitted, "but Cane is like an uncle to her."

"How do you know?"

"Dawn talks about it sometimes. She said Cane never really had an interest in children until Lexy came along," Bishop explained. "She said he enjoyed having someone around he could mold."

52

"That's wild," Kelley commented. "I just can't see Cane in that light. Did Lexy like spending time with him?"

Bishop nodded. "From what I understand, the two were inseparable for a while."

"That's sweet, in a kind of sick and twisted sort of way," Kelley said with a smile. "I like Cane and all, but I don't think I would want him to have an active role in my children's lives—if I had any."

"Why not?" Bishop asked, slightly bemused.

"Because they would turn out like you," Kelley said with a snicker.

"Are you implying I'm like Cane?"

Kelley laughed out loud. "In more ways than one."

"What's that supposed to mean?" Bishop asked incensed.

"Nothing," Kelley said. "I'm just teasing. Trying to lighten the mood a bit. I mean, none of us even talked the entire flight here." She looked forward at Cane, then back at Bishop. "Ever since Chairman Weiss broke the news, there's been a dark cloud hanging over Cane's head. It's affecting us all."

"Can you blame him?" Bishop asked. "This is practically his niece we're investigating."

"What do you think drives a person to such heinous acts like murder?" Kelley asked after a brief pause.

Bishop shrugged. "I hope I never find out."

Chapter Five

Hayden Collins sat alone in his apartment in downtown Seattle. The floors were bare, having moved all the furniture up against the front door and windows. He could see the lighter areas on the floor where less dust had settled, creating outlines of his furniture. He was curled up in the exact center of the room, his knees drawn tightly to his chest, while his eyes scanned the shadows for movement. He hadn't even taken the time to clean up, or put on a fresh set of clothes. Not after what he had seen last night.

The sound of footsteps outside his door chilled his soul. He listened as they grew louder. They seemed to be in sync with the rhythm of his heart. It was pounding in his chest, threatening to burst at any moment. Subconsciously, he began to hold his breath so as not to make even the slightest sound. If he could stop the thump of his heart, he would have. It was looking for him. He had seen it, and it had vowed to find him. What else could he have done but run?

He hadn't even taken the time to call in to work. If anyone called, he quickly picked up the receiver and slammed it back down. He had to keep the line open. Nothing was as important as his safety at this point. He had thought about keeping a small radio or a television out to keep tabs on the local news, but the sound might draw it here. He had no way of knowing if the police had caught it, no way of knowing when it was safe to go out.

Hayden listened as the footsteps began to recede. Letting out a long slow breath, he returned to his vigilance. It would not be able to make good on its promise. Hayden was going to make sure of that. He reached over and ran his fingers along the barrel of the pistol sitting next to him.

***

He felt miserable as he came to. The tattered clothes he was wearing were drenched with rainwater and his muscles and joints ached. He slowly opened his eyes and glanced around at his surroundings. He was lying amidst a pile of wet cardboard boxes he had apparently been using as a provisional shelter. Looking up, he could see the steel and concrete monstrosity of an overpass spanning four lanes of highway below. He was curled up just above one of the stilts, the concrete less than a foot above his head. He could hear the rumble of vehicles passing overhead with regularity.

Glancing to his left, he could make out a few small convenience stores and a gas station through the drizzling rain. Their lights, as well as the red, yellow and green of a nearby stoplight, were creating a rainbow in the ever-changing puddles below. Turning his attention in the opposite direction, he could see only a lonely highway leading off into the darkness.

Jax straightened up and pulled his coat tightly around his body. There were no familiar landmarks. He had no idea where he was, or for that matter, how he had gotten there. Crawling down the slope of the overpass, he heard the familiar jingle of change in his pocket. Fishing his cold hand in, he pulled out a few quarters and dimes. It was at least enough to get a warm cup of coffee at the gas station. He clenched the money tightly in his hand and moved out of the shelter the overpass had been providing.

The large raindrops were hitting hard against his face and exposed hands. Dropping his head down, he doubled his speed, all the while carefully avoiding the lakes of rainwater masquerading as puddles. Jax glanced down at his legs as he moved. There was an odd discoloration on his jeans. He couldn't quite make it out in the darkness, but it probably wasn't important. It was probably a result of sleeping under the overpass.

His mind was buzzing with questions. How did he get here? Where was here? There was a piece missing there, as if it had been wiped clean. That didn't make sense to him, though. He knew his name was Jax, he was married to a woman named Sara, and he was a struggling writer. *Could amnesia be selective*? he wondered.

He crossed the wet parking lot toward the gas station. The large lights above the gas pumps made him feel slightly better, but his body was aching, as if he had been exercising too much. His muscles were tired and weak and screaming for him to stop, but Jax continued on. He couldn't stand another minute in the rain.

Reaching out with his empty hand, he pulled open the door to the gas station and stepped inside. He could smell the familiar scent of burned nacho cheese and continuously warming hot dogs. It was comforting in an odd sort of way. He quickly wondered if he had enough change for a dog. He hadn't even realized it before, but he was starving.

Jax stopped on the large black mat in front of the door, wiped his feet and tried to shake off some of the rain. Looking up, he spotted a lone cashier standing behind an octagonal shaped checkout. She hadn't yet turned around to acknowledge Jax as she looked to be busy stocking the cigarette rack.

Glancing around the small station, Jax spotted two coffee machines to the right. Quickly making his way over to them, he spotted a clearly labeled price sheet on green. He ran his eyes down the list, then counted the change in his hand. A smile crossed his face. He had just enough for a cup. Reaching to his left, he pulled a thick white Styrofoam cup from a stack and set it on the counter. He then slid his hand around the black handle of the coffee pot and lifted the glass container of the dark fluid toward his nose. He took a long, deep breath, then exhaled. It smelled especially wonderful tonight. He carefully filled the cup and replaced the pot on its warmer. Searching over the items next to the coffee, he grabbed two sugars and a white plastic lid. Jax moved swiftly toward the cash register, eager to partake of his drink. He stopped and laid out the change on the counter.

The cashier heard the rattle and turned around. A quick gasp escaped her lips. "Are you going to rob me?" she said through quivering lips.

Jax's eyes widened. "What? Why would you say that?"

The blonde cashier, who couldn't have been more than seventeen years of age, took an uneasy step back. "Please don't hurt me."

"Listen, lady," Jax said quickly, "I don't know what you're on about, but I just want to pay for my coffee." He pointed down to his change on the counter. "I already…." he stopped. Jax stared at his hand. Setting the coffee on the counter, he quickly checked over his other. He felt several moments pass as he stared in disbelief. Taking a step back, he looked down at his clothes and the stain on his pants…it was blood. Everywhere. He was covered in it. His fingers up to the second knuckles were pure red, and several splatters extended up to his wrists. He turned to face the large window at the front of the store and stared in horror at his reflection. Several large streaks of blood extended across his unshaven face and down his neck.

Jax stumbled back. "Dear God."

"Take what you want and get out of here!" The cashier sobbed. She had sank down into the fetal position behind the counter. Her eyes, however, remained intently focused on Jax.

"What happened to me?" Jax asked softly. A realization crept into his mind. "What have *I* done?" Jax started to press his hands to his face, but quickly pulled them away out of revulsion. "I'm sorry," he said as he charged out the door and into the night.

***

Spenser tipped his dark gray fedora back as the rain began to subside. It had been coming down lightly all morning, which wasn't unusual for this time of year. Stuffing his hands into the deep pockets of his black trench coat, he continued on his way. He didn't mind the rain; it was the cold that accompanied it that bothered him.

He hated to admit it, but he was getting old. When he was young, he was built like a tank. Nothing could stop him. Now, however, it was a different story. His piercing blue eyes had dulled, and he had been coddling his left knee for quite some time. He had completely blown it out while chasing a suspect early in his career, and it had never quite been the same. Even after several surgeries to repair the damage and numerous months of physical therapy, he knew he would never be one hundred percent again. After a lifetime of abuse to his body, he could feel the weather in his joints. It was a dull ache that came just before the storm. He considered for a moment if he should retire to Florida. A smirk crossed his face and he shook his head. *I don't think so,* he said to himself. *A lot of weird shit happens in Florida.*

Spenser stopped and looked around. He was in the same rundown neighborhood the crime had been committed in the previous night. This part of town was a mess. It was a far cry from the pristine streets and buildings of downtown Seattle. Turning to his left, he spotted the alley where the officers had found the body. A long band of yellow police tape still ran across its mouth. If this were any other neighborhood, the tape would be gone, but this one was different. Residents here just wanted to be left alone. They had no need to pry into the lives of their neighbors. Solitude was their only desire. Finding a witness here would prove to be a difficult chore. Spenser had heard stories of drug busts in the middle of the street and not a single person had even peeked out their window.

Spenser moved slowly toward the alley. Lifting the tape, he ducked beneath it and began to work toward the rear. It was a blind alley littered with trash, garbage bags, boxes and junk that had outlived its usefulness. There was a lone ladder extending down from a fire escape, but it was too far off the ground to reach. His mind snapped into analytical mode. The killer had to leave the same way they came in. That meant someone could have seen them exiting after the crime. He wondered for a moment if the victim had screamed.

Stopping just short of the end, he glanced down at the white chalk outline on the ground they had drawn around the body exactly as it had been found, which was curious to Spenser. The woman's body was lying almost perfectly straight. With the exception of her left arm, she was lying with her feet and arms together, flat on her back. He pondered the possibilities. It probably meant she was dead before she hit the ground, or that the killer had arranged her in such a fashion after they finished their work. Did it mean anything? Was there significance to the pose? His mind worked back over the previous four murders. None of the other victims had been found in the same condition. Their bodies were flailed wildly about as if there had been a struggle. Or did the killer want Spenser to think that?

Spenser was giving the killer too much credit. He knew from experience not much thought was put into a murder. Usually, it was done out of lust or rage, and those were two emotions that negated the presence of clear and concise thought. This was also the reason Spenser held little respect for criminal profiles. They often tried to tell the tale of a well-planned crime and of a killer's motives that were clearly defined. Spenser knew in the gritty truth of reality, there was often no reason why. And that was the frightening aspect of human nature, that we are all capable of something this grotesque with enough provocation.

The pose raised a red flag in his mind. *Was this crime connected to the previous four? Or are we looking for two separate killers?*

His eyes moved quickly from the chalk outline to the almost black stain beneath it. It was blood, completely oxidized. Some of it was beginning to wash away due to the rain, but there was still enough left to work with. Kneeling down, he reached into his coat pocket and removed a pair of latex gloves. Snapping them on, he ran his finger through the crusty substance on the concrete. Turning his head to the left, he noticed a similar coloration on the wall. Moving closer, he realized it was also a blood splatter. It was very near the bottom of the wall, indicating the killer had splashed it there while they worked on the body. Spenser stood. It was too low for the killer to have slit her throat right here, but he knew they did. *They must've done it on the ground,* Spenser reasoned, *but why?*

He took a few steps back and examined the entire crime scene again. He remembered what the agents had said earlier to him, and he began to agree with them. The killer must've snuck up on his victim and strangled her, or knocked her cold with a blunt object. Spenser shook his head. That would have left a clearly definable mark.

Maybe he was looking at this from the wrong perspective. Maybe it wasn't the Weiss woman after all. Spenser glanced around the boxes at the end of the alley searching for more tell-tale marks of a crime, but there were no more to be found. He wondered if the rain had washed them away before they had a chance to examine them this morning.

"Detective?"

Spenser turned slowly to his left. The two FBI agents had entered the alley and were only a few steps away from him. *I must've been so deep in thought, I didn't hear them.* "What can I do for you, Agents?" Spenser asked casually while trying to pretend he wasn't shocked at his lack of focus.

"We came down to look at the crime scene," Fowler replied equally as casual.

Spenser nodded. "The rain's washed a lot of the evidence away, but you can still make out the rough outlines of what happened."

"Thanks," Fowler said, dismissing Spenser, "we don't need a guide."

"Look, goddamn it," Spenser said slightly, raising his voice. "We're all here for the same thing. We all want to catch the son of a bitch who did this, so I'm not going to take any of your 'holier than thou shit'. Do you understand?" Fowler smiled politely. "Of course."

"This is my case," Spenser protested.

"This *was* your case, Detective. Now, it's in the hands of the government. So if you'll excuse us," Fowler started to push past Spenser.

Reaching out, Spenser grabbed Fowler by the collar of his trench coat and spun him around. "You arrogant piece of shit," Spenser growled. "I should rip out your fucking eyeballs and piss in your dead skull."

Fowler quickly pushed Spenser away and adjusted his coat. "Assaulting a federal agent," he began, his demeanor never faltering. "That's a serious offense, Detective. I wouldn't want to see you end such a distinguished career that way."

Spenser felt the urge to charge again, but stopped himself. A wicked smile curled his lips. "I'm not getting into a pissing match with you, Fowler. If you want to run this investigation, fine. I won't help you at all, but I want you to know that you're losing a valuable resource."

Fowler nodded as he moved past Spenser. "Noted," he said with his back to Spenser.

Looking at the two agents, Spenser pulled his fedora down and started to move out of the alley.

Chapter Six

Bishop glanced down at his watch as he hastily made his way through the halls of the Seattle Hilton. It, as was the case with the majority of the chain, was drably decorated throughout the hallways. An off-white paper dominated the walls, occasionally interrupted by a light jutting out. The carpet was red with a gold and black pattern weaving through it. It was horrendous, but Bishop understood why most hotel and motel chains used this kind of carpeting: vomit stains were much harder to see. Disgusting, but true. Years ago, he had the fortune of chatting with a hotel maid he met in a bar. The stories she told about the people who stayed in motels were amazing. Bishop quickly made a mental note to look her up again when he returned to D.C.

He was running late by almost half an hour. He was so tired when he finally made it to his room the previous night, he had fallen asleep without setting the alarm or arranging for a wakeup call. After a quick spin in the shower and rummaging through his suitcase, he had settled on a pair of jeans, a dark t-shirt and his traditional black leather jacket. A pair of tan boots rounded out the ensemble. Running his hand through his still wet hair, he tried vainly to make something of it before he reached Cane's room.

Turning another corner, he glanced at the numbers on the doors and made his way to room three-thirty-five. Knocking on the door, he heard Cane's familiar voice inside. Bishop reached down and slid his hand around the doorknob. Twisting it open, he moved quickly into the room. He patted the air with his hands as he saw the looks on his teammate's faces. "I know, I know," he said quickly.

The room was decorated rather elegantly, a far cry from what they were accustomed to. Chairman Weiss had spared no expense on this trip, putting each member up in their own room. Lately, the OPR had been trying to cut costs by pairing the male and female members in joint rooms. Glancing around, Bishop noted this room looked fairly similar to his. The room was divided into two halves.

The first contained a closet, the bathroom and a queen-sized bed. The second, separated by a short wall, held a small coffee table, a couch, two chairs and a small desk. Rows of cabinets were built along the wall that held a microwave, a small refrigerator and a shallow sink.

Cane, Dawn and Kelley were sitting around the coffee table with several papers and files scattered around them. Dawn was holding a paper cup in her hands, the dark liquid inside still steaming. Likewise, Cane was also nursing a warm cup of coffee while Kelley flipped through several pages in a folder. All three looked up as Bishop made his way into the meeting.

"Nice of you to join us," Cane said slowly. "The meeting started half an hour ago."

"Sorry," Bishop repeated as he grabbed a chair and pulled it toward the table. "My body is still on east coast time."

"Wouldn't that mean you got up earlier since the east coast is three hours ahead of the west?" Dawn conjectured.

Bishop glared at Dawn. She was making things worse. "I don't know." Cane looked from Dawn to Bishop, then back at the papers in front of him.

"Regardless of the time shift, I think we should get started. We have a lot to accomplish today."

The three partners nodded at Cane's suggestion and sat forward in their seats. Their minds switched from personal to professional mode.

Cane flipped aside a sheet of paper revealing a small photograph of a young woman. Holding the picture up, he showed it to each member of the group. "This is Lexy Weiss," he said quickly. "You all know she's the daughter of our own Chairman Weiss and that she was charged with murder yesterday by the Seattle Police Department." He handed the photo to Bishop, "Please pass that around." He quickly readdressed the group, "What you don't know are the details." Lifting a stapled stack of papers off the table, he flipped over the first page and creased the corner roughly between his fingers and thumb. "According to the police report that Chairman Weiss provided us with, Lexy called 911 at approximately three-thirty yesterday morning."

"She called 911?" Dawn asked with amazement.

Cane nodded. "About twenty minutes later, police and ambulance crews arrived to find her cowering in the corner of her shower. She was babbling incoherently and trying to wash blood off her body. Upon further investigation, the police found her bedding also soaked in blood and there were bloody foot and fingerprints all over her apartment."

66

"This doesn't make sense," Bishop interjected. "Why would they automatically arrest her? Wouldn't they assume she was suffering from some kind of massive trauma and take her to the hospital?"

Cane flipped a page and nodded. "Indeed they did. She was admitted to the county hospital at four in the morning. I don't have the sheets here, but in the police report, it states the doctors found nothing wrong with her and released her into police custody."

"A kind of stigmata?" Kelley posed.

"No," Cane said quickly. "The lab work on the blood proved it wasn't hers. It was actually the victim's."

"Who's the victim?" Dawn asked.

Cane flipped another page. "Mary Glass, mother of three and known prostitute. Apparently, no connection to Lexy."

"Unless Lexy was working the streets," Bishop thought.

Cane turned and scowled at Bishop, daggers of anger shooting from his eyes.

"Whoa," Bishop said quickly, "I was just theorizing."

"Keep your theories to yourself, Mr. Bishop," Cane growled.

Bishop sat back in his chair. He realized, just as everyone else had at that moment, this was going to be a deeply personal case for Cane. He wasn't looking at the problem rationally. Instead, they knew he had the fifteen-year-old image of Lexy stuck in his mind. Bishop knew he would have to keep his thoughts personal for a while, at least until—or if—Cane started to look at the case analytically.

"I'm sorry," Bishop said finally. "Please continue."

Cane's glare continued for a moment longer. He finally turned back to the papers. He scanned the sheet for his place, then started again. "As I was saying," he shot Bishop another look, "there was apparently no connection between the two women, except for the blood."

"But that's strong enough evidence to convict her," Kelley said.

Cane nodded, "Hence why they have her in county lockup." He flipped over to the next page. "The statement she gave is very strange. She wrote three complete pages, basically describing her dreams."

"What?" Dawn asked.

"Lexy claims that's how she knows so much about the murders. She sees them in her dreams," Cane replied.

"'Murders'? Plural?" Kelley wondered.

Cane nodded. "Although there is no mention of other victims in this report, Lexy makes several references to seven other victims, all women." Cane dropped the papers in his lap for a moment and gazed up at the ceiling. "This could mean that she's psychic, or telepathic."

Kelley nodded. "You're thinking she has somehow tapped into the subconscious mind of the actual killer and her dreams are somehow broadcasting that information to her?"

"Like a television," Cane concluded.

Dawn tapped her fingernail against her front tooth. "Have her powers been previously documented?"

Cane shook his head.

"Does Chairman Weiss know something we don't?" Bishop asked.

"I don't think so," Cane said after a moment. "I just don't think he wanted his little girl involved in this world. Lexy was as normal as you or me," he said, pointing to Kelley. A smile crept over his face when he realized whom he had singled out. "Sorry, bad choice."

Kelley smiled softly. "It's okay. I wish I was as normal as you guys."

"But the bottom line here," Dawn said, pulling the group back to the topic, "is that she, and her apartment, were covered in the victim's blood when the police arrived. How do we explain that?"

"Working on that one," Cane admitted. He slowly sat back in his seat and looked around the group. "Suggestions?"

"I think we should interview the doctors who performed the examination yesterday," Kelley said. "Maybe we can find out a little more from them and her medical records."

Cane nodded and turned his focus to Dawn. "Can we talk with Lexy?"

"Unknown," Cane said quickly. "I don't know if we'll be permitted."

"I'll work on getting us clearance," Dawn added.

Cane turned slowly to Bishop.

"We need to track down eye witnesses," Bishop said after a moment. "That will be the fastest way to clear Lexy's name."

Cane tossed the papers down on the coffee table and stood up. "Good, we all know our assignments. Let's go."

Dawn looked up at Cane. "What are you going to do?"

"I'm going to visit an old friend," he said as he started out of the room.

***

Lexy lay quietly in her cell. Pulling her arms up from her sides, she folded them gently on her chest. She watched as her fingers laced together perfectly. Lifting two of her fingers she steepled them and frowned. This was the church she remembered from the old children's rhyme. This was where she was supposed to get married, and now, she would never get that chance. Lexy looked away at the drab walls of the cell and let out a long sigh.

She thought of her students for a moment. She wondered if the substitute teacher was covering the material or just giving them busy work. She wondered about the conversations she knew must be taking place in the teacher's lounge.

What they must think of her now? But all that didn't matter, as she would probably never see any of them again.

Lexy shook her head. Why was she being so negative? There was always hope, she tried to convince herself. A knot welled up in her stomach. And why was she so guilty? Was it because she saw those women die and did nothing to stop it? How could she? It was only a dream, she reminded herself, but that wasn't the truth. A woman was dead, a woman with a family to support. It was the same woman she had seen murdered in her dreams, but how was that possible?

She had read about cases on the net where people would sleepwalk and act out their dreams. These were extremely rare cases where subjects actually had to be lashed to their beds, but Lexy had never experienced that particular problem. She had always been a very sound sleeper. She wondered if something in her life could have triggered a change in her sleeping behavior. It was not completely unheard of, but at the same time, the chances of that occurring were slim. Perhaps she could claim insanity during her trial. That way, she could live out the rest of her days in a nice, padded room by herself, instead of trapped in a tiny cell with one or two other women.

Lexy sat up and held her face in her hands. She was starting to believe she had killed someone. She didn't know how, but all the clues pointed to her. She was even beginning to question her own sanity…for what that was worth.

She pushed herself up and walked across the cell. Propping her arm against the wall, she forced herself to remember. *It was the only way*, she had to know the truth. Closing her eyes, she reveled momentarily in the darkness. It was so soothing, she almost began to lose herself. It would be so easy to retreat right now, but she had to remain focused. Taking a deep breath, she began to shuffle through the random thoughts in her head, digging toward the

71

dreams. As all dreams are, these were fleeting. Only fragments remained in her conscious mind. The remainder had retreated deeply into her subconscious to be locked away. *Perhaps that was best,* she thought. Maybe she didn't want to face those images again, those terrible, grotesque images, but she had to.

She traveled back to that night and found herself standing outside a bar. It was rundown, the neon lights in the windows had ceased to work years before. Only a nearby streetlight illuminated the sign above the door. She couldn't make out the name, but she was vaguely familiar with what part of Seattle she was in.

It was a bad neighborhood, not for the people who lived there, but for the savages that terrorized it. It had, at one time, been a hub of commerce, but now, it had mostly been forgotten. Turning to her left, she saw a long car passing on the street, its headlights shining brightly in her eyes, yet she made no move to duck out of the light. There was no danger of her being recognized, there was no fear of capture.

She turned her attention skyward and caught a glimpse of the moon peeking out between dark storm clouds. Its white light was casting a beautiful silver coating atop the clouds, giving them the appearance of having a satin lining. The rain was beginning to fall now, lightly at first, the storm saving its full brilliance for later. A single arc of lightning danced between the ground and the heavens, lighting up the night.

Hearing the door open with a clack, she returned her attention to the small bar. A man and a woman stumbled out arm in arm, the former clearly drunk. He lost his footing for a moment, almost pulling his female companion to the ground, but she helped him regain his balance. He patted her on the shoulder with his meaty paw and smiled through his haze of alcohol. The woman giggled politely as they moved away from the bar.

The man was clad in a dark suit and wrinkled white shirt. His formerly neat red tie was hanging loosely around his neck and the top four buttons of his shirt hung open, exposing his pale flesh. His dull brown hair, usually slicked back against his head, now hung in sweat and beer-soaked strands from his scalp. Lexy theorized he was a businessman looking for a little adventure in an unknown part of town. No one would think to look for him here, and that was exactly what he wanted.

The woman, by comparison, was thin, but full at the hips with a well- endowed chest. She was wearing a short, black dress and a pair of four inch black "fuck me" heels. Her long, brown hair was teased up beautifully in curls that just licked her bare shoulders. She had a dark tattoo on her back that peeked out over the top of the dress. She had to be in her late forties, but she was still quite striking with her alabaster skin, ruby red lipstick and well-defined facial features. Her eyes screamed "sultry".

Lexy stood beneath the streetlight, allowing the light to cast deep shadows over her as the couple passed. It was the woman she wanted. She thought about the man for a second, but quickly changed her mind. He would be too easy a target in his inebriated state. There would be no challenge. At least the woman would put up a struggle. He would probably pass out before Lexy could go to work. Pushing herself off the lamppost, Lexy began to follow the couple discreetly.

They moved through the thickening raindrops, went around a corner, and finally ducked into an alley. The woman pressed her hands against the man's chest and slowly pulled his shirt open. She bent down slowly and pressed her lips to his flesh, kissing up toward his neck. She dragged her bottom lip up his throat toward his ear where she stopped and whispered something quietly.

Lexy had taken up position at the mouth of the alley, hiding behind a large dumpster. Dropping down to her knees, Lexy peeked out around the edge of the dumpster. She saw the man dig into his pocket and produce a small wad of bills, then hand them to the woman. The woman smiled slightly and accepted the money, which she then slipped into a slim black purse she had been carrying. Slipping off the purse, she set it on a stack of boxes next to her, then worked her hands seductively down her body to the bottom of her dress. Grabbing it with both hands, she pulled it slowly over her hips, then her breasts, finally, completely off. Dropping it next to her purse, she presented her now naked form to the man.

Lexy felt dirty as she watched, but at the same time, couldn't look away. There was something striking about the way the rain hit the woman's body and how it glistened in the moonlight. She watched the man place his hands on the woman's hourglass shaped hips and slowly work up her stomach toward her chest. He rubbed his fingers over her nipples for a moment before diving in with his mouth. The woman let her head fall back in pleasure. Lexy knew she was a whore, but she obviously enjoyed her work. She could hear the woman's soft moans echoing off the brick walls of the blind alley.

After a moment, the woman pushed her client away and slowly turned around. Placing both of her hands firmly on the wet walls as she bent over, the woman waited to earn her money. The man began to pull quickly at his belt and trousers, but couldn't quite manage the simple operation with so much alcohol in his system. Finally loosening the belt and his pants, he exposed his erect penis to the brisk air. He took a step forward, his pants falling to his knees, and placed his hands on the woman's hips. Moving a hand down between her legs, he quickly inserted his penis and pressed hard against her.

Lexy rocked back, turning away from the display. She felt a presence. Slowly turning her head, Lexy spotted two dark figures standing motionlessly in the rain. Each appeared to be a woman garbed in black, their faces covered with veils. One stood a few feet away beneath a flickering light, while the other was across the street. The rain didn't seem to touch them as it pounded to the ground. There was a sense of doom hovering around them. Lexy couldn't understand why, but something deep inside told her not to worry about the dark figures. They were not there to harm, rather to observe.

Wiping the rain from her brow with her free hand, she saw a glimmer of light next to her. Focusing her attention, she brushed away the bits of trash to see the broken edge of a mirror lying on the ground. Picking it up, she moved it in front of her and angled it toward her face. She gasped as her reflection came into view and dropped the mirror.

Opening her eyes, Lexy became aware that she was still in her cell. Moving quickly back across the room, she planted herself in the middle of the cot and pulled her knees up tightly to her chest. Wrapping her hands around them, she began to rock back and forth while shaking her head. "It wasn't me," she muttered. "It wasn't even human...."

Chapter Seven

Pushing through his office door, Spenser dropped his fedora on one of the outstretched arms of a thin, gold coatrack. He slowly pulled his arms from his trench coat and deposited it on another arm of the rack. Adjusting his suit, he glanced around his office. It was only slightly smaller than Captain Hart's. His desk was large and wooden, stained a dark shade of brown. It had several battle scars notched in its wooden frame from various cases and suspects who had gotten a little too unruly. A large black blotter sat in the center, flanked by a rectangular desk lamp and a computer monitor on the other. A stack of pens was contained in a tall, dark green coffee mug with a handle shaped like a fish's tail.

Walking toward his desk, he straightened his nameplate and sat down in his chair. His wooden chair creaked in agony as he leaned back. It was an old chair, almost as old as he was. He was just glad his joints didn't creak in protest as he sat down, yet.

Spenser pulled out a small tray from beneath his desk producing the computer's keyboard and mouse. Grabbing the mouse with his right hand, he wiggled it back and forth until the dark screensaver on his monitor was replaced with the now familiar desktop image. He made his way quickly over the GUI and double-clicked the web browser icon. He heard the tower beneath his desk whirr to life as it worked to complete his task. Spenser knew he was getting on in years, but the one thing he never wanted to be accused of was being computer illiterate. He made sure to take the time to learn the latest operating system and hardware. He despised being lumped in the group of elderly that couldn't program a VCR. He would never need to have an eight-year-old show him how to work his technology (plus, he didn't even own a VCR anymore. He had converted his entire library to DVD some time ago).

The desktop image was replaced with the browser. It quickly located his home page and called for the appropriate data to be displayed. Moving his cursor over the page, he clicked on the e-mail icon in the upper right-hand corner and was instantly transported to the login page. The nice thing about working in Seattle was everyone felt they had to have the latest computer technology. He enjoyed working with the department's high-speed internet connection. It made his job a lot faster when he was using the net as a research tool.

Moving his fingers nimbly over the keyboard, he typed in his username and password, then tapped the enter key. A white screen appeared, then one by one, the pieces of his web-based e-mail replaced the login screen. Opening his inbox, he was instantly greeted by a swarm of spam. Clicking through the junk mail, he stopped when he saw a familiar email address.

"Ginger," he said with a smirk. He opened the message and began to read out loud.

Had a great time the other night. Was wondering if you wanted to get together for dinner again…and maybe more?

Love, Ginger Spenser let out a grunt of approval as he closed the message. He would definitely have to reply to that e-mail before he left today. Cycling through the remaining letters, he closed the browser window and sat back in his chair. A knock on his door pulled him from his thoughts. "Yes?"

He watched as a brunette woman peeked around his door and smiled. "Detective Spenser?" she asked softly.

Spenser nodded, his demeanor stiffening.

The woman pushed open the door and strode inside confidently. She extended her hand to Spenser. "My name is Dawn Lassiter."

Spenser reached up and shook the woman's hand. "What can I do for you, Mrs. Lassiter?"

"Ms.," Dawn corrected him.

"Sorry. What can I do for you, *Ms.* Lassiter?"

"I was given your name by Captain Hart," Dawn began. "He informed me that you were working the Weiss murder case."

"If you're a reporter," Spenser said abruptly, "I have no time for this. You can get an official statement through the department's PR officer."

"I'm not a reporter," Dawn conceded as she sat down in one of the chairs that faced Spenser's desk. "I represent the law firm of Cane and Bishop out of Washington D.C.," she said with a smile. "We were hired by Ms. Weiss' father to represent her."

"You're a lawyer," Spenser said with an apparent air of dismay in his voice. He had high hopes for her up until that point.

Dawn was unwavering, "That's correct."

"First the feds, now the lawyers have descended," Spenser said half to himself. "Pretty soon, I'm not going to have a corpse left for you vultures to pick over."

Dawn ignored the comment. "Did you say the FBI is here in Seattle?" Spenser nodded.

"Is there any way I can get in touch with them?"

"I wouldn't know," Spenser said gruffly. "Try contacting them through the field office here in Seattle."

Dawn was surprised at the venom spewing from this man. "I need to see my client, Detective Spenser," she said abruptly. It was clear to her this line of enquiry was going to end before it even started.

Spenser stood and moved toward the door. "Come on," he said motioning with his hand over his shoulder.

***

Kelley strode inside Seattle General Hospital. The first thing she noticed was the sterility of the lobby. Glancing down at the glistening tile floors, she was sure this room was clean enough to perform surgery in. It was a far cry from the hospital she had worked at in Stone Brook, Florida. She recalled her work as a nurse and the conditions she worked in. She had, on occasion, spotted the fleeting edge of the colony of cockroaches that lived in the walls of the building. It sickened her that a place of healing was so infested. She didn't even want to think about the stories she'd heard in the breakroom of monster rats that lived in the basement.

She glanced around the lobby. It was clearly divided into two sections.

80

The first was all white walls and tan tile floors. A large, circular reception desk sat off to one side, surrounded by several large plants. The opposite side of the room housed the gift shop, filled to the brim with bouquets of flowers and stuffed novelty items that all read 'get well soon' or 'thinking about you'. She had always found items from gift shops particularly tasteless in nature. It signified to her the person visiting the hospital hadn't put any thought into a gift or even a card and had scrounged at the last minute. It was very unsentimental in her opinion.

The second section of the room was all carpeted with a dark gray weave. Rows of couches and chairs sat around numerous coffee makers and a large television in the rear. A bank of elevators was situated on the far wall to the right. It boasted twenty-foot ceilings, giving the room a grandeur missing from most hospitals. It was the architect's way of telling visitors the patients were in good hands.

Kelley smiled. Maybe she should pick up an application while she was here. Shaking her head, she let out a little laugh as she made her way toward the reception desk. She stopped and rested her hands on the simulated wood top, waiting to be noticed. The nurse was a heavy-set woman wearing a white smock with balloons and teddy bears imprinted on it. Her dark, curly hair was tied up with a rubber band and pencil behind her head, while a pair of dark rimmed glasses sat low on her nose. She was working over what looked like a general admittance form, probably trying to catch up on some paperwork.

Kelley cleared her throat loudly.

The nurse spun around in her chair to face Kelley. Using the back end of her thumb, she pushed her glasses up to the bridge of her nose. "I'm sorry," she said politely. "I didn't hear you come in. What can I do for you?" The nurse folded her hands neatly in front of her and waited like a child ready to hear a bedtime story.

Kelley's mind whirred for a moment. She hadn't taken time to work up a cover story on the way over here. She had been too preoccupied with the theory Lexy Weiss might also be telepathic. She had never met another like herself and was anxious to find out if it was true.

Kelley opted for the direct approach. "My name is Kelley Windel, and I'm with the Office of Paranormal Research."

"What can I help you with, Ms. Windel?" The nurse asked.

"I'm working on a case and I need some information." Kelley dug into her purse and produced the photo of Lexy. "Do you recognize this woman?"

The nurse took the photo from Kelley and poured over it. "Was she a patient here?"

"Yes. She was admitted early yesterday morning."

"I think I do remember her."

"Great," Kelley said with a smile. "Is there anything you can tell me about her?"

"Like what?" the nurse asked while handing back the photo.

"Like," Kelley paused for a moment, "what condition she was in when she arrived?"

82

"Oh yeah," the nurse nodded. "I remember her because I was conned into working a double shift yesterday. She came in on my second shift."

Kelley quickly probed the woman's thoughts. She wasn't lying to her. "She had to be strapped down to the gurney," the nurse continued. "The EMTs were afraid she might hurt herself, or one of them for that matter." The nurse stopped for a moment, realizing she was gossiping to a complete stranger. "I'm sorry, who did you say you were with again?"

"The Office of Paranormal Research," Kelley said clearly.

"Without proper credentials or permission from the Chief of Staff, I can't discuss this," the nurse had just realized she was committing a breach of protocol.

"I understand," Kelley said sympathetically. "I spent quite a few years as a nurse myself. Is the Chief of Staff available?"

The nurse picked up a white phone next to her on the desk and began to dial a number. "Let me check."

***

Bishop walked slowly through the rundown streets in the area where the murder had been committed. A light rain was falling, but it didn't bother him. He loved the rain. He would go out of his way to walk in the rain, or at least smell the fresh, clean scent of it. Stuffing his hands into his jacket pockets, he listened to the patter of the droplets as they hit the leather shoulders of his coat.

Looking up into the sky, he could see patches of blue beginning to peek out through the dark clouds. He uttered a silent prayer for the rain to continue. It was peaceful; he wasn't entirely sure why. Stillness hung in the air when it rained or snowed, but that wasn't it. He began to wonder if it was because most people stayed inside when the weather grew wet, making the city seem empty. Either way, there wasn't a soul to be seen on the streets and that was perfectly fine with Bishop.

Spotting the yellow police tape cordoning off an alley, Bishop stopped. In the back of it he could see a faint chalk outline on the ground amidst a litter of trash bags and waterlogged cardboard boxes barely retaining their shape. Glancing left, then right, he ducked under the tape and made his way into the alley.

His eyes worked analytically across the alley floor and walls. He took in every piece of trash, every scrap of rubble. He was going in blind. There wasn't much here the police hadn't already combed over and catalogued. Stopping near the end, he glanced down at the partial chalk outline on the ground. Inside the outline, he could see the vague discoloration of a bloodstain. Bishop turned away. It felt somehow disrespectful to be staring. A woman had lost her life here, for whatever reason, her remaining years had been ripped away. Bishop began to make his way away from the crime scene. There was nothing for him here.

Stopping at the mouth of the alley, he glanced out over the neighborhood. There was no joy in this place. He could tell it was a haven for those who didn't wish to partake in life anymore. No flowers grew in the various planters hanging from windowsills and the small areas that had been left open in the sidewalk to plant trees and grow grass were nothing more than piles of trash on dirt. Multi-colored patches of graffiti littered the walls of buildings signaling this turf was under dispute by several gangs. Looking across the street, Bishop's eyes wandered up the side of a three-story brick apartment complex. He stopped on a second-floor window. There was someone staring at him. Quickly, the face disappeared as a curtain dropped, covering the window. Bishop stared at the window for a second longer. The face reappeared, then vanished again when it saw Bishop was still watching.

That person knows something.

Moving quickly across the street, he made his way up the small flight of stairs that led to the apartment's front door. Glancing right, he saw a directory of tenets in the building. The individual buzzers had long since been removed and the gold plating had tarnished over time. Reaching for the door, he easily pulled it open and stepped inside. The lobby was in a similar state of disarray as the rest of the neighborhood. Bishop conjectured in its heyday, this was probably one of the nicer apartment complexes in Seattle. An old circular couch stood in the center of the room with a tall marble statue of an angel perched above it. One of the angel's wings was missing and the other was broken just below its elbow. Studying the room, he could find no elevators, only a narrow staircase toward the rear. Bishop shrugged and moved toward the stairs.

Standing at the bottom, he glanced into the gloom at the top. Apparently, the lobby was well maintained compared to the second floor. He took several uneasy steps up, then stopped. A musty odor was wafting down from the upper floors. "Smells like someone's dead up there," Bishop commented to himself.

"I assure you, there's not," a voice said from behind him.

Spinning around, Bishop glanced around the lobby. He spotted a short, balding man moving toward the stairs. He was wearing an old, yellow sweater vest with tan slacks and a wrinkled white shirt. His gray hair was slicked back to the sides of his head while his scraggly mustache had long since grown over his lips. "Can I help you?" Bishop asked.

"I think that's my line, partner," the man said with a gravelly voice.

"You must be the manager," Bishop reasoned. He held his position on the stairs.

"Owner," the man corrected. "The name's Harold, and you are?"

"Nick," Bishop said evenly, still not sure what to make of the man.

"I have a strict rule," Harold started, "no unannounced guests in the building. The neighborhood isn't what it used to be," he confessed. "I'm gonna have to ask you to come down here to the lobby. We'll call up to the apartment your visiting and make sure you're okay."

Bishop turned and glanced up the stairs, then back at Harold. He nodded once and moved down toward the man.

"Who were you here to see?" Harold asked as they moved toward the front desk.

Bishop wasn't sure if he should make up a lie, or tell the truth. "I'm working on a case," he said after a moment. "I'm looking for people who might've seen a murder across the street last night."

"Who are you with?" Harold asked while picking up the receiver of a small black, outdated phone.

"No one. I'm a private investigator."

Harold seemed to swallow the lie. "Who were you here to see?"

"I'm not sure," Bishop confessed. "I saw someone watching me from the second floor of this apartment complex. I don't have a name or—"

Harold quickly set down the phone. "I'm afraid I can't let you up there, then. The people in this building count on me to protect their privacy and I do not take that job lightly."

Bishop cringed. He hated the way Harold pronounced the word "privacy". As was apparently the trend now, he emphasized the shortened the 'I'. His entire life, he had been taught it was said with a long 'I'. He wondered why he let such a trivial thing bother him. Maybe he was just a little perturbed with Harold.

Harold smiled, but it was barely visible beneath his mustache, "I'm sorry, but I'm going to have to ask you to leave." He lifted a small business card from the desk next to him and handed it to Bishop. "Next time, call ahead."

Bishop took the card and slowly slid it into his pocket. Shooting an insincere glance at Harold, he turned and slowly began to walk out of the hotel. He hoped Kelley, Dawn and Cane were having better luck than he was.

Stepping back outside, he hiked his collar up as the rain fell heavily around him. In the time he had been in the apartment building, it had gone from a light sprinkle to a drizzle. Moving across the street, he took cover in the same alley where the woman had died. Keeping his eyes trained on the second story window, he leaned his shoulder against the alley wall.

A dull thud behind him startled him.

Snapping around, he saw a large, fresh blood splatter on the ground. Curious, he dropped down to one knee and examined it. He could see traces of green flesh inside, as well as a few indiscernible organs scattered about. Rubbing his hand on his chin, Bishop stood up just as he heard another thud. Turning, he spotted a similar blood splatter on the sidewalk in front of the alley. Looking up, his eyes widened. Running further into the alley, he dodged the green projectiles raining down around him. Ducking behind a dumpster, he listened as the thuds became more frequent. Leaning his head around the corner, he watched in amazement as the street was actually becoming red with blood. He was startled as something hit the top of the dumpster. Standing up, he peered over the top to find a partially smashed frog.

"It's raining frogs," Bishop mumbled. "I have a bad feeling about this." He moved out of the way as two more frogs hit the ground next to him.

Chapter Eight

"Absolutely not," the Chief of Staff said to Kelley. "I can't share any of that information with you."

Kelley sat back in her chair and recrossed her legs. Folding her hands neatly in her lap, she looked carefully over the Chief. He was an older man with solid white hair and beard. He was wearing a pair of dark glasses that seemed to be thick enough to be used as binocular lenses. He was dressed in the standard white smock of his profession, but nary a spot was visible on it. In fact, it looked to be ironed into crisp folds at the collar and sleeves. Kelley secretly wondered how long it had been since he had seen actual hospital duty. She calmly stared into his wrinkled face, "It would really help me."

"Who did you say you were with again?" the Chief asked. "The Office of Paranormal Research."

The Chief adjusted his glasses as he leaned back in his chair. His hands went instinctively for the knot of his tie and tightened it. "I've heard of you. Can't say any of it was flattering, though."

"I can assure you," Kelley said with a calm and level tone, "we are professionals. We take our research very seriously."

"You realize there are laws against me letting out that information?" Kelley nodded. "I was a nurse for several years. I know the rules." The Chief was perplexed. "Then why did you even ask?"

Kelley smiled devilishly. "I had to try." Standing up, she extended a hand to the Chief. "Thank you for your time."

The Chief shook her hand gently and nodded. "Perhaps next time, we can meet under better circumstances," he added with a coy smile.

"Perhaps," she said diplomatically. Turning toward the door, she walked briskly out of the Chief's office into the hallway. Stopping a few feet short of the elevator, she stumbled toward the wall. Using her hand to brace herself, she began to rub her temples with the other hand. That was a hard hack. More difficult than even those damned shadows....

Shaking the cobwebs loose, she stood up and straightened herself.

Taking a long breath in through her nose, she then exhaled it through her mouth. She needed to sit down, but she also needed to get someplace she could write down all the information before she lost it. She remembered a notepad on the back seat of her rental car. It would have to do. Normally, she used a miniature tape recorder and dictated the information, but she had forgotten to bring one with her. It was still packed with her clothes back at the motel.

Kelley didn't like probing around in people's minds. They were generally full of trivial information and it took a great deal of concentration to push that aside for the pertinent facts. The Chief was no exception, and in truth, was probably worse than most. His medical education was still resting heavily in the front of his mind, as were the political happenings of the hospital. He was a very cluttered individual. She had eventually wound her way to what she wanted in his mind and took it. That was the easy part. Getting back out proved to be a challenge in most cases.

Kelley had performed her Mind Hack several times since joining the OPR, and the more she did it, the more distasteful it became. When she reached out with her mind, she created a telepathic link between her and her subject. She likened it very much to a bridge. The only problem was information could pass both ways on the bridge. If she wasn't careful, her subject could end up with several of her memories as well. It was a dreadful, sticky process. She often felt like the connection was a tongue rooting through her subject, the muscles contracting and tensing as they pushed random thoughts out of the way.

Adversely, she couldn't rip the "tongue" out of her subject when she was done. She was afraid she would be detected, or worse, it could do permanent damage to their brain. She didn't want to be accused of accidentally lobotomizing someone just for some information. She knew from previous experience that even the most uneducated subject could tell when someone was rooting around in his or her mind. Kelley knew everyone possessed a certain level of psychic ability. It stemmed from deep within inactive areas of the brain humanity had yet to fully explore, but *she* knew it was there.

She reached out and tapped the elevator call button with her thumb. She heard the ding of the elevator as the doors slid open. Stepping inside, she pressed the first-floor button and waited for the doors to slide shut. The stolen memories were quickly beginning to fade. She had to hurry and write them down.

**

Cane moved briskly through the Seattle streets. He knew exactly where he was headed. Taking a corner sharply, he narrowly missed a couple heading in the opposite direction. His shoulder brushed against the woman's, and without a word, he continued on his way. He could hear the man shouting behind him. If this were any other day, he would enjoy stopping and teaching him some manners, but this wasn't any other day.

Glancing up for the first time since he left the hotel, he spied his target: The Golden Crow. It was a dive, but the best kind. Stopping in the doorway, Cane took a deep breath. It had been a long time. Could she really still be here after all these years? He suddenly began to question his course of action. He had moved on, why couldn't she? Was he so arrogant to assume that nothing was allowed to change in his absence? He looked at the battered door in front of him. There was only one way to find out.

Pushing the door open, he stepped inside. The atmosphere of the bar immediately assaulted his senses. There was the lingering but faint smell of mold in the air, one of the hazards of living in such a damp climate. Music was blaring from an ancient jukebox in the corner, while several fans chugged noisily overhead, their motors threatening to burn up at any moment. Cane glanced amidst the few splashes of light to see a smattering of patrons and a lone woman standing behind a long bar at the rear. She *was* here.

Moving slowly through his old haunt, he worked his way toward the bar. Glancing to his left, he had to do a double take. Sitting at a small, round table was Ernie Miller nursing a beer. Cane smiled. Some things never changed. That comforted him. Miller was a professional boozer. He and Cane had raised some hell in their day, and they had always sat at the round table in the corner.... Cane would have to stop and say hello to his old friend before he left. Stepping up to the bar, he ran his fingers slowly over the finished surface. Stopping for a moment, he moved his hand under the lip and felt around. He smiled as his fingertips ran over several recesses. It was still there. He had carved his name there over thirty years ago while the bar was being built.

Shaking his head, he looked up at the woman tending the bar. She hadn't noticed his approach since she was busily wiping down several freshly washed glasses. She was still beautiful, even with the added years. She had aged perfectly, her dark hair still perfectly kept, her eyes still sparkling. She was wearing a dark skirt with a white floral pattern along the hem with a matching t- shirt. A silver cross still dangled from her neck, a keepsake from an old adventure.

Cane cleared his throat. "Hey, barkeep."

The woman looked up with a soft smile. As her eyes focused on Cane, the smile quickly vanished. She moved slowly down the bar. "What the hell do you want?"

Cane's eyes narrowed. He had expected a slightly warmer welcome. "Is that any way to greet your ex-business partner?"

"Is that what you called yourself?" The woman asked. "I thought you drank our alcohol all day and flirted with the female customers."

"Well, I did a bit of that as well," Cane smiled. Her stern glance was unwavering.

"Lydia," Cane said with a sigh, "do we really have to pick up where we left off? Can't you let the past die?"

Lydia slammed her hands on the bar and leaned dangerously close to Cane. "How can you, of all people, say that, you son of a bitch!" She straightened up, glanced at her customers, who hadn't taken any interest in the fight, and back at Cane.

Cane reached out for Lydia's hand, "I'm not here to—"

Lydia ripped her hand away from Cane. "Don't touch me. You lost that right thirty years ago."

Cane slammed his fist against the bar while glaring at her. "Bloody Hell, Lydia. I didn't come here to fight with you, but you are the same stubborn witch I knew when I left. It wasn't the past that drove me away," he had never told anyone, let alone Lydia, this, "it was you. That was just an excuse. It was like hitting the eject button just to escape."

Lydia's eyes hardened, "You self-centered limey prick. Now I have a new reason to hate you, liar."

Cane turned away. "To hell with this," he started out of the bar. "Wait," Lydia's voice beckoned from behind him.

94

Cane spun on his heel and looked at his ex-lover. "What?" Lydia turned her glance away from Cane. "Don't go."

Cane stopped. That wasn't the response he'd expected. He started slowly back toward the bar. "Why?" It was the only thing he could think of.

"I…." Lydia stammered.

Cane wasn't sure she had expected to say that either.

"I can't take you leaving again without saying goodbye." She was standing strong, but her eyes had become misty.

"After the welcome I just received, I didn't think you would care either way," Cane said slowly, still standing a few feet from her. "Why did you bark at me like that?"

"Did you expect anything different after what you did?" she asked while wiping her eyes. She slowly moved around the bar to face Cane. "I hated you for what you did to me," she said softly, now less than a foot from Cane.

Cane started to reach for her, but stopped. He wasn't sure if it was the right thing to do. "I'm sorry," he said after a moment.

A tear escaped her eye. "That's all I wanted to hear." She moved quickly and wrapped her arms around Cane.

Cane slowly returned the gesture. It was familiar, yet different at the same time. She still smelled the same. Her body pressed against his was…enthralling. He could die here. Right now. He was complete. He let his hands run down her back as he held her tightly, her face pressed against his shoulder. He had dreamt of this moment, but let out a long sigh. There were more pressing matters at hand. He slowly pulled away from Lydia. "I need your help," he said slowly.

Lydia's hand slowly made its way up to the cross around her neck. She began to rub it gently between her thumb and forefinger. Those words had almost cost her life last time and were the reason she *always* wore the cross. "Anything," she said without hesitation.

"Thank you," Cane said. The two moved back to the bar and onto two empty bar stools. "Do you still have connections in the Wiccan community?"

Lydia nodded. "Still practicing. I even have my own coven now." Cane let out a soft laugh.

"What?" Lydia asked.

"The one thing I was always afraid of was that you were going to curse me or something after I left," Cane admitted.

Lydia smirked. "Who says I didn't?"

Cane laughed uncomfortably. "I'm looking for information on a killer."

"For the Office of Perpetual Repudiation?"

Cane looked at Lydia crossly. "Is that what they're calling us now?" Lydia nodded.

"We're doing good work there," Cane argued. "It's a good organization." Lydia nodded again.

Cane sighed. "Yes, I need the information for the OPR."

"What are you looking for?" Lydia asked.

"Not sure," Cane admitted. "This is a strange one. A young woman has been arrested under suspicion of murder, but she says she didn't do it. She was found covered in the victim's blood."

96

"Sounds like 'case closed' to me," Lydia admitted.

"Yeah, but she claims she sees the actual murder in her dreams and that the killer's been terrorizing her."

"A Psychic Stalker?"

"Possibly."

Lydia thought for a moment. "As a favor for an old friend, I'll look into it." Cane reached over and placed his hand on her knee. "Thanks. This one's important to me."

Lydia only nodded.

Cane retrieved a business card and a pen from his jacket pocket. He quickly jotted the hotel's number on the card as well as his room number and handed it to Lydia. "Let me know as soon as you hear anything."

Chapter Nine

Agents Fowler and Allen stood waiting on one side of the darkened morgue. Around them was a sea of white and silver. Every surface was polished to a high shine and smelled of disinfectant. The odor was starting to churn Allen's stomach. He turned to look at his partner. Fowler was solid as a rock. *As usual*, he thought.

Allen glanced across the room to a silver autopsy table. It had a body resting on top of it with a white sheet draped over it. Only the feet were visible, giving away that it was a woman. Allen's eyes moved to the wall of silver doors on the far wall. He wondered how many of them housed other corpses. How many of those were senseless deaths?

The double doors burst open as another gurney was wheeled in. Two people appeared next, slowly steering the table into the room. They were both young men dressed in light green scrubs. Sliding the gurney up to the nearest autopsy table, the two men lifted the body and deposited it in the center of the table. Turning away, they pulled the gurney out of the room without a single word or glance at the agents.

Before the doors had even come to rest, a dark-skinned woman pushed them open again. She was dressed in blue scrubs and a white lab coat with her dark hair pulled up away from her face. She walked briskly toward the two agents, a clipboard in hand. "You Agents Allen and Prowler?"

"*Fowler*," Fowler corrected.

The woman glanced down at her paperwork, double-checking. "Sorry. I'm Dr. Moran."

The two agents nodded.

Moran turned and began to walk toward the body the two men had just brought in. "This is what you came to see, gentlemen." Placing her clipboard down on a nearby table, she pulled a pair of latex gloves from a box and snapped them on. "For the record," Dr. Moran stated, "I don't like this. You could have easily waited for my completed report in the morning."

"In case you haven't heard, Doctor," Fowler said coolly, "we have a murderer on the loose. Every moment is precious."

Moran shook her head as she rolled her eyes. Like she had never heard that one before. Reaching down, she grasped an edge of the sheet. "Ready?"

Fowler nodded. "Pull it."

Moran pulled the sheet away from the body in one fluid motion, revealing the naked, disfigured corpse of Mary Glass. Allen coughed as a gag reflex, quickly balling his fist in front of his mouth as he turned away. Fowler made no motion, only stared at the body. Moran turned and snatched her clipboard. Flipping over the top sheet, she began to study the police report.

Fowler studied the body. It was no longer the healthy pink of life. Bodies slowly turn a grayish white after death. The human body is an ingenious creation. It has built-in mechanisms to dispose of itself in the end. Breakdown begins on the cellular level and continues until the flesh has completely rotted away. Even in death, the body has a purpose.

He looked over the massive wound in her throat, then down to her exposed abdomen. He could clearly see where intestines had been

99

removed. The open wound ran from just above her pubic area to the base of her rib cage. The cut was jagged, angry. This was not done precisely, rather in the heat of the moment. It looked torn, rather than cut. Fowler looked up at Moran. "Professional opinion?"

Moran glanced at her notes. "As you can see by the wound in the abdomen, this was done with a sharp object, probably a knife of some kind, although the blade couldn't have been too sharp to do this kind of damage to the surrounding flesh. The wound on her throat," Moran paused, "was probably done with the same instrument."

"Anything unusual?" Fowler asked.

Moran shook her head. "She recently had intercourse. We found traces of sperm in her vagina. She was probably a hooker."

"Not a news flash," Fowler said slowly. "Any idea why the intestines were removed?"

"No idea," Moran admitted. "At this point, it just looks like they wanted to defile her corpse."

"Toxicology?"

"Won't be back until tomorrow morning," Moran said. She flipped the pages on her clipboard back over and placed it back on the table. "Anything else?"

Fowler shook his head. "Thanks. You can take off."

Moran snapped off her latex gloves. "'Bout time." She started toward the door. "I'll have the orderlies pick up the body shortly."

Fowler watched Moran stride through the double doors and quickly moved around the table. Pulling a glove from the box, he slipped it on his hand. Reaching up, he pulled down the light closer to the body and focused it on the open cavity. "Take a look at this," he said to Allen.

Allen took a few tentative steps toward the body. "What?" Fowler glared at his rookie partner. "Get over here, you sissy."

Allen took another uneasy step. "I'm just not used to seeing a dead body this badly mutilated." He watched Fowler dig his gloved hand into the body and felt another wave of nausea grip him. "What are you doing?" he asked, trying to fight through it.

"I noticed this a moment ago, but I didn't want to say anything in front of the good doctor." Fowler lifted the remaining bit of intestine and slid his finger into the open end. He pulled slowly revealing a small, folded piece of paper. "I saw the corner sticking out," Fowler admitted.

"How could she miss something like that?"

Fowler shook his head. "No idea." He slowly began to unfold the piece of paper.

"John," Allen said quickly, "you're tampering with evidence."

Fowler didn't even acknowledge Allen's statement. He moved his finger to the outer edge of the paper and slid it inside. Gently, he folded it open. Quickly scanning over the note, he slowly handed it to Allen as he snapped off the glove.

Allen turned the piece of paper in his hand and stared at the thick, black foreign lettering on it. "What does this mean?"

Fowler turned and began to make his way out of the morgue. Folding the paper in two, Allen dropped it into his pocket and followed his partner.

He had never seen Fowler this rattled before. It unnerved him. Thoroughly.

***

Dawn stood outside Lexy's cell watching. The young woman had curled herself up into a ball in the far corner behind the cot. Her arms were wrapped tightly around her knees, which were pulled up to her chin. Dawn had met Lexy on a few social occasions, but the two had never been friends, rather little more than strangers. At this moment, Dawn hoped Lexy wouldn't recognize her. It could completely blow her cover.

Dawn turned and looked back down the cellblock. Spenser had just finished conferring with the officer on watch and was moving her way. In his right hand, she could clearly see a set of keys on a large ring. The sight struck a nerve deep in her subconscious. It was a scene from every prison movie she had ever seen. If she weren't in such dire circumstances, she might laugh out loud at the preposterousness of the image. Dawn held her composure and returned her gaze to the cell.

Spenser moved in front of Dawn and lowered the keys to the lock. "I'll be just down the hall if you need me," he said while twisting the key. He opened the door just enough for Dawn to slip inside and firmly locked it behind her. Giving both women a quick glance, Spenser sighed and moved away.

Dawn turned her attention to Lexy. An involuntary burst of fear gripped her. She had no idea what to expect. As far as she knew, Lexy could well be the killer, and Dawn was placing herself in harm's way. Dawn quickly quelled the irrational sensation. She had no reason to believe any of that. She was here to save this woman, not condemn her for what the law had accused her of. Slowly setting her briefcase on the cot next to her, she took a cautious step toward Lexy.

"Ms. Weiss?" she asked carefully and waited. There was no response. No movement. "Lexy?"

Lexy leisurely lifted her head. There were dark bags under her eyes and her hair hung in matted strands around her face. She was a mess. She gave Dawn the once over, searching for a spark of recognition. "Who are you?" a meek voice trickled from her lips.

"My name is Dawn Lassiter. I'm a lawyer sent her by your father." Lexy perked up slightly. "My dad? Is he here?"

Dawn shook her head, "No, but you're in capable hands. Zachary Cane has brought a team to investigate."

Lexy laughed. "Uncle Zach. I don't think ghosts killed that woman," she said with a hint of anger in her voice. "He's not going to be much help."

"Why do you say that?"

Lexy cocked her head slightly. "Have you ever met the man? He's a certified nut case."

"Be that as it may," Dawn started slowly, "you need all the help you can get." She moved to the cot and sat down on the edge, confident that Lexy posed no threat. "I need to talk to you about the case, Lexy. We need as much information as you can provide."

"It doesn't matter."

"Why?"

"There will be no justice for the man who did this," Lexy said painfully. "There can't be."

Dawn looked warily over Lexy. "I'm not following you."

Lexy turned away from Dawn. "You won't believe me. No one does." She buried her face in her arms. "I've told the same story a dozen times and I always get the same thing. Why should you be any different? Why should I waste my time? After all, with the way things are going, I'll be getting the electric chair in a few days. So why does it matter?"

Dawn recoiled from the venom in Lexy's voice. It wasn't her fault. She knew she would probably share a similar sentiment if the situation were reversed. "Listen, I'm here to help, not to denounce you, but I need to hear your side of the story, Lexy. You have to trust me."

"Trust you?" Lexy looked up again, a lone tear streaking down her cheek, "I don't even know you." She wiped the tear from her face. "It doesn't matter anymore."

Dawn stood in front of Lexy. "I'm not going to sit here and listen to this garbage," she said in a commanding tone. "Stop feeling sorry for yourself and start fighting."

Lexy looked at the woman before her in dismay. "Feeling sorry for myself?" she echoed. "How do you know what I'm feeling? I'm sitting in a jail cell, accused of a murder I didn't commit, and you think I don't have the right to feel sorry for myself? Best case scenario, I go to jail for the rest of my life. That's not something I can live with, so you'll have to excuse me if I want to sit here and feel sorry for myself."

"Lexy," Dawn started to reach out her hand but stopped. "Don't bother," Lexy spat. "I've had enough of you. Guard!"

Dawn shook her head frantically. "I'm here to help you. Don't you understand that? We want to clear your name!"

Lexy was ignoring her. "Guard!"

Spenser appeared at the cell door, his hand firmly on the pistol in his holster.

"Get her out of here," Lexy growled.

Dawn looked from Lexy to Spenser, and back again. Shaking her head disapprovingly, she lifted her briefcase from the cot and moved toward the cell door. Waiting for Spenser to open it, she glanced back one final time at Lexy. She had once again curled herself into a ball in the corner. Dawn knew all her defenses were up. Every wall in her psyche had been reinforced. She wasn't letting anyone in.

Dawn returned her attention to Spenser. "Thank you. I'll be in touch."

***

Hayden slowly pulled the hammer back on his weapon and cradled it between his sweaty palms. He looked at the barrel of the gun. It was exquisite in its blackness, much like dark storm clouds that rolled in just before dusk. Setting the handgun on the floor next to him, he pulled himself up off the floor. He stretched his tired, worn body and looked around the room. It was still in a complete state of disarray. He was exhausted from having sat in the same spot for almost a full day with no sleep, but he had to be sure. He couldn't allow himself a moment of rest, as it would let his guard down. He had cursed himself for allowing that man to see him through his window earlier in the day. It was just clumsiness on his part. It could've gotten him killed. He knew that.

Crouching back down, he glanced across his darkened apartment. A wisp of yellow light was bleeding under the crack in his door. It ran and tumbled across the floor until it died somewhere near the middle. He could easily make the restroom from where he was without passing any windows or doors. He glanced to his right and saw an empty milk carton. Hayden shook his head. Even he wouldn't go that far.

Crawling on his hands and feet, he scurried across the hardwood floor. He stopped just short of the door as a noise caught his attention. He froze. He could hear his pulse quickening in his ears and feel a light residue of sweat forming on his brow. He heard the noise again. It was almost a scraping sound, he decided, but not quite. Hayden exhaled slowly and rocked back onto the balls of his feet. The silence around him became deafening as he listened for the sound again.

His pulse jumped as he heard it. This time, it was louder and much closer.

Hayden swallowed hard and stood up. It was coming from the door. He moved slowly atop the creaking wooden floor, his attention focused completely on the wooden rectangle that separated him from the outside world. He could feel the blood draining from his face as he neared it. He stopped and glanced at the loaded weapon on the floor, then back at the door. He had pushed several pieces of furniture up against it, including his couch. He was confident no man could break through that door, but that wasn't what he was worried about, was it?

This is stupid, he told himself as he inched closer to the door. Resting one knee on the couch, he leaned his ear against the door and listened intently. The scraping sound appeared again. It was sharp, not like that of fingernails, but more like a piece of metal, or a blade.

He ripped his head away from the door just as a knife exploded through the shoddy wood. He watched in terror as the blade wiggled back and forth as the attacker tried to free it. Thinking quickly, he grabbed a nearby phone book and slammed it against the broad side of the knife. He hit it again, then again until the blade started to bend. Rearing back, he threw his weight into another attack. The spine of the mammoth book landed firmly against the silver blade and succeeded in bending it almost in half. Taking a step back, he watched the blade wobble in the door one last time, then fall still where it had become entrenched.

Silence.

Hayden took a deep breath and wiped his forehead with the back of his shaking hand. He felt as if at any moment, his knees would buckle beneath him. He knew his desperate act had required a heavy dose of adrenaline, and that it was slowly wearing off. He listened again, waiting. There was nothing. He looked at the blade still hanging limply in the door. He hoped that had assuaged the attacker. Sighing deeply, he turned his attention to the telephone. He knew he should call the police. Reaching down to the floor, he snatched his cordless phone up into his hand. Using his thumb, he tapped the talk button and held it to his ear.

Nothing.

He pulled the phone away and glared at it. Tapping the talk button again, he waited for a moment, then repeated the action. Holding it to his ear again, he waited for the dial tone, but it was silent. There was nothing but an empty hiss in the receiver. His heart jumped up into his throat as he dropped the cordless to the floor. He had just seen a dark shadow pass in front of one of his apartment's three windows. Kneeling down, he slowly took his gun in his hand and steeled his nerves.

At that same moment, the middle window shattered inward. Slowly rising to his feet, Hayden lifted the weapon toward the window. He ran his thumb over the hammer and cocked it. He watched the window intently as his hands began to waver. Fear was eating him alive.

Again, there was nothing. Hayden let out a long-exasperated breath as he wiped the beads of sweat from his brow. Cradling the weapon in both hands, he slowly uncocked it and let it fall to his side. Taking a few tentative steps toward the window, he peered through the shards of glass, nothing but the cool Seattle night outside. The gears in his mind began to whirr. Something wasn't right he—

A dark form swept in the window hitting Hayden squarely in the chest. Hayden skittered to the floor, his back hitting hard against the broken glass. He could feel the tips jutting into the soft flesh of his back. His eyes went wide in the darkness as he scanned the room for his attacker, but there was no sign of him. Making a split-second decision, he lifted himself off the floor and quickly retrieved his weapon. Quickly sweeping the room, he moved slowly toward the barricade in front of his door. With one hand still firmly on the weapon, he pushed the pile of rubble out of the way.

Taking one final look around the apartment, his hand moved rapidly to the door handle. Moving on instinct alone, Hayden bolted out the apartment's door and hit a dead run down the hall toward the emergency stairs.

***

The steady flicker of tall, black candles cast a golden light over the hard surfaces of the room. It was not designed with comfort in mind, rather pure practicality. From the walls, the black marble floor, to the ancient iron chandelier hanging overhead, this room had but one purpose. A lone figure sat cross-legged in the center. She wore dark garments and a lace veil over her face as she sat motionless. Her current task required all her attention. She couldn't allow so much as an out of rhythm heartbeat to break her concentration or use some of her precious energy. She had to focus. She felt her energy gathering in her feet and begin to work up her body. It moved slowly through her stomach and into her chest and finally, to the top of her head. With one fluid motion, she snapped her head back and released the energy. A solid blue, white stream of power surged from her eyes and mouth toward the ceiling, flooding the room with an intense light.

As the stream diffused, the woman slowly stood and opened her eyes. Vague shadows could be seen traveling in and through the light. She had done it. She spared only a moment to savor her triumph, then returned her full focus to the task at hand. As if her mind were a searchlight in the fog, the shadows were revealed to be people in their daily routine, unaware they were being watched. She stopped momentarily on a figure, but quickly continued on. She was searching for something very specific.

There was another, then another. Frustration began to build in her mind. It was imperative to find her quarry. All thoughts of despair suddenly washed away as she focused on a single woman. A faint, bubbling blue aura could be seen around her. She was bent over her computer typing effortlessly.

The witch smiled and relaxed. Flexing all her muscles at once, she raised a hand and twirled it counter clockwise over her head. The white light of the room vanished as quickly as it had appeared, leaving only the golden glow of the candles. Turning by no visible means, the witch moved toward the far side of the room, her feet never touching the floor. She motioned with her left hand and the tall, wooden door creaked open. She could see her companion before a large open window peering out into the city. It was not her place to interrupt. She had to be addressed before speaking. She folded her hands neatly and waited.

110

The second witch slowly spun to face her. "You, who are Horus, the Son," she said in a low, quiet voice, "what do you wish of me?"

Horus moved effortlessly into the room. "I kneel before Osiris, the Father," Horus said as she dropped down to one knee. "I have news."

Osiris extended her hand and lifted Horus out of her kneeling position. "What is it?"

"I have found another match," Horus hissed. "I have also seen that several new players have entered our arena." She paused, "They mean to stop us."

Osiris turned away from Horus and back to her window. "This is a regrettable turn of events." She scanned over the city with her mind. She could also feel their presence. "I hadn't expected so much outside interference, but they won't stop us." She turned back to her younger counterpart, "I have foreseen it."

"As have I," Horus agreed.

"Do we have a collector available to us?" Osiris asked. "There is already one collector on the streets."

"I do not like his methods," Osiris shook her head slowly. "He will serve us well in other capacities, but he is not delicate enough for our needs. Use another."

Horus produced a small colorful poppet from a satchel slung over her shoulder. "This woman has served us well."

Osiris nodded. "Well, indeed." She smiled beneath her veil. "Proceed, and soon we will be the Abydos Triad again and all prisoners will be released."

Horus lifted her open palm to Osiris. Lifting a knife out of her satchel, Osiris pulled it across Horus' hand opening a large gash. The wound immediately began to bleed a thick, almost black blood. Horus lowered her hand and pressed her bloody palm against the poppet doll. "By the Gates of Hell, we summon thee," she said slowly as she covered the poppet in her blood.

"By the power of our master, the Dark Lord, we command thee," Osiris continued.

Horus lifted the poppet high above her head. While cradling it in both hands, she spoke the final words of the incantation. "Let no mortal or impasse turn you away from your course. By the power of three times three, you belong to us, so mote it be!" The poppet burst into flames in her hands. Bringing it slowly down in front of her face, Horus watched her blood burn in a bright blue flame around the doll.

Osiris smiled. "It is done."

***

Lexy's head snapped back unnaturally in her cell. A low, guttural moan escaped her lips that seemed to emanate from the very bowels of hell. Her eyes closed slowly and began to jerk frantically behind her eyelids as a shiver ran up her body. She pressed her palms to the sides of her head trying to stifle the pain. Her body convulsed, knocking her to the floor. Twisting an arm around her body, Lexy slowly pushed herself into a sitting position. She slowly opened her eyes. The once dark pupils were now replaced with a thin, milk-white membrane, much like the one some species of shark use to protect the delicate flesh of their eyes during an attack. Flicking her tongue out of her mouth, she ran it quickly over her teeth. She could feel them becoming sharper, even hardening.

Standing from the cot in her cell, she moved to the rear. There was a small one foot by one foot window high on the wall. She glanced down the wall, then back up to the window. It was at least six feet off the floor.

Pressing her fingertips against the wall with unimaginable strength, she watched as they slowly dug into the concrete. Quickly, she climbed up until she was level with the window. Balling up her fist, she threw it hard into the window, shattering the thick glass, but in the process, breaking the small bones in her hand. She pulled her oddly deformed hand back and stared at it for a moment. It would heal. Reaching her arm out of the window, she began to squeeze through; first her head, then her shoulders. She felt her ribs crack one by one as she pushed her torso through. Now hanging out the window, she glanced down at the ground beneath her. It was easily twenty feet. Moving her hands behind her, she pushed off the wall and freed the rest of her body from the window.

She sailed into the asphalt below, her head hitting first with a sickening crunch, then her body, a broken sack of bones and organs, followed. Lexy lay motionless on the ground, her body twisted into an unnatural position, as a steady stream of blood seeped from the corner of her mouth.

Her eyes snapped open.

Chapter Ten

Bishop lifted his cell phone and clicked it on. He waited for a moment until the signal meter filled up. Using his thumb, he scrolled through a dozen pre-programmed numbers in the memory until he found the one he wanted. He tapped the send button and held the slim device to his ear. He glanced around the street as he listened to the ring on the other end. He had taken up a position just outside the apartment complex for most of the day, just in case his target had decided to leave. He wasn't going to let this one go.

He heard the familiar click on the other end. "Dawn? It's me."

"What's the word, Bish?" Dawn asked.

"There's little to nothing on this end," Bishop assessed grimly. "I thought I might have one lead, but my best efforts have been blocked."

Dawn sighed. "I haven't had much luck either. Why don't you head back? We'll regroup and try and attack this from a different angle."

"Sounds—" Before Bishop could complete his sentence, he was knocked to the ground. The cell phone skidded out of his hand along the pavement. Snapping his head up, he saw another man also picking himself up off the ground with what appeared to be a pistol in his hand. Bishop's eyes widened at the sight. It was his target. The man looked back and recognized Bishop as well. He took off at a dead sprint down the sidewalk.

Rolling onto his hands and feet, Bishop quickly pushed off like a sprinter. He moved easily between the trash and other discarded junk on the sidewalk.

114

He was a good twenty paces behind his target and wasn't gaining. Bishop pushed himself harder, his eyes firmly focused on the man ahead. He didn't want to lose him in the twilight that had settled over the city. Dark clouds had begun rolling in again after the brief rainstorm that afternoon and were threatening once more. If Bishop didn't catch him by time it got completely dark, he knew his target would have a thousand places to hide. He couldn't let that happen. He was running for a reason, and Bishop needed to know why.

Skittering around a wayward dumpster, Bishop saw his target duck into an alley, almost losing his footing in the process. Bishop stopped at its mouth. He suddenly remembered the target had a weapon, and probably wouldn't hesitate to use it. Craning his head slightly around the corner, Bishop smiled. The alley came to a dead end. His eyes quickly scanned the shadows. There were several places to hide there, and any mistake on Bishop's part could be a deadly one. He took a deep breath and stepped into the open. Raising his hands above his head, he continued to peer into the darkness. He had a plan.

"I just want to talk," Bishop said evenly. "I just want to ask you a few questions."

Bishop heard the crack of the weapon and the bullet whizzing past his ear. Diving to the left, he hit the ground and rolled away from the alley. "Shit," he muttered under his breath. "I knew that was coming." He took a deep breath as he pulled himself up into a sitting position and rested against the wall. "There's no way out," he shouted into the alley.

"I have the gun!"

115

"Yes, you do," Bishop conceded dully, a bit shocked hearing his target's voice. "Listen, I just want to talk. I don't want to hurt you." Bishop shifted up onto the balls of his feet.

"It's not you I'm worried about."

Bishop was puzzled at the statement. "What are you talking about?" No reply.

Bishop slowly peeked around the corner. He cursed under his breath. He was quickly losing the light. It was getting harder and harder to make anything out in there. He spotted a tall dumpster just inside the alley. He knew he could make it there if he just stayed low. "I can help you, if you'll let me," he said as he started to move.

"I don't think so."

Bishop pressed his back flat against the wall as he began to slink inside. Slowly at first, he used his hands to guide him along the wall. Due to the echo in the alley, he couldn't get a fix on his target's voice. He could easily be at the very end, or on the other side of the dumpster for all Bishop knew. "Listen to me, I work with a group who helps people. All you have to do is lay down your weapon and come out." Bishop felt a small chunk of broken concrete next to him. He slowly cradled it in his hand.

"That's not going to happen."

The voice, it was…Bishop snapped his head up and felt his heart sink. His target was standing on a fire escape directly above him. He had seen Bishop's every move and had his weapon pointed directly at him. Bishop dived forward just as the target pulled the trigger again. He heard the bullet ricochet off the ground just behind him. Bishop rolled hard to his left coming up on his feet. He reeled back with the concrete and tossed it as hard as he could toward the target. He let out a grunt of satisfaction as the chunk hit his target just below the bridge of his nose.

Bishop snapped his head to the right and spotted the ladder leading up to the escape. He leapt ahead and latched on. Glancing back up at his target, he watched as the man quickly regained his balance. Bishop moved briskly up the ladder and onto the fire escape. He charged the target, stuffing his shoulder directly into the man's midsection. The target let out a gasp as the wind was knocked out of him. He tried to retaliate, but Bishop was already on top of him. Grabbing him by the shirt collar, Bishop swept his leg behind the target's knees and dropped him to the iron grating. The pistol fell onto the edge of the railing, teetering on the brink of falling.

Bishop jabbed a knee into the man's midsection while pinning his arms down. "I'm not here to hurt you."

A trickle of blood from Hayden's nose ran down over his lips. "Could've fooled me," he said with a gasp.

Bishop watched as the man's eyes focused on something just over his shoulder. "What?"

"You're going to die," Hayden whispered in fear. "Not by your hand," Bishop noted.

"No," Hayden swallowed hard, "by its."

Bishop peered over his left shoulder to see a dark form standing on the edge of the roof just above them. It was watching them. Bishop drew a deep breath, "Oh crap."

Kelley ducked around a corner just as an orderly went by. She caught herself marveling at the cleanliness of the hospital again and mentally reprimanded herself. This wasn't the time for that. The doctor on call had just come on duty and she had to catch him before he started making his rounds. Kelley had been sitting in the waiting room most of the evening, sifting through old magazines and waiting. The information she had culled from the Chief of Staff had told her which doctors had been on duty last night, and who probably handled Lexy's case. Kelley knew it was imperative she talked to him. It was only then she would begin to get answers.

She glanced down at her watch. It was nearing eight-thirty, well past visiting hours. She had to be cautious. Closing her eyes, she reached out with her mind and scanned the hospital. She smiled. He was here. She could sense him. She also felt several other doctors and nurses on this floor, as well as a few orderlies. It would be easy to work her way around them. That was one of the benefits of being able to read thoughts. She knew, almost before her subject did, where they were going and what they had to do. When all the information was available, evasion was simple. Even if she was spotted, she could easily plant a false image. She had even, on a recent case, planted the image in a police officer's mind that she was a detective on the same force, even though they had never met. The police officer trusted the image as his thought and revealed every

118

detail of the case to her. She hated to do that, but sometimes, it was necessary.

Kelley stepped out into the hall and proceeded down a long corridor. She could feel the doctor near, but she couldn't quite get a fix on him. There were so many different patients on this floor, it was hard to single out an individual person, but she trusted her instincts. Turning the corner, she zeroed in on her target. Glancing to her left, she spotted a small cart and smiled. Quickly moving to it, she grabbed a piece of paper and a pen off of it.

Dr. Rhys David pulled off his jacket and slung it onto one of the arms of a nearby coatrack. Stretching his arms out wide, he arched his back, feeling it pop twice. He rolled his head forward, then back as he tried to stifle a yawn. He hated graveyard shifts. If they were more regular on the schedule, they probably wouldn't be so bad, but as a physician, he lacked that certainty.

He patted his hands against the slicked back hair on the sides of his head. He wanted to make sure he hadn't upset it when he took off his coat. Slowly moving down his face, he felt slight stubble on his cheeks. He thought momentarily about shaving, but then decided against it. Tonight, he would just have to go with the rugged look. He hated to do that, as it was his experience that patients were often more trusting of a doctor that was well groomed and dressed, but at the moment, he just didn't care. This was supposed to be his night off after all. He'd even had reservations at one of the harder to get into restaurants downtown and had to cancel at the last moment. He shook his head

119

and smiled a crooked smile. This was his chosen profession. He would have to make sacrifices.

Moving to a bank of lockers in the small dressing room, he stepped in front of the second to the left. Reaching down, he popped it open and browsed over the inventory. Several personal effects sat on the second shelf, while two of the standard white smocks hung beneath. He began to reach in as he heard the dressing room door creak open. "James," he said without looking, "you're late." He turned to see a lovely blonde woman standing in the open door with a quizzical look on her face. "Oh, I'm sorry. I thought you were someone else."

"It's quite all right," Kelley said evenly. "I get that a lot," she joked. "What can I do for you?" Dr. David asked as he pulled on his coat.

Kelley focused her thoughts quickly and connected with David's mind. She transferred a new image in; only slightly different from the one he already had of her. She paused for a moment, allowing the new image to take hold. Kelley pointed to a folded piece of paper she had hanging out of her shirt pocket. The letters FBI were clearly written in dark pen.

"What can I help you with, Agent…?" David said after a moment. Kelley smiled at her success. "Agent Windel," she said. "I have a few questions about a patient you worked with last night." She fished the picture of Lexy out of her pocket and handed it to David.

"I'm sorry, I don't think I recall seeing her," he answered honestly.

"Her name is Lexy Weiss. She's our main suspect in a rash of homicides." Kelley paused,

120

"She came in here early this morning covered in blood."

"Oh," David said, snapping his fingers. "I remember her now. She was a bit of a nut case, screaming and carrying on. We had to restrain her and then sedate her to even examine her."

"What can you tell me about her, Doctor?"

"Not much, I'm afraid." He pulled his favorite pen out of his locker and slid it into his shirt pocket. "She was in pretty good health, all things considered."

"What was she screaming about?" Kelley probed.

"It was mostly nonsensical. One minute, she would be ranting about this all being a dream, then the next, she would be crying about something. She kept saying something about a," David searched for the word, "triangle? No, that's not right."

"Focus, Doctor, this could be very important."

David began to rub his chin between his forefinger and thumb. "I think it was tri- something. I can't quite remember. Maybe triad?" David said with a shrug.

"Is that all you remember?" Kelley asked.

"Pretty much. Honestly, Agent Windel, there isn't much to tell. She came in here, we sedated her, performed a very cursory examination, then released her to the Seattle Police Department."

"Did you have time to perform a toxicology on her?"

David shook his head. "The SPD didn't request one. If you ask me, it would've been a good idea. That woman was obviously on something."

"Why do you say that?" Kelley asked.

"She was displaying all the characteristics of an addict coming down from a high: bloodshot eyes, slow pupil dilation and poor reflexes. There was definitely something in her system."

"Why wouldn't the police request a toxicology report?" Kelley asked more to herself than the doctor. "That's a bit odd."

"I agree."

Kelley mulled over the information for a moment, rolling the word "triad" around in her mouth. She wasn't familiar with it, but she thought, it might not even be the right word. She returned her attention to the Doctor. "Thank you, Dr. David. If I need anything else, I'll be in touch."

David nodded. "Any time, Agent Windel."

Kelley turned and moved out into the hallway, retracing her steps toward the main elevators. *What did it all mean? And why had there been no toxicology performed?* There were too many questions. She had to report back.

Chapter Eleven

Dawn pushed open the door to Cane's hotel room without knocking and strode inside. Dropping her briefcase on the floor, she quickly kicked off her shoes and dropped down into a chair in the back of the room. Propping her elbow up on the arm, she ran her fingers through her hair as she let out a long breath. She had the sudden realization that she wasn't alone. Sitting straight up in the chair, she glanced over the room until her eyes settled on a figure seated on the opposite side.

"You're not a lawyer," a low voice spoke.

Dawn clicked on the small lamp sitting on the table to her right. "Detective Spenser," she exhaled. "You know this is a serious invasion of my privacy."

"It's also a serious offense to lie to a police officer." Spenser ran his thumb over the brim of his fedora. "I dug into your records, Ms. Lassiter. There is no mention of anyone named Dawn Lassiter ever passing the bar exam in any state, and there was also no mention of the firm you claim to work for." Spenser stood up and moved closer, "So who are you?"

Dawn leaned forward and began to rub her hands slowly together. "Are you going to arrest me?"

"Depends."

"On?" Dawn asked quizzically.

"The answers I get from you." Spenser slid his lanky frame into a chair opposite Dawn. "Who are you," he paused, "really?"

123

"My name honestly is Dawn Lassiter," she started, "and I work for the Office of Paranormal Research."

Spenser sat back in the chair and rubbed his chin thoughtfully. "I've heard of that group," he stated. "You guys run around the country chasing ghost stories, right?"

"Not exactly," Dawn said with a smile. "We investigate and research claims of the paranormal. Oftentimes, we are called in to work with local law enforcement on cases just a bit outside the norm. With our help, the Fort Worth Police recovered an abducted child earlier this year."

"How is that related to the paranormal?"

"Turns out the abductors were a group of Satanists planning on eating her. With our knowledge of the occult, we easily infiltrated the group and recovered the girl."

Spenser smiled. "Couldn't the FBI do that very same thing? I mean, they have experts on those kinds of things."

Dawn nodded. "That's true, but the parents didn't want to involve the Bureau. We were their only other option in the situation."

"Okay," Spenser said slowly, "then tell me why you're here."

"This is more of a special case," Dawn said after a moment. "Your main suspect, Lexy Weiss, is the daughter of our chairman, Thomas Weiss. This was a special request on his part."

"So what you're saying," Spenser dropped his fedora onto his right knee, "is that you are here because of a conflict of interest?"

Dawn looked puzzled. "What do you mean?"

"Your chairman sent you to clear the name of his daughter, so you're not looking at the situation with enough detachment. This is personal."

Dawn thought about the comment for a long moment. "While I can certainly see how this could be perceived that way, we are nothing if not researchers. We are trained to look at events through the eyes of science, not emotion." Dawn leaned closer to Spenser. "Detective, we're here to solve a case. It doesn't matter if it involves the chairman's daughter or a complete stranger.

Our course is clear."

"Persuasive," Spenser finally said.

"Detective Spenser," Dawn said softly, "why are you really here? You could have easily sent an officer down here to arrest me, if that was your intention."

"True."

Dawn waited for a more complete answer. "And?"

"I'll admit it," Spenser smiled mischievously, "coming down here, I already knew you worked for the OPR. I just wanted to hear you admit it," he paused, "and ask a favor."

Dawn laughed softly. "And that would be?"

"I want your help on this case."

"Why?"

"I contacted several police forces you've worked with and they all recommend you very highly," Spenser admitted. "Truth be known, I could also use the help."

Dawn's curiosity had been piqued. "Why?"

"There's some strange shit going on out there right now," Spenser said gravely. "I'm talking about end of the world omens like frogs raining from the sky, locusts invading downtown and water turning to blood, among other things. I don't think I can handle this one alone."

"What about the FBI?" Dawn wondered.

"They've already succeeded in burning all their bridges and they've only been in town one day. The Bureau has officially taken over this investigation, but I can't help feeling like they're on the wrong track."

Dawn nodded. "What can we do to help?"

***

Cane was standing alone in the darkness. He had left Lydia's bar several hours earlier and since then, had been wandering the streets. This had been his home so many years ago, as well as his first exposure to the American culture he had come to embrace. In and around, he had been visiting his old haunts looking for familiar faces, but none were to be found. He felt a strange sense of belonging when he came back here. He knew where he needed to be was in Washington D.C., but this is where he belonged. The city had been ingrained on his very soul.

Cane dug his hands into his pockets as he ducked beneath a small overhang. He needed a reprieve from the rain for a moment. That was one thing he could safely say he didn't miss about this place: the rain. It seemed like it was always raining here, but he knew that wasn't true. Seattle, just like any other place, had its share of sunny days. It was just the rain everyone remembered.

126

His mind wandered back to Lydia. They had been wonderful together. But he came up wanting. An offer from his friend Thomas to start a business had been too tantalizing to pass up, even if that meant leaving everything he knew behind. Sacrifices were required, he told himself, but in retrospect, he wondered if he made the right decision. He could have happily lived out his life here in Seattle with Lydia, and maybe he could again. After all, he was getting older, and chasing specters was a job for the young.

He thought about his team. Dawn was qualified enough to lead the team, and he knew he saw a reflection of himself in Bishop. With the recent addition of Kelley to the roster, he knew his people had every tool they needed to succeed.

Would it be worth it?

He couldn't help wondering what Lydia's response would be if he told her that he was coming home. Would she take him in with open arms, or would she be unwilling to risk losing him again? It was a difficult decision he had ahead of him. What would his colleagues say? How would they take this? He shook his head. They would have to understand, he told himself. This was his life. His decision. They had to respect that.

He returned to the question plaguing his mind. Would it be worth it? He couldn't be sure of that until he took the leap. He would be with Lydia…but that hadn't been enough once, would it be this time? He hated to admit it, but the woman he had the longest relationship was Dawn. No other had even come close to that. He allowed himself a brief smile. Maybe that was a sign.

There were a lot of maybes. Too many to consider right now. He had a task at hand, one that he was determined to see through to the end, and then he would see. That was all he could promise himself. Nothing more. There was work to be done. All else would have to wait, even if it meant the biggest decision of his life.

The ring of his cell phone distracted him. When he had first bought the phone, Dawn had set it on one of those God-awful musical rings that drove him up the wall. Unfortunately, he had never learned how to change it. He pulled the sleek black phone out of his pocket and folded it open. He tapped the send button with his index finger, then pressed it to his ear.

"Cane here."

"It's Dawn."

"What's up?" Cane asked quickly, not in the mood for any sort of small talk.

"I have a guest here in your hotel room, one who wants our help."

"Who is it?"

"Detective Spenser of the Seattle Police Department," Dawn said confidently.

"We weren't approved to work with the police on this mission," Cane said disapprovingly.

"I know, but he came to us."

"I'm on my way," Cane said as he snapped the phone shut. Sliding it back into his pocket, he glanced around the darkened city one more time, then set off back to the hotel.

***

Bishop took a deep breath as he rolled off Hayden, his eyes squarely focused on the dark figure looming above. He expected at any moment that a pair of glowing red eyes would materialize and it would be on top of them. He slowly moved toward the pistol and took it into his hand. Sliding his thumb up the handle, he carefully cocked back the hammer.

"Don't make any sudden movements," Bishop said quietly to Hayden. "We don't know what we're dealing with yet."

In one fluid motion, Hayden rolled onto his feet and snatched his weapon from Bishop's hand. "To hell with that."

"No," Bishop yelled as he struggled to regain control of the gun.

Without another moment's hesitation, Hayden pulled the trigger, sending the bullet careening toward the figure.

Bishop turned his head just in time to see the figure stumble back as the projectile tore through its shoulder and fall out of sight. "You shouldn't have done that," Bishop said, quickly ripping the gun from Hayden's hand. "We need to go.

Now."

"I'm not going anywhere with you," Hayden said quickly.

Bishop stood and moved toward the fire escape. "Fine. You stay here and take your chances with whatever that was. Just remember, I could've helped you." He started to climb down the ladder.

Hayden looked from Bishop back up to where the figure was standing, then back at Bishop. "Don't leave me," he shouted as he ran toward the ladder.

Allen tapped lightly on Fowler's door. Standing outside, he glanced nervously around the hallway of the motel the two were staying in. Fowler hadn't returned any of his calls or pages all afternoon. Since finding the note, Fowler had locked himself in his room, refusing to come out. Allen didn't know why, and it frightened him. His partner wasn't scared of anything, and yet, when he opened that note, it appeared as if all the life had drained from his face. He had to know what was going on.

Allen knocked again. "John?" He heard motion inside the room and slowly took a step back from the door. The doorknob rattled once and then stopped as if Fowler grabbed the handle, then changed his mind. Allen pounded on the door with the meaty side of his fist. "John! Let me in!"

The door suddenly swung open revealing a frazzled Fowler. His shirt hung open with his undone tie dangling from the collar, while his usually well-kept hair was sprouting in several different directions. "Keep your damned voice down," Fowler whispered angrily, "and get in here."

Allen stepped inside the room and was abruptly pushed out of the doorway by Fowler. He spun around to see Fowler throwing the door shut and locking the dead bolt. Allen slowly turned to look at the single occupant room the Bureau had afforded them. The single bed was awash with piles of crumpled papers and notepads; all with computer printed or hastily scrawled notes upon them. The familiar sound of a printer drew Allen's attention to a small table situated in the corner. Fowler had a small, white laptop sitting in the middle with a portable printer on the side spewing out what appeared to be an endless stream of documents. An ashtray sat on the opposite side heaped with half smoked cigarette butts. Allen turned back to Fowler, who was still standing in the doorway, his back against the door. "John, what the hell is going on here? We have an investigation to continue."

Fowler shook his head. "Something more pressing presented itself." He pushed past his partner and retook his position in front of his laptop. "Come look at this."

Allen moved across the room and peered down at the screen. "What am I looking at?"

"This is a brief, but relatively complete picture of the Egyptian culture at its peak," Fowler said as he scrolled down the web page. "The answer is here."

"What answer, John? What are you talking about?"

Fowler reached for his shirt pocket. Digging his fingers inside, he stopped. "Where is it?" Quickly standing up, he patted down his pant pockets then straightened up. "It's not here." Fowler pushed past Allen again as he started rooting through the piles of paper on the bed. "Where is it?" he asked almost frantically. "It should be right here!" He flung pages in all directions as he searched, then stopped. His eyes narrowed. Moving to the back of his chair, he pulled his dark jacket off and dug his hand into the pocket. Fowler let out an audible sigh as he pulled a scrap of paper from the pocket. "It's this," he said handing the scrap to Allen.

131

Allen unfolded the scrap to see the same writing he had earlier in the day. Refolding the paper, he placed it on the table next to his partner. "John, I need to know what's going on. That little scrap didn't tell me anything."

"The answers are there, you just have to decipher them," Fowler said confidently, "and I think I have." He double-clicked a link near the top of his browser's window, opening up a new page. "I recognized the writing as soon as I saw it. I had seen it before," his eyes seemed to glaze over for a moment, "a lifetime ago."

Fowler highlighted several graphics on the page and pointed to them. "Are you familiar with Egyptian culture?"

Fowler shook his head.

"This is Osiris," he said, pointing to a picture of a man. "He was the ruler of the underworld."

"Like the devil?"

"No, not exactly. The underworld was where the good went after the souls were balanced and weighed by Anubis. The Christian equivalent is Heaven. In Egyptian mythology, Osiris with his wife Isis, son Horus, and brother Seth, were very important figures. Osiris represented the resurrection into eternal life."

"I don't understand what this has to do with anything," Allen said with an exasperated sigh.

"I'm getting to it," Fowler said slyly. He turned back to his computer. "The story goes that Seth, Osiris' brother and lord of all that was evil, was jealous of his brother, so he killed Osiris and separated his body into fourteen pieces. He then scattered them about the land. Isis took it upon herself to recover the parts, and resurrect her husband. Osiris was reborn into immortality. With their son Horus, Osiris and Isis form the Abydos Triad of gods." Fowler closed the browser window and turned to Allen. "There was a sect of Osiris and Isis followers several years ago that held the belief they too could attain immortality through the use of the Osiris Myth and ancient Egyptian Magicks. They abducted several children and sacrificed them in their rituals."

Allen sank down onto the edge of the bed, intrigued by Fowler's story. "How do you know all this?"

Fowler furrowed his brow. "I was there." He grabbed his pack of cigarettes and slid one out. Lighting it, he took a long drag and slowly exhaled. "I couldn't save those kids, Greg. I was too late. It was one of my first cases out of the academy: infiltrate the cult and retrieve the children." Fowler stared at his half-smoked cigarette, then crushed it out in his ashtray. "I successfully infiltrated the cult, but that's where things started to go wrong.

"I became enchanted by them. They were extremely persuasive in their beliefs. I became one of them, Greg. I was there the day they killed those kids. I watched the High Priestess tie those innocents to poles, then slit their throats, and I did nothing."

Allen watched his partner become visibly shaken. "I never knew."

"No one does. It was buried under a mile of paperwork. If the media caught wind that one of the FBI's latest recruits had joined a child killing cult, the Bureau would never have recovered. It was hidden to protect all involved."

"What happened to the cult?"

Fowler smiled. "They got what they deserved, but by then, it was too late. Another agent working the case led an ATF raid on the Abydos Compound, killing several of the followers and Isis, the High Priestess." Fowler lit another cigarette. "After that, I wasn't allowed on active duty for almost two years. I had to undergo rigorous psych evaluations almost daily. I probably would've been drummed out, but they felt by keeping me under their thumb, they could better control the information, and me."

Allen clasped his hands and just stared at his partner for a long moment. "I don't know what to say, John. That's a horrendous story, but I still don't see how that connects to our current case."

"Don't you see?" Fowler said with a deep pain in his voice. "That scrap of paper I pulled out of the dead prostitute, it's an Egyptian spell. They placed those with all their children victims to ensure their souls wouldn't leave their bodies, but rather join the collective power of the High Priest and Priestess. It's happening all over again. The cult has returned and they're operating right now here in Seattle."

Allen stood up and started toward the phone. "We need to contact our SAC. This is going to require more than two agents."

Fowler bolted from his chair, slapping the phone out of Allen's hand. "No!"

"What the hell are you doing?"

"Not this time, not again," Fowler muttered. "This time, I stop them." Allen's cell phone interrupted the moment. Digging it out of his pocket, he clicked it on. "Allen here," he said evenly. He listened for several moments. "I understand. Thank You." He returned the cell phone to his pocket and turned to his partner. "Bad news."

"What?" Fowler said with anticipation. "Lexy Weiss has escaped."

Chapter Twelve

Cane opened the door to his room to find most of the team already assembled. Dawn and Kelley were seated in the corner speaking to whom Cane could only surmise was Detective Spenser. Bishop was notably absent. Moving inside, Cane dropped his jacket on the edge of the bed and sank down into a chair near the others. After a moment, he leaned forward and addressed the group. "What's everyone's situation?"

Dawn spoke first. "Zachary Cane, I would like you to meet Detective Jim Spenser."

Cane made no move to shake his hand.

Dawn continued, trying to ignore her leader's odd behavior. "He's offered to share all information with us, as long as we fully cooperate with his investigation."

Cane nodded, then turned his attention to Kelley. "What do you have?" Kelley took a deep breath, "I think I struck ou—"

"Cane, what are you doing?" Dawn interrupted.

"I'm sorry, Kelley." Cane looked at Dawn crossly. "Excuse me?"

"You've treated our guest very rudely. He's offering to help us." Dawn stated. "You could at least take the time to find out what he knows."

"He obviously doesn't know any more than we do, or he wouldn't be here trying to leech off us," Cane spat.

Dawn was taken aback. She shot up from her chair and grabbed Cane by the arm, almost yanking him from his seat. "Can we speak outside?" she asked as she pulled him toward the door. Pushing

Cane into the hallway, Dawn closed the door slowly. She turned to her friend with fire in her eyes. "What the fuck is wrong with you?"

"Bloody hell. Me?" Cane asked insolently. "What about the way *you* acted in there?"

"Goddamn it, Cane, we don't have time for your bullshit. A life hangs in the balance here and you're fucking around!"

Cane's face contorted with rage. "How dare you accuse me," he growled. "Do you think I'm so arrogant I would actually take Lexy's life for granted? You obviously have no idea of who I am."

"My God," Dawn said slowly, "what is wrong with you, Cane?"

Cane took a deep breath and turned away from his partner. "I'm tired, Dawn. Tired of it all." He leaned his head against the wall. "If you haven't noticed, I'm getting old. I just don't have the desire I once had. I think it's finally time I settle down and start a real life."

Dawn took a step toward her oldest and dearest friend and placed a hand on his shoulder. "I didn't know you felt this way."

"It's been brewing in me for some time, but I guess it was just the nature of this case that finally tipped the scale," Cane admitted. "I can't stand to watch the people I love hurt anymore. I keep sending you into battle and one of these times, we're not all going to come back. I don't think I could handle having one of your deaths on my conscience."

Dawn was at a loss. She had every intention of screaming at Cane when she stepped out here, now

137

she was consoling him. "Is there anything I can do?"

Cane nodded. Slowly turning around, he took Dawn's hand. "I'm leaving the OPR. I want you to take over as team leader."

Dawn shook her head as she stepped back. "You can't leave!"

"I have to. I have outlived my usefulness, Dawn. I don't want to be known as the 'Old Sod' on the team. I can't contribute anymore. I'm just," Cane tried to smile, "worn out."

Dawn shook her head. "I won't accept this, Cane. You can't leave. You helped start this organization."

"That's part of the reason why I'm leaving. I left my life behind to start the OPR, everything I knew. I really would like to get back to that now. It's been far too long." Cane rubbed his hand through his hair. "You don't need me to hold your hand anymore. You're in charge now."

"Is that it?" Dawn asked angrily. "After all this time, you're just going to walk out and leave me?" Tears were welling up in her eyes. "How can you do that?"

"I didn't make this decision lightly," Cane said softly, "but it was a long time coming. You know I can't stay here forever."

"But why now?"

Cane smiled. "I became an American here. I lived in Seattle a long time. My life was here, my friends were here, and," he paused, "my wife is here."

Dawn was shocked by the admission. Her mind was reeling. "I can't do this alone," she whispered.

138

Cane smiled again and started to turn. "You'll do fine." Without another word, he turned and walked away.

Dawn felt her knees beginning to buckle. She reached out to the wall to steady herself as she watched her friend, her mentor, heading for the elevators. She was taken by the sudden urge to run after him and drag him back kicking and screaming, but she held her spot. She knew there wasn't anything she could say to change his mind. For probably the last time, she watched the elevator doors close on Zachary Cane. Turning back toward the door, she just stared.

She didn't want to go back in there. Now she was in charge with no one to turn to. She was alone.

***

Bishop charged around a corner with Hayden in tow, the pistol still firmly in his hand. He glanced back over his shoulder quickly to see the dark figure still following them at a distance. The figure didn't seem to be trying to catch up, rather, it was just tailing them. Returning his gaze in front of him, Bishop spotted a large mall looming just ahead. Pushing on, he crossed through the rows of cars toward the front doors. At the very least, they could hide in there. They had to get out of the open into a well-lit area with lots of people.

"I don't think this is a good idea," Hayden protested through heaving breaths. He definitely wished he hadn't let his gym membership expire last year.

"Shut up," Bishop yelled as he cut around an oncoming car, barely missing it, and continued on. Upon reaching the mall's sidewalk, Bishop spun on his heels. The figure had no intention of giving them up, even if they went inside. He had almost bridged the gap between them, hopping along the roofs of cars as he cut across the parking lot. Bishop watched the figure move easily along the rooftops. Its movements were dynamic and forceful. He appeared much more like a predatory animal than a person. Each step, each jump, seemed to be perfectly timed and executed for maximum efficiency.

"Shit," Bishop muttered. Stuffing the gun into the waistband of his jeans, he threw open one of the large glass doors and pushed Hayden inside. "Move now."

The mall was packed wall to wall with people. Bishop could smell the potpourri of scents from the food court wafting through the air, and the not-so-subtle smell of chemicals used to clean the floors. The floor was covered with cream-colored tile, while the walls were the standard white with splashes of bright color applied evenly over them. Glancing to his left, there was a jewelry counter, followed by an optical center and finally, a toy store. Through the maze of people and stores, Bishop couldn't see the opposite side of the mall.

Swallowing hard, he pushed Hayden into the looming traffic. Glancing over his left shoulder, he could see the figure clinging to the overhang just above the bank of glass doors. Pulling back from the glass, he lunged and crashed through, landing on his hands and feet. He wasn't on the floor for more than a second before he sprang toward the roof and latched on. There, he began to scuttle like a spider toward Bishop and Hayden.

Screams filled the corridors as shards of glass from the window rained down on the crowd. People began to scatter wildly as they spotted the figure climbing along the roof. A lanky, dark-haired woman was knocked to the ground as she tried to push her child away from the panic. The cries of her child filled the air as she tried to get up, but kept getting trampled. The crowd seemed to be moving in unison for the exit.

Bishop and Hayden pushed forward while trying to wade upstream against the flow. The figure moved easily along the ceiling, stopping just above them. Letting go, it twisted its body upright in mid-air and landed flat on its feet. Seeing no other option, Bishop threw Hayden aside and charged at the figure, finally getting a clean look at him. He was, or used to be, human. His clothes were ripped and stained, while his face and hands were covered in dried blood. His eyes were glazed over white, revealing no hint of an iris or pupil. The creature leaned forward and emitted a high-pitched shriek.

Not missing a step, Bishop broadsided the creature, hitting it squarely in the chest with full force. The two toppled to the floor, but the creature was quickly back up and on Bishop. He reared back and tore his clawed fingers over Bishop's back, cutting him deeply. Bishop cried out in agony as the creature struck again. The cuts felt like canyons of pain crisscrossing his back. He could feel blood spilling from the wounds.

Reaching back, Bishop snagged the creature's head and delivered a vicious reverse head butt. The creature, momentarily stunned, toppled off Bishop, but was quickly back on his feet. Rolling onto his back, Bishop drew the gun and fired off a quick round. The bullet hit the creature directly in the chest with no effect. Bishop fired again, hitting him in the neck this time. The creature wailed as a chunk of flesh was torn away. It again leapt off the floor. Bishop watched in amazement as the creature latched onto the roof and quickly scurried toward the wall.

"Hold it right here!"

Bishop snapped his head around to see a shaking security guard dressed in a blue and black uniform with his weapon drawn on him. "Get out of here!" Bishop yelled.

"I said, hold it," the guard yelled again. He couldn't have been more than nineteen years old.

Bishop began to move to his feet to intercept the guard, but not before the creature was on top of him again. The creature had leapt from the wall and hit Bishop in the back with both feet, smashing him to the hard tile and knocking the wind out of him.

"Jesus Christ," the guard muttered. "Don't you move!" he yelled at the creature. "I know how to use this!"

"No," Bishop struggled for breath.

The creature cocked its head to the side and flicked out its black forked tongue. It shifted its weight from one leg to the other as it looked over the guard, its white skin glistening under the hard fluorescent lights. The guard snapped back the hammer on his weapon, his hands trembling so

142

badly, he could barely hold it. He pulled the trigger, but the creature was too fast. It dodged right and attacked the guard. With one hand pressing against the young man's chest, it used the other to rip its claws across his throat. Blood sprayed out over the floor as arteries were severed. The creature wailed again as he knocked the gun from the guard's hand. It lifted its clawed hands high above its head as it prepared for the deathblow.

Bishop rolled onto his knees as he took a labored breath. Lifting up onto the balls of his feet, he prepared to spring at the creature. As he was about to jump, a gunshot echoed through the mall. Bishop watched the creature topple to the ground lifelessly. Snapping around, he saw Hayden standing just behind him with the guard's gun in his hand.

Slowly standing up, Bishop moved toward the motionless Hayden and pulled the gun carefully from his hand. "Good shot. Now call 911."

Hayden nodded and turned away.

Cradling the gun in his hands, Bishop walked slowly toward the guard and creature. Kneeling down, he pressed two fingers against the guard's throat. He breathed a sigh of relief when he found a pulse. It was weak, but it was there. Stepping over the man's body, he glanced down at the creature. Hayden's shot had ripped right through its head, obliterating the upper section of its skull and face.

Crouching down, Bishop stared at the creature. There were no signs of breathing. Using the barrel of the gun, he pressed it hard into the creature's shoulder. No movement. Sliding the weapon into his jacket pocket, he carefully rolled the creature onto its back. Lifting one of its hands, he examined the nearly two-inch claws protruding from its fingers. They hadn't grown from its fingernails; rather, they looked like extensions of the bone that had burst through the skin. Setting the hand down, Bishop slowly opened the creature's mouth and peered inside. He could see it's long, black forked tongue and several rows of razor-sharp teeth. He ran his finger over its skin. It was pliable, much like a balloon. Beneath the grey white flesh, Bishop could see a network of dark blue veins all leading toward the milky eyes. The bullet had ruptured one of the eyes, but the other was still intact.

"Let's see who you are," Bishop said as he reached into the creature's tattered jacket, "or who you used to be." He felt around for a wallet or any kind of ID in its pockets, but came up empty-handed. Rolling back onto the balls of his feet, he heard the echo of approaching footfalls. Bishop glanced up to see Hayden returning.

"The police and an ambulance are en route," Hayden said, stopping just short of the creature. "Is it," he paused, "I don't know if 'dead' is the right word, but is it dead?"

Bishop shook his head slowly. "I'm not sure, but we need to get out of here, just the same."

"Where are we going?" Hayden asked.

"We need to meet up with my partners. Cane will know what to do," Bishop said calmly. He stood up and started to move toward the door.

Hayden stopped. "We're just going to leave that thing here?"

Bishop turned around and looked at the creature. "Do *you* want to take it with us?"

Hayden thought for a moment, then furiously shook his head. "Fuck that."

***

Captain Mark Hart pulled the collar of his dark coat up around his face. Holding the envelope tightly in his hand, he made his way down the street toward a dilapidated building. It was almost in ruins. The brick it was built of had long ago begun to crumble, revealing large sections of the second floor. There was no glass remaining, it had all been broken some time ago, leaving only the rotting wooden sills. Hart knew this used to be an inn a long time ago, housing some of history's most important, and infamous, figures here in Seattle, but now it was nothing more than a derelict, a haven of evil.

He could feel the darkness emanating from the very walls. It radiated out like heat from a furnace, threatening to scorch everything with its touch. Reaching into his jacket, he pulled his necklace out from his shirt. He ran his thumb nervously over the silver talisman hanging there. He hoped it would provide some protection, as each time he traveled here, the evil furthered its plans to consume him. He would let it eventually, of course, but not yet. There was still a reason to keep his wits about him. It was very important not to give away the game, not when they were this close, so very close. They had already collected ten of the fourteen required. She would return soon, and then all would pay for their insolence. Hart allowed himself a chuckle. All religions kept promising the return of their

145

"messiah", when in reality, something very different was about to be unleashed on Earth.

Stopping at the door, he opened the top of the envelope and peered inside. There was time for one final check before it was out of his hands. Several black and white photos sat inside the envelope, along with pages of police reports. It was everything he had…no, wait, there was more. Why didn't he think of that? Spenser's files had duplicates of all the reports. Hart cursed under his breath. It was imperative he retrieve those.

Kneeling down, he slid the envelope under the front door. Before he had it fully under, an unseen force snatched the envelope and ripped it inside. Hart stumbled back from the door. He would never get used to that, no matter how many times it happened. Glancing around nervously, he started quickly away from the door. He had to be back at the office soon.

Chapter Thirteen

"Working late, Alice?"

Alice spun around with a start. Placing her hand on her heart, she sighed at the sight of Garret Wilkins, the office manager, leaning on the edge of her cubicle with his dark brown jacket slung lazily over his shoulder. Alice smiled at her supervisor. "I have to get the last of these reports done before the board meeting tomorrow. I promised Mr. Stahl I would have the complete summary ready."

Garret laughed. "Working late for old man Stahl. I don't envy you."

"What are you doing here this late?" Alice wondered.

"I, uh," Garret pointed his thumb over his shoulder at his office, "I just had a few things to take care of."

Alice caught sight of one of the cleaning crew, a slender Latino beauty with long dark hair named Lupe, sneaking out of Garret's office. She was still buttoning up her powder blue blouse, her black lace bra draped over her shoulder. Alice slowly returned her attention to Garret. "How's your wife?" she asked pointedly.

"Good," Garret said cheerfully, unaware of what Alice had just witnessed. "Cheryl dropped the kids off with their grandparents tonight and went out with her girlfriends. Well, I better be getting home." Garret started toward the elevators. "Don't work too hard, Alice," he advised over his shoulder.

Alice furrowed her brow. "Pig," she muttered under her breath. Standing up, she stretched her weary body and glanced around the office, then down at her clock. It was almost ten-thirty. Pulling off her black jacket, she dropped it on the back of her chair and walked toward the large windows that dominated one side of the office. Placing her hands on the glass, she peered out over the city and yawned. It was going to be a long night. She still had three budget reports to complete, and she had to be back here at seven in the morning for the meeting. She needed coffee.

Turning away from the window, she moved through the maze of gray cubicles toward the break room. Stopping just inside the door, she surveyed the room. It was a mess. Multiple dirty coffee mugs lay scattered about with two open bags of cookies and one half eaten yogurt. It was a small room, only being able to accommodate four or five people at a time, but nicely equipped. On the far side of the room, next to the full-sized refrigerator, there were four coffee pots, a microwave and a dishwasher built into the cabinets. Alice frowned at the sight of the coffee makers. All four were empty, and she didn't have the time or patience right now to brew her own. Digging into her pant pocket, she felt just enough change to buy a soda. Alice spun and headed for the elevators. She would have her caffeine after all.

She hit the call button once, then again. She cocked her head back to see the numbers above the door. The elevator was slowly rising. She hated having to run all the way down to the lobby to get a soda, but that was the only place in the building that had a pop machine. She usually brought her own drinks to work, but in a rush this morning, she had forgotten. She had drunk enough burnt coffee today to kill a small animal. Alice laughed to herself. She knew she would never get to sleep tonight. One late morning and she would be paying for it for a few days. Alice brushed her wavy brown hair over her shoulder as the elevator announced its arrival.

Alice stepped forward as the doors began to slide open, but stopped dead in her tracks. There, in a broken, bloody heap, was Garret's body. He had been torn apart, then thrown in a pile in the center of the elevator. Huge swaths of blood were splattered across the sliver walls. The change fell from Alice's hand as she covered her mouth. Stumbling back, she had to turn away from the body. Garret was still twitching.

Running instinctively toward the nearest phone, she lifted the receiver and punched in 911. She listened to the rings on the other end as she kept her eyes firmly attached to the elevator. One of Garret's arms had rolled forward and was blocking the door so it couldn't close. Alice finally heard someone pick up on the other side. "Help me, he's dead!" she screamed. She waited a moment for a response, but heard nothing. "Hello?" Alice glanced down at the phone to make sure she had indeed dialed an outside line. "Is anyone there?" she asked in a panic.

Alice had to tear the phone away from her ear as a high-pitched whine erupted from the receiver. Dropping it to the floor, she ran to another phone. Picking it up, she heard the same angry whine. Letting out a gasp, Alice slammed the receiver back down on the base and stepped back.

Then the lights went out.

She staggered back, fear gripping her. She waited for a moment for the emergency lights to

149

kick on. Glancing up at the unit on the wall, she saw the familiar red light blinking, but no floodlights. Pulling a chair to her, Alice carefully stepped into it. The lights now within reach, she twisted and tapped both of the bulbs. She slammed her fist against the beige plastic cover and stepped down from the chair. A noise from behind startled her. Spinning around, she peered into the darkness, waiting, watching. Her heart was thumping in her chest, threatening to burst out at any moment.

"Is anyone there?"

The sudden flash of light blinded Alice. Holding her hand up to her eyes, she saw the vague outline of a person approaching her. "Alice?" a familiar voice called out from the darkness.

"Lupe?" Alice asked slowly. The light was pulled from her eyes revealing the same woman she had seen earlier leaving Garret's office. "Lupe," Alice said again with relief. "I'm so glad to see you. What's going on?"

"I don't know," Lupe answered. She was standing in the mouth of an adjoining hallway, her flashlight in hand. "I was cleaning the offices in the other room, and suddenly, the lights went out. I think we blew a fuse or something. I tried to call maintenance, but all the phones are dead, too."

"Did you," Alice paused, "hear a kind of screaming when you picked up the phone?"

Lupe shook her head. "No, it was just dead."

The image of Garret's dead body in the elevator flashed into Alice's mind. She couldn't let Lupe see it. Not that way. "Lupe, do you know where anymore flash…." Alice stopped. A figure was looming just behind Lupe. "Get out of the way!" Alice screamed.

An inhuman scream cut through the air, then Lupe was gone. All Alice could see was the flickering beam of her flashlight on the floor. Alice took a step forward, then stopped. Whatever had Lupe was still in there, and it was probably the same thing that butchered Garret. Alice turned around and ran for Garret's office. At least in there, she would have four walls and a locked door to protect her. Pumping her legs hard, she was almost at the door when she heard the wail. Taking a chance, Alice threw herself at the door, hitting it hard with her shoulder. Chunks of wood flew from the doorframe as the door exploded open. Alice moaned in agony. She had easily broken her collarbone in the impact. Picking herself off the floor, she turned around to see a creature charging toward her. Controlling her fears, Alice flung the door shut and pressed herself firmly against it. She felt the creature hit the door with a thud which, through sheer force alone, almost pushed it open.

Alice cringed at the sound of another wail. Bracing her feet against the legs of Garret's desk, she held the door against the creature. She could hear the monster shrieking wildly outside. Alice was in excruciating pain. Every time she took a breath, pain would shoot from her collarbone. She could feel the tears welling up in her eyes. "No, goddamn it," she scolded herself. "I'm going to survive. I've got to fight!"

A clawed hand burst through the door to her right and grabbed onto her broken shoulder. Alice screamed in pain as she tried to break free from the grip. With one motion, the hand had moved from Alice's shoulder to her throat. It squeezed hard, sinking its thumb claw deep into her flesh. Alice heard a gurgling noise as she tried to cry out again. He windpipe had been ruptured. The creature pushed Alice's head away from the door, then repeatedly slammed it back. After a moment, Alice's body fell limp.

Extracting its arm, the creature forcefully threw the door open, crushing Alice between it and the wall. Stepping in, the creature pulled Alice into the open. A single ray of moonlight broke through the clouds and spilled across Alice's body on the floor. The creature crawled on top of her and sneered. Alice's eyes slowly opened. Groggy at first, she had a concussion. She fought through the fog to focus. Her eyes widened at the sight of the creature. Alice tried to scream out, but again, only produced a gurgling noise. She shook her head back and forth pleading with the creature for her life.

Lexy flicked her forked tongue out, then smiled through razor sharp teeth. Reaching back, she sent her clawed hand deep into Alice's chest.

***

"What the hell was that thing?"

Bishop shook his head. "I wish I knew."

Hayden, at least five steps behind Bishop, was moving quickly to keep up. The two hadn't spoken since they left the mall, leading Hayden to further question Bishop's involvement. Here was a man, who at the time, didn't even know Hayden's name, who risked his life for him. One thing was clear:

Hayden knew he was safe. For the first time in days, he wasn't constantly checking over his shoulder. This man, Bishop, was a hero and he owed him his life. "So, you never told me what you do."

"You're right," Bishop said acknowledging the question. He started to pick up his pace.

"And?" Hayden probed.

"I work with a group of paranormal investigators known as the Office of Paranormal Research." Bishop slowed slightly as they passed an open alley. Glancing inside, he again picked up his pace. "We research supernatural phenomenon."

"I know," Hayden said with a slight bounce in his voice. "I've been following the exploits of the OPR for years. At first it was hard, because you guys didn't release much, but when they started publishing you guys in various scientific magazines, it became a little easier." Hayden stopped dead in his tracks and snapped his fingers. "I knew I recognized you!" he said with a giddy laugh. "You were on *Ghost Chasers, Inc.* almost a year ago! You were a part of the now infamous 'Halloween Episode'!"

Bishop peered over his shoulder at Hayden. "You actually watched that?" Hayden took a step closer to Bishop. "Who didn't? I mean, in paranormal chat rooms and message boards, that episode became the Holy Grail of ghost hunting. Although, there were those who said the whole thing was hoaxed, but those guys are idiots." He again scooted closer to Bishop, "Aren't they?"

Bishop smiled and nodded.

Hayden jumped up and down, but quickly tried to regain his composure. "I knew it. I just knew it. I can't wait to log on to the net the next time and…." The gravity of his situation again caught up with him, killing his train of thought. The joy melted out of his face. He had no idea if there would be a next time.

Bishop patted Hayden on the back. "Come on, we need to keep going. We're almost there."

***

Fowler and Allen moved easily through the hospital. Moving toward the elevators near the back of the lobby, Fowler checked a small scrap of paper with instructions hastily scrawled on it. Committing the information to memory, he punched the call button with his thumb. He turned and looked at his partner, who was dusting a bit of lint off the collar of his jacket. Allen was holding it all together very well, all things considered.

Allen flicked the lint with his finger, then turned to his partner. "Did they mention anything else?"

Fowler shook his head. "No, just that they had a body they felt we would be very interested in."

"How do we know this is pertinent to our case then?"

"We have faith," Fowler said quickly as the elevator doors slid open.

***

Spenser snapped his cell phone shut and stood up. "We need to go now." Dawn and Kelley stared up at the older man. Dawn was the first to speak.

154

"What's going on?"

"We have a new body."

"Another murder?" Kelley asked.

"No," Spenser said as he slipped on his fedora, "we think we have our killer."

Chapter Fourteen

Chairman Weiss sat alone in his office. He laid his palms flat on his large wooden desk and stared at his beige telephone. No word, not even a progress report had been issued so far, but, he reminded himself, it had only been one day. Standing up, he walked around his desk to the row of bookshelves on the far wall. Running his finger over the spines, he searched for one that he hadn't read before, or in a while, for that matter. He needed something to take his mind off the case.

Finally settling on an old, dusty volume, he pulled it from the shelf and moved toward the green leather couch he kept in the corner. Sinking down into it, he carefully opened the book, careful not to break the spine. This book was older than he was. Weiss flipped through the first few pages, then settled in. Glancing over the first paragraph, Weiss stopped and closed his eyes. He pinched the bridge of his nose between his thumb and forefinger trying to relieve some of the pressure. After a moment, he took a deep breath and sat forward on the couch.

Placing the book on a small, glass table, he glanced around his office. It was huge, by any standard. On the right side, sat his desk, bookshelves, couch and anything he needed to conduct business. To the left, he had a full-sized pool table (red felt, of course), perpetually stocked bar, personal bathroom and sauna, and a state-of-the-art entertainment center, complete with big screen television and a surround sound system. He thought about playing a quick game of pool or popping in a movie, but he knew he wouldn't be able to keep his mind on it for long.

He just wished he knew what was going on.

Weiss leaned back on the couch. They should have reported in by now, after all, that was standard procedure. He should know something…anything. He hadn't heard from his team, the police or even the media. He knew those vultures were just waiting for an opportunity to bash both him and the OPR in the press. *Those arrogant bastards*, Weiss thought, *never concerned with how much work or sacrifice had gone into a project. They were only worried about their deadlines, and money. They didn't care what they destroyed as long as they had both.*

Why didn't he know what was going on?

Picking the book up, he slid it under his arm and stood. Maybe he would be more comfortable in his chair. Walking back across his office, he stopped in the middle of the floor and stared at his phone. It was well after two in the morning on the east coast, and he had no intention of leaving the office until he heard from his team. He had to know something. They could at least call and tell him that his daughter was all right. They could at least have that courtesy, but there was nothing. Weiss began to pace back and forth in front of his desk. Minute by minute, he became more agitated.

Why in the hell did he not know what was happening?

Lifting the book into his hand, he flung it hard across the room. The book hit the wall and in a cloud of dust, crumpled to the floor. This was unacceptable. He was in charge for God's sake. This was his company and his daughter. Running

157

around his desk, he perched on the edge of his chair and picked up the phone. Punching in a familiar number, he waited for someone to pick up. He began to tap his knuckles on the desk. "Come on, come on," he said impatiently. He perked up when a human voice came on the line.

"What's your earliest flight out to Seattle, Washington?" Weiss asked quickly.

***

"My God," Allen said. "What the hell is that thing?"

Fowler moved around the body, examining it. "There were claims they had made them back then, but I never saw one for myself," he said quietly. "This is extraordinary." Fowler held his hand just over the body, "I can feel the darkness in it. It's like a black hole sucking all life into it." He kept his hand where it was for a moment longer, then pulled it away. "The power they must have to create something like this."

"What is it?" Allen asked again. He moved around the table and grabbed his partner by the shoulder. "John," he said firmly.

Fowler looked up into his partner's eyes, almost shocked he had let himself get drawn in that far. He wrung his hands together and took a step back. "That is the product of some very dark magick. It's what's known in Voodoo as a zombie." He glanced down at the body again, "Not quite living, but not yet dead."

"Do we have an ID on this guy yet?" Allen asked the attending doctor. The doctor shook his

158

head. "He was rigged for silent running. He had no fingerprints and his teeth have all apparently been filed into points. It's going to be very difficult to get a positive identification on this...*thing.*"

Fowler picked up a pair of forceps off a nearby table. Bending down to the body, he suddenly stopped and glanced over at the doctor. "You mind?"

The doctor lifted up his hands. "I don't even want to touch that thing. Be my guest."

Nodding, Fowler turned back to the body. Opening its mouth with his fingers, he slid the forceps in and grabbed the tongue. Slowly pulling back, he revealed the long, black, forked tongue. Laying it gently over the creature's bottom jaw, Fowler took a step back. "What the hell do you make of that?"

Allen shook his head. "It looks like a snake's."

Fowler nodded. "Except for these two barbs on the end of each fork," he said pointing with the forceps. "They could be part of some kind of venom system." He glanced up at the doctor for confirmation.

"I'll have to run some tests," he stated.

Reaching up, Fowler pulled the examining light down closer to the body. Grabbing a pair of latex gloves, he snapped them onto his hands and pulled open the creature's eyes. "Look at that," he said. "No pupil or iris. It looks like it's all been taken over by sclera." He bent a little nearer, "And you can see a fine web of blue veins just below the skin." Fowler stood up and snapped off the gloves. "Doctor, we have to get this thing open. I need to know what makes it tick."

159

"Isn't it enough that it can be killed?" The doctor asked, hesitant to even get near the body. "I mean, there it is. It's dead. Case closed. If you see another one, shoot it in the head."

Fowler shot the doctor a very stern glance. "Shall I put in my report that you were very uncooperative in our investigation? That could look very bad on your record, Doctor."

The doctor gave Allen an "is-he-serious?" look. Allen nodded.

Turning away, the doctor headed for a nearby sink to scrub up. "I'll need a few minutes before we begin."

"Take all the time you need, Doctor," Fowler said with a smirk.

Pushing open the double doors, Spenser, Dawn and Kelley entered the morgue. They quickly moved toward the body. "Agents," Spenser said with a tip of his fedora. "What have we got here?"

Fowler snapped his head toward the three. His expression turned dark as he quickly stepped up to meet them. "This is a restricted area. You're all going to have to leave right now."

"On whose authority has the city morgue become a restricted area?" Spenser questioned, while at the same time trying to get a peek at the body.

Fowler strategically placed himself in front of Spenser's line of sight. "The Government's," Fowler answered. "If you don't leave, I'll have to arrest you all."

"Agent," Dawn said slowly, "we're all working on the same case here. Why can't we share information?"

160

Fowler smiled slyly. "I'm sorry, miss, we haven't been introduced. You are?"

"Dawn Lassiter, OPR," she answered.

"Ah," Fowler said with a laugh, "they've called in the ghost hunters." He turned and sneered at Spenser. "Show's how desperate they've become."

Kelley closed her eyes and focused on Fowler while he was occupied with Spenser and Dawn. Reaching out with her mind, she struggled to connect with her target. His was one of the most difficult minds she had ever attempted to crack. Thick walls had been built up around even thicker walls guarding some deep, recessed secret. As she broke through one wall, another was built up around her, blocking her progress. She started again.

"You arrogant piece of shit," Spenser spat. "I should kick your ass right here." He stepped up into Fowler's face.

Fowler didn't back down. "If you think you're man enough, let's go." Spenser balled up his fists readying for an assault, but Kelley was quickly on him. "Not now," she whispered, wrapping her hands around his arm. "You will have a chance later."

Spenser remained tense for a moment, but headed the advice. "I'd better." Dawn darted around Fowler toward the body, stopping just short of the table. "A zombie," she said with a gasp. "I've only read about these things." Fowler snapped around, pulling his pistol from beneath his jacket. "Step away right now or I will fire."

Dawn slowly stepped back, her hands raised.

Allen was quickly assessing the situation from behind the table. If the need arose, he would have to act.

Fowler moved around in front of Dawn, his weapon pressed into her chest. "Get back right now."

"I'm going," Dawn protested. "Put the gun away."

"I said, fucking move!" Fowler shouted. "Now!" Fowler glanced over his shoulder at his partner. "Allen, get up here and move these people back."

Allen moved up from the rear, hesitantly drawing his weapon. "Do as he says," he warned. "We're authorized to use deadly force."

Spenser finally nodded his head. "Okay, we're going."

Spenser turned to find Kelley with her eyes still closed. He quickly tapped her on the shoulder. The three started to move toward the door, flanked on both sides by Allen and Fowler. Once outside the double doors, they heard the latch slide shut. Dawn instinctively went for the small windows on the door and began to peer inside, but stepped back as Fowler's gun was slapped against it.

"I really hate that guy," Spenser said.

Dawn nodded and turned to Kelley. "Did you have enough time?"

Kelley shivered. "It's a very dark place in there." She rubbed her temples with the tips of her fingers. "I had to really work for the information I pulled out of him. He has more secrets than any man I've ever known."

Dawn patted her partner on the back. "Good work. Let's get out of here. That body gives me the creeps, and we need to find Bishop."

Back inside, Fowler watched intently as the doctor started the autopsy with the Y incision. He dug the scalpel deep into the creature's chest just below his collarbone, spilling a viscous, dark fluid out of the cut. As doctor began to slowly peel the flesh aside, the creature blinked.

***

Alice screamed as she sat straight up. The last thing she remembered was that horrible creature and the pain, horrible, searing pain. Grabbing her chest, she ran her hands quickly over her shirt. Ripping it open, she began to examine herself. There was nothing wrong. Not a single cut or scrape could be seen, not even a bruise. Running her hand up her face, she wiped an errant lock of hair from her eyes. She looked nervously around her surroundings. She was home and in her bed but she had no idea how she'd arrived there.

A spattering of sunlight had begun to seep through her curtains into her room. Glancing at her alarm clock, she became even more confused. It was just shy of five in the morning. Lying slowly back down into bed, she pulled her thick comforter up to her chin. Alice stared at the roof while she tried to sort out her thoughts. She remembered being at the office, then that thing....

What was it?

She tried to close her eyes as she felt very tired, but they refused to remain shut. Alice again found herself staring at the textured, white ceiling. It was all she could do. She tried to ignore the nagging thoughts in the back of her mind and just enjoy the warm comfort of her bed, but there was something out of place here. There was a sense of foreboding doom surrounding her. It floated about her, making the air dense and difficult to breathe. She slowly panned her eyes over the area. Everything seemed to be in place and was immaculately clean.

The white decorum of her room showed dust and dirt very easily, making it important to clean regularly. That was one thing she hated about it.

Alice started to close her eyes again, but suddenly snapped her head to the right. Tossing the covers away, she swung her feet off the bed and walked across the room. She stopped in front of a large, framed painting on the wall. Alice ran her fingers slowly up the silver frame, then onto the glass. She took a step back. This wasn't right. The floral patterns of the painting were certainly beautiful, but they didn't belong here. They should be two thousand miles away in Maine. Alice had given this painting to her mother two months ago. It had been painted by Alice's grandfather and her mother had always treasured it, but why was it here?

Alice gasped and took a step back as the painting vanished, replaced with a portrait of herself she had commissioned earlier in the year. That *was* what was supposed to be hanging there, but how had it happened? Was she still in some kind of bizarre nightmare?

Turning away from the picture, she ran toward the bathroom. Once inside, Alice immediately turned on the tap and cupped her hands beneath the running water. Leaning over, she splashed the cool liquid against her face. Reaching blindly for a towel, she knocked over the cup that held her toothbrushes. Wiping the water away from her eyes, she immediately bent over to retrieve them. Once back on the sink, Alice pulled a white towel from a nearby rack and dried her face. She held the soft linen in place for a moment, enjoying the sensation, but something snapped her out of it. Standing straight up, she felt the hair on the back of her neck stand up. Alice snapped around to see a woman standing in her bedroom. Alice couldn't budge. The woman was dressed entirely in black with a dark veil covering her face. The only flesh exposed was that of her long, slender hands. Even her nails had been painted black.

"It's all right, dear," the woman said softly. "I'm not here to hurt you." Alice cocked her head to the right, studying the woman. The sense of doom had not left, instead it had thickened. It was almost choking her now. "You're evil," Alice stated boldly. She was startled at her own comment. She would never say anything like that. It almost didn't even sound like her.

The woman lifted slightly off the ground and hovered toward Alice. "Why would you say that, dear? I'm here to offer you a choice. Would an evil person give you a choice?"

Alice nodded, "If they knew that no matter what the outcome, they would still win."

"You are very distrustful, Alice," the woman said slowly, "but you have no reason to be. My name is Isis."

"How do you know my name?"

"Because we are in your soul right now, the very thing that makes you who you are. I know

165

everything about you, Alice," Isis said almost malevolently. "Come, we need to talk," she said, extending her hand.

Alice felt compelled to take Isis' hand. She slowly lifted her am and grasped her thin hands. Alice shuddered for a moment. Isis' hands were cold and clammy, feeling corpselike.

Isis moved slowly across the room, guiding Alice back onto the bed. Sitting her down, Isis ran her hand over Alice's hair. "Do you feel better now?"

Alice nodded, even though she felt like she could jump out of her skin at any moment. She didn't want to do anything to anger or insult this woman. Alice could feel she had power. It radiated off her in waves. "What do you want from me?"

"I think the question you should be asking is, 'what can you do for me'?" Alice was confused.

Isis nodded. "I understand. You're in a very complicated situation. You are hanging between life and death right now. One step in either direction could mean salvation, or damnation."

The words struck Alice bluntly, as if she already knew. "What can I do?"

"You have to make a choice," Isis said. "Do you know what that is?"

Alice nodded. Standing up, she looked Isis straight in the face. "I will never become part of you," she spat.

"That's unfortunate," Isis hissed. Lifting her hand, she pulled the veil away from her face.

Alice stumbled away from the sight in horror.

Isis' face was mostly exposed bone with a few sparse patches of rotting flesh hanging off it. Her

166

eye sockets were deep wells of blackness that seemed to stretch forever, while her rotting teeth seemed to be on the very verge of falling out of her head. Isis sneered at Alice and held up her hand. In it, she held a still beating heart. "Do you know what this is, child? This is your heart. My minion tore it from your chest and brought it to me. I intend for it to become mine."

"No," Alice moaned.

"I am offering you the choice. Either you give yourself willingly to me and become part of me, or I hold your soul in an eternal state of limbo, never letting you pass on to your final destination." Isis squeezed Alice's heart.

Alice tumbled to the ground, pain shooting through her body. She doubled over and grabbed at her chest. "Why are you doing this to me?"

"Because you have something I need," Isis said. "I offer this same choice to all who have come before me."

"You mean all those you steal from? You are taking our organs and our souls, our very essence, so you can live again," Alice sneered in defiance. "You are nothing but a thief. You don't care about us, so why do you even offer the choice? You will do what you want either way."

"Never let it be said that I am an uncaring Goddess," Isis smiled. "Choose now."

"I will not," Alice said in agony.

"You will not choose?" Isis asked.

Alice shook her head. "I will not help you!"

Isis stood up, looking down at Alice. "Damn you and your foolish pride. Don't you see that I offer you great power if you become part of me?

167

The remaining two gods of the Triad are rebuilding me, and you could be a part of that. You would be immortal within me. Do you not wish this?"

"I do not," Alice groaned. "You and your Triad can go to hell!"

"I would rather rule in hell…." Isis trailed off. She took a visible deep breath and sighed out loud. "That is unfortunate. Now you will never find rest." Isis dropped Alice's heart to the ground. Lifting her foot high off the ground, Isis sent it crashing down onto Alice's heart, smashing it.

Alice dropped flat to the ground, paralyzed. The familiar world around her began to fade away, replaced with darkness. Only Isis remained, barely visible against the blackness. "This is what you have chosen for yourself, girl, eternal darkness. There is no beginning, no end, only darkness. After a short time, you will begin to go mad, but you will find no relief, as even death cannot touch you here. You are now mine forever." Isis laughed out loud as she vanished.

All at once, Alice began to fall. Wind screamed past her face, twisting and throwing her around. She was helpless and alone for eternity.

Chapter Fifteen

Lexy lifted her head and slowly peered around. Confusion set in as she took in her surroundings. Her last memory was of sitting next to her cot in the jail. Then there was nothing. Only vague shadows creeping across her mind. She had been somewhere, done something, but she couldn't remember what it was. Perhaps it was nothing more than a dream, but that still didn't explain where she was, or how she had gotten here. Lexy lowered her head as she massaged her temples. She begged for a moment of clarity.

Pressing her hand against the cold, brick wall, she lifted herself off the floor. Her knees almost buckled beneath her when she applied her full weight. Holding herself up against the wall, she glanced around.

She was in an empty room, her only company the debris scattered about the floor. This place was dilapidated. She could hear the wind whistling in through several cracks in the walls. Several pools of rainwater had begun to gather on the floor. The roof obviously wasn't sound either. The only light was emanating from a small, burnt-down candle situated in a nook on the far wall. A lone door was carved out of the brick, filled with black, iron lattice locking her in.

Moving cautiously to the door, Lexy propped herself against the wall next to the lattice work and peered through. What little she could see was lit with candles as well. The rest of this place was in a similar state of disrepair. Large chunks of the building had caved in, leaving gaping holes looking out into the darkened sky. Ancient, yellowed pieces of paper littered the floor. They were being picked up and tossed about as the wind whipped through the building.

On a whim, Lexy touched her hand to the lattice. With a groan of protest, it swung open. She pressed herself against the wall, sure that someone had heard that the noise. She waited, holding her breath. After a moment, she peeked through the door. Empty. Mustering up her courage, Lexy took a cautious step outside the room. She stopped in front of the first hole. Placing her hand on the edge, she glanced outside. She was on the second floor of this building, and while she could easily make the jump, she needed to know what was going on. This place, and the secrets held within, were the key to it all. It had to be.

Turning away, she looked into the darkness. Was it worth it? The odds were that even if she did escape, she would be picked up by the police again and locked back in her cell. This could be her only chance at finding any answers.

She knew she had to take it. Lexy desperately wanted her life back. She took a step away from the wall, carefully avoiding the debris on the floor.

With her hands in front of her, she worked her way down a long corridor connecting her cell with the rest of the building. As she moved through the dimly lit area, her foot caught on a bit of brick that had crumbled to the floor. She spilled to the ground, her hands hitting first, tearing along the chaos. Rocking back onto her knees, she cradled her scraped palms for a moment as pain radiated up her arms. Biting her lip, she suppressed the pain and picked herself up off the floor. She shook her hands and continued on.

Through the darkness, she began to see the outline of a heavy wooden door. It looked as if it belonged more in the splendor of a gothic castle than this dilapidated place. Running her fingertips down the door, she came to the recessed handle. Slipping her fingers inside, she pulled back. Light began to spill out around through the cracks, flooding the corridor Lexy was in. Placing her slender fingers around the edge, she glanced through the crack. The room inside was much larger than Lexy's cell and showed none of the distress the rest of the building did. The floors were covered with lavish black marble, while the walls consisted of brick. Tall, red tapers burned in every corner of the room. Lexy guessed there were at least two hundred candles. She could feel the heat from the flames radiating out through the open door. A large stone altar stood in the middle, flanked by two huge statues representing what she believed to be Egyptian gods. On the altar itself, there were several old books, tools of a sort she wasn't familiar with, and three ceremonial knives. Two more black candelabras rested on the altar, filled with three more candles each.

Lexy glanced around the rest of the room. There was no one to be seen, but surely there was someone here. Someone had to light all those candles and place her in the cell, but why wasn't she locked in? That thought didn't occur to her until this moment. Perhaps she wasn't a prisoner after all. Pulling the door open the rest of the way, Lexy took a few cautious steps toward the altar, careful to avoid the candles. In the center of the floor, a large stone circle had been carved. Inside the circle, Lexy recognized Egyptian hieroglyphics, although she couldn't translate them. Lexy took a step back, noticing for the first time several drawers built into the altar. Carefully pulling open a drawer, she gasped and stepped back. Inside, she could see the translucent tops of several jars, each containing what appeared to be a human organ.

Steeling herself, Lexy reached into the drawer and lifted one of the bottles. Inside was a heart with several of the major arteries and veins still dangling from it. Lexy swallowed hard trying to bury the revulsion she felt. Replacing the jar, she studied the others. Each contained a different organ ranging from a liver, intestines, stomach, lungs and kidneys. All in all, there were fourteen bottles, but only ten were in use. Each one also appeared to be, she hesitated to use the word "fresh", but no decay had set in.

"Why have you entered here?"

Startled, Lexy jumped away from the altar. She spun on her heels searching the room. "Who's there?"

"This place is forbidden. Return to your cell at once," the feminine voice boomed again. It seemed to come from nowhere and everywhere simultaneously, echoing and bouncing off the walls until it folded back over itself.

"Who are you? Lexy asked bravely. "I want answers."

"What makes you think you are entitled to answers? You are nothing more than a tool for our use."

172

"A tool?" Lexy echoed. "I am no one's *tool*! I am a human being!" A pause.

"Are you so sure?"

Lexy was shocked by the question. "I don't understand."

A large mirror appeared on the opposite side of the altar. "See for yourself."

Lexy held her position. "This is a trick." She waited for a response, but there was none forthcoming. "Fine," Lexy said angrily, "I'll play your little game." She strode quickly around the altar to the mirror and stopped in front of it. Her eyes widened at the sight. Stumbling back, she tripped over herself and tumbled to the floor. Pushing with her feet and hands, she scrambled away from her reflection. "That's not me," she said in horror. "What did you do to me?"

Nothing.

Lifting off the ground, Lexy turned around and cleared the altar with her hands. The books and candles went crashing to the ground. "Tell me!" she screamed. "What did you do to me?" Lexy rushed toward the nearest statue. Using all her strength, she toppled it, watching it shatter across the floor.

Turning around, she began to run for the second statue, but stopped suddenly. Her body became rigid and she was lifted off the ground. She held firm, unable to move, until what felt like an unseen hand tossed her aside. Lexy sailed across the room hitting the far wall. Her body crumpled to the floor with a crunch. Her body and mind in shock and still unable to move, she drew a painful breath and passed out.

Horus and Osiris entered the room through an unseen passage. They both stood over Lexy's broken body staring at the disaster that had been wrought on their altar. Osiris waved her hand over the room. A dark grey haze settled in, filling every corner. After a moment, the haze receded and the room was completely repaired.

Horus turned to Osiris. "What are we going to do about her?"

"She is of no concern to us now," Osiris revealed. "We will deal with her at a more appropriate time."

"She is dying," Horus said.

Osiris turned away from Horus and Lexy. "Let her die then."

"We still need her," Horus argued. "There are several more pieces we need to attain, and our other collector has been detained."

"You question my methods?" Osiris asked.

"No," Horus answered quickly, "but we have encountered some unforeseen difficulties."

Osiris glanced from Horus then to Lexy. "Place her back in her cell," she thought for a moment, "and you may restore her. You may be right. She may yet be of use to us."

***

Cane stood just below the hanging sign of The Golden Crow. He waited, savoring the moment, wondering how Lydia would take the news. After all these years, he was finally coming home to her. Taking one of his hands out of his pocket, he reached for the door handle. Pulling it open, he again let the smells assault his senses. After taking a deep breath, Cane stepped inside. Glancing across the bar, he spotted Lydia faithfully standing there, chatting with a few patrons.

She radiated good feelings, as if she was a sun filling the room with warmth and light. Even in this downtrodden place, Cane felt safe and at home. He knew if she ever left, the place would fail instantly. It was her alone that kept the Crow open all these years. Lydia had no marketing plan, no advertising budget, and it certainly wasn't the quality of the drinks, because God knew there was more water in each than alcohol. It was all her.

Lydia glanced up from her conversation to see Cane standing there. A soft smile appeared on her face. She placed her hand on the nearest man's shoulder, ending their discussion. Pulling the towel off her shoulder, she moved around the bar toward Cane. Opening her arms wide, she embraced him. Stepping back, but keeping her arms around his neck, she glanced into his eyes. "I have news for you on your case. You were right. There are some extremely powerful witches, dark witches, operating in this area."

Cane shook his head, "That doesn't matter anymore. All that matters is that I'm here."

Lydia cocked her head to the side. "What are you talking about?"

Cane smiled slyly. "I've resigned from the OPR. I've decided to stay here…with you."

Lydia took an uneasy step away from Cane. "Why did you do that? I didn't ask you to do that," she said, clearing herself of implication in the matter.

"I know you didn't," Cane said. "I did it of my own free will. I thought it would be what you wanted."

"How can you say that?" Lydia asked incredulously. "Are you so self- centered that you are deciding what I need now? Jesus Christ, Cane," she said angrily and turned away. "You've only been back in town for two days and we're back to where we were when you left."

"What the hell are you talking about? I'm doing this for us," Cane said slowly. "I want *our* life back."

"How do you know that life even exists anymore?" Lydia looked angrily at Cane. "How do you know I haven't moved on?" Cane laughed. "You're still here, aren't you?"

Lydia began to fume. "How dare you pass judgment on me? You seem to be under the assumption that as soon as you returned to town and walked into my bar, I should have dropped everything to be at your side. Should I kick off my shoes and go cook you dinner, too? Or maybe you would like your pipe and slippers, you son of a bitch."

"What's wrong with you?" Cane asked in anger. "I didn't come here to start a bloody war with you."

Lydia laughed in Cane's face. "How could you not think that was going to happen? That's all we did when you were here! Why should we change our ways now?"

The truth hit Cane across the face, snapping him out of his rage. He took an uneasy step away from Lydia shaking his head. "I'm so sorry," was the only thing he could think to say. It was the only thing that made sense. "I really didn't come here to fight, or to force you to do anything," he assured. "I truly came here to ask for a second chance at the life I left behind." Cane turned to a small, nearby table and pulled out a chair. Sinking down into it, he let his head fall into his hands. "It's empty. I don't have anything except my work," he admitted to her. "I've thrown away so much time," he looked up at Lydia through misty eyes, "I just want a second chance."

Lydia pulled up a chair next to his, moved by his sentiment. "You're life isn't empty," she said after a moment. Reaching over, she wiped the tears from his eyes and ran her hands softly down his face. "Your life is what you make it, Cane. Nothing else. *You* chose to leave here and start the OPR. No one else made that decision for you and you have to live with that."

"What are you trying to say, Lydia?"

Lydia took his hand. "I've moved on, Cane. I have a good life now and I'm happy. I love you very much. I always have, and Goddess knows why, but I probably always will, but there's no room for you here anymore."

Cane sat back in his chair and looked at Lydia. "Can't we give it another shot? At least try?"

Lydia shook her head. "No, Cane. We don't belong together anymore. You went your way, and I have gone mine. We need to leave it at that."

Cane started to argue, but stopped abruptly. "You always were right. I should've listened to you more often."

Lydia nodded. "Yes, you should have."

"What now?"

Lydia thought for a moment. "We both need to get back to work." Cane swallowed his pride and nodded. "You said you had some information for me?"

Chapter Sixteen

"What are you doing to me?" Fowler asked.

Horus said nothing. Locking the last restraint in place, she continued with her work.

"You can't do this! I'm an agent of the Federal Bureau of Investigation! People will come looking for me."

Horus turned to look at Fowler and laughed. "Soon, it won't matter."

"I know what you're doing here, Horus," Fowler said quickly.

Horus stopped. She hadn't heard her name spoken by a mortal in a very long time. "How do you know that name?"

"I know all about you because I'm the reason you're here." Fowler grinned. "I led the FBI and ATF agents to your compound all those years ago."

Horus stepped back, her emotions hidden beneath her black veil. She stood staring at Fowler for a long time, her slender fingers clenched into a fist. "I must consult Osiris on this matter." She turned and quickly exited the room.

Fowler looked down. He had bought himself some time at least. He had been shackled to the wall, his arms stretched out above his head with his feet dangling at least three feet off the ground. The heavy iron restraints were cutting into the flesh of his wrists. There was no way he could relieve the pressure, nothing he could brace against. And he was sure that was the way they wanted it.

He glanced around the room. His eyes focused on a woman lying limp on the floor in the corner. He could see a trail of blood running down her chin

179

from her mouth. It was Lexy Weiss and she was dead. *So much for the police's main suspect,* he thought grimly. Moving away from Lexy, his eyes darted back and forth trying to take in everything. He was in some kind of holding cell, the brick walls and ceiling decaying around him. It looked as if it were going to collapse at any time.

His head was throbbing. That creature in the morgue packed quite a wallop. He could feel a deep bruise forming on his chest where the creature had broken two, possibly three of his ribs. Fowler was a mess. A long wound carved its way down his face, starting just above his right eye and moving down to his chin. Dried blood caked the wound and his face. He didn't know how he survived the attack. Fowler dropped his head. At least he had survived. He couldn't say the same for Allen. In the first moment of the attack, the creature had slaughtered his partner. It had all happened too fast. He didn't even have a chance to draw his weapon before the creature was on him.

The doctor, on the other hand, was much more fortunate. He had turned tail and ran as soon as the creature moved, but then, why wouldn't he? If he was elbow deep in a cadaver that turned out to be alive, even as he removed its vital organs?

Allen didn't deserve that. Fowler knew Allen was destined for much greater things in life. Eventually even surpassing Fowler in his accomplishments, but now, it was all gone. Wiped out in a single moment of brutality. The image of Allen's dying face was seared into Fowler's mind. He could hear the final gasp of breath from his partner as he tried to fend off the creature.

It was a swift blow to Fowler's head that ended the struggle and left him with the wound on his face. He had drawn his weapon and fired three rounds point-blank into the creature with no effect. The creature then lunged at him, his chest still gaping open from the autopsy. It hit him square in the chest, knocking him up against the examination table and breaking his ribs. The creature lifted Fowler by the head, its long claws digging into his flesh and slammed him to the ground. It was then Fowler knew he was about to die, but something strange happened. As his vision began to blur from the concussion, he watched the creature prepare for the final strike, but then he stopped. The last thing Fowler remembered seeing was the creature bending down to pick him up and then he was here…with the witches and a dead girl in the corner. Things couldn't possibly get any worse.

He heard a soft groan from the corner of the room. Snapping his eyes to the right, he watched Lexy slowly roll over onto her back. An unseen force lifted her off the ground and levitated her in mid-air. A dark blue mist formed around her entire body. Inside the mist, Fowler could see what looked like sparks. The sight transfixed him as it moved and undulated around Lexy. Her body slowly angled from a lying position to upright. The mist, as if it was a pair of hands, deposited Lexy on her feet and vanished.

Fowler watched as Lexy swayed unsteadily for a moment. His eyes widened as a transformation began to take place in front of him. Lexy's body began to mutate into the same kind of creature he had seen in the morgue. Her head suddenly snapped hard to the left, then raised back into position. Her eyes shot open revealing a milky-white color. Lexy crouched down on her hands and feet and glanced around the room as claws sprouted from her fingertips. She spotted Fowler. Leaping forward, she attached herself to the wall just above him and stared down at him. She emitted a horrid shriek as she inched closer to him, stopping just inches from his face, her head bobbing back and forth like a bird's. Fowler slowly turned his eyes to look at her. She recoiled momentarily, then opened her mouth wide. Her long, black, reptilelike tongue shot out and hit Fowler on the neck. He could feel the two small barbs sink into his flesh. Darkness immediately followed.

***

Dawn was the first one out of the elevator. She moved briskly down the hall toward Cane's room. She wasn't sure if he would be using it anymore, but it had become the designated meeting place. Spenser and Kelley were closely in tow. Fishing the key out of her pocket, she slipped it into the lock and twisted it to the right. Grabbing the handle, she pushed open the door. Dawn stopped. She knew she had left the light on earlier. Someone was in there. She signaled for the others to stop and peered into the darkness. Only the vague outline of objects were visible as a tiny amount of moonlight spilled into the room. Taking a deep breath, she began to reach for the light switch. A hand shot out of the darkness and grabbed her arm. She was yanked forcefully into the room and knocked to the floor. A man quickly climbed on top of her and pressed a cold gun barrel to her head.

Light suddenly flooded the room. Looking up, she found Bishop sitting on top of her. Reaching up, she angrily pushed Bishop off and yanked the gun from his hand. "What the hell were you doing?"

Bishop rolled forward onto his knees. "I am sorry. I didn't know it was you."

"Who did you think it was?" Dawn asked.

"A monster that's been tracking us all night," Bishop admitted. Dawn fast-forwarded past the monster comment. "Who?" Bishop pointed across the room. "That's Hayden Collins."

Dawn quickly turned and acknowledged the man. She then returned her attention to Bishop. "Who is he?"

"Witness," Bishop stated.

"That's kind of a moot point right now," Dawn said. "We already know what's going on."

Bishop straightened up. "Did I mention we were chased around the city by a monster?"

"Congratulations, you're a member of an ever-growing club," Dawn said sarcastically. She turned to see Spenser and Kelley still standing in the doorway, her hand still resting on the light switch. Dawn motioned for the two to enter. "Kelley can fill you in on the details." She pointed to Spenser. "This is Detective Jim Spenser with the Seattle Police Department. He's offered to help us with our investigation, as well as share information."

Bishop reached up and shook Spenser's hand. "Nice to meet you." He turned back to Dawn. "What do you mean 'an ever growing' club?"

"There have been more deaths, Bish, and Lexy Weiss is missing," Kelley stated. "Somehow, she managed to escape from her cell. We don't know how yet." She sat down in a chair just behind Bishop. "From what I pulled from Agent Fowler's mind, we may be in over our heads on this one. He believes there's a cult operating here in Seattle based on ancient Egyptian mysticism. They are apparently creating zombies to harvest organs from people. Their purpose is still unknown."

"They're trying to resurrect the third member of their triad."

Everyone in the room turned to see Cane standing in the doorway. Dawn jumped up, but quickly stopped herself. "What are you doing back here?"

Cane smiled. "I couldn't let you go on the hunt without all the facts." Dawn smiled and nodded. "Fill us in."

Cane moved into the room and sat down on the edge of the bed. "My sources tell me that two powerful witches are behind all this. They apparently stumbled onto an Egyptian Ritual designed to make the caster immortal."

"That confirms the information I took from Fowler," Kelley said. "So why are they stealing human organs?" Spenser asked.

"Apparently, they are trying to resurrect their High Priestess, Isis, into an immortal body. My sources also tell me the ritual must be completed by the next full moon," Cane added.

"That's good news," Dawn said. "The next full moon is tomorrow night. All we have to do is stop them from completing their task."

"I wish it were that easy," Cane said, rubbing the bridge of his nose, "they have at least two unstoppable zombies working for them. They will make this task very difficult."

Kelley stood up. "We stopped the Phantoms, didn't we? We can do this." Bishop pointed his thumb over his shoulder. "What about Hayden?" Dawn looked at the young man sitting in the corner. "What do you think, Hayden?"

Hayden smiled. "Do you think I would pass up a chance to work a case with the Office of Paranormal Research?"

Bishop turned to Dawn and smiled. "He's a bit of a groupie."

Dawn laughed. "That's fine. We need all the help we can get." She slowly turned her attention to Cane, "And you?"

Cane looked at his team. They were counting on him. He was needed and useful. "I respectfully withdraw my resignation."

Dawn moved quickly to Cane, wrapping her arms around him. "I'm so glad you're back."

Cane patted his friend on the shoulder. "So am I, dear."

"You resigned?" Bishop asked incredulously. "I'm out of the loop for a couple hours and all hell breaks loose."

Kelley laughed and placed her hand on Bishop's shoulder. "We couldn't do it without you, Bish."

Cane slipped out of Dawn's arms and moved to the center of the group. "All right, you know the drill. We need some quick research on any kind of resurrection and immortality rituals. Kelley, you

185

and Dawn are on that one. Bishop, take Hayden and round up our equipment."

"Anything specific you had in mind, Cane?" Bishop asked.

Cane shook his head. "Whatever you can track down. Detective Spenser," Cane turned to face him, "looks like you and I are on recon."

Spenser smiled. "Fine by me."

Cane looked at each member of his team in turn. They were his family now. "Everyone has their assignments, let's get a good night's rest and get on it first thing in the morning." Cane looked down at his watch, "That gives us a little under twenty-four hours to stop this. I need each and every one of your personal bests. The lives of many are resting in our hands now. If we fail," Cane paused, "we *won't* fail. We can't fail. The stakes are too high on this one." He looked around the room one last time. He was fulfilled. He hadn't realized it, but he had everything he wanted right here. "Let's get some sleep."

Each member of the team stood and began to shuffle single file out of the room until there was only Cane and Dawn. Dawn sat down in one of the chairs behind the table. She slowly crossed her legs and folded her hands. She wasn't moving without an answer, Cane knew. Closing the door behind him, he dug his hands into his pockets and moved slowly across the room. After a moment, he sat down in a chair opposite Dawn's.

"What happened?" Dawn asked after what seemed like an eternity of silence.

"It turns out," Cane said without looking at her, "you can't go home again." Dawn nodded. "I think

I've heard that somewhere. What were you trying to do here, Cane?"

Cane shook his head slowly and sighed. "I honestly don't know. Ever since this case was given to us, even before, it just feels like...." he intentionally let his words trail off.

"Feels like what, Cane?" Dawn waited for an answer, but after a moment went by, knew she would have to prod a little harder. "I'm your best friend, Cane. We've worked together for almost eleven years now. Anything you tell me will not leave this room. I swear."

Cane looked up at Dawn as if for the first time. "I'm old," he said bluntly. Dawn would've laughed if the situation weren't so serious. It sounded to her like the punch line of a bad joke. She searched for an appropriate answer, but none were forthcoming. "That doesn't mean anything anymore. The whole concept of age is in your mind," she soothed.

"To hell it is," Cane argued. "I can feel it in my joints and I see it every morning on my face."

"So what if you are?" Dawn asked after a moment. "You are still the same grouchy bastard you've always been. That hasn't changed."

"People my age start to think about settling down."

"So you want to quit? You want us to put you in a nice home in Florida, where we can wheel you out on the beach every so often and feed you prunes?"

"That wasn't exactly the sentiment I was looking for," Cane admitted. "What the hell do you want?"

"I—" The question startled Cane. He hadn't been asked that in a long time. He leaned back in his chair and stroked the gray hairs of his goatee. After a moment, he finally sat forward and rested his elbows on the table. "I don't want to see anyone get hurt anymore."

Dawn smiled softly. "You're worried about Lexy."

Cane nodded. "I can't see her get hurt."

"So you would rather walk away, holding that pristine image of Lexy in your head, than risk losing her through this investigation?"

"I know that sounds horrible," Cane admitted.

"No," Dawn interjected quickly. "It makes sense. All these years, you've been investigating cases you had no personal connection with. You had no stake in the matter, but now, things are different and you don't know how to operate."

"All the old rules are out the window on this one," Cane agreed.

Dawn reached over the table and placed her hand on Cane's. "We won't let anything happen to her."

Cane smiled. "I hope that's true."

"Whom were you running off to?" Dawn asked.

"Why do you assume it was a who?" Cane asked with a sly grin. "Because I know you too well."

"Her name is Lydia," Cane confessed. "She's a very old friend of mine." Dawn smiled. "I remember hearing stories about Lydia. I didn't know she lived here in Seattle."

Cane nodded. He got up from his chair slowly and walked toward the kitchenette. Lifting a small, plastic glass, he pulled the plastic off and held it under the tap. "Have I ever told you the story of how I met Lydia?"

Dawn shook her head and settled in. She loved Cane's stories.

"I was twenty-five and fresh off the boat from England. Most people tend to migrate to New York, but I hopped a boat that took the long way around. We stayed for a week in Australia, but that's a different story," Cane said with a smirk. "I was working at a local beef processing plant, and renting this horrid little one room apartment down by the waterside. I tended to work a lot of night shifts at the plant as I was the new kid and fairly gullible. It was then I noticed a strange amount of orders for pig and cow blood at night. At first, I paid it no mind as we were a butcher shop as well, but the frequency of the sales began to trouble me."

"So you've been interested in the paranormal all your life apparently," Dawn said.

"Yes," Cane agreed, "but up until that point, I had only read about it, or experienced it in small doses that I couldn't explain. I was fascinated by everything supernatural, but I really had no inkling of to investigate it."

"So why did the blood pique your curiosity?"

"I had read a lot about Pagans and blood rituals and other such nonsense when I was younger. Of course, now I know all that's rubbish, but then I was just a starry-eyed kid. I began to follow up on the orders in my free time, and actually did trace one of them to a small coven of witches in the area. That's where I met Lydia. At the time, she was just a first-degree witch learning the ropes, but we hit it off

189

immediately. She owned a small bar, and still does, I might add, called the 'Golden Crow'. That became my home away from home."

"That doesn't explain the blood," Dawn said.

"This one gets a little strange, so bear with me," Cane warned. "It turned out the coven had captured a member of a gypsy clan of vampires. They had him chained up in the basement and were keeping him alive with the pig's blood."

Dawn sat back astounded. "I've never read any of the OPR member accounts of vampires. The general consensus is they don't exist, or at least no longer exist. How could you keep this from me?"

"We all just wanted the events of those terrible nights to go away. Things that happened were better off left unsaid."

"So what happened?" Dawn probed.

"The vampires were using the blood to sustain themselves when they couldn't feed on human blood, which wasn't very often. They were a ravenous bunch, and they stacked up quite the death toll by the time we stopped them. Unlike much of the literature you've read that states if you kill the head vampire, all will be released, it's simply not true. Once you kill the head vampire, you just really piss the rest of them off.

"As the coven tried to 'persuade' the answers out of their captured vampire, Lydia and I traced the other orders of blood back to the vampires. In classic movie style, we snuck in during the day and found their coffins. We staked a few of them, including the leader, but inadvertently, awoke the rest of them. They captured us and kept us chained up in the wine cellar of their building. I guess they

190

decided they were tired of pig's blood, so when they had a slow night, they would feed off Lydia and I."

Dawn's eyes widened to the size of saucers. "My God," she gasped. "They would actually drain you of blood?"

Cane nodded, "But not to the point of death. They just snacked on us."

"What happened?"

"Lydia's coven contacted a group of vampire hunters in Europe. They were known as the 'The Gwyliad Wraith', The White Guard. They were an ancient Celtic order that had been hunting vampires since before time. They came in, wiped out the vampires and saved us."

"That's incredible," Dawn breathed.

Cane nodded. "That's the reason, even though Lydia is a Pagan, that she wears a cross around her neck to this day."

"What about you?"

Cane smiled. Reaching up to his shirt, he produced a small gold cross dangling on a chain around his neck. "Never can be too careful." He lifted his glass of water and took a long sip. "You better get some sleep," he advised her.

Dawn laughed out loud. "After a story like that, you expect me to sleep?" She thought for a moment, "If you've been keeping that from me all these years, what else do you know about?"

Cane smiled broadly and escorted Dawn to the door. "You know those little green men from outer space they're always talking about?"

Dawn nodded as she stepped into the hallway. "Yeah?"

"They're not green," Cane said as he closed the door.

***

"I guess you're bunking with me tonight," Bishop said as he slid his key into the lock. Turning back to Hayden, he gave the man, who was not much younger than him, the once over. "Is that okay with you? I can get you your own room if you want."

Hayden shook his head. "No, this is fine. I spent two days locked up in my apartment by myself."

Bishop had the sudden flash of Hayden snipping off a lock of his hair in the middle of the night to show to his other groupie buddies. "You're not going to do anything weird, are you?" Bishop asked as he stepped inside.

"What do you mean?"

"Anything groupie-ish?"

"You mean like tying you to your bed and breaking your ankles so you have to write me a novel?"

"Yeah, something like that."

Hayden laughed. "You really think that of me? I'm not a Trekkie, for God's sake."

"Yeah, right," Bishop said uncomfortably, but slightly amused. "It's just that I've never had a fan before. I don't know how to act, you know?"

"Understood," Hayden said with a grin. "Fame is a hard mistress."

192

Bishop laughed. "Knock it off." He pointed to a small couch in the corner. "That okay for you?"

Hayden nodded. "Why don't I get the bed?"

"Because *I'm* the celebrity," Bishop said mockingly. "That's why." Hayden slumped down onto the couch and yanked off his shoes. He looked at Bishop who was in the process of digging through his suitcase. "What are you looking for?"

"My toothbrush," Bishop said, still working through the clothes.

Hayden looked nervously around the room, then back at Bishop. "Do you mind if I ask you a question?"

Bishop smiled as he pulled his trusty yellow toothbrush from his suitcase. "Sure. Shoot."

"The things you've seen," Hayden began, "was it ever hard for you to truly believe?"

"That's an odd question," Bishop replied. "Why do you ask?"

"I've been a bit of an amateur paranormal investigator all my life. I've read every book I could get my hands on and seen a great many documentaries, but I still find it hard to believe."

"Do you mean when we track down a ghost or ghoul, do we expect to rip off a rubber mask and expose Farmer Billy-Bob Jimbo just trying to keep a bunch of meddling kids and their dog away from his crops?" Bishop asked with a laugh.

"Yeah, something like that."

"As a part of the OPR, we always look for the scientific answer first. In a sense, you could say we're a group of debunkers. We go into a case with the full expectation of finding a UFO hung on fishing line, or a ghostly apparition that's just an

193

electromagnetic disturbance. That's the point, though," Bishop added. "We want to separate the kooks from the actual phenomenon."

"You didn't answer my question," Hayden reminded.

"Yes, I still find it hard to believe sometimes, but in the end, that's okay. You don't want to automatically run into every situation in blind faith. That could spell bad news for everyone. I have always been more of a 'hands on' kind of guy. I won't allow myself to believe something outright, no matter how convincing the evidence is," Bishop essayed. "I always have to go and see for myself to make my decision, but there again, that's part of being a researcher."

Hayden nodded. "I understand."

"Don't let faith get the best of you," Bishop warned with a grin. "Recent studies have proven faith is a psychological disorder."

***

Kelley and Spenser had adjourned to the small bar in the lobby of the hotel. They both knew they needed some sleep, but that none was going to happen. They had both agreed perhaps a drink would help calm their nerves a bit and allow them to rest. Moving inside, they peered around. The place was lavishly decorated in deep red with gold highlights. Tall ferns sat in every corner of the room and flanked the bar on both sides. A lone man in a red satin vest stood behind the bar wiping down glasses with a white dishtowel. Kelley and Spenser

194

pulled out a stool and sat down, looking away from each other at first.

"Name your poison," the bartender asked from the other side of the bar. Kelley looked at Spenser, then at the bartender. "I'll have a scotch rocks." Spenser chuckled. "Same for me."

Kelley turned to her companion. "What's so funny?"

"Nothing."

"Come on, tell me," Kelley urged.

"It's just that I've never met a woman who ordered scotch on the rocks. That's more of a man's drink."

"That was a sexist remark," Kelley smirked. "I bet I can drink you under the table."

Spenser leaned back in his stool and assessed the young woman sitting next to him. "Of that, I have no doubt."

The bartender slid the drinks in front of them and returned to his previous task.

"I'll buy." Spenser pulled a few worn dollar bills out of his pocket and placed them on the lip of the bar. Lifting his glass, he took a hard gulp of the liquor. Setting the glass down, he held his breath and waited for the burning to subside. Shaking his head once, he turned and looked at Kelley. She had already finished her drink and was signaling the bartender for another. "Slow down, honey," Spenser said with a laugh.

Kelley turned to Spenser. "I'm sorry," she said with a guilty laugh, "this whole case just creeps me out. Every time I think about it, my skin just crawls."

"I know the feeling," Spenser agreed. "I've never seen anything like this before." He lifted his glass and worked the ice around carefully. "How do you bring something like this to justice?"

"You just have to have faith," Kelley said as she took her new drink from the bartender.

"Faith in what?"

"*Faith* that there is a Heaven and Hell and that these creatures are getting what they deserve in the afterlife," Kelley said dryly and gulped down her drink again. "That's the only way you can make it through."

"How can you have faith in a profession like this?" Spenser asked. "The things you see must rattle your beliefs every once and a while."

Kelley nodded. "They have, but that's when my faith becomes the strongest. I have to hold onto something, or I would probably lose my mind."

"But these creatures, these *things*," Spenser said, emphasizing the word, "they go against what we're taught in Sunday school. If these things exist, then surely God does not."

"Why do you say that? Even the Bible talks about ghosts. If anything, seeing these things should reaffirm your belief in religion," Kelley stated.

"I can see your point," Spenser agreed. He lifted his glass and knocked down the last bit of amber liquid. "This is all so new to me."

Kelley nodded. "It doesn't get any easier either."

"That's reassuring."

"So what do you do besides being a police detective?" Kelley asked after a moment.

Spenser thought for a moment. "Not a whole lot. That pretty much consumes most of my time."

"Come on," Kelley smiled. "There has to be something you do to unwind at night after a long day."

"Well," Spenser said slowly, "I love to read detective novels."

Kelley laughed out loud. "You're a detective and you read detective novels when you're off the job. Isn't that like taking work home with you?"

Spenser laughed, "I never thought of it that way, but I guess it is. I've been reading them since I was a boy. It was just something I could always lose myself in."

"I understand that. Anything else?"

"I watch a lot of hockey."

"Professional?"

"That's the only kind."

"What team do you follow?" Kelley asked.

"I grew up in Detroit, so I've always been a Red Wings fan," Spenser said. "It was great to see them win the Cup recently."

"I bet," Kelley agreed as she started her third drink. "Me, I've never been much of a sports fan. When I was young, I used to watch football with my dad, but my mom always encouraged me to do more 'girly' things, like play with dolls, or something like that."

Spenser ordered another drink from the bartender. "This time, hold the ice," he instructed him. He turned back to Kelley. "So what did you do before the OPR?"

"I was a nurse at a hospital in Florida."

"Did you like that?"

Kelley nodded. "It was what I thought I always wanted to do."

"That didn't answer my question."

Kelley smiled slyly. "Yes, it was fulfilling for a while. I got the opportunity to help people, to actually save lives in some cases."

"But…." Spenser lead.

"*But*," Kelley said slowly, "it just wasn't for me. I couldn't handle scrubbing patients, or cleaning out bedpans. It got to the point where I felt like I was doing most of the doctor's work for a quarter of the pay."

"I'm not following."

"What does a nurse do?" Kelley asked. "She comes in, takes your temperature and blood pressure, weighs you, writes down all your symptoms, and then sends in the doctor, who diagnoses based on what she wrote. Does that seem fair to you?"

"No I guess it doesn't."

"Then, if it's an emergency, the nurse has to put in IVs, trach tubes, give injections and generally try and stabilize the patient. The doctor will then come in and take all the credit."

"I think you're oversimplifying things, Kelley," Spenser started. Turning toward Kelley, he caught a dark glance and quickly backed off. He knew he needed to change the subject. "So what do you do with your time off?"

Kelley was still fuming slightly. She looked at Spenser, then back at her drink and took a deep breath. "I'm like you. I just read a lot," she finally said. Before Spenser had a chance to ask another question, Kelley had finished her drink and stood up. "If you don't mind, I think it's time I got some sleep."

Spenser nodded. "Sure. Goodnight."

Kelley nodded and made her way out of the bar.

Spenser watched her head for the elevator and climb on. Once the door was closed, he lifted his glass and drank the last bit of alcohol. Setting it down, he slipped a few more bills onto the bar and headed out into the lobby. As he approached the large glass doors, he checked his watch. It was closing in on three in the morning. That wouldn't give him much time to get home, get cleaned up, catch a quick nap, and be back here by seven, but he needed the sleep.

Stepping out into the rainy Seattle night, he walked to the curb and began to hail a cab. A strange sensation passed over him as he waited. The tiny hairs on the back of his neck stood up. He shook off the feeling and hiked the collar of his coat up around his neck. The sensation hit him again. Lowering his arm, he slowly turned to look behind him. There was nothing but the well-lit front of the hotel. Shaking his head, he returned his attention to the street. A yellow cab had pulled up in front of him. Grabbing the door handle, he quickly slid into the backseat and gave the cabbie his address. Laying his head back against the seat, he heard a thump on the roof. He shot forward, looking around nervously.

"Did you hear that?" he asked the driver.

The cabbie glanced up into his rear-view mirror, locking eyes with Spenser. "I hear nothing," he said in broken English.

"I could've swore I just heard something hit the roof of the cab," Spenser insisted.

The cabbie shook his head and returned his eyes to the road. "It late. You need sleep. I hear no sound."

Spenser slowly began to relax. Maybe his nerves were a little frazzled after the day's events. Leaning back into his seat, he glanced out the rain-streaked window at the city as it whizzed past.

On the roof of the car, Jax dug his claws in and held on. He quickly flicked out his tongue twice. He could smell his prey. Leaning his still disfigured head close to the roof, he listened intently to the people inside. He could hear them breathing, their hearts beating. Rolling back onto his heels, Jax lifted a clawed hand and stared at it for a moment. Flattening it out, he tore through the roof of the cab, exposing its passengers.

Spenser flattened himself in the seat and drew his weapon. Snapping the safety off, he blindly fired off three quick rounds into the roof. The cabbie screamed profanities in his native language as he swerved the car in and out of traffic. Spenser fired again as Jax's claws reached for him. The cabbie glanced into his rear-view mirror with wide eyes as a clawed hand erupted from the roof. Cranking the wheel hard to the left, he sent the taxi up onto the sidewalk, barreling through mailboxes and trash cans.

The force of the impact knocked Spenser from the seat, his gun hitting and skidding under the passenger's seat. "Keep it steady," he barked at the cabbie.

"Doing best I can," the cabbie shrieked as he turned the car back onto the street. He swerved, narrowly missing an oncoming vehicle, and finally made it back into his lane. He glanced over his shoulder at his passenger. Jax was still clawing wildly through the roof. "Crap," the cabbie breathed. "There go insurance."

Grabbing Jax's hand, Spenser twisted it to the right, immobilizing it for a moment while he searched for his weapon. Turning his attention away, he dug his hand under the seat and patted frantically for his weapon. His fingers finally connected with the barrel. Pulling back, he heard the hard clink of metal on metal. It was stuck.

Jax took the opportunity. Grabbing the edge of the tear in the roof, he pulled with all his strength. The metal groaned in protest as it bent and split away from the frame. Finally free, Jax tossed the chunk of now worthless material away, hitting a trailing car in the windshield. He watched with glee as the metal tore through the glass and sent the car careening into a light pole.

Leaning his head in while still perched on what remained of the roof, Jax shrieked at Spenser and flicked out his tongue. Spenser snapped his head around just in time to avoid the attack. Rolling back onto the seat, he finally pulled his weapon free. Spenser quickly took aim and fired four rounds into Jax's chest. The creature shrieked again, pulling his hand free. Moving quickly around the top of the taxi, he swatted wildly at Spenser.

The cabbie frantically turned and looked behind him just as Jax's claws sawed through the steel mesh separating him from the passenger section.

201

Ducking down into his seat, the cabbie stared through the steering wheel out the window. He spotted a solution.

With one mighty swat, Jax knocked the gun away from Spenser. It sailed up through the air, finally colliding with the nearest window and shattering it. Satisfied, Jax took a step into the back of the cab. With both feet on the back seat of the cab, he hovered over Spenser almost gloating, his head and shoulders exposed above the roof.

"Passenger!" the cabbie yelled. "Hold on!"

It took a moment for the warning to register with Spenser. Taking a deep breath, he rolled off the seat again and braced himself. The cabbie smashed the accelerator to the floor as he cranked the wheel to the right. His headlights focused on a large light pole on the sidewalk. Jax snapped his head up and his white eyes narrowed in anger. He leaned forward and shrieked in defiance as the cab hit the pole dead on. The front of the cab was shredded instantly as the pole cut through it. The force of the impact sent Jax flying forward. His midsection hit the jagged edge of the roof and was sliced cleanly in two. His legs buckled and landed on Spenser while his torso was flung into the pole, then onto the ground.

Spenser slowly lifted his head and looked around the demolished cab. His eyes settled on Jax's legs. Lifting them off, he pulled himself up onto the seat. He pressed a hand to his temple to try and stop the throbbing pain. His head had collided with the metal frame of the seat in front of him during the accident. After a moment, he glanced up at the cabbie sitting motionless in the front seat. He reached his hand through the gash in the metal and pressed his fingers to the man's neck. There was a pulse, but it was weak. Looking around for a way out, he finally settled on the hole torn through the roof. Standing up, he braced his hands on each side of the tear and vaulted his legs up and over the roof. He landed flat on his feet next to the car.

Spenser moved to the driver's side door and tried to pull it open, but it wouldn't budge. He yanked again, but the door was firmly wedged in its spot. Glancing in the window, he could see that the dash and wheel had come forward and were pinning the cabbie against the seat. He couldn't see any physical damage to the man and no blood was visible, but that didn't mean anything, his injuries could be entirely internal. Reaching into his pocket, he pulled out his cell phone and dialed 911. Turning to his left, he glanced nervously at Jax's motionless torso. He expected at any moment that it would start clawing its way toward him to finish the job. He finally heard a voice on the other end of the line.

"This is Detective Spenser of the Seattle Police Department," he said quickly. "I need an ambulance ASAP."

Chapter Seventeen

Sleep didn't come easily for any of the group and Dawn was no exception. Each found themselves embroiled in their own personal struggles, tossing and turning in bed. Thoughts turned to the well-being of Lexy Weiss, then back again. Each knew the group was beginning to unravel. They were showing signs of cracks in the foundation. Such was the way when a group bands together to become a fighting unit. None were from a common background or were friends beforehand. They had been thrown into the grinder together by circumstances beyond their control, and it was beginning to show.

Each, in their own way, was valuable to the team, bringing their own personality and knowledge, but perhaps that wasn't enough. They needed a unifying force, someone to act as the glue that bound them. The team needed a person who knew all their special talents and personalities and could utilize them to their fullest potential. Dawn knew that even though Cane had returned, the role of leadership was still resting on her shoulders. She knew they couldn't survive with a leader that wanted to be somewhere else, no matter what he said to their faces. He *would* eventually leave the group, she knew, and then it would all fall to her. She wasn't looking forward to that day.

The others were still too new to be counted on in that capacity. Of the group, Bishop was most akin to Cane, containing the same streak that pushed them to know the truth. They both lived the paranormal. It consumed them, becoming the only thing in their lives that brought them passion. If there ever was a nonperson, Dawn knew, it was Cane and Bishop. They were nothing without their work. It was heart-breaking to a point. Cane, for the most part, had been lost to the cause. He was, and always would be, the OPR. There was nothing else out there for him, and he had proved it today. With his big, grand speech, he had come crawling back to the group as if nothing had happened. Lydia had rejected him, Dawn knew. It was that simple. He had hoped to slide back into his previous life with no questions asked, but found it didn't exist anymore. People move on.

That was the sad truth of the matter. Dawn wondered for a moment if presented with the opportunity, if she would ever wait for someone. Would loyalty outweigh her own happiness? She hoped she would never find out.

Dawn rolled onto her back and clasped her hands behind her head. Indigestion was tearing up her stomach. She thought about getting up for an antacid tablet, but then reconsidered when she glanced at the clock. It was approaching six in the morning and she would have to get up soon anyway. Reaching over the side of the bed, she grabbed her laptop off the floor and set it in front of her. Pressing a hand to her abdomen, she let out a long breath. Hitting the release button with her thumb, she lifted the computer's screen and tapped the small power button located just above the white keyboard. The familiar sound of the hard drive whirring to life filled her ears. Standing the computer on its side for a moment, she checked to make sure that the power and phone cables were securely connected.

After logging in, she moved the pointer to the modem icon and clicked it once. She listened as the computer rapidly dialed her ISP. Tapping her fingernails on the keyboard, she waited for a connection. Reaching over to her nightstand, she lifted a half empty can of Coke and swallowed down the flat remnants. She let out a dissatisfied breath as she returned the can to the stand. She watched the scrolling 'dialing' status indicator at the top of the screen change to the word connected. Moving the mouse, she clicked on her browser icon and waited for it to launch.

Pushing the laptop away for a moment, she got up out of bed and moved to the kitchenette. Dropping down on one knee, she opened the half-sized refrigerator and surveyed its contents. There wasn't much to choose from, as she hadn't had time to stock it yet. As a ritual, if she were going to be in a hotel room for more than two days, she always filled up the fridge with sodas, bottled water and a few choice snack foods. She had a propensity for working late and snacks always seemed to help. Grabbing the only bottled water in there, she unscrewed the top and returned to bed. She smiled quickly when she saw her home page had loaded.

"I hate dial-up," she muttered as she clicked the email icon on the page. She moved quickly through the log on screen and into her mailbox. After sorting through the dozens of junk letters in her box, she glanced over the few real emails. She stopped at the first one. It was a letter from a man she met almost two years ago. She had made the mistake of giving him her email address when she thought he was sincere. It turned out some time later that he was a spook. His tales of the supernatural were nothing more than recycled books and television shows. After a quick (and illegal) search of his personal records, she had found he had been prescribed some really heavy antipsychotic drugs. She had been trying to get rid of him ever since, but he always seemed to find her new address. She shook her head as she read the subject line of his letter.

"I finally have proof! I abducted one of them!"

She instantly clicked the delete key and went back to her inbox. Scrolling through the remaining three messages, she stopped. There was an email from Captain Hart of the Seattle Police Department. Her finger hovered over the mouse for a moment, searching her memories. She hadn't met the captain, nor had she given him her email address. She had, however, given her fake lawyer card to Detective Spenser. She was too curious to pass up the letter. Clicking it open, she scrolled down to the message:

Ms. Lassiter, my name is Captain Hart of the Seattle Police Department. Detective Jim Spenser gave me this email address. I have tried repeatedly to contact you via the phone number on the business card you left, but have been unable to reach you. All I get when I contact your office in Washington D.C. is a voice mail recording.

I need to meet with you urgently regarding your client Alexis (Lexy) Weiss. There have been several breakthroughs in the case and I think you should be apprised of them. Contact me as soon as possible. It is urgent.

Hart closed the letter with his own email address and office phone numbers. Apparently, Spenser hadn't told Hart who she really was yet. Perhaps that was for the better. She could still play up the lawyer angle and probe him for details.

Dawn clicked the reply button and began to type.

***

Kelley reached down and picked a small yellow flower. Holding it up to her nose, she inhaled the fragrance and smiled. Never let anyone accuse her of not taking time to stop and smell the roses, she laughed. Brushing her hair back, she slid the flower behind her ear and continued on. It was a beautiful spring day. Most of the snow had already melted, leaving only a few muddy patches and puddles. The sky was clear above her, allowing the sun to shine down in its full magnificence.

She stood in the middle of the sidewalk and spread her arms wide, palms up, and accepted the warmth of the sun. It had been a long and hard winter here. Many farmers had lost part of their herd, but at least this summer, they wouldn't have to worry about drought conditions.

She glanced around the small park. Children and parents were busy enjoying the weather as well. Frisbees sailed through the air and couples readied homemade kites to fly. This was easily Kelley's favorite time of year. Pulling off her light jacket, she slung it over her arm and continued down the cobblestone path. It cut straight through the center of the park and was only interrupted by a small bridge that crossed an active stream. Stopping just short of the bridge, she sat down on a bench and relaxed. Two of her long-time friends passed through a glade of trees and waved. Kelley smiled and returned the gesture. This was her hometown in Colorado, she only wished she could visit here other than in her dreams. She hadn't been home in years, but for now, it was nice. Soon, she would wake up and again have to face the world.

She turned and watched a beautiful young woman walking up the path toward her. The woman was wearing a long, black dress with formal high heels. Her dark hair hung straight down almost to the center of her back and appeared to shimmer as she moved. Her skin was pale, but had just enough color to seem healthy. It probably seemed that way because of her dark hair and eyes, Kelley remarked to herself. She had never seen this person before, but that wasn't entirely uncommon in her dreams. Sometimes, she accidentally found herself connected psychically to another person, sharing their thoughts and fantasies. It had, on occasions, made for some very interesting dreams.

The woman stopped in front of Kelley and smiled. Her lips were painted a deep, ruby red. "May I sit down?"

Kelley nodded. "Be my guest."

"Thank you," the woman said as she slowly slipped onto the bench. "It's a lovely day here."

"Yes it is. This is my favorite time of year. Everything is fresh, alive and new. Animals are starting to reappear after the winter and life generally starts to renew."

"This is a time of birth," the woman agreed. "Witches celebrate this time of year as Beltane, the union between the Goddess and God. For many, this is a time of new beginnings and great celebration."

Kelley smiled. "Are you Wiccan?"

The woman laughed softly, "Once upon a time, but things never remain the same."

"What do you mean?" Kelley asked, now positive she had tapped into another's dream.

"There is always a turning point in every life. For you, it was when Joanne lost her life. That sent you on an entirely different path."

Kelley was unfazed by the personal material the woman seemed to know about her. It was her experience that when she tapped into another's dream, it was a two-way link. "And you? What was the turning point in your life?"

"It's complicated," the woman said as her eyes sparkled in the sunlight. "It would take too long to tell."

"In here," Kelley said, tapping her forehead, "we have all the time in the world."

The woman smiled and nodded. Opening her hand, she produced a small, gold ankh. Kelley marveled at the symbol in the light for a moment. It was truly beautiful. "This is what changed my life."

The ankh was nothing more than a cross with a loop on top. Kelley could see what appeared to be Egyptian Hieroglyphics carved around the loop. "How could that small thing change anything?"

"I was a Sociology teacher at a little high school when this came to my attention," the woman said, still admiring the ankh. "It was part of a traveling Egyptian exhibit at our local museum.

Being the good teacher that I was, I took the kids on a field trip to see it. I had come across a lot of Egyptian mythology in my Wiccan studies, but nothing could've prepared me for what I found there."

Kelley was becoming enthralled by the story. "Please continue."

The woman nodded. "They had several pieces that once belonged to the Pharaoh Tutankhamen. This piece and an ancient book were among them. They were exquisite. I knew from the moment I laid eyes on them, I had to have them. At the time, I wasn't sure why, but later, I learned they had called to me to be set free."

"Set free?" Kelley echoed.

"Yes, from their wood and glass prisons."

"You mean the display cases?"

The woman nodded again. "That night, I broke into the museum and took them. It was relatively easy, even with my limited magick. Once I brought them home, I began to understand their power." The woman glanced down at the talisman in her hand, "I could not read Egyptian, but I found that if I concentrated on the book hard enough, the knowledge would come to me. I found incredible secrets locked away in the book I believe even the researchers had no idea of. They professed a mighty power, one I couldn't even begin to comprehend.

"After that night, I moved to a different town and spent all my time trying to unlock the knowledge of the book. It took many years, but I found it. I finally found it."

"Found what?"

211

The woman held up the ankh, "Its secrets. Why this symbol means 'eternal'."

"What are the secrets?" Kelley asked.

The woman shook her head vehemently. "You are not ready for them, but if you join me, I will instruct you. I can teach you how to become more powerful than you ever imagined and," the witch smiled, "become immortal."

A shiver ran down Kelley's spine. She bolted from the bench and stood staring at the woman. "I know who you are."

"Of course you do," the woman replied. "I have made no secret of my identity. I come to you as a friend, not as your enemy."

"But you're killing people."

"One of the unfortunate side effects of being dead," Isis smiled, "is that you need a new body to come back to. I am simply gathering spare parts."

Kelley suddenly stopped. "This is the real you," she said, looking over Isis. "You haven't shown your true face since you found the book."

Isis smiled. "When you look like a rotting corpse, you don't go around flashing your smile everywhere."

Kelley slowly moved closer to the bench again. There was no feeling of evil about Isis; she just seemed to be a normal woman sitting there. "Why did you come to me?"

"I already told you, dear, I want you to join me." Isis stood. Kelley took an uneasy step back.

"I'm not going to hurt you," Isis reassured. "I've seen what you can do, what powers you already possess, you would make a welcome addition to the Triad."

"But there are already three of you," Kelley said, recalling the information she took from Fowler's mind.

"You misunderstand, Kelley. I am not offering you a position in the Triad, I need a new body until my more," an evil smile crossed her face, "permanent vessel can be created. You will have access to power you've never dreamed of." Isis held out the ankh in her hand. "Take this and be with me."

Kelley took another uncomfortable step back. "This is not what I want, you know that."

"I know many things," Isis stated. "I also know power corrupts the good." She pushed the ankh toward Kelley. "Take it," she whispered naughtily.

"I will not," Kelley said again. "I want to wake up now," she told herself. "Wake up now."

Isis stopped and looked up at the beautiful blue sky above. "It appears you're still here with me," she laughed. "Let me put it to you this way," Isis said slowly, "I have taken control of your mind. If you join me, I will release you, if not, well...." she snapped her fingers.

Kelley snapped her hands over her ears as the sound echoed through the park like a sonic boom. She glanced up in horror as the pristine area around her turned gray and died, then slowly slid from view like wet paint running on a canvas, leaving only darkness around them. Turning back to Isis, Kelley jumped back, startled. She had changed into a solid black dress with her veil drawn over her face, leaving only her hands exposed.

Isis once again presented the ankh to Kelley. "I have the power to crush your pitiful mind, no matter how powerful it has become. If you do not join me, I will make sure you stay in this dark place."

Kelley felt her hand lifting toward the ankh. A moment of true terror gripped her mind as her fingers opened around it. She held them there, hovering over it. She could feel its power, and Isis was right, it was what she wanted. She ran her tongue quickly over her parched lips as she stared intently at the ankh. "I could have anything," she said slowly. She felt herself drawing near the ankh. Then suddenly, she ripped it away and took a step back from Isis. Standing proudly in front of the witch, Kelley laughed. "I will never join you."

Isis shook her head as she retracted the ankh. "So be it." With lightning quick reflexes, the witch shot out her arm and wrapped her hand around Kelley's face. Using only a fraction of her strength, she snapped Kelley's head painfully to the right. She felt Kelley's body become limp. Letting go, Isis watched the woman crumple to the ground. "Such potential. What a waste," Isis said with a hint of regret in her voice. Opening up her opposite hand, she looked at the gold ankh. Slowly rolling her hand over, she let it fall on Kelley's body.

***

Cane awoke to the annoying chirp of his cell phone. Slowly sitting up in bed, he yawned and stretched before grabbing the small phone from his nightstand. Flipping it open, he pressed it to his hear. "Cane," he said groggily.

"Cane," the voice said.

"Yes?" Cane asked, a little more awake. "This is Chairman Weiss."

Cane sat straight up. "I forgot to check in with you yesterday," he said apologetically. "It was such a busy day, we just didn't have time. Would you like our progress report?"

"There's no need for that now, Cane," the chairman responded.

Cane listened for a moment. "Where are you? You sound like you're in a car."

"I am in a cab right now."

"Heading?"

Silence.

"Tom?" Cane asked.

"I'm in Seattle right now, Cane. I should be at your hotel in about twenty minutes."

Cane felt the acid level in his stomach suddenly jump. "Why are you here?"

"I've come to take over this investigation," Weiss said quickly. "Have the team prepped and ready for a debriefing as soon as I arrive." With that, he hung up.

Cane held the phone to his ear for a moment longer, almost stunned. Slowly snapping the phone shut, he rubbed the bridge of his nose between his finger and thumb. "Bloody hell," he muttered under his breath. Depositing his phone on the nightstand, he picked up the white hotel phone next to it and dialed the front desk. "This is not going to make anyone happy," Cane quickly assessed. "Especially me."

Chapter Eighteen

Fowler opened his eyes and tried to move his head. Panic set in when he couldn't feel his body. Below his neck, all sensation was gone. He could still feel the two puncture wounds in his neck, however. They felt like gaping canyons of pain. Moving his eyes around the room, he found himself still chained to the wall. Glancing right, he saw three long streaks of blood running down his exposed arm. They were probably from his wrists, he thought. He wondered how long he had been up here. Looking up, he could see a small ray of sunlight beaming through a crack in the ceiling. At least he knew it was daytime, but when, he wasn't sure.

His mind suddenly recalled the image of Lexy Weiss hovering over him, her fingers dug deep into the bricks as she clung to the wall. Fowler nervously searched the room for the woman, but found no traces of her. The panic subsided for a moment. Concentrating on his body, he tried to wiggle his toes. He thought for a moment he could feel it, but the sensation went by too quickly. Fowler closed his eyes and took a deep breath. At least he could still feel that.

"Welcome back to the land of the living, Agent Fowler," a woman's voice echoed in his head.

Fowler glanced around the room, but there was no one to be seen. He felt completely helpless. "Who said that? Who's there?"

"You are in no danger...yet," the voice said playfully. "That voice," Fowler muttered to himself.

"I'm hurt you don't remember me," the voice said. "You killed me!" The voice became shrill as it screamed.

"Isis," Fowler breathed.

"That's right, Agent Fowler. I certainly remember you," Isis added. "It just happened to be pure coincidence our two paths crossed again, but I was going to find you eventually, you realize."

"I didn't do anything to you, Isis," Fowler argued. "You were killed by the ATF agents during the raid. I wasn't even there."

"That much is true," Isis said slowly, "but it was because of you that they were there. You betrayed my trust, John. I accepted you into my fold and offered you the deepest, darkest secrets of life." Isis paused, "And how did you repay my kindness and generosity? You had me killed!"

Fowler closed his eyes tightly together as Isis' screams echoed around in his head. "Stop!" Fowler shouted.

"Why should I?"

Fowler gritted his teeth in pain. "Please." In that moment, the pain was gone and he could feel his body again. Fowler let out a long sigh, then became aware of the deep cuts the shackles were making in his wrists.

"I can make this all end, John," Isis said after a moment. "With one wave of my hand, I can make all the pain and suffering go away. Isn't that what you want?"

Fowler nodded.

"But you have to do something for me."

Fowler furrowed his brow. "Never," he forced the word through his gritted teeth.

217

"That's not the answer I was looking for, John."

Fowler's head snapped back as once again, Isis' screams filled his mind.

His temples throbbed as if pressure was building up inside. At any moment, he felt his head would explode. "All right!" he finally shouted. "What do you want?" His head fell forward in exhaustion as the sounds subsided once again.

"I need a temporary vessel in this world until my new body is prepared. I have chosen you for this privilege."

"Is that what you call it? A privilege?"

"I should think so," Isis said coolly. "After all, you will be the bearer of the soon to be empress of the world."

"You've spent too much time by yourself, Isis." Fowler lifted his head and sneered, "You've obviously gone insane."

Isis hit Fowler with another sonic attack. Fowler took a deep breath, but refused to cry out. "You are brave," Isis commented, "but foolish. Because of you and others, my plans have fallen well behind schedule. If we do not complete the ritual by midnight tonight, the Triad will lose its tenuous grasp on the physical world."

"I will never help you," Fowler said as a trickle of blood erupted from his nose.

Isis' voice became very agitated. "I tire of these inane games. I have offered several this gift and all have refused. Do you not know the power you will have? Do you not understand what you will be capable of?"

"I know that I will cease to be me," Fowler snapped.

Isis appeared in front of Fowler, her body draped in the now familiar black dress and veil. However, she didn't appear to be complete. Her form seemed to be shimmering in and out of this plane of existence. Reaching up, she lifted her veil revealing her ghoulish visage. Her dark, empty eye sockets began to glow with a soft orange light as she approached Fowler. "I have given enough chances," she said gravely. "I do not need a willing host, but it would have been easier that way."

Thrusting her hand forward, she buried it in Fowler's chest. "I will take your body, John, just as you took mine."

Fowler lifted his head and screamed as Isis worked her way into his body. He could feel her like a disease spreading into each organ and cell. He felt as if he were drowning in his own body as his very essence was ripped away, in favor of Isis'. Fowler's body convulsed with pain. Isis moved rapidly though Fowler toward his brain. Scurrying up his spine, Isis' spirit erupted into Fowler's brain. Both screamed in pain as they fought. As Isis moved, muscle groups began to transform, fitting to their new host. Lurching forward, they ripped the shackles free of the wall. The two tumbled to the ground in writhing pain. Hair that was once short, instantly grew several inches down their back, then withered and fell off. Isis was gaining the upper hand. With one final push, Isis ejected Fowler's soul from his body.

Clumsily standing up, Isis worked to move Fowler's body. She stumbled across the room to a small mirror lying half broken on the ground. She could feel her essence filling in the spaces and transforming this body. Leaning over to the mirror, she saw her own face beginning to take shape. Soon, this body would have no memory of its previous occupant and she would be strong enough to complete the ritual.

Turning away from the mirror, Isis walked slowly toward a door in the far corner, still learning her new body. Pulling it open, she leaned her head against the edge for a moment. She needed rest. After a moment, she adjourned to a small room the other members of the Triad had prepared for her. In the back of it was a large, comfortable bed with red satin sheets. On both sides stood tall, black candelabras, their slender white tapers already burning. Slipping onto the bed, Isis rolled onto her back. A large, evil smile crossed her still changing face. Soon, it would all be hers. The end was approaching.

**

The team had gathered in a small conference room downstairs, just off the main lobby, allowing easy access to the restaurant, pool and modestly equipped gym. It was decorated in faux wood, with several tall, fake ferns scattered about. Everything in the room, from the large, oval conference table to the chairs and the smaller tables to the rear was a deep shade of mahogany. This room had been completely designed with business in mind.

Dawn was the first inside, her arms loaded with her laptop, several folders filled with notes and reports. She was sipping coffee from a white mug with her free hand as she moved to the end of the table. Leaning over awkwardly, she tried not to spill her coffee as she dropped her papers. She glanced up to see Bishop and Hayden enter the room next.

They were each carrying two small duffel bags, and each had what looked like a laptop case slung over their shoulders. Bishop was garbed in his now traditional black leather jacket, his ever-present messy hair and cleanly shaven face, but for a small patch just below his lower lip. Hayden appeared to be in the same outfit from the previous day, minus a different shirt Bishop probably loaned him.

Pulling the case off his shoulder, Bishop deposited it on the table in front of him. He sat in the nearest chair and glanced over at Dawn. "Morning," he grumbled.

Dawn nodded without looking up from her paperwork.

Bishop turned to Hayden, who had taken the seat next to his. "Did you remember to pick up that cable I asked you to?"

Hayden smiled and pulled a black cord out of his pocket. "Got it."

"Good," Bishop exhaled.

The three sat quietly in the room staring at the walls waiting for the others to show. After several moments, one would turn to the other with something to say, but no words were spoken. Dawn worked steadily on the papers in front of her. She wanted to have something documented to show the chairman when he arrived. Bishop, on the other hand, had taken to resorting the equipment in his duffel bag.

221

Lifting out a rectangular shaped black box, Bishop set it gently on the table next to his laptop case. Reaching over, he unzipped the case and propped open the top revealing his white laptop. Thumbing the release latch on the front, he popped open the screen and hit the power button. He snatched the black cord from Hayden and snapped it into a port on the left side of the computer. Running it around the back, he attached the other end of the cable to the black box. The box instantly whirred to life and began to unfold revealing the sensitive equipment inside. Bishop tapped a series of buttons inside the box, then sat back for a moment. The machine began to emit a high-pitched whine that only seemed to increase.

Dawn looked up from her paperwork just in time to see a bright flash of white light fill the room. She fell back in her chair and covered her eyes quickly, but had, unfortunately, taken the full brunt of the light. "Goddamn it, Bish!"

Bishop snickered, "Sorry, I didn't know it was going to activate like that." He leaned forward and checked several readings on his monitor. "It worked, though."

"What did?" Dawn said glancing over the unrecognizable piece of equipment in front of her. She could now clearly see the flashbulb perched near the top of it.

"I had this custom built for me back in D.C." Bishop said proudly. "Over the past few months, I've taken enough electromagnetic readings to understand that ghosts operate on an almost set frequency. This device sends out a pulse of light and phosphorescent dust that blankets the area and attaches itself to spirits, rendering them visible."

"Is the dust harmful to humans?" Hayden asked.

"Probably," Bishop said with a smile. "I call it the Visi-Spook 2000."

"Lame name," Hayden said as he shook his head. "Sounds like a vacuum."

Bishop laughed out loud. "I guess it does. I'll have to work on that."

"So I have dust all over me right now?" Dawn asked as she looked down at her clothes. "I don't see anything."

Standing up, Bishop moved to the front of the room and rested his finger on the main light switch. "Ready for this?" He clicked off the lights.

The room, and everything in it, was glowing a sickly green. Dawn stood up and looked at herself. Her outfit, from about her waist up, was glowing the same color, looking as if a bucket of Day-Glo paint had been splashed on her. She shot a disgusted look across the room at Bishop, who was also glowing. Reaching down, she picked up her cup of coffee but stopped with it just in front of her face. The usually dark liquid was also glowing.

"How do I get this stuff off?" Dawn asked, setting the mug back on the table.

"It just washes off," Bishop said as he flipped back on the lights. "After a while, the glow will fade as well."

Hayden leaned back in his chair laughing at the two.

"Laugh it up, dork," Dawn said angrily.

Bishop broke down and started to laugh as well. "I don't know, Dawn, I think green is a good color for you."

The three were interrupted by Cane striding into the room. "I just heard from Chairman Weiss again. He'll be arriving in a few moments. Let's get started." He placed a small stack of papers on the table and looked around. "Where's Kelley?"

Bishop shrugged, "I'm sure she'll be down here in a few minutes. It's not quite seven yet," he said, glancing down at his watch.

"We're still waiting on Detective Spenser, too," added Dawn.

"The detective won't be joining us this morning," Cane said as he flipped open his folder of papers.

"Why not?" Bishop asked, still wiping the dust from his jacket. "Apparently, he was involved in some kind of car accident last night. I didn't get all the details," Cane admitted. "He's still trying to wrap things up down at the station."

"Is he all right?" Dawn asked.

Cane nodded. "I'm meeting him there directly after this meeting."

Bishop retook his seat at the large table. "Cane, why is Chairman Weiss here?"

"I really don't know," Cane admitted. "All I can think is that this is his daughter we're investigating and he wants to make sure it's done right."

"So he doesn't have any faith in our abilities," Dawn stated.

"I wouldn't say that," Cane said quickly. "Let's just let this play out and see where it goes." He checked his watch. "Will one of you go and get Kelley?"

Bishop stood up and started to move for the door. "I'm on it." He reached down for the door handle but had to quickly step out of the way as it swung open. "Chairman," Bishop said respectfully.

Chairman Thomas Weiss walked into the room and surveyed his team. Even after the long flight, he looked immaculately kept. His dark suit showed no sign of wrinkles, and his hair was perfectly styled. His tie was cinched up tight around his collar and his dark overcoat was slung neatly over his arm. He was only carrying a single brown briefcase. Adjusting his glasses, he moved into the room and sat down at the head of the table. "It's good to see all of you," he said as he flipped open his briefcase. Lifting several pages out, he began to pass them out. He stopped in front of Hayden. "Who are you?"

Hayden felt suddenly uncomfortable. "My name is Hayden Collins, sir." Weiss shook his head as he turned to Cane. "Pick up another stray?"

"No," Bishop interjected, "Hayden is the only eyewitness in the case.

We've placed him under our protection."

Both Cane and Weiss turned and glared at Bishop. Dropping his head, Bishop moved around the table to his seat without another word.

"I had time on the flight to work these out," Weiss said of the papers. "They are an outline I think we should follow in this investigation. It will bring us the best results."

"Tom," Cane said as he took a cursory glance at the pages, "we've already begun our own investigation. It would be a complete waste of our time to start over."

"Plus," Dawn added, "we're on a deadline. From what Kelley gathered, we know all this will come to a boiling point tonight during the full moon."

"Where is Ms. Windel?" Weiss asked.

Dawn looked at Cane, then returned her gaze to Weiss. "We're not entirely sure at this point. She hasn't checked in this morning yet."

Weiss nodded. "I want to speak to her as soon as she comes in." He glanced down at the papers, then back at his group. "You all have your written assignments. Let's get to work, and remember, lives are at stake here."

Cane turned and nodded to the team. They quickly went about their assignments.

"I want full paperwork on this one," Weiss called after them.

"Want my opinion?" Cane asked after everyone else had left the room. "Do I have a choice?"

Cane thought for a moment, "No. I think you're making a big mistake here, Tom. I know this is your daughter we're investigating, but that makes it all the more important you aren't here. We can't risk you letting your emotions cloud your judgment."

"I know what I'm doing, Zach. I have worked plenty of field cases before," Weiss added.

"I know, but none that involved your daughter." Cane stopped and decided to try a different angle. "Look, all I'm saying is the best place for you is back in Washington D.C."

"Do you take me for some kind of damned old fool?" Weiss asked. He moved around the table, his

226

gaze intently on Cane. Stopping in front of him, Weiss smiled. "I have made my decision. I'm staying here and taking over this investigation. Nothing you can say will change that, Cane. I'm here to help Lexy," he said softly. Turning, he lifted his briefcase off the table. "Now if you'll excuse me, I want to go clean up a bit."

Cane watched Weiss walk out of the room and head down the hall. Turning back inside, he closed the door slowly. "God help us all," he breathed.

Chapter Nineteen

Bishop knocked again on Kelley's door. He waited patiently outside, Hayden, standing behind him like a pack mule, had their equipment slung over his shoulders. Leaning up against the door, Bishop pressed his head against it. He lifted his hand to knock again, but stopped himself.

"She's not in there," Hayden assessed grimly.

"She has to be," Bishop muttered in return. "There's nowhere else she could be."

"Maybe she left late last night to follow a lead and just hasn't come back yet," Hayden suggested.

Bishop turned away from the door. "That's not like her. She always checks in."

"Unless she can't."

Bishop shot a nasty glance toward Hayden, then returned his attention to the door. Pressing his ear against it, he listened for a moment.

"Do you want me to see if I can get someone from housekeeping to let us in?" Hayden offered.

Taking a step back from the door, Bishop shook his head. "That won't be necessary." In one motion, Bishop had twisted to the side and kicked his leg straight out, knocking the door open. He smugly glanced at Hayden and walked straight into the room.

"This is breaking and entering," Hayden said nervously. "We have just cause."

Hayden shook his head, "We're not cops!"

Bishop waved the younger man off with his hand. "Look around for anything that might suggest where Kelley is."

Hayden nodded, dropped the bags and set about the task.

Bishop stood in the center of the room, slowly working his eyes over the scene. The bed was in a complete state of disarray. The mattress was hanging off the edge of the box spring, while the sheets were a tangled mess around it. One of the lamps next to it had been knocked to the floor and the phone was off the hook. Bishop could hear the repetitive squawking from the receiver. Leaning over, he slipped the phone back into its cradle. He didn't like this at all. There were clearly signs of a struggle. Bishop was suddenly hit with a deep sense of despair. He knelt down and lifted a lone shoe off the floor and held it in his hand.

"We can call off the search," Hayden called from the opposite side of the room.

Bishop quickly stood, dropping the shoe. "What?"

"She's here," he said quietly. Hayden glanced into the bathroom, then down to the floor.

Bishop moved across the room, stopping just short of the bathroom door. He looked from the door, to Hayden, then back again. Bishop swallowed hard. "Is it bad?"

Hayden nodded. "You don't have to go in there."

Bishop reached over and placed his hand on Hayden's shoulder. He gripped it firmly and shot the younger man a reassuring glance.

Hayden understood. He stepped away from the door and moved toward the telephone.

Bishop took a step forward, but stopped. He wasn't ready. Summoning up all his strength, he gritted his teeth and stepped into the bathroom. Out of the corner of his eye he saw her, but he couldn't bring himself to look directly at her. His vision moved from the tan towels hanging on the wall to the faux marble sink and to the floor. He could see her foot clearly now. Moving slowly up her body, Bishop saw that she was still in her pajamas. She always wore a pair of boxers and a tank top to bed. His eyes followed her legs up to her chest and then to her head. Stumbling back, he hit the wall and slowly slid down.

Kelley was lying with her head propped up between the wall and toilet. Her arm was crossed uncomfortably over her body and her usually well-kept hair was a mess. Her opposite arm was resting against the wall, where her fingernails had ripped small gashes into the wallpaper. Her eyes were wide and still bore the recognizable emotion of fear. Crusty trickles of blood led down from her nose and onto the strap of her white shirt.

Bishop ran his hand slowly down his face, then back through his hair. Leaning forward, he stared at the white linoleum floor. The urge to vomit gripped him, but he fought it. He would not allow himself to lose control. Looking back up at Kelley, he lifted himself off the floor and moved toward her. Lowering the lid of the toilet, he sat down next to her. Tenderly, he placed his hand on the cold flesh of her shoulder. He moved his hand to her face and carefully closed her eyes. Reaching into his coat pocket, he retrieved two coins and placed them gently on her eyelids.

"This was done in ancient times by the Greeks, Kelley," Bishop said with a slight crack in his voice.

"It was so the departed could pay Charon the ferryman of the River Styx and have a safe journey into the afterlife, instead of being doomed to wander the river's edge until they found the pauper's entrance to Hades." Bishop paused. "I couldn't take care of you in this life," he said regretfully, "It's the least I can do for you now." He caressed her shoulder gently and stood up. "Goodbye, Kelley." He looked up to see Hayden standing in the doorway.

"That was nice," Hayden said with a subtle smile. "I only hope someone says something like that at my funeral."

Bishop patted Hayden on the shoulder as he moved out of the bathroom. "So do I." He moved back toward the center of the room and dug his hand into his pocket. He cursed under his breath. "My cell phone's gone." He vaguely remembered losing it during the escape from the creature the day before. "You have a phone?"

Hayden shook his head, but pointed to the hotel phone resting on the floor next to Kelley's bed.

"We can't use that phone anymore," Bishop said slowly. "This is a crime scene and we've already contaminated it enough just by being here. We have to get out of this room." Bishop stopped. All he could see was his friend, a woman he had come to respect and love lying dead on the floor. He thought back to the crystal he had bought for her two days earlier and how it had broken. Someone was trying to tell him something back then, but he chose to ignore the message and pass it off as random chance. Bishop stopped and lowered his face into his hands. He was reading too much into

231

this. There was no way he could've prevented this. He knew everyone had his or her own course in life, and unfortunately, this was Kelley's. He didn't have to like it to make it true.

Looking back at Hayden, he pointed toward the two bags of equipment on the floor. "Let's get out of here and find Cane." As Bishop moved past the pile, he lifted his laptop case and a duffel bag from the floor and strapped them over his shoulder. Hayden quickly followed, scooping up the rest of the equipment.

"Shouldn't we wait for the authorities?" Hayden called after him.

Bishop walked briskly down the hall, not even acknowledging Hayden's comment. It was all he could do to keep his mind off the dead body…Kelley, he quickly corrected. This wasn't just some random person they had found, rather a member of the team, part of the family. Anger began to well up inside him. He would find the people responsible for this, and he would have retribution. They all would.

***

Isis rolled onto her back and slowly opened her eyes. She smiled softly. Her servants had attended her while she was resting. They had tucked her neatly into bed and removed the horrid clothes Agent Fowler had been wearing. She was now swathed in a red, silk nightgown that hugged her freshly formed curves. Isis slid into a sitting position and glanced around her room. A large mirror hung on the wall next to the bed. Swinging her legs over the edge, she took a cautious step. She stood carefully for a moment, shifting her weight back and forth between her legs. They now felt firm and solid, rather than the awkwardness she had encountered earlier. Taking another step, she became more confident. She easily traversed the floor toward the mirror.

Stopping in front of it, her eyes widened. She was not exactly as she remembered. Probably, she theorized, a result of being in an alien body. Her frame was long and slender, but her eyes were no longer brown, they had changed to a shade of green that almost appeared white in the light. She lifted her hand and ran it through her hair. It used to be shimmering black, but now it was blonde and hung to her shoulders. She smiled through luscious, full lips at her reflection in the mirror. The new colors suited her, she decided. Perhaps that was why her servants had dressed her in red rather than her traditional black. This was much more appealing.

She ran her hands down her newly created body with satisfaction. This vessel would serve her purposes well until her more permanent one could be created. She slowly cocked her head to the right playfully. Perhaps she wouldn't even need her new body. This one was lovely. She lifted her arms above her head and stretched her aching muscles. Closing her eyes, Isis brought her arms down across her body in the Goddess position and began to focus her energy. She felt a quick sputter of power, then nothing. She reopened her eyes and stared dolefully at herself. That was why she needed a new body. She was unable to use her powers to their full extent in this one. It had taken her years to master the magicks she used. In this vessel, it would take at least that long to learn them again. Muscles had to be taught, connections had to be altered, chemistry had to be changed. She didn't have that kind of time. At least she could do enough to complete tonight's impending ritual, then she could be free of Fowler's body. She wrinkled her nose. She could still smell him.

Clearing her mind, she mentally called for her servants. She waited for a moment, then repeated the call. Mere seconds had gone by before her chamber door creaked open and two figures moved inside. Isis turned to face the two. They were both her zombies. The one on the right was Lexy Weiss, the other, she didn't recognize. Isis moved slowly toward the two. Raising a hand, she placed it on the face of the second zombie. It was a man, but it wasn't her first creation, Jax. This one was new. She glanced over the creature's facial features, then down to his tattered clothes.

Moving her hand up his face, she stopped when she reached his forehead. Pressing her fingertips firmly against his skin, she delved into his mind. The process was difficult for her. In her previous incarnation, she wouldn't have had to even touch her subject, but now her powers were weak and unfocused. She shuffled through the random thoughts on the surface of his mind to the more important ones buried beneath. She saw flashes of his parents, school, college and then…Fowler. She saw his face clearly. Reaching deeper inside, she suddenly smiled and broke the connection. The creature panted hard and almost fell to the ground as Isis removed her hand.

"Sorry for the harsh treatment, love, but I had to be sure. You were Agent Fowler's partner." A name suddenly came to her. "Agent Greg Allen, I believe it was." She sized up her new creature. He was lean, looking as if he could slay an entire army by himself. Isis laughed to herself. She knew he could. "You were an accident," she said after a moment. "When Jax killed you, there was a mingling of blood and you were created."

Allen nodded happily, much like a puppy would when its master was speaking to it. He had no idea what she was saying to him, but he liked being spoken to. A side effect of the zombie transformation was a limited understanding of vocabulary.

Isis smiled again. "You'll do fine." Turning away from the two, she moved back to her mirror and held her arms wide. "Dress me," she commanded.

The two creatures moved to Isis' side and quickly set about their task. As they reached for her nightgown, each retracted their claws. Lexy and Allen lifted the nightgown up Isis' body and carefully slipped it over her head revealing her naked body. Without a second glance, the two moved to a large chest located at the head of Isis' bed and opened it. Inside, they found the traditional trappings of an Egyptian Queen. One by one, they removed the pieces made of brass, copper and gold and laid them gently on the bed. Lexy lifted a white cotton dress from near the bottom and hung it over her arm. Moving back to Isis, she carefully slid the dress on and adjusted it until it hung perfectly from her shoulders. Allen came next, with a large gold collar that he snapped around her neck. The collar hung heavy and spread out like a bird's wings on her chest. The gold was interwoven with green stones and intricate pattern work.

Lexy then lifted a headband and slipped it onto Isis' forehead. The gold band sat perfectly and presented itself in its full glory. The head of a cobra arched up from the band, its hood spread wide. Two almond-shaped emeralds had been used for its eyes, giving it a sinister, regal appearance. Allen, dropping down to one knee before his Goddess, presented her with the final piece: a six-foot-tall gold staff with a similar cobra head atop it. The cobra's golden body weaved its way down the staff to the very bottom where it terminated. Isis admired the staff for a moment as she took it into her hand. Switching it to her opposite hand, she felt the weight of the instrument and smiled. She could feel the waves of power emanating from it as they were absorbed into her body. She turned the staff head toward her. The cobra head came to life, its tongue working rapidly in and out of its mouth, smelling the air. Its green eyes focused on Isis and hardened. The snake bowed its head in reverence. Everything was in place.

Isis extended a hand to her two servants. They both took it in turn and gently kissed it. "Rise," she commanded. Moving toward the door, she smiled seductively at the two. "Come, we have work to do." She waited patiently for one of her servants to open the door. Glancing behind her, she shot an evil glance at the two. Allen looked at Lexy, then back at Isis. Apologetically, he slunk forward and

236

reached for the door. Bowing his head, he waited for his Queen to pass.

Moving slowly, Isis walked through the altar room and stopped in front of a blank wall at the rear. Lifting her hand, she carefully waved it, palm forward, over the blank space. As she worked her way down the wall, a large, wooden door was revealed. Waving her hand again, it swung open revealing a new chamber. Isis took a step inside and smiled.

The room shimmered. Unlike the other rooms, this place was in immaculate condition. Candles filled every nook of the room, radiating light in every direction. The floor was polished white marble with a few sparse veins running through it. Several six-foot tall golden statues stood guard in the corners and beside the raised throne near the back. It was constructed of white stone with golden highlights and inset with several different colors of gems. It stood in the center of a platform, three steps off the floor. Two tall torches burned just behind it and a long red carpet ran from the door to its foot.

Isis walked quickly along the carpet and took her position on the throne. Laying her hands gently on the arms, she stiffened her posture. Isis looked regally down upon her subjects. Allen and Lexy had dropped to one knee at the foot of the throne and bowed their heads. "Bring me the other members of the Triad," she commanded them. "We have much to discuss."

***

Bishop caught up with Cane just outside the hotel. Cane was in the process of hailing a cab when Bishop tapped him on the shoulder. The elder man turned to see Bishop standing there, his face long with grief. Cane's heart dropped, but he quickly regained control of his emotions.

"I found Kelley," Bishop said softly.

Cane waited, not wanting to rush his young friend through what was clearly very difficult for him. He placed a firm hand on Bishop's shoulder.

Bishop took a deep breath. "She's dead."

Cane let his head fall forward. "Jesus," he muttered. He took a moment to gather his thoughts before he continued. "What happened?"

"We're not sure yet," Bishop admitted. "We found her," he paused as his voice cracked, "in her bathroom. There were no clear indicators of how she got there, but the room was in a clear state of disarray. There could have been a struggle."

"With whom?" Cane asked. "Again, we don't know."

"Could this be the same creature that tried to kill you and Hayden last night?"

Bishop thought for a moment, but then shook his head. "I don't think so. The previous victims were mutilated and organs were removed. Kelley had no cuts, bruises," Bishop stopped, "but she did have a bloody nose."

"Theories?"

Bishop shrugged. "None that I find in any way feasible. This just doesn't make sense. It looks like she just died."

Cane leaned close to his young protégé, "You and I both know she didn't die of natural causes."

238

Bishop nodded. "I know."

"We will find them, Bish. I promise."

Bishop looked up into the older man's eyes. "What now?"

Letting out a long sigh, Cane patted his friend on the shoulder. "We have to continue. Lexy Weiss still needs our help."

"We have another problem. Kelley picked that FBI agent's mind for information. As far as I know, she never told anyone or wrote down what she found. It's probably completely lost to us."

"Get with Dawn," Cane instructed. "We need that information. Maybe Kelley told Dawn."

Bishop nodded. "They were together most of yesterday. That's a possibility."

"See what you can find out," Cane said as a cab pulled up to the curb in front of him. "I'll be in touch." Cane slid into the cab and pulled the door shut.

Bishop watched from the curb as the cab turned into traffic and sped off. Slowly turning, he looked at Hayden, who was standing quietly in front of a large, potted plant. He had several regrets flash through his mind. "Hayden," Bishop breathed as he took a step closer.

"I know what you're going to say."

"How do you know?"

Hayden pointed to Bishop's face. "You have that 'I don't want to see you get killed' look in your eyes." He set the equipment down and moved toward Bishop. "I can take care of myself."

Bishop shook his head. "I really think you need to head home, kid." Hayden was incensed. "Who are you calling 'kid'? You're only three years older than I am and I can take care of myself."

"Like hell you can," Bishop spat. "I had to haul your butt out of the fire twice yesterday."

"If I recall correctly, I also saved you."

"That's not the point," Bishop argued.

Hayden shrugged, "Then what is your point?"

"I don't want to see anyone else hurt. You don't have to be here. We already know everything you do. You're just slowing me down. I can't spend my time taking care of you, when I should be trying to solve this case."

"I can't believe you!" Hayden said in disgust.

Bishop reconsidered his strategy and took a new approach. "Look, I really appreciate all you've done, but I can't, in good conscience, allow you to go any further," Bishop said sincerely.

"I have an obligation to help these people."

"Bullshit." Bishop crossed his arms. "If that creature hadn't come along, you would still be barricaded in your apartment, wetting your pants every time someone walked past your door. You weren't going to do anything except save your own ass."

Hayden took a step back stunned. "I want to help," he muttered.

Bishop reached down and picked the equipment up off the ground and turned away from his young fan. "Go home, Hayden." Bishop started to walk away.

Hayden stood there stunned as he watched Bishop move away. He had, for all intents and purposes, been talked down to by one of his heroes. Hayden was emotionally crushed. Dropping his

240

head down, he started in the opposite direction. He paused for a moment to glance back over his shoulder, but when no requital came, he continued on. With his heart firmly in his hand, Hayden did exactly what Bishop wanted him to: he went home.

Chapter Twenty

Hart lifted the glass of liquor to his lips. Closing his eyes, he took a deep sniff, then swallowed it down. Holding the glass between his index finger and thumb, he let it tumble to the desk. Cradling his face in his hands, he let out a long breath. This wasn't what he'd asked for. Slowly, he pulled his hands away from his face and peered at the tall bottle sitting in front of him. There was no more than a swallow of the amber liquid left, and that was fine by him. *That should at least slow things down,* he thought, but in the long run, he didn't know what would happen. He hooked his finger around the knot of his tie and pulled it away from his neck. He then unbuttoned the collar of his shirt and reached inside. His fingers ran over the necklace he was wearing. Grabbing it between his fingers, he yanked hard, pulling it free. He dropped the broken necklace to his desk and stared at it.

Captain Hart....

It was a long silver chain with a bit of beadwork around the symbol at the bottom. Using his thumb, he spun the symbol to face him. It was a circle with a star inside, a pentacle, the traditional symbol of witches. The small silver figure of a woman with wings was superimposed over the star. He knew it was a representation of the Goddess Isis in her full glory.

What do you think you're doing?

She had used him. He'd been lured in with the promise of power and immortality, but she'd used him. He'd given her details no one should have been privy to, much less *her*. How could he have been so blind? He was spying on the very people he was sworn to honor and protect. Hart glanced down at his hands and furrowed his brow. It was coming. He hadn't even slowed it down. Lifting the necklace off the desk, he dropped it in his top desk drawer. Better there than hanging heavy around his neck.

You are mine now....

Hart leaned back in his chair uncomfortably. He should leave right now, he knew. He could save at least one. All he had to do was stand up and head for the door. Once there, it was a few quick steps to his car, then a short drive to the nearest bridge. That was how he could win, the only way he could win. He wouldn't do her dirty work anymore. All he had to do was get out of the office.

You will finish this right now.

Placing his hands on the arms of his chair, Hart sat right where he was. His body wasn't his own anymore. He was quickly starting to understand that. He belonged to her now. He cupped his hands over his ears. He could still hear her.

FINISH IT!

Hart leaned forward and slammed his head against the desk. Lifting up, he hit it again, then again. Pulling back, he slammed his head against the desk one final time. Hart fell back into his chair dazed. He ran his fingers over his brow. He was bleeding profusely, but it wasn't enough. He could still hear her. She was in his mind now. Even his thoughts weren't his own anymore. Glancing down at his fingers, he watched the tips begin to tear open. Blood spurted from the wounds as four small points began to emerge.

You dare disobey me?

Yanking open the top drawer of his desk, he sat motionless for a moment, just staring at it. There had to be another way. This couldn't be the end. He was a respected veteran of the force. His men would die for him if he asked them to. How could he even think of throwing away his life like this? A spike of pain tore through his midsection doubling him over. Wrapping his arm around his stomach, Hart gritted his teeth and tried to fight the pain. One moment of clarity was all he needed; one moment when he could wrap his hand around his pistol and draw it to his head. Another wave of pain hit him. It felt as if a fire had been lit in his brain. It washed over him, sending threads of pain down through his spine. She was punishing him.

A knock on his door startled him. "Go away," he moaned.

The door slowly creaked open. "Captain Heart?" a female voice asked.

"I said…" another burst of pain erupted behind his eyes, "go away." Dawn poked her head in the door. Her expression quickly faded into concern. She rushed into the room and placed her hand on Hart's back. "Captain? What's wrong?"

Hart slowly raised his head to look at Dawn. "Ms. Lassiter?" he asked in agony.

Dawn nodded.

Hart's eyes glazed over white. "Run."

Dawn staggered back from Hart watching his body convulse in his chair. His body contorted into several unnatural positions before coming to rest. Dawn took an uneasy step toward Hart, her eyes locked on his motionless body. Carefully, she lowered her hand toward the desk and reached for

244

the phone. Lifting the receiver, she pressed zero. Momentarily turning her eyes away from Hart, she focused on the door while she listened to the phone ring.

A large shadow passed over her.

Letting the phone fall from her ear, she carefully spun around. Dawn gasped. Hart had risen from his chair and was now perched on the desk just above her. He was a zombie now. Hart swung at her with his claws. They ripped through the exposed flesh just below Dawn's neck. Falling away, Dawn skittered frantically toward the door, but was stopped short by Hart. The large man leapt off the desk and landed in front of her. He leaned forward and shrieked in Dawn's face, his white eyes staring directly into hers.

Take her now!

Dawn lifted her leg and kicked hard into Hart's midsection. The large man fell back holding his gut and shrieked. Standing up, Dawn moved quickly to the opposite side of the room. She watched as Hart lifted off the ground into a crouching position. He held his arms wide exposing his jagged claws, then leapt. Before Dawn could react, Hart was on top of her. He landed with both feet in the center of her chest, knocking her to the ground. Once down, he pinned her arms and legs down. Hart leaned close and shrieked again. His long, black tongue slipped out of his mouth toward Dawn. She could see the fangs on the ends dripping with venom.

Hart ran his tongue over the bleeding cuts on Dawn's chest, then slowly moved up to her face. He pulled his tongue back and tasted her blood. His eyes closed for a moment with pure pleasure, savoring the flavor. Opening his eyes again, he focused on Dawn's neck. His mouth opened and his tongue lashed out, the fangs breaking Dawn's skin. Using newly formed muscles in the back of his mouth, he pushed a generous portion of venom into her body, then retracted the fangs.

Sitting back, he watched Dawn writhe in pain for a moment before her body became still. Sliding his hand under her back, he slung her over his shoulder. Standing up, he moved for the large window behind the desk. Breaking into a dead sprint, he tossed himself through the glass.

***

Spenser sat alone in his office, running his hand over the slanted brim of his hat. He had yet to remove his coat and he had been in the office for well over three hours now. After a morning full of paperwork and questions, he didn't feel much like being comfortable. He had a single image burned into his mind, haunting him. Tossing his hat on the desk in front of him, Spenser leaned back in his creaky wooden chair. He slowly rubbed his chin with his thumb. He had clearly seen it dead on a slab in the morgue. Hadn't he?

A knock on his door interrupted his thoughts. He looked up at his door for a moment. "Come."

Cane opened the door and stepped inside. He immediately moved to a chair opposite Spenser's and sat down. "Detective," he finally greeted him.

"Mr. Cane," Spenser returned the gesture.

The two sat in silence for a long moment, each looking in opposite directions. Finally, Cane turned to Spenser. "Kelley's dead," he said dryly, as if speaking of the weather in passing.

"What?" Spenser asked, not sure if he had heard correctly. Cane nodded. "Bishop found her this morning in her room."

"How?"

"We're still unsure on that one." Cane shifted positions in his seat. "I heard you had an interesting morning."

"I think that's an understatement. It was—" Spenser stopped when he heard another knock on the door. He glanced at Cane, who was rubbing his hand down his face. Spenser looked up at the door. "Come."

Chairman Weiss walked briskly in and stopped in front of Spenser's desk. He extended his hand. "Detective Spenser?"

Spenser stood and shook the man's hand. "And you are?"

"This is the OPR chairman, Thomas Weiss," Cane introduced them. "Weiss?" Spenser asked.

Weiss nodded. "Lexy's my daughter." He immediately turned to face Cane. "Why didn't you wait for me?"

"I'm sorry," Cane smiled. "I thought you had your own investigation to start."

Weiss shot Cane an angry glance, then took his seat. "Detective Spenser, I've been told we have your complete cooperation in this matter." Spenser nodded once.

"Before we get started, I would very much like to see my daughter." Spenser sat forward uncomfortably. "Didn't anyone tell you?"

"Tell me what?" Weiss asked quickly.

Spenser looked away from Weiss, then at Cane. He felt uneasy when he looked back to Weiss. "The Seattle Police Department is no longer in possession of your daughter. She escaped yesterday."

Weiss stood up and placed both his palms flat on the desk. "What?"

"We don't know how she got out, but she—" Spenser stopped. A loud crash caught his attention. Shooting up from his desk, he moved quickly to the door, followed by Cane and Weiss. He stopped just outside Hart's office.

A young officer was standing outside as well with his hand on his weapon. "It came from in there," he said with a deep breath.

Spenser nodded. Reaching into his jacket, he pulled his pistol. Nodding to the officer, he took up position next to the door. The young officer pulled his weapon and cradled it in his hands. Taking a step back, he counted to three in his head, then kicked Hart's office door open. Spenser spun around the doorframe, his weapon at the ready. He quickly surveyed the office and spotted the broken window. Moving swiftly, he peered outside to see the fleeting image of a figure rushing around a corner outside. Spenser slowly holstered his weapon and leapt through the window. The young officer, Cane and Weiss stopped short of the window just as Spenser dove through.

"What the hell is he doing?" Weiss asked.

Not stopping to find out, Cane followed him out the window. Hitting the ground running, he charged after Spenser. Charging around the corner, Cane spotted Spenser a few paces in front of him. Up ahead, Cane could clearly make out the form of a large man moving easily through the alley. He appeared to be carrying something over his shoulder. Cane weaved left and narrowly missed a large garbage can. Stumbling away, he skidded to the concrete, his hands flailing in front of him. He looked up just in time to see the figure and Spenser disappear around a corner.

Lifting himself off the ground, Cane worked into a light jog down the alley. His knee had hit the ground hard and was bruised. Favoring the knee, he tried hard to catch up with the others, but they were gone. He slowed to a trot and then finally, stopped. Leaning an arm against the alley wall, he took a moment to catch his breath. A hand reached out and grabbed him and quickly stifled his mouth. Cane struggled to break free from the grip.

"Quiet," Spenser instructed him.

"What the hell are you doing?" Cane broke free of Spenser's grasp. Spenser pointed past Cane. "Look."

Cane turned and scanned the alley. "I don't see...." He spotted a dark shape sitting in a high fire escape. "Who is it?"

"I think it's one of your zombies," Spenser whispered. Cane nodded. "What's the plan?"

"We should try and follow him. He could lead us back to whoever is orchestrating all this."

"Agreed. I'll contact Bishop and Dawn. We need to be at full strength if we're going to have any chance of stopping this." Lifting his cell phone out of his pocket, Cane pressed the memory button with his thumb, all the while keeping his eyes on the dark figure across the way. He scrolled through the entries until he reached Dawn's. Pressing the send

249

button, he lifted the phone to his ear. He listened intently to the ring, silently urging his partner to pick up. A sharp sound caught his attention.

Lowering the phone, Cane listened intently for a moment. He heard the sound echo through the alley again. It was the ring of a cell phone. The ring repeated. His eyes shifted up to the figure on the fire escape. He watched the creature move frantically over the other body as the ring continued. It lifted an object into the air then slammed it against the alley wall. The ringing stopped. Cane once again lifted his phone to his ear. The ringing on his end had also stopped.

"The customer you are trying to reach is unavailable. Please try your call again later."

Cane's eyes widened. "Dawn...."

***

Lexy lifted a small stone from the ground and tossed it away. Sitting in the corner, her knees pulled up tightly to her chest, she lifted her bruised hand and ran it through her hair. Lexy took a deep breath, every part of her ached. It felt like she was falling apart, which couldn't be too far from the truth. After all the various transformations, she wondered how her body was still going. It had to be the magick. It was keeping her alive.

Lexy closed her eyes as a chill ran down her spine. The fog in her mind had been gradually lifting. She was now starting to experience memories she had accumulated as a zombie in a waking state. They were horrifying. It actually made her sick to her stomach to think about them. She had killed that woman in the alley that night, as well as several others she could now remember. The police were right. She was a murderer. With each passing moment, the past became clearer. Her soul would surely be damned to hell for this. There was no hope for her, in this world, or the next.

Lexy dropped her head down and rested it on her knees. Wrapping her arms around her legs, she tried to calm herself. She thought about her students for a moment. She wondered what chapter they were now working on. Her mood worsened. Her life had been taken and shattered against the wall by these people. Everything she held dear had been ripped from her in one sweep of their hands. It wasn't fair, but that was the nature of life, wasn't it? One moment, she was sitting high in the saddle, the next, she was face down in the mud. Lexy shook her head. Not only was she face down in the mud, she was drowning in it.

Lifting her head, she swept a piece of hair out of her eyes and stopped. She glanced at her hand. It was bruised and battered with deep lacerations running the entire length of it. Large scabs had formed on the tips where the claws sprouted. Her nails, which were usually immaculately kept, were broken and bloody. She wiped her hand against the orange jail jumpsuit she was still wearing. Even it had seen better days. It was dirty and torn so badly in places, she wondered how it was staying on.

She looked around the room. It was the same place she had originally been in. Glancing across the floor, she spotted two lumps. Her eyes focused in the dim light and slowly began to make out what they were: two men lying unconscious. Lifting up, she fought against the pain in her legs and feet and moved toward the first man. He was wearing a frayed suit that, in its better days, looked expensive. Taking a step closer, Lexy reached out, but stopped. Fear was coursing through her veins, threatening to paralyze her. Biting her lower lip, she reached out again, this time, more slowly. She held fast when her fingertips made contact with the man's shoulder. An image flashed in her mind. She recognized him. This man had stood by her side earlier in the day as they attended Isis. He was another unfortunate soul who had been taken from his normal life.

Wrapping her fingers around his arm, she carefully rolled him onto his back and stared at him. His face and body were a patchwork of cuts and slashes. His white shirt, what was left of it, was stained a deep red from all the blood he had lost. A large wound ran from his forehead, down past his jaw and terminated just above his collarbone. Lexy could easily imagine one of her claws inflicting that. She stopped. What if she *had* done this? She shook her head. She had no memory of this man before today. Softly, she ran her fingers down his cheek. He was extremely handsome. Maybe, if the situation were different, she would have the chance to get to know him. Maybe.

Turning her attention away, she focused on the other man in the room. Standing up, she took several uneasy steps toward him. As she neared him, her eyes widened. She clasped her hand over her mouth. This one surely had to be dead. If not, he was in the greatest pain of his life. His chest was completely laid open, probably part of some kind of surgery. A lone silver clamp hung from one side of his chest. Circling around him, Lexy let out a gasp. The man was completely missing the lower section of his body. Lexy had to know. Dropping down to one knee, she carefully pressed two fingers to the man's bloody throat. She uttered a silent prayer of thanks when she found no pulse. Luckily, he was dead. Through no action of his own, he had escaped this place. Lexy wished she could be so lucky. Pulling her fingers away, she rocked back onto the balls of her feet and stared at the corpse in front of her. Was this the fate waiting for her as well?

Standing up, she moved back to her corner of the room and leaned against the wall. Why had she been chosen for this? Surely it couldn't be purely coincidence. There had to be, as with everything, a reason. She scanned through all her recent memories, but came up empty. There was nothing there to even suggest how her involvement came to be. Three days ago, she was a teacher wondering if she should get a pet. Now, she was a zombie.

"You don't remember me, do you?"

Lexy straightened up and glanced nervously around the room. "Who's there?"

"It is I, your queen, Isis."

Lexy squinted her eyes in the darkness.

"Don't bother looking for me. I am not in the room with you."

Lexy became enraged. "Get out of my head!"

"Poor child. You still do not fully comprehend my power. I can do anything I want and be anywhere I want. You have no choice in the matter. You still haven't answered my question."

Lexy slid down the wall into a sitting position. "What question?"

"You don't remember me?"

"How could I?"

"I gave you what you wanted. You should."

Lexy pressed her hands against her temples and started to rock back and forth. "Get out of my head," she muttered again.

"You came to me wishing for a better life, and I gave it to you freely. Now I find you resenting me? I don't think that's the appropriate way to thank someone."

"What are you talking about?"

"Close to three months ago, you visited a fortune-teller."

Lexy sat straight up.

"As the woman read your fortune, you confessed you were unhappy with your life. You wished you could be free of your mortal trappings. Do you recall?"

"I...." Lexy couldn't find the words. As soon as Isis mentioned it, the memory sprang into her head. She had never held much faith in fortune tellers, but had sought one out of boredom more than anything. She recalled the woman sitting behind a small, round table with her crystal ball. Like all the fortune tellers she had seen in the movies, this one was garbed in purple and black and wore excessive amounts of jewelry. She was an older woman with a hunched back that spoke with an accent Lexy wasn't familiar with. Lexy allowed herself a laugh. The gypsy had told her good things were coming in her life.

"To that complete stranger, you confessed your sorrows and desires, so I helped you."

"How did you think killing people would help me?" Lexy shouted.

"I freed you of all your problems. I took you from that life and gave you a better one. You are now in my service. You are working for the soon to be queen of this world."

"I didn't ask to kill anyone!"

"Nothing is free, my dear. With your new life came certain chores that had to be completed. For all that I gave you, I asked very little in return."

"You stole my life from me," Lexy sneered. "Everything that is, *was* me," she corrected, "is gone."

"I am shocked. I gave you everything you asked for, and now you whine for the very things you complained about, the very things that made you miserable? I find this lack of gratitude very disturbing. I freed you!"

"I want my life back!" Lexy wailed as a tear rolled down her cheek. "I want to see my family, and my students! I want you to leave me the fuck alone!"

"Ingrate. You are mine now, and no amount of tears or pathetic whining will change that! You belong to me, girl!"

Lexy cocked her head back and screamed at the top of her lungs. "I will not serve you!"

"You have no choice."

Lexy felt her eyes begin to melt to white.

"I have a job for you."

Chapter Twenty-one

Bishop checked his watch and shook his head. It was almost noon. Half the day had vanished. The full moon would be up soon and he was no closer to an answer than he was yesterday. His mind wandered to Kelley again, but he quickly thought of something else. He couldn't keep torturing himself like this. There would be time to mourn her, but for now, he had to focus. There was an answer here, somewhere. As if buried in the sands of time, he had to begin excavating the site; dig through the rubble until he came to a clear and concise picture of the events unfolding. This is what he had been taught in the FBI before he dropped out, and it was the key. "Think clearly and examine the evidence from all sides," was a saying one of his instructors had been fond of, but there was nothing here that seemed to connect.

Bishop leaned over the small desk in his hotel room rubbing his forehead. The facts just didn't seem to add up. There were no underlying themes to latch onto from his perspective. To him, it appeared to be multiple killings that somewhat followed the same modus operandi, but that was as far as the trail went. Each victim had been mutilated in a slightly different way, and different organs had been removed. It reminded him of the old urban legend about the missing kidney.

A man is away on a business trip and finds himself drinking alone in the hotel bar. After a short time, he spots a woman across the bar flirting with him. Thinking that while away from the wife a little adventure might be in order, he meets the woman

256

and buys her a drink. The two immediately hit it off as she tells him that she is in town for the same conference. With a mutual interest, the two talk late into the night, and with several drinks in him, the man finally invites the woman up to his room. Once there, they decide to have one final drink. The woman moves to the bar, picks out an appropriate beverage and serves it to the man. After a moment, the man becomes dizzy and disoriented. He passes out on the bed. Later, he wakes up to find himself naked in a bathtub full of ice. On the counter next to him are a cell phone and a note that reads, "Call 911 if you want to live." The man panics and digs through the ice to find a gaping wound in his side where his kidney has been removed.

Of course, Bishop knew this could never happen. It was just a basic reflection of society's fears. First of all, the legend was preposterous. Why would the man need to be submerged in ice? It would be the kidney that needed to be kept cool, not him. Secondly, no hospital in the world would accept a kidney brought in that condition. All donors are carefully, and exhaustively, screened. Even on the black market, that kidney would be of no value. From the hack and grab surgery, it would surely be damaged beyond use, and third.... Bishop shook his head. There was no third. The story was idiotic.

Leaning back in his chair, he glanced over his yellow notepad. He had scribbled notes randomly across the page, but still no order could be brought to it. They were harvesting organs, this much he knew to be true, but for what purpose? They would be useless, unless used in some kind of ceremony....

Or Ritual. Bishop stopped and sat straight up.

Reaching over to his laptop, he quickly opened his browser and connected to the net. Running his fingers over the keyboard, he typed in his search string and hit enter. He waited anxiously as the result page was built. Once open, he scrolled through the hits. About halfway down the page, he smiled. Clicking the link with his cursor, he waited for the page to display. He had his answer. It had been staring him in the face the entire time. It all seemed to come together now. Tapping the print key, he listened as his printer whined to life.

Standing up, he strutted triumphantly around the room. Turning back to his desk, he stopped and became very still. A dark shadow had just passed outside his window. He had caught it out of the corner of his eye. Taking a deep breath, he crept toward the window, but stopped dead as the shadow went by again. Turning frantically away, Bishop ran to his desk and snatched the printed documents. Snapping his laptop shut, he quickly disconnected the cords and tucked it under his arm. It had all of his answers. Less than three steps from the door, Bishop heard a now familiar sound behind him. It chilled him to the bone.

Glancing over his shoulder, he saw a zombie pressed to his hotel window, its tongue working over the glass. It slowly raised a hand and pulled its claws down the window. It was taunting him.

Bishop found himself mesmerized by the creature's glare. Looking it over, he felt a pang of recognition in its distorted face. He had to remind

258

himself to take a breath when it hit him. It was Lexy Weiss. She was a zombie now. Bishop watched Lexy's feminine form struggle against the window. It almost looked like she was trying to fight against whatever it was that had been done to her. A moment of sorrow and urgency passed over Lexy's face as if she were screaming for Bishop to run. Bishop shook his head. The pain faded from Lexy's face, allowing the demonic visage of the creature to return. She had given him time to run, but it was too late.

Looking down, Bishop spotted his black duffel bag sitting near the edge of the bed. Crouching down, he unzipped it and slid his laptop and papers inside. At that same moment, the creature reared back and sent its head into the window. Shards of glass exploded into the room and rained down on Bishop. Slipping the strap over his shoulder, he sprung up and hit a dead sprint toward the door. Not looking behind him, he reached for the door handle and twisted it to the right. He had the door only slightly open when the creature hit him solidly in the back. The momentum of the creature carried the two into and through the door in an eruption of wood. Bishop hit the ground and quickly rolled to his right, narrowly missing the creature's claws. Leaping onto its feet, the creature leaned forward and shrieked at Bishop. Still on his back, Bishop pulled off the duffel and swung hard. The bag, with all of his equipment, connected with the creature's head and sent it tumbling to the ground. Seizing the moment, Bishop rolled to his feet and charged down the hall toward the elevator. Glancing over his shoulder, he could see the creature skittering from the floor to the wall, and it was gaining.

He could feel blood pouring down his forehead, threatening to go in his eyes. When they had burst through the door, Bishop had felt a chunk of wood tear along his face and scalp. He was in pain, but he had to keep going. He pumped his legs harder as he skidded around a corner. He could see the elevators looming at the end of the hall. He knew he would be safe if he could just get there. Reaching out, he tagged the call button with his hand. Spinning around, he braced himself for the impact that was surely coming.

The creature was gone.

Bishop scanned the hallway nervously. Behind him, he could hear the ding of the elevator as it crawled toward his floor, in front of him, there was emptiness. Every muscle in his body tensed. It was planning something. Behind him, he heard the elevator doors slide open. Turning around, he moved uneasily toward the doors.

He snapped his head up as a shriek echoed through the hall. The creature was latched to the ceiling above him, glaring at him. It had intentionally allowed Bishop to call for the elevator to trap him. Bishop knew it meant to corner and kill him. Releasing, the creature fell head first toward Bishop, its claws spread wide. Falling to his back, Bishop kicked upward connecting with the creature's head. It wailed once and fell back as its neck contorted painfully. It crumbled to the ground, but wasn't down for long. Bishop watched in horror as the creature rose to its feet, its neck twisted back. Lifting its hands, the zombie twisted its head around

260

and snapped it back into place. Bishop cringed. It sounded like a bowl of Rice Crispies popping as the creature twisted its head back and forth to realign it on its spine. Thinking quickly, Bishop skittered backward into the elevator just as the doors had begun to slide shut. The creature flung its hands toward the fleeing man, only to catch Bishop by the boot. The door closed on Bishop's leg, but the safety mechanism kept it from crushing his appendage. An alarm bell sounded as the door slid open again.

The creature yanked hard, pulling Bishop out of the elevator. Spreading his arms, Bishop latched onto the sleek silver walls of the elevator and held tight. The creature yanked again, but Bishop held firmly. Moving his free leg, he kicked the creature hard across the face. Pulling back, he kicked again, but this time, the creature intercepted the blow with its hand. Snapping its fingers around Bishop's ankle, it twisted hard. Bishop quickly twisted onto his stomach to avoid a broken ankle. The creature released Bishop's ankles and swung down hard, tearing a gash in his leather jacket, its claws narrowly missing flesh. Tucking his knees under his chest, Bishop bucked and connected with the zombie. The creature rolled back, hitting the ground flat on its back.

Lifting up, Bishop shot forward just as the creature started to recover. Hitting the floor of the elevator, Bishop spun around and hit the door close button. He watched in nervous anticipation as the creature rolled onto the balls of its feet to strike. It leapt out just as the doors were about to close. Bishop heard a solid thud and a shriek as the doors finally closed. Lying back, Bishop let out a long sigh of relief.

He pulled his duffel close and unzipped it. Digging his hand inside, he lifted out his laptop. Snapping it open, he stared at the LCD screen. Shaking his head, he folded the laptop closed again. The screen had been completely shattered. He wouldn't know if it was operable until he had a chance to hook it up to a new monitor. Dropping it back into the bag, he took comfort in the fact he still had the printed hardcopy of the information.

Bracing his hands against the elevator's rail, he lifted himself off the ground with a groan. He could feel several new bruises forming on his chest. Pulling his sleeve over his hand, he tried to wipe some of the blood off of his forehead. He placed his fingers carefully on the edge of the wound. He followed the jagged cut back into his hairline and cursed under his breath. As the elevator chimed one final time, he wiped his fingers off on his shirt and slung the duffel over his shoulder. As the doors slid open, he moved out amidst a crowd of staring eyes. Ignoring them, he fought his way to the front door. He had to find Cane and Dawn. Glancing down, he checked his watch again and frowned. Time was quickly running out. Moving to a bank of pay phones, he fished some change out of his pocket and plunked it into the slot. Pressing the receiver to his ear, he dialed Cane's cell number.

***

Lydia stood and walked to the center of the circle. Folding back the hood of her long, black robe, she glanced over her group. It had taken many years and several false starts, but she had finally branched off and created her own coven of witches. She, along with her partner, Conroy, had only recently become third degree witches, meaning they could operate a coven as High Priestess and Priest with complete autonomy from the mother coven. This had been a blessing in her life. Now she was the one initiates sought out for guidance. Lydia had become the wise old sage. It had given her a renewed love for the craft and all those in it.

The group was seated in a circle around an old tree stump well out of the city. The leaves around them were just beginning to sprout after a long winter. Each was wearing a long, dark robe that completely enveloped them. While all appeared similar with their hoods up, each had a streak of individualism clearly present. This had been their meeting place for as long as many of them could remember. Lydia had stumbled across it some years ago while on a nature walk with Conroy. It was secluded, with the trees forming a natural wall around them, and perfectly suited for their needs. A cauldron sat in the middle of the tree stump, burning brightly in the night. Several familiar tools of the craft surrounded it as well.

Glancing around her group of nine (including herself), she couldn't help but smile. Lydia felt she had assembled a very talented flock of witches for her coven. Their skill levels ranged from beginner all the way to seasoned veteran. There was a small smattering of men in the coven, but mostly, it was made up of women. Lydia understood this. It was easy to see why more women than men were drawn to Wicca. Here was a religion where the women were equal to men. No longer would they be forced to live under a vengeful male God. Here, they found a loving Goddess and a God. This was not a place where they had to cling to outdated rules of feminine subjugation. Here, all were equal. Lydia would have it no other way.

Her mood became grim as she thought about what she was about to suggest to the group. "This is a crisis," she stated. "As most of our Elders have already discovered, our ability to use magic has been greatly lessened, and some of us have even been magically assaulted by a dark force during spells and rituals."

"What is going on, Lydia?" a young woman asked.

"Something truly evil is in Seattle," Lydia said grimly. "I'm not sure how, but it appears it is leaving the rest of us unable to perform."

"How is that possible?" an older witch asked. "I thought magick was infinite?"

Lydia paused. "I wish I had an answer for you, but this defies logic. I tend to liken it to a power generator, and we are all plugged into it. When one requests more power, the rest suffer a power loss. That could be what's happening. The big evil is sucking so much juice, we're all experiencing a brown-out." She waited for a moment so her explanation could sink it. "I have an old friend here in town, who is, as we speak, on his way to try and stop this. He is going to fail, and everyone he holds close is going to die, unless we intervene." Lydia glanced over the worried faces of her coven.

"I am asking you now, will you help me? Will you fight?" Reaching down, she lifted her staff off the stump and held it vertically in front of her. "I can't promise anything, but at least we can try to make a difference."

Galen, an elder male witch, immediately walked to his High Priestess' side and placed his hand alongside hers on the staff. "I will fight," he proudly said, momentarily looking at Lydia, then at the group.

The two watched as the coven stood from the circle one by one and placed their hands on the staff. Lydia raised the staff with all hands attached to the heavens. "Goddess and God be with us," she prayed.

***

The power flickered in his apartment for a moment, but he paid little attention to it. In a city this size, brown-outs were a common occurrence. Leaning back in his chair, he waited for his browser to fully load up. As the only one of his friends to still be working with a dial-up connection, the net was decidedly slower. To pass the time, he drummed his fingers on his desk. He shook his head and quickly stopped. It was just making him more anxious.

Turning away from the computer, Hayden glanced over his apartment. It had taken him a little over an hour to put everything back in its place. He was lucky he even had furniture after the way he left his apartment door open. He nodded. Lucky *indeed*. He glanced up at his door. There was a large crack in the door the landlord was sure to throw a fit over. At least he had removed the knife. A chime from his computer gathered his attention. Spinning back around in his high-backed chair, he clicked open his email. At the top of the long list was a message from his boss. Warily, he opened the letter. After scanning through the contents, he rubbed the bridge of his nose and let out a long breath. He had been fired. After three days off from work with no explaining phone call, how could he expect anything different?

Closing his email account, he opened his favorites menu. A massive list of paranormal related sites appeared. Clicking the second from the top, he waited for the page to load. Grabbing the scroll bar with his pointer, he quickly browsed over the page. The familiar headlines were all present, featuring stories on ghosts, Bigfoot and UFOs. A headline near the top of the page caught his attention.

"Wiccans across the northwest report loss of powers."

Hayden opened the story and was immediately redirected to a new site. The page, being mostly text except for a banner graphic across the top, loaded quickly. Leaning forward on his elbows, Hayden sped through the article. His curiosity had been piqued. He never really paid much attention to stories on Wicca, because he felt they had no true power. They, in his opinion, were a group of tree hugging hippies hiding behind a pseudo-pagan religion actually invented in Britain in the fifties. There wasn't much there for him to latch onto. They were the least supernatural "witches" he had ever met.

As he read through the article, he came upon several glaring facts. He leaned back in his chair and reread the first paragraph. "Wiccans report their power has severely diminished, and every time they try to conduct a ritual or spell, they are confronted with an evil presence," Hayden summarized. "Seems like someone is sucking up all the witch's power," he thought out loud, "something evil. Something evil...."

Hayden sat straight up in his chair. "It's here."

Jumping up, he snatched his coat off the wall and pulled it on. Picking up his keys from a nearby table, he dumped them in his pocket and headed for the door. Reaching for the door handle, he stopped himself. "Where am I going?" Moving back across the room, he slumped down in his couch. "Who am I going to tell?"

His first instinct was to take this new information straight to Bishop. If it meant something to him, it would surely be important to the members of the OPR, but that wasn't the case. He wouldn't have the chance to even tell him. Hayden understood Bishop's concern, but he really could take care of himself. He had been doing so, and successfully he might add, for twenty-three years. And even if something horrible happened to him, it wouldn't have been on Bishop's conscience. Hayden wanted to be there of his own free will. He wasn't Bishop's ward.

Hayden took a deep breath as he let his head fall back against the couch. What had begun as a small case had turned into a full-blown apocalypse for team OPR. They needed all the help they could get. Hayden smiled, even if they didn't want it.

267

Jumping up from the couch, he ran to his computer and launched his chat client. Opening up a dialogue box, he started a mass email to all his friends on the list. "Hold on, Bishop, the cavalry is on its way."

***

Cane glanced behind at Weiss. He was easily keeping pace, but his face was a mass of stress and grief. Slowing his pace slightly, he allowed Weiss to catch up. The two of them and Spenser had been tracking the creature through alleys by foot for some time now. Spenser, who was leading, had kept a healthy distance from it so as not to spook it. Cane, meanwhile, had kept his eyes firmly focused on Dawn. She was still hanging motionlessly over the creature's shoulder as they moved from rooftop to rooftop. During the chase, they had moved from the nicer part of the city into a more rundown district.

"Are you all right?" Cane asked after a moment. Weiss nodded.

"Even though we're not the best of friends anymore, you can still talk to me," Cane advised.

"I know," Weiss said as he continued on. Cane huffed and began to move away.

Reaching forward, Weiss grabbed Cane's arm and stopped him. "Wait." The two men stopped and faced each other. It had been a long time since the two had spoken on a personal level, and even longer since they had been in the field together. This was a rare opportunity for them both, and one that neither would recognize. Stubbornness was a trait both men had in spades. Weiss bit his lower lip regretting reaching out to Cane. He was afraid, but he didn't want anyone to know that. Since the phone call two days ago, he had been torn up inside. He began to feel useless and following Cane around the city blindly wasn't helping.

"Cane," Weiss started again, "Zach, this is my daughter we're trying to help."

"And my friend, remember?" Cane corrected hastily. "I've already lost one of my team on this one, Tom."

"I'm sorry," Weiss said sympathetically, "but we need to use any means necessary to ensure the safe return of Lexy."

"How many lives are you willing to sacrifice to save your daughter?" Cane asked angrily.

"All of ours," Weiss shot back without hesitation. "Including mine," he added.

"How can you say that?"

"She is everything to me." Weiss paused, "She is the one thing in my life that makes it all worthwhile. She is my heir to the future as she is the last of the Weiss bloodline."

"That seems a little selfish, don't you think? You're willing to throw away all our lives, just so the Weiss family can live on?"

"No, you blithering idiot," Weiss spouted, "she is my daughter. Being such, I would without a second thought lay down my life for hers, and I insist on the same from my employees...especially you."

"That's asking a lot, you realize."

Weiss nodded. "I would expect nothing less." What happened to us?"

Weiss shook his head, "What do you mean?"

269

"We used to be inseparable, you and me. We started this company together. How did we get here?"

"Will you two shut up and come on?" Spenser whispered loudly.

The two men nodded at Spenser, then quickly returned their attention to each other. Things were being said here that should've been said years ago. This was far too important a moment to let pass.

Weiss smiled. "After all this time, I still really don't know. It all started when I created the board. When I offered you a position, you flat out rejected me. To this day, I don't understand why.."

"I felt like you were taking the company from me," Cane admitted. "I was still out in the field every day, researching and doing all the leg work, while you were sitting back in your posh office. I resented that."

"But that was the way you wanted it, if I remember correctly. You always told me that you had no mind for business. You just wanted to be a ghost hunter."

"Yes," Cane nodded, "but it was still partially my company."

"I still don't understand. Everything was the way you wanted it," Weiss argued. "I was running the day-to-day stuff while you were in the field. That was the way you set it up. How could you resent that?"

Cane shook his head. "I'm not sure."

"Listen, old friend, you still own half the company. That much has never changed. Anytime you want your own posh office, you just let me know."

"You know I would never be happy," Cane admitted. "It's just not what I want."

Weiss laughed. "Then what the hell have you been complaining about all these years?"

The epiphany hit Cane like a ton of bricks. He really had no idea of what he had been so upset about. Everything was the way he had always wanted it to be, and yet he was still bitter inside. Maybe that was it. He was just bitter. Even though he was living the life he wanted, the way he wanted, he still felt empty and angry. Cane shrugged, perhaps that was just the way he was. All this time, he had been blaming Weiss for his problems, when the door had always been open for him. He had just refused to take it out of some unknown personal issue. A deep sense of shame passed over him. He was truly a rebel without a clue. Moving away from Weiss, he again took up position behind Spenser.

A moment later, the chime of his cell phone interrupted his thoughts. Quickly digging into his coat pocket, he tapped the send button. "Cane," he answered.

"It's Bishop, where are you?"

"Following one of those creatures downtown."

"There are more of them? One just tried to whack me in my hotel room."

"That makes two," Cane said grimly. "I wonder how many there actually are?"

"No telling. Cane, I have information for you. I think it's vital to this case."

"Hit me with it."

"I think we are chasing after a group that's trying to become Gods.

Whoever is doing all this has been harvesting organs from the victims, very specific organs. They are trying to recreate the Osiris Myth."

Cane nodded. "I am familiar with the myth. Go on."

"They have been trying to collect fourteen different organs for a kind of 'resurrection' ritual. I found news on the net of a similar group trying to do the same thing about ten years ago. Apparently, they had all the required organs back then and were preparing to complete the ritual, but the FBI and ATF busted in and all hell broke loose. The High Priestess was killed during the raid."

"Okay, I'm following you. You think this is a group trying to finish what the first started?"

"No, I think this is the same exact group. Witnesses to the event said that when the High Priestess died, the other two members of the Triad seemed to vanish, but their screams could still be heard through the commotion. I think the ritual was broken up before it was completed, and it backfired on the remaining members of the Triad."

"Meaning what?"

"I'm not entirely sure yet, but the one thing Kelley did tell us was that they had to complete whatever they were doing by midnight tonight, or they would be lost forever. My theory is they are trying to complete the ritual, while at the same time, resurrecting their fallen High Priestess."

"Interesting," Cane said as he digested the information. "We're coming up on a Starbuck's Coffee. Why don't you meet us there?"

There was silence, then a laugh.

"Cane, we're in Seattle. Which of the hundreds of Starbuck's are you talking about?"

"The one just across from the old power mill downtown, smartass."

"Is Dawn with you? I've been trying to get a hold of her."

"In a manner of speaking, she is." Cane paused. "The creature has her."

"What?"

"We're following her now. Meet us down here ASAP." Cane snapped his phone shut and deposited it back into his pocket. Following Spenser around a corner, he watched the creature vanish from sight.

The three turned to face each other. Cane quickly took the initiative. Pointing to Spenser, he motioned for him to continue ahead. Looking at Weiss, Cane pointed in a different direction. "If we don't find the creature and Dawn, let's meet back at that coffee shop in half an hour."

Each man nodded and headed off in a different direction. They had to relocate the creature, even if it meant splitting up the group.

Chapter Twenty-two

"Something unexpected is happening," Osiris said as she peered out the window. "Events have been set in motion that threaten our goals."

Horus wrung her hands together, and nodded. "It is troubling indeed."

"Our fate has become uncertain," Osiris added. "A shroud has fallen. Everything has become clouded."

"We must move quickly to remedy this," Horus said immediately.

"I concur," Osiris nodded. "If we act quickly enough, this could be averted." Isis got up from her throne and marched toward the other two members of the Triad with her staff firmly in hand. She stopped just short of them and slammed her staff into the ground. A large, dark shadow crept up around her, extinguishing all light as it went. "I will hear no more of this," she hissed. Her mood softened slightly as the shadow began to fade, "You two have done nothing but complain. Try to do something constructive."

The two bowed before their High Priestess. "What would you wish of us?" Angrily, Isis lifted her staff and swung it at the two. The golden shaft slipped through the center of both, not even touching them. "I wish I could hit you," Isis smirked.

Osiris nodded apologetically. "We are non-corporeal beings. That makes it impossible to strike us. Even after we complete the ritual tonight, we will not be able to touch anything physically, or be touched. We were doomed to this life when the ritual was not completed correctly the first time."

"Osiris," Isis said softly, "you are my oldest and dearest friend. Didn't you used to be the vice president of a major corporation?"

Osiris nodded. "It seems like a lifetime ago."

"And you, Horus, you were a dancer."

"I loved the ballet," Horus said.

"I fail to see your point in all of this," Osiris admitted. "Dwelling on the past does us no good in the present."

"I was merely stating a fact," Isis smiled. "Don't you miss your physical lives?" She ran her hands down her new body. "I can give this back to you."

The two looked shocked, not anticipating this turn of events. They had assumed when the ritual was complete, their life forces would be merged with Isis', as was called for in the ritual. "What about the ritual?"

Isis smiled slyly, "I have something better in mind."

"You presume a false assumption, High Priestess," Osiris pointed out. "You were able to take a physical body because you are a spirit. We have no such ability."

"*Nothing* is beyond my capabilities." Isis moved slowly back to her throne. "When I died, I became aware of powers greater than any one mortal could ever possess. Many have called this the 'Universal Consciousness'. It is the root of all, and I have learned how to harness it over time." Isis smiled. "Think of it as a monstrous spider web that connects every living thing on this planet and

275

others. As a mortal, you can sometimes feel this connection, but can do nothing with it. As a spirit and a witch, I learned how to make it bend and flow to my bidding. I can give you anything you want. Anything *I* want."

"But—"

Osiris began to question her, but Isis quickly waved it off with her hand. She looked at the two in front of her. "Rally your soldiers, this war is about to begin." Horus and Osiris turned and began to leave. "Wait," Isis commanded. "Horus, bring me your best soldier. I have a special task."

***

Spenser had lost sight of the creature. He had been following it for a short time since splitting from the others, but it seemed to have fallen off the face of the Earth. He stopped and rested his hands on his hips, dismayed. There were literally millions of places to hide in a city this size. The creature could be anywhere with Dawn. He had to find them.

Turning down a nearby alley, he jumped up and pulled down a fire escape ladder. Climbing up, he quickly made his way to the top of the escape. Propping his foot up on the edge of the railing, he pulled himself up and stood precariously as he reached for the roof. Steadying himself against the sill of a nearby window, he stretched up a hand to the ledge. His fingers wrapped around as he tried for a firm grasp. Lifting his other hand, he started to pull himself toward the roof. Swinging to the left, he kicked a leg up and caught it on the ledge. Using all his strength, he pulled himself onto the roof.

Spenser rolled onto his back and tried to catch his breath.

Lifting himself up, he surveyed the rooftop. It was completely empty. He had no idea what happened to the creature and Dawn. Climbing to his feet, Spenser moved briskly over the uneven surface the sun and time had helped warp. Resting his hand on the ledge, Spenser squinted and searched the horizon. There was no sign of it anywhere. Turning, he sat down. Reaching into his coat pocket, he removed his cell phone and typed in a text message. He hit the send button, then tucked it back into his coat. After a moment, Spenser headed back for the fire escape as an unseen figure lurked behind him.

***

He lifted his clipboard and looked at the body in front of him. She was completely naked on the exam table, except for a large toe tag. The man shook his head. She was extraordinarily beautiful. Every curve of her body was perfect and her blond hair, though matted now, was still lovely. "Where were you when you were alive?" The examiner rubbed his gloved hand along the side of her face. He was interrupted as another younger man entered the room. He looked up, "Daren."

The younger man, dressed in similar green scrubs, nodded at the man. "Walter," he acknowledged. Moving to a nearby sink, he washed his hands and pulled on a pair of white latex gloves. "What've we got?"

Walter shook his head. "A real beauty. This was Kelley Windel, currently resides in Washington D.C., but here on business."

Daren moved to Walter's side and nodded. "How'd she end up here?"

"The report says natural causes, but I think they're just guessing." Walter pointed to the blood on her face. "That's a little strange."

"Nah," Daren said quickly. "She could've easily fallen as she died and bloodied her nose, or she could've coughed or sneezed so hard, she burst the tiny capillaries in there."

"I see your point."

"Who ordered an autopsy?

Walter checked his clipboard, "SPD."

Daren lifted a scalpel, "Let's get to work then."

Walter waved his hand, "It's almost lunch time. We'll wrap this one up later." Walter smiled. "She's not going anywhere."

Daren laughed, "Why do you always use that tasteless joke?"

"Mortician humor," Walter dropped his clipboard on the table next to him. He peeled off his gloves and started toward the door. "Where do you want to eat today? I have this real craving for a taco."

Daren snapped off his gloves as well. "I'm brown bagging it today. The wife and I are trying to save up cash to move into a new apartment."

"You can't spend fifty-nine cents on a taco, cheap ass?" Walter pushed through the doors followed closely by Daren, leaving the room empty.

The room fell silent; the only noise was the slight buzz of the ceiling lights. Moments later, the

278

doors began to creep open. The creek of the hinges echoed throughout the room filled with hard steel and tiled floors. A shadow crept into the room as the lights flickered and died. A hand rose up over Kelley's body and slowly came down on her forehead. In the darkness, a figure rose up over the body and hovered motionlessly. It slowly began to run its hand down from her head over her body and stopped. The master would be pleased. Pushing one hand under the body's knees, it slid the other under its back. The creature lifted the corpse and turned toward the door. Moving with great stealth, it exited the building the same way in which it had entered: unnoticed.

***

Cane's cell phone chirped. Lifting it up, he saw a message displayed on the screen.

LOST IT—SPENSER.

Cane gritted his teeth as he dumped his phone back into his pocket. Turning around, he looked over the alley he was standing in. It was dark and damp with trash littered haphazardly about. A man, wrapped in torn clothes, sat in the back of the alley with a half empty bottle pressed to his lips. Turning away, he walked slowly out of the alley. He didn't have time for this. He had to meet Bishop in a few minutes. Why couldn't monsters just be predictable? They should just show up as you walk around the corner.

Cane stopped. A dark shadow passed over him as he rounded the corner. Glancing behind him, he could see only the litter filled alley, but ahead was a main street. He watched the cars whiz by through the crack between two buildings. Tilting his head up, he caught a glimpse of what looked like a man leaping from one roof to the next. He muttered a profanity under his breath as he sped out of the alley and around the building. His eyes remained focused at the top. He weaved through the crowds of people on the sidewalk as he tried to follow the dark figure above. Cane looked ahead just in time to see a man stopped in front of him. With no time to stop, his momentum sent him barreling into the man, knocking him and two of his friends to the ground. Quickly dusting himself off, Cane leapt up and continued on his way without a parting word. The three men shook their fists at Cane as he skittered around another corner.

***

Lugging his duffel over his shoulder, Bishop moved briskly along the sidewalk narrowly missing pedestrians. He swerved in and about trying not to knock anyone over in his rush. Stopping at the corner, he anxiously waited for the light to change so he could cross. Glancing around, he noticed a man standing on a milk crate on the other side of the street. A white sandwich board was slung over his shoulders with large black letters emblazoned on it.

THE END IS NEAR! REPENT NOW! JESUS SAVES!

Bishop shook his head and turned away. It was a familiar sight in all major cities: a religious zealot with too much time on his hands trying to save the world. To them, the end was always near. They liked it that way, he guessed. It gave their work meaning. In their minds, they were actually saving people, when in reality, all they were doing was frightening and driving them further from a religion that seemed to have no answers.

The man was old and gray with a large beard that hung over the top of the board. His clothes were worn and ragged, and the brown gloves he wore were fingerless. He had been doing this a long time. Bishop wondered what it must be like for the man to wake up every morning and, to his dismay, find that the world hadn't ended. Did that just strengthen his resolve, knowing he had that much more time, or did it become disheartening? After all this time preaching Armageddon, was he actually looking forward to it? Was he waiting for the first day of the afterlife, where he could stand in front of all those who passed him by and say, "I told you so"? It was surely a bleak existence.

Bishop closed his eyes for a moment and took a deep breath. The end *was* near.

The light finally changed, allowing him to continue on his way. Bishop's mind was buzzing with questions to the answers he had found. Every time he felt like two and two equaled four, he would come up with five. Somewhere in the equation, things just didn't add up. Every new answer would ask another question, and that question would generate two more. He had no answers, and

281

wouldn't until he stood toe-to-toe with the thing that killed Kelley. Then he would be able to find out…and kill them with his own two bare hands. The answers were important, but not as much as the retribution. They had taken an innocent life, someone very close to his heart. There would be justice, Bishop had to believe that. If not in this world, then surely in the next. He had to believe.

Hiking the bag a little higher on his shoulder, he stopped to catch his breath. He had been moving almost nonstop since he left the hotel. He would much rather have taken a cab, but he'd left his wallet in his room and had no intention of going back. Now that the Triad knew where the OPR was staying, it wouldn't be safe there until everything was finished.

Turning his head to the right, he began watching a small television in the window of an electronics store. Although he could hear no sound, he knew it was a news program, and a local one judging by the quality of the set and on-screen graphics. Images of floods, fires and other disasters unfolded before his eyes. He glanced down at the graphic at the bottom of the screen and his eyes widened. These images were all from the Seattle area. Rivers had begun jumping their banks, while fires ravaged buildings. The scene cut to a mess of brown insects on the sidewalk and the word "Locusts" appeared. The scene cut again to show a swarm of them looming above sections of the city. An anchor appeared on the screen and began to read off his teleprompter. A small box materialized over his left shoulder with yet more images of disasters. Bishop recognized several shots of dead frogs that

282

had rained down from the sky yesterday. He turned away from the television.

Glancing back over his shoulder, he caught sight of the old man again, still wearing his sign and preaching the gospel to all who would listen. Bishop's eyes worked over the words on his sign. "Maybe the end truly is near this time, old timer." An odd sensation rolled down Bishop's spine for a moment. Lifting his hand, he rubbed the back of his neck as the tiny hairs began to stand up. "My Bishop Sense is tingling," he muttered with a wry smile as he tried to bury the sensation. He couldn't let despair seep in.

Tapping into his strength reserves, Bishop took off again down the sidewalk. He had to get to Cane. Too much time had passed since their last conversation and he had no idea what was going on with Dawn. He cursed himself again for losing his cellular phone. That was a rookie mistake and had already come around to bite him on the ass. Diving around a corner, he pushed his legs harder until it felt like battery acid coursed through his veins.

***

Weiss propped a hand against a nearby wall as he tried to catch his breath. His mind, as well as his heart, was racing. His thoughts were flooded with images of his daughter as a little girl. He was letting his emotions get the better of him, but how could he not? It was, after all, his daughter they were here to find. He knew he had to have faith, but it was becoming increasingly difficult as the minutes ticked off his wristwatch. He was getting closer and closer to losing her, and that scared him to death. She was the only good thing he had ever accomplished. His entire life after she had been born had been dedicated to her. How could he stand to lose that?

He had always envied the bond that existed between Lexy and her mother. That was something they would always share, and he would never truly experience. Sure, she was daddy's little girl, but that wasn't the same as having a child growing inside of one. Pregnancy, in Weiss' eyes, was truly a wonderful process and he was jealous he would never experience it. His sole purpose in this life was to care and provide for Lexy. He was the hunter/gatherer. It was his job to put food on the table and make sure there was fire to keep his family warm. He had learned long ago that everything in life had a purpose. If one recognized it was a different matter altogether.

Pushing off the wall, he slid his hand inside his coat and adjusted something. Once satisfied, he patted it with his hand, feeling the cold, hard metal under his fingertips. This would be his insurance that he would get his daughter back, and he was not afraid to use it, if it came to that. He would protect her at all costs. That was what a good father did.

Weiss glanced down at his watch. This was taking too long. It would be dusk very soon and the moon would begin rising over the horizon. If they had not found Lexy and Dawn by then, it would be too late. The ritual would have already begun. Taking a deep breath, he pushed forward again, fighting his body's urge to stop and shut down. Stepping out of the alley, he glanced up at the sky.

Ominous dark clouds had begun to gather in the west and were quickly heading this way. Hiking up his collar, Weiss moved quickly as he scanned for the creature.

Chapter Twenty-three

Isis was pleased. Lexy walked into the room with Kelley hanging lifelessly in her arms. Stopping short of Isis, Lexy turned her attention to her Goddess. Isis moved several items off her altar and tapped it with her knuckles. Lifting the body, Lexy set it gently down. Kelley's arms, shins and hair spilled over the edges of the altar. Her flesh had become an even paler shade of white as the blood had begun to pool lower in her body due to gravity.

Isis stood above her and grinned. Resting her hand on Kelley's forehead, she used her thumb to lift open her eyelids. Kelley's eyes were dull and dilated as they stared off into what Isis could only assume was the afterlife. Pulling her hand away, she lifted a bottle of herbs and twisted off the top. Digging slender fingers inside, Isis lifted several of them into her hand. Setting the bottle down, she pulled open Kelley's mouth and pushed the dried herbs inside.

Taking a step back, Isis turned to her Book of Shadows resting on a pedestal next to the altar. It was an ancient tome; the pages had long since become yellowed and brittle. Grabbing the upper corner of the page, she carefully turned it over. Each page was lovingly inscribed by hand with Egyptian, Celtic and Runic symbols as Isis was fluent in all. Scanning over the page, she quickly read the incantation. Turning back to the altar, she raised her arms and waited for Lexy to attend her.

Without a spoken word, Lexy moved to Isis' side and began to remove her clothes. Piece by piece, she gently set them on the floor next to the altar. Standing tall, she lifted Isis' dress over her head and pulled it off. It was a long- standing tradition that Witches practice in the nude. It was believed any article of clothing, barring a few spare pieces of ornamental jewelry, would interfere with a Witch's power. They began opting for the now familiar robes when different religions began imposing their belief systems on Pagans. They felt it was shameful to show your flesh, while Pagans had always treated nudity respectfully.

Isis called for Osiris and Horus to enter the room. She watched as two dark forms passed through a wall in front of her and stopped on the opposite side of the altar. Osiris lifted her hands, palms up to the sky and let her head fall back while Horus stood silently next to her. She was ready. Isis lifted her staff and twirled it clockwise above her head. Several candles she had prearranged in a circle around the altar sprang to life as tall flames erupted from them. The circle was now closed. The ritual could begin. She waited a moment for Lexy to slink out of the room. There had to be absolute silence for her to concentrate. She paused and looked at Osiris, then at Kelley.

Lifting a knife off the altar, she held it aloft in both hands until she could feel her natural vibrations matching its own. Wrapping her right hand around the pommel, she slowly brought it blade down above Kelley's chest. Closing her eyes, she pressed the tip of the blade into Kelley's flesh. In her mind's eye, she traced the image of a pentacle and several runes below it. Lifting the knife, she looked down at the body. She had carved the exact same image into Kelley's chest.

Placing her hand on the carving, Isis raised her left hand to the sky. Around her, she became aware of every candle, every brick and tile in the room. Her mind was expanding. To complete the ritual, she needed to tap into the very essence of life and return it to this body. It was useless to her dead. Only in life could it serve her purpose. She reached out with her thoughts and connected with Osiris and Horus. Their powers began to merge and instantly increased threefold. Lifting her other hand, Isis waited. She needed to finish drawing the power.

The flames of the candles around the room tripled in size. One by one, they melded into each other creating a circle of flame around the altar. The circle grew quickly in size and intensity as it burned in mid-air. Rising up around Isis, the circle snapped and arced into her hands. The fire popped and crackled as it jetted in through the very pores of her skin. Isis felt the fire move down her arms and into her chest as it gathered in her black heart. As she blinked her eyes, a wisp of smoke escaped.

Bringing her hands slowly down, she rubbed them together. Taking a deep breath, Isis slapped both hands down on Kelley's chest and exhaled. She felt the fire course through her veins and muscles as it exited her body. Kelley's corpse arched up as the magical flame invaded every corner of her body. Her mouth spewed smoke as her eyes shot wide open. The corpse convulsed under Isis' hands as the last of the flame ruptured from her fingers.

"Now," she said to Osiris.

Closing her hands, Osiris placed them on either side of Kelley's head. Osiris moaned in agony as her life force was sucked inside. She struggled against it as it pulled her down. Her hands sank inside Kelley's head, followed by her arms. In an instant, Osiris was gone. Isis ripped her hands away from Kelley's body and stumbled uneasily back. She fell to the floor in exhaustion. With her last conscious thought, she opened the circle.

A stiff wind whipped through the room carrying a foul stench on its wings as if released from the very mouth of Hell. Every flame in the room was quickly extinguished and all fell dark. Horus moved through the altar and knelt down next to Isis. She probed her High Priestess with her thoughts, looking for a remaining spark of life. A moment of doubt moved over her, but quickly vanished. Isis had simply used too much power in her weakened state. It had taken its toll and now she needed to rest. Horus called for Lexy.

Lexy moved briskly into the room carrying an oil lamp. Setting it down on the floor, she lifted her Goddess up and hauled her toward her chambers. Horus stood and turned around. She was momentarily taken aback. In the dim glow of the lamp, she came face to face with Kelley's body. It was now sitting straight up on the edge of the altar, its arms resting in its lap. Horus peered into the woman's eyes. The spark of life had returned.

Kelley, now Osiris, lifted her head and smiled at Horus. Pushing off the edge, Osiris planted both feet on the ground and stopped. Lifting her hands, she could still feel her essence seeping into the last remaining corners of this new body. Clenching her fists, Osiris raised her arms above her head and stretched, as if just waking up from a long nap.

Horus took an uneasy step back. "How do you feel?"

Osiris screamed at the top of her lungs with glee. After a moment, she glared down at Horus, her fists still clenched.

"Powerful."

Lifting her hand, she slowly opened it. A flame jumped from her palm and burned in a halo just above it. Moving her hand away, she blew softly on the halo and transformed it into a solid block of ice. She watched it fall to the ground and shatter about her feet.

***

Hart stopped. He knew he had been followed. Lifting his head, he sniffed at the cool breeze with his tongue. There was someone near, but he couldn't tell where. Too many signatures in the city confused his senses. Laying Dawn down on the rooftop, he moved swiftly to the edge and peered over. His milky eyes scanned the landscape, but he couldn't see any of the men who were tracking him. He knew one of them, but he didn't know from where or why. It was more like a fleeting image than anything else, but it still stuck with him. In his mind that had become more animal than man, it was troubling.

A sharp pain stabbed him in the chest. Lurching back, Hart grasped his breast as he tumbled to the floor. Immediately, he doubled over as he gasped for breath. The pain slowly moved up his chest to his neck and finally settled in his head right between his eyes. He pressed hard against his forehead waiting for the sensation to subside. Deep in his mind, he could feel his master's grip. She was calling to him, punishing him for taking so long with his task. Rolling onto his knees, Hart slammed his head against the floor. A dull throb masked the pain for a moment, but it was fleeting. He could feel her grip tightening. His brain felt like it was on fire as her bony fingers moved through it. She was severing nerves as she went, removing that which he no longer needed.

Horus, standing inside the Triad's compound, moved skilfully over Hart's brain finally locating her quarry. Reaching deeper inside, she found a small glob of cells connected only by a few thin synapses and veins. Using her powers, she transformed her fingertips into surgical blades and began to slice away at the affected area. Hart shuddered and fell to his back with a long moan of pain. She was cutting away his memory. Everything that made him who he was, Horus stripped away. As she cut the final nerve, she pulled her hand away from Hart's brain. She took a step back and waited.

The once writhing man took a deep breath and stood. All traces of Hart were gone. He was now the perfect killing machine. No conscience, no feelings, no memories, and no remorse. Horus' work was done. She now had only to wait for her new body to arrive, and the Triad would be complete again.

Hart glanced around the rooftop with new eyes. All at once, he had no memory of this place, but felt exhilarated by it. Turning around, he scooped Dawn off the roof and headed for the stairs. He had a task to finish. He would not invoke the wrath of his master again. That was a lesson he only had to be taught once. With Dawn firmly on his shoulder, he sprinted forward and crashed through the locked wooden door protecting the stairs. He had to get back to street level.

***

Bishop reached for the door and pulled it open. The warm aroma of coffee and cookies filled his nostrils and invited him inside. He glanced around the small coffee shop built into the corner of a strip mall. The outer wall was entirely glass allowing the sun, if there was any, to shine in and warm the customers in the morning. At least a dozen small, round tables were arranged around the shop with a tall bar at the back. A long rack of greeting cards and knickknacks ran the length of the opposite wall, while a shiny, golden antique cappuccino machine sat silently on the bar, overseeing everything. The walls were painted a creamy white with green trim and the carpet matched perfectly. Several waitresses in green aprons buzzed around the few patrons. Looking to his left, he spotted Cane and Weiss sitting together at a table near the doors to the restrooms. They were each sipping from tall white cups.

Bishop moved briskly toward the table. Grabbing an empty chair, he spun it around and sat down with his two supervisors. "What's the word?"

Cane finished his drink and set the empty cup back on the table. "We lost her."

"Dawn's dead?" Bishop asked in a panic.

"No," Cane said quickly, "the creature eluded us."

292

Bishop let out a long breath. "Where's Detective Spenser?"

Weiss shook his head. "He hasn't checked in yet. In fact," he said, glancing at his watch, "he's fifteen minutes overdue."

"We were going to head back out and look for him," Cane added, "but we wanted to wait for you."

"Cane told me you had information," Weiss said, cutting to the chase. "What did you find out?"

Bishop unzipped his duffel and lifted out several bent and creased papers. Setting them on the table, he ran his hand over them to try and smooth them out a bit, but it was no use. He handed them to Weiss. "This is what I found."

Weiss began to scan over them.

"Give me the Cliff Notes version," Cane instructed.

"I think we're dealing with a cult that worships an ancient Triad of Egyptian Gods and Goddess. I found proof that a similar cult tried this same thing almost ten years ago: zombies, missing organs, dead women, the whole shebang. You name it, we have it."

"I'm assuming they didn't succeed," Cane guessed.

"Right," Bishop said with a nod. "Their whole operation was busted up right in the middle of the ceremony when the feds raided their compound. I pulled these pages off a paranormal website that tracks this kind of stuff."

"Do you trust the source?" Weiss asked without looking up.

"Yes. The guy who runs the site is an old college buddy of mine. We may have smoked too much pot together, but he was always on the level."

"Illegal drug use," Weiss said condescendingly.

Bishop shook off the guilt trip and continued. "The ring leaders of the cult were a trio of witches who took on the names Horus, Osiris and Isis. Their followers worshipped them as if they were actually *the* Egyptian Gods and Goddess embodied."

"Kind of like the Pharaohs," Cane said. "They were gods incarnate."

"Right, except these women had no intention of leading their followers to anything other than a quick death. They were using them as batteries in a way. They would gather them in some ludicrous ritual of their own design, and suck the life force out of them. They would then use this power for their own nefarious plans."

"Such as?"

Bishop shrugged. "Whatever they wanted. That's how the feds got involved. Cultists started turning up dead after too much of their life force was taken from them."

"So they had a 'Waco' on their hands," Cane summarized. "Where did this happen?"

"Chicago. Want to hear the most interesting part?" Bishop asked like a child telling a story.

Cane nodded for him to continue.

"Agent Fowler, the one who accosted Dawn, Kelley and Detective Spenser in the morgue, was sent in as an undercover operative to survey what was actually happening. He, unfortunately, fell under the thrall of the cult and joined. He was later

294

exonerated of any charges, but he was kept under permanent psychiatric evaluation."

"You think he's picked up the fallen banner and ran with it here in Seattle?" Weiss asked.

"Couldn't hurt to look into it," Bishop said with a smile. "What happened to the Triad back then?"

"Not sure," Bishop admitted. "No charges were ever brought against them. They just kind of vanished after the whole thing came crashing down. There were reports, however, that the High Priestess, Isis, was killed during the raid."

"Could this be substantiated?"

Bishop shook his head. "No body was ever positively identified as hers." Each man fell silent for a moment.

Cane rubbed his goatee. "So you think she and Fowler hooked up again and are trying to finish what they started here in Seattle?"

"Makes sense."

Weiss looked up from the pages. "What were they trying to do?"

"From the statements of arrested cultists I found, they were trying to re-enact the Osiris Myth."

"I'm not up on my ancient Egyptian," Weiss admitted. "Who was Osiris?"

"He was the god of the underworld, husband of Isis and father of Horus.

Along with his son, he would pass judgment on souls passing into the afterlife. His brother, Seth, envious of everything he had, killed him and dismembered his body. He then scattered the fourteen parts around Egypt. It was Isis who recovered the parts and breathed life back into her husband making him immortal."

"So how can they re-enact this?"

"They have been harvesting body parts from women around the city. I think they mean to put them together in some kind of immortality ritual. I don't have all the details yet," Bishop admitted. "It could mean they are building a new body with the parts, or what's more likely is that they are using them to make the bodies they already have immortal."

"You said they had a compound they worked from ten years ago," Weiss said. "Does it stand to reason that they would again?"

"It's possible," Bishop nodded, "but I don't think they would've bought anything here in the area. Their paper trail was part of their downfall back then. I don't think they would repeat the same mistake twice."

"So they're squatting somewhere." Bishop nodded.

Cane nodded. "Get on that, Bish. We need to find the Triad before nightfall." He turned to Weiss. "Are you going to argue with my authority on this?"

Weiss shook his head. "We're running out of your playbook, Cane."

"Good. Then you and I need to track down Spenser."

Bishop pointed to the rear of the coffee shop. "They have internet terminals here. I can use them to search for abandoned buildings in the area."

"What happened to your two-thousand-dollar laptop we bought for you?" Weiss asked.

Bishop patted his duffel. "It's now a two-thousand-dollar paperweight, thanks to one of the zombies." He suddenly flashed back to that moment and saw Lexy's face pressed against his hotel window. Should he tell Weiss that he knew what happened to his daughter, or should he let it alone? Bishop decided that some secrets were better left unsaid. "One of them attacked me in my room. I was lucky to escape at all."

"How many does that make now, Bish?" Cane wondered.

"At least three, counting the two I've encountered and the one you were following."

Cane glanced at his watch. "We'll meet back here in an hour. After that, we have no more time for research. We have to get on this one. Time is short. Let's move."

"Wait," Weiss said, holding up a hand. "What about my daughter? How does she fit into all this?"

Cane looked at Bishop. With an apologetic look, Bishop shrugged his shoulders. "We still don't know. She could have been turned into one of the zombies we encountered, or at the very least, she may have been set up to take the fall for this whole thing."

"A patsy," Weiss gritted his teeth. "Thank you, Mr. Bishop." Bishop nodded.

"Let's get going on this," Cane said after an uncomfortable minute. "Nightfall is only a few hours away."

***

Isis sat up in her bed with a groan. Still completely naked, her body ached. Lifting her hand,

297

she frowned. They were scorched a deep black and the flesh of her fingertips was beginning to flake off. Large burn marks also ran the length of her arms. Balling her fist, she held it in front of her mouth as she coughed. Her muscles tightened as the spasm of coughing increased. Dropping back down onto her pillow, she tried to take a deep breath. Her lungs were on fire. She could feel it every time she took a breath. Lifting up her hand, she saw several splatters of blood from her coughing fit. She closed her eyes. This body was dying. She had burned it out too quickly. Too much power, too fast, she knew.

Rolling onto her side, she brushed the hair out of her eyes and coughed again. Her body was in pain. Every nerve seemed to be lit up like a Christmas tree. She rested one of her scorched hands on her stomach and took a deep breath. The flame she had taken into her during the ritual, even though it was magical in nature, had still done a number on her innards. She wondered if they looked the same way as her hands and arms.

Pressing her fingertips to her temples, she quieted her mind and focused on the pain. She followed the synapses to the very root of her brain where the pain was being processed. Using a bit of her power, she temporarily masked that area. Lying flat on her back, she felt the pain drain from her hands and arms until there was nothing. She smiled and took a deep breath. That would only last for a little while, but hopefully, it would be long enough to finish the ritual. She cursed under her breath. How could have she been so stupid?

Scooting back slightly in her bed, she carefully pulled up her covers with her fingertips. She could see several bloodstains on the covers where her hands had cracked open and bled while she slept. It was disgusting, but tolerable for the moment. She would just have one of her servants replace the entire bedding set before she slept here again. It was as simple as that. She was about to close her eyes and drift off again when the sound of her chamber door opening startled her. Isis sat up in bed again. Osiris strode confidently into the room, now garbed in a tight, black full sleeved dress. If her hair had been black, she would've looked very much like Morticia from the Addams Family. Isis had the sudden urge to ask her how Uncle Fester was. She allowed herself a brief smile, but it quickly faded.

Osiris moved to Isis' bedside and bowed her head. "I am glad you are well, Horus and I worried about you as you slept. We feared you had used too much power and damaged your new body."

Isis quickly slipped her hands under the covers before Osiris noticed. "I'm fine, and you appear to be as well."

Osiris nodded and ran her hands over her hips. "You were right, my Queen, I did miss this. This new body is wonderful."

"You did not feel the need to alter its appearance to suit your own?"

"It's been so long, I had almost forgotten what I actually look like," Osiris admitted. "Besides, I like this face. It is quite beautiful."

"Agreed, but how do you feel?"

"Never better. This woman took excellent care of this vessel before she died. I feel right at home in

299

here." Osiris blinked, allowing a wisp of smoke to escape her from under her eyelids.

Isis stared at her ominously. Her birth by fire may not have went as planned. She's still showing some residual effects of the ritual. "Good," Isis said slowly. "What is it you need that made you disturb my sleep?"

"Horus' new vessel is almost here. We were wondering if you were going to perform the ritual, or if you would rather have me do so?"

Arrogant suggestion, but Isis was in no position to perform another. It would surely kill her. "I will stand in the circle with you, but I think this will be a wonderful test of your skills. You shall lead the ritual."

"Thank you, my Queen," Osiris bowed her head. "Rest now. I will send a servant to awake you when we require you presence."

"Thank you." Isis laid back and once again pulled the covers up to her chin. She slowly closed her eyes and drifted off.

Turning away, Osiris walked out of the room and shut the door behind her. Standing in the middle of the altar room, she allowed herself to smile. "She is weak indeed."

Horus materialized out of thin air in front of her. "I do not like this course of action."

"After you receive your new body, you will," Osiris assured her. "I had forgotten the simple pleasures that human form allowed. Every sensation is wonderful. I have no intention of giving this up."

"But for the ritual to succeed, we need to combine our life force with Isis'." Osiris nodded,

300

"Leaving us dead in the process and her immortal. I will not allow that to happen."

"Dare we speak such mutinous words this close to the High Priestess' chamber?" Horus asked nervously.

"I don't care. I will not give this up."

"What's your plan?"

Osiris smiled slyly. "We will kill Isis and take her powers. Then we can use our servants to complete the ritual. We need two for each of us to become immortal."

"I cannot with a clear conscience plot to kill my Queen," Horus turned away. "We swore to live and die at her command. How can we even fathom such a course of action?"

"I promise, once you regain flesh, you will feel different. Everything will be ours, Horus. Imagine the possibilities."

"I will not participate in this insurrection." Horus vanished.

Osiris balled up her fists in rage. If Horus would not help, then she would do it herself. Isis was weak, and would prove no challenge for her. She would take everything that was rightfully hers…finally. Before the day was over, Osiris would be High Priestess. She assured herself of that.

From inside her chambers, Isis pulled her ear away from the door. Distraught and angry, she wandered back to her bed and sat down on its edge. Hundreds of thoughts whirled through her mind as she processed the information she had just overheard. Rage welled up inside her. After all she had done for Osiris, this is how she repaid her kindness? She had even risked her own life to return her to the flesh. This indiscretion would not pass lightly. Her eyes narrowed to slits as she furrowed her brow. *If it was mutiny Osiris wanted, then that was exactly what she was going to get*.

Getting up from her bed, she lifted her red nightgown from the edge of the bed and slipped it on. She moved to a large armoire situated at the back of her chamber and pulled open a drawer. Reaching inside, she lifted out a long, silver athame bearing an image of the Goddess Isis, her wings spread wide. Turning the knife over in her hand, she pulled the tip across her wrist. A small bead of blood welled up and began to run down her hand. Dropping the knife, she lifted a small, glass vial out of the same drawer. She held her wrist over the container, allowing a small amount of blood to drip inside. Isis quickly capped the vial and pressed a cloth to her wound to stop the bleeding. Lifting the glass, she smiled broadly as she stared at the thick red liquid inside.

Chapter Twenty-four

The rain was falling around them as they moved. Ducking in and out of alleys and connecting streets, Cane and Weiss searched feverishly for Spenser. There had been no word from him, and each call to his cell phone had gone unanswered. They had seen what the creatures could do to people. They knew they were all in danger. It went unspoken between the two, but they had already lost one member of the team, could others follow?

Stopping outside an old dry cleaner's, Cane sucked in a deep breath. He dug into his pocket and retrieved his cell phone. Dialing Spenser's number, he lifted his head into the rain, allowing the large drops to fall on his face.

"Give it up," Weiss said. "If he didn't answer the first ten times you called, he won't answer this time."

"We have to keep trying," Cane asserted. "I'm going to use every tool at my disposal to find Spenser. If that means calling his cell twenty times before he answers, then that's what I'm going to do."

"I know you want to find him," Weiss said, patting his old friend on the shoulder, "but our hour is almost up. We have to meet Bishop back at the coffee house."

Cane nodded. Snapping his cell phone shut, he dropped it back into his pocket. Turning back, he dropped his head. He suddenly stopped. "Wait."

Weiss turned around with an exasperated look on his face. "He'll show up."

"He's not a damned stray cat, Tom. We can't just put a dish of food out on the porch to coax him back." Cane dropped down to one knee. "Look at this." Cane pointed his finger at the base of a rain drain. Crystal clear water was pouring out of it onto the sidewalk and running into a nearby gutter.

Weiss glanced up the drain. It ran all the way to the roof. "I don't see...." Cane lifted his finger to his lips to silence Weiss. "Look now."

Weiss reluctantly looked down at the drain again. At first he didn't see it, but after a moment, it became very clear. "Is that what I think it is?" Sporadically, a stream of red liquid would mingle with the water as it splashed onto the pavement. After a moment, it was gone again.

Cane nodded. "I think so." Standing, Cane rushed toward the nearest door. "To the roof, Bat-Lad!"

Weiss shook his head as he followed his old friend into the dry cleaner. A few stray racks of clothing could still be seen scattered about, but for the most part, this place was dead. The cleaning equipment had long ago been taken, or looted by the looks of the place. All that remained now was a front counter and a broken, battered washing machine spending its final days in silence. Cane moved to the rear of the building. Turning to the first door, he twisted the handle and pushed it open.

Inside, a homeless man cowered in the corner beside the toilet. "Don't hurt me," he moaned. He was visibly drunk and the vomit stains on the front of his worn green coat indicated he had been for some time.

"We're not here to hurt anyone," Cane said quickly and shut the door. Turning to the next one, he glanced back at Weiss. "What do you think we'll find behind door number two?" Cane jiggled the handle, then stepped back. "This one's locked."

"Bust it down."

"All right, Mel Gibson," Cane said sarcastically. "I was getting there. Give me a minute to center my chi." Taking a deep breath, Cane kicked hard into the door just above the handle. The old wood splintered on impact, sending up a cloud of dust around the two.

Weiss coughed as he waved the dust out of his face. "That door was so old, you probably could've pushed it over."

"I didn't see you stepping up to help, Chief."

The two moved through the settling dust to find an equally old staircase. Cane wasted no time. Rushing up the stairs, he turned the corner at the top and headed up the next flight. Stepping over the broken carcass of a table and chairs, he reached the top. He stopped in front of the door and reached down for the handle, but stopped. The creature could still be out there, he reasoned.

"Bloody hell." Taking a step back, he dropped his shoulder and rushed the door full force. The weight of his impact knocked it open and sent him skidding along the wet roof. Rolling onto his feet, he went into a three-point stance. Cocking his head, he searched the roof with his eyes. A dark, solid form snagged his attention. Cane stood up and walked cautiously toward the form. It was laying awkwardly over the edge with its legs draped

305

toward Cane. Moving closer, he could make out a now familiar fedora next to the figure.

"Spenser."

Rushing toward him, Cane dropped to his knees. He reached over the edge and fished Spenser's head back up. Leaning him against the waist-high wall, he pressed his fingers against Spenser's throat. "I have a pulse."

Weiss stopped just behind Cane and looked down at the detective. He had three long claw marks torn into his chest and another that arced over the bridge of his nose and down his cheek. Stepping forward, Weiss leaned over the edge to see the rain gutter filled with blood. Shaking his head, he knelt down next to Cane. "We need to call an ambulance."

Cane nodded. "There was a payphone down on the corner. Go now." Weiss, not wasting time with semantics, stood up and rushed back toward the door.

Cane placed his hand on Spenser's face and pulled open one of his eyelids with his thumb. "Spenser," he said quickly. "Wake up," he shook him by the collar of his coat.

Nothing.

Cane closed his eyes for a moment, then glanced back at Spenser. "Detective!"

Spenser's eyes slowly opened, then threatened to close again. He was disoriented and in a great deal of pain. The loss of blood was severely affecting his mental capabilities. "The frog smiled at me," he mumbled, obviously keying on some past memory as he drifted in and out.

"Detective Spenser," Cane said firmly. "Help is on the way, but I need you to focus." Cane wiped the blood away from Spenser's eyes with the heel of his hand.

Spenser ran his hand over his face, cringing when he accidentally hit the cut. His hand fell limp. "I can't."

"Stay with me, Detective. Listen to the sound of my voice and stay with me." Cane spoke calmly to Spenser, "How did this happen?"

"Hart...."

Cane glanced down at Spenser's chest. "I don't think the cuts were deep enough to hit your heart."

"No," Spenser gasped. "Captain Hart." Every word was labored.

Cane could hear the agony in his voice. "Everything is going to be all right, Detective, you just have to hold on. Did you see Dawn?"

Spenser nodded. "Is she alive?"

"Yes." Spenser's head fell backward against the wall.

Lifting his eyelids, Cane watched his eyes roll back as well. "Don't die! Detective, don't you dare go into the light!" Cane shook the man by the collar. "Detective Spenser!"

Spenser made a gurgling sound as he exhaled his final breath. All at once, every tense muscle relaxed. He was gone. He had lost too much blood before they had found him. Lifting his hand, Cane pulled the detective's eyelids closed one final time.

"Rest now. You've done enough for one lifetime."

Leaning his back against the wall, Cane pulled his knees up and crossed his arms over them. He dropped his forehead down on his arm and let the rain wash over him. He took a long, deep breath. He looked up when he heard footsteps on the roof. It was Weiss.

Weiss started to ask, then abruptly stopped. Cane shook his head. Spenser was gone.

***

Dawn lifted her head. It felt like a rock on her shoulders. A wave of pain thrust up from her neck and exploded in her brain. She gasped and pressed her fists against the side of her head. Rocking back and forth, she waited for the pain to pass. After a moment, she opened her eyes and slowly looked around. She carefully kept her head in the same position to ward off another surge of pain. She was in a dark, damp place she didn't recognize. Her last memory was of being attacked by Captain Hart.

Carefully rolling her head back, she held her breath as a dull thump ran over her brain. She slowly stood up against a nearby wall. Pinching the bridge of her nose with her thumb and finger, she felt the throb pass. *It could be a concussion, or just the result of getting the crap kicked out of me.*

Above her, a large chunk of the roof was missing allowing the rain to fall freely inside. She tilted her head back and let it hit her face for a moment. The cold water felt somewhat refreshing. Lifting her hand, she wiped the water away from her eyes and mouth, then ran her hands through her hair. She straightened her clothes and began to assess her situation. She had no idea where she was, had no idea how she got here and was scared out of her wits. That about summed things up. There was very little light in the room. She wondered if night had already fallen, or the clouds were just blocking out the sun. Dawn had no way of telling for sure. She had forgotten to put on her watch this morning.

She quickly reached into her back pocket for her phone, but felt a wave of despair when she found it missing. Moving slowly through the room, her foot caught on a piece of rubble and threatened to trip her. Her body recovered quickly, saving her from the fall. She smiled. Reaching into her coat pocket, she produced a small, silver flashlight. She'd placed it there last night and forgotten about it. Clicking it on, she waived the tight beam of white light over the room. There was nothing there but debris. There were no windows and no visible door. How the hell did she get in here?

Swinging the light around, she gasped and stumbled back. Buried under a bit of rubble and dirt was a partial corpse. Taking a cautious step closer, her eyes widened. She recognized it as one of the zombies. In fact, it was the very same one she had seen in the morgue last night with the FBI. It was a horrid mess. Its flesh, at least what was still left of it, had begun to rapidly decay. Its milky white eyes looked as if they had deflated and sunk back into its skull. The legs were missing just below the rib cage and the smell was awful. Dawn turned away from the body. She had no idea of how long it had actually been in this place, but it looked as if it had been decomposing for at least three months.

Looking up through the gouge in the roof, she watched a bolt of lightning arc across the sky. Snapping the light off, she slipped it back into her pocket. She would much rather be in the dark with that thing, than have to look at it. Leaning back against the wall, she waited. For what, she didn't know.

You are brave.

Dawn snapped to attention. Fishing the light back out of her pocket, she snapped it on and scanned the room. She was sure she had heard something.

You did.

"Who's there?"

Kelley materialized in front of her.

Dawn suddenly felt at ease. She took a step toward her friend. "Thank God it's you, Kelley. I was...." Dawn's sentence fell flat as what had just happened registered. She stopped dead in her tracks. "Who are you?"

She smiled softly. "I am Osiris."

"I thought Osiris was a man," Dawn shot back.

"I can be whatever I chose to be," Osiris replied. "You are indeed brave, or perhaps foolish. I could kill you where you stand, and yet you mock me? Do you not understand?"

Dawn was a bit shaken. It was Kelley's face and her voice, but definitely not her friend. "If you had wanted me dead, I would be already. You need me for something."

"Your reasoning holds water," Osiris replied. She pointed to her body. "This was your friend, yes?"

Dawn nodded slowly.

"I saved her from death." Osiris smiled. "I can do the same for you." Dawn started to take a step

310

back but stopped. She couldn't allow herself to show any fear.

"I know you are frightened. I can smell it all over you, but you needn't be. I am not here to harm you." Osiris reached out her hand. "I can offer you anything you desire. All you have to do is take my hand."

Dawn found herself reaching for Osiris' hand. She snapped to and yanked her hand away. "Why should I trust you?"

"Who else do you have?" Osiris paused, "They have abandoned you." Her voice was soft, yet persuasive. "I can save you. I can take you away from all this death. Look at my face, Dawn, this is a face you know and trust."

"It may be Kelley's face, but you're not my friend." Dawn crossed her arms. "My team would never abandon me. We don't leave people behind."

"Cane tried to leave you, or have you already forgotten?" Osiris had tapped in to Kelley's latent psychic ability and was reading Dawn like an open book. "He left you right in the middle of a case to fend for yourself and complete the investigation."

"He did…." Dawn was unaware she was being sucked in. Osiris was psychically breaking her will.

"Did he even stop to consider your feelings before he went off and left? No," Osiris said evenly. "Then he had the gall to come back as if nothing had ever happened."

"He never even apologized."

"Because they don't care about you," Osiris continued without missing a beat, "but I do. I want to help you. All you have to do is take my hand."

She extended her open hand again. "Come, be with those who want you."

"What will happen to me?" Dawn asked as she uncrossed her arms and took a step forward.

"Take my hand and find out."

Dawn lifted her hand slowly and inched it toward Osiris'. Her hand dangled perilously over Osiris' waiting palm, but she made no motion to grab it. Dawn looked up at her. It was Kelley staring back, that same soft smile and warm, inviting eyes. Her resolve began to melt away. Taking a deep breath, Dawn took Osiris' hand.

***

"I found three places in the greater Seattle area that might be suitable for the Triad's purposes," Bishop said as Cane and Weiss walked into the coffee shop. "You're late, by the way."

Cane nodded as he slumped down into a chair. Weiss quickly followed suit. "We had to fill out paperwork with the SPD."

Bishop sat in a chair opposite Cane's. "What the hell happened out there?"

"We found Detective Spenser," Weiss said slowly. He ran his hand over his face as if trying to wipe away some of the guilt. "This wasn't our fault," he tried to convince himself. "He would've been investigating the case even if we had never shown up." He looked up at Bishop with eyes wide. "We couldn't have known."

"Tell me," Bishop urged. The two men fell silent.

"Spenser's dead," Cane said gravely. "How?"

"Zombie," Cane answered. He began to tap his fingers on the table nervously. "We think it was Police Captain Hart."

"My God," Bishop breathed. "What about Dawn?"

"We…" Cane swallowed hard, "we don't know. We lost the trail completely. As far as we know, they could be halfway to San Francisco by now."

Bishop, unfettered by the bad news, set a printout on the table in front of Cane and Weiss. "This could be where the Triad is holed up," he said while tapping his finger on the sheet. "These three locations have all been set for demolition by the city. They are all well secluded and sit on a large piece of land. I think these would be our best bet."

"How far from here are they?"

"I asked a local here in the shop. He was familiar with two out of the three addresses and he indicated they were both at least an hour's drive from here." Bishop ran his finger down to the third on the list, "This one's only ten minutes away."

Cane rubbed his goatee. "We need to check all of them out. If we split up—"

"No," Bishop interrupted. "I don't think we need to do that. I have a gut feeling it's the third house on the list. Why else would that creature be heading in this direction?"

"We were chasing him. He could have just been trying to evade us, nothing more," Weiss speculated.

Bishop held up a finger as he stood up. He moved quickly to the front counter and asked something of the waiter. The man nodded and handed Bishop a copy of the local phone book. Rushing back to the table, he slammed the spine down and flipped it open. He quickly ruffled through several pages until he found a map of the area. "Look," he pointed to the center of a mass of streets. "We're here." He ran his finger across the map and stopped. "The house is here. It's a straight line from the police headquarters to the house. That must be where the creature is heading with Dawn."

Cane glanced to Weiss. "Sounds like a good possibility, Bish. Tom?" Weiss nodded in approval. "Should we alert the police?"

Bishop shook his head. "Not their game."

Cane smiled. "Let's move. Sunset is less than an hour away."

The three stood up. Much like the Wyatts marching toward the OK Corral, they stood tall as they headed for the door. Stepping through the glass doors of the coffee shop, the men stood on the sidewalk facing west. They watched the yellow sun sinking down toward the Pacific Ocean. A vast stripe of pink, red and orange danced across the horizon in front of them. It was almost sundown, and they were being called out. Pulling their Stetsons down tight on their heads and adjusting their six-shooters, they marched off with their spurs jingling toward what they knew could be their last showdown. Good men and women had already been lost. Innocent blood had been spilled. It was their task to stop this, not because they could, but because they had to.

Chapter Twenty-five

"This has to be the place," Bishop said as his eyes wandered over the building in front of him.

Each looked over the decrepit, crumbling building. It was three stories, but looked as if the third floor had long since collapsed into the second. The entire place was constructed of a deep, red brick with wooden trim which, many years ago, had lost its paint covering. Gaping wounds were carved into the sides allowing the elements to seep in. In the courtyard, a jungle of overgrown vegetation, a tree had sprouted under the front wall and had grown up in and through it. A tall iron fence surrounded the entire property, but the gate had rusted off some time ago. The air around the house was dense with evil. It choked the men as they waded through it toward the gate. Above them, the overcast sky crackled and broke loose again, letting the rain fall. It was light at first, but the rain quickly increased in strength.

Weiss, displaying his best poker face, held his ground. His unblinking eyes remained focused on the front door. They had made no effort to sneak up or disguise their approach; instead, they had marched unhindered toward the gate.

If the Triad were as powerful as they feared, there was no reason to hide. They already knew the three of them were coming.

Bishop, on the other hand, was hunched over his duffel bag with a familiar piece of equipment in hand. He jotted down several notes on a clipboard as he checked the display on his Electromagnetic Field Meter. Occasionally, he would let loose a grunt of approval, but for the most part, he remained silent as he worked. It was all he could do to take his readings and keep his papers dry. Lifting his head, he glared at the compound. "This place is definitely hot with paranormal activity. The EMF is off the scale."

Cane glanced at Bishop, then back at the compound. The only word he could find to describe the place was *ominous*. He felt that fit rather well. There wasn't a window left in the place. All had been broken or had caved in, along with a section of the wall. He wondered how the place was even still standing after all this time. Working his eyes up to the second floor, he stopped on the second window from the right. He thought for a moment he had seen a flash of light. It could have been anything, but it was not a reflection. There was no glass in the window. He fought the urge to blink for a long moment as he kept his eyes trained on the same spot. Taking a deep breath, he finally allowed himself to relax. *It was probably nothing*, he told himself.

A stiff wind whipped through the building and over them. It had the rancid smell of death about it. Bishop, snapping off the EMF Meter, slid it and his clipboard back into his duffel bag. A shiver ran down his spine. Standing, he slipped the bag over his shoulder and shook it off. He glanced over at Cane and Weiss. They were standing shoulder to shoulder with their eyes fixed on the brick building in front of them. They were afraid, but this had to be done. Each man readied himself to enter the compound.

"Wait."

Spinning around, Cane came face to face with Lydia. She was dressed in a long black robe with the hood up around her face. A dark blue sash bound the robe around her waist and hung down just past her knees. "What are you doing here?"

Lydia smiled. "We've come to help."

"We?" Weiss asked.

Lydia pointed triumphantly over her shoulder. The other members of her coven emerged from behind trees and bushes. They moved swiftly toward their High Priestess. Each was dressed similarly with a black robe and blue sash, but had added their own personal flair. "This is my Wicca Coven," Lydia announced. "We knew you could not do this alone." She turned to the nearest witch and held out her hand. The woman placed three items in Lydia's hand. "We made these for you."

"What are they?" Bishop asked as he took a step forward.

Lydia opened her hand revealing three necklaces. Each was made of a long black cord and had several beads, as well as a silver pentacle dangling from the bottom. "These have been blessed by the coven and should help keep you safe." She placed the first one around Cane's neck. "The pentacle, our most holy symbol, is silver, the color of the Goddess. May she watch over you this night." She hung the other two around Bishop and Weiss' necks. "Blessed be," she whispered to each.

Cane lifted the necklace and held it in his hand. "Thank you for this, but we can't ask you to go inside."

"And you should not," Lydia nodded. "We are here of our own free will. Tonight, just like the old days, we battle side by side."

Cane smiled and placed his hand on Lydia's shoulder. "Thank you."

"You're not going in without us either."

Bishop looked past Lydia to see Hayden standing with five men and women of similar age. "Hayden," Bishop walked past Lydia and extended his open hand.

Hayden shook his hand. "These are my friends, the local Seattle chapter of the OPR Fan Club."

Bishop couldn't help but laugh as he looked at them. Each was dressed completely in black with tall combat boots and a backpack slung over their shoulder. Several of them were wearing sunglasses, although there was little light to block. A sudden pang of guilt hit him, but he pushed it away. He knew they needed all the help they could get. "The more the merrier," he smiled. "What have you brought to the party?"

Hayden slipped off his backpack and zipped it open. Reaching inside, he produced a black, rectangular object and held it up. "We're each packing a taser."

Bishop nodded. "Good," he said slowly. He looked over the faces of everyone. They were so young. "I want you all to know that there is the possibility we may not all come back." He paused, watching their faces. There was no fear, only determination. He patted Hayden on the shoulder. "I was wrong earlier."

Hayden nodded. "I know."

Bishop shook him with his hand. "Good to have you back." He turned back to Cane. "Here are six more for our army."

Cane nodded. Taking a step back, he addressed the entire team. "I want three teams. I'll lead one, Chairman Weiss and Bishop will lead the others. Split up as evenly as possible so there are witches and paranormal investigators on each team." He looked over each face. "We are here to rescue Lexy Weiss, but also, to stop the Triad. They can't be allowed to escape or to complete the ritual. We have to end this before midnight, or all is lost. Do you understand?"

Each member of the team nodded.

Cane clapped his hands. "We have amassed an army, now it is time to storm the castle."

***

Inside, the Triad was also amassing an army. Isis moved slowly around her altar room looking over her servants. In front of her stood Lexy, Allen, Hart and the newly restored Jax. Isis was dressed in a white robe with gold trim. Her blonde hair was pulled back behind the large gold headdress she wore. It was done in the traditional style of the Pharaoh, with large cobra like flairs on the sides that hung around her face to her shoulders with alternating lines of gold and blue. In her right hand, she held her serpent staff.

Turning to her altar, she lifted a golden bowl filled with a thick, black liquid. "Kneel," she instructed them. Dipping her thumb into the bowl, she moved to Lexy. "This is a ceremonial mixture

319

the Egyptians used to wear into battle. It contains a small amount of my blood and several herbs that will ensure our victory." She pressed her thumb to Lexy's cheek just below her eye and pulled it down her face. Turning to her other servants, she repeated the process. Each now had a thick, black line running down the right side of their faces. "The ritual will begin shortly. It is your job to make sure we are not interrupted," she placed the bowl back on the altar. "Do not fail me," Isis held her staff toward her servants. The golden cobra lifted its head and hissed at them. "Or your fate will be most horrible. I assure you of that." She took one final look at her servants and nodded. "Go now. Protect your Queen."

The creatures stood up and headed for the door. Once outside, they made off toward a different area of the compound. Isis turned her attention to the altar. Each of the necessary organs was arranged there in a jar. Everything was in order for her transformation. Cautiously slipping her hand under the lip of the altar, she felt a glass vial taped in place. This was her insurance. She would not be double-crossed on the most important night of her life. She quickly pulled her still charred hands away as the nearby door creaked open.

Osiris walked inside, stopped and bowed her head. "My Queen, we may have underestimated the attacking forces. They have already made their way into the compound and they have white witches with them."

Isis brushed away the fear. "It is no matter. Soon, the ritual will begin and we will be unstoppable. Is Horus ready to begin?"

"Not quite yet," Osiris answered. "She is still adjusting to her new body."

"Very well," Isis smiled. "We still have plenty of time." She walked across the floor to a solid brick wall. Waving her hand over it, the wall became transparent. Isis took a deep breath. "The sun has just about set," she said as she looked into the west.

Osiris joined her. "We must exercise caution, my Queen. We should not underestimate these mortals."

"Indeed," Isis nodded. "They are nothing more than mortals. What hope do they have to stop a God?"

***

"This is Delta Team," Bishop said into the small walkie-talkie. Hayden had given one to each of the team leaders before they'd split up. "We're ready to enter."

"Hold for one minute," Cane's voice replied. *"We should all go in together."*

"Acknowledged," Bishop said and slipped the walkie-talkie into his jacket pocket. He looked back at his team. Hayden had chosen to come with him, along with one of his crew, a young brunette girl named Piper. Lydia had also given him two witches, an older man with a thick, gray beard who had taken to calling himself Galen, and a tall blond woman known only as Jinx.

Delta team had moved around the back of the compound at the suggestion of Jinx to find a gaping hole sitting on the first floor of the building. This

321

would be the easiest way for them to enter and would put them on a straight path to the altar room. The three men and two women moved cautiously amidst the tall grass and weeds that accounted for a majority of the landscape. They were only a few steps from the outer wall. Craning his head around a nearby tree, Bishop checked their path. It appeared to be clear. Keeping low, he moved the team to the wall, but stopped just short of the breach. He had to wait for Alpha and Beta Teams to reach their positions. He glanced up at the sky just as a lightning bolt tore across it. Lifting the walkie-talkie out of his pocket, he nervously waited for the signal.

***

Weiss led Alpha Team to the front door. He assumed this would be the least guarded of the entrances, considering no one just walked in the front door. "Alpha Team is in position," he said into the walkie-talkie.

His team, much like Bishop's, consisted of two members of the OPR Fan Club, a man and woman named Sam and Jean, and two women of Lydia's coven, Krista and Glimmer. Krista was a second-degree witch, while Glimmer had only just been initiated to the first degree. Krista was, in fact, Glimmer's teacher, and had brought Glimmer to the coven only two weeks prior. Weiss knew this would be a hard learning experience for the young witch.

He glanced over at Sam and Jean. They were hovering over a small piece of equipment. "What do you have there?" he whispered.

Sam looked up and wiped a wet piece of brown hair from his face. "This is a device of Jean's personal design," he said proudly.

"It's a Protoplasm Meter," Jean replied in a soft voice. "It was designed after reading a paper published by Zachary Cane that all spirits seem to have a consistent electromagnetic field. This is designed to detect that."

"Why not just pick up a standard EMF Meter?" Weiss asked. "This was more fun to build," Jean smiled.

"Any readings?"

Jean shook her head. "This is its first field test, and it doesn't appear to be working."

"Or maybe there are no ghosts in there," Weiss countered. His radio squawked. Lifting it to his mouth, he pressed the talk button. "This is Alpha Team, go ahead."

"Let's go," Cane's voice announced.

"We're ready," Weiss replied. He turned back to his team. "Stay close to me. We're going in." Snapping the radio to his shirt with the belt clip, he turned and reached for the front door handle. To his amazement, it twisted open. Pushing it open, Weiss took a cautious step inside. Glancing around the foyer, he waved his team inside. Moving slowly into the room, Weiss glanced around in the low light. "Anyone have a flashlight?"

Sam and Jean immediately started digging into their backpacks, but it was Krista who stepped forward first. She smiled at Weiss. "This should help." Reaching her hand into a pouch on her robe, she produced a small vial filled with a milky

323

substance. She smashed it on the floor in front of her. Instantly, a soft, warm light filled the room.

Weiss smiled. "Nice work."

The foyer was devoid of any decoration and relatively free of rubble. There was a large staircase that led up to the second floor. To their right stood a partially collapsed archway that led further into the house, and on the left was another archway that had completely collapsed. Large portions of the wall and roof had caved in over it, permanently blocking it. The same brick pattern on the outside of the house was replicated within with the same wooden trim. The floors were primarily wood, with a few areas of linoleum and carpet still remaining.

Weiss turned back to his team. "Suggestions?"

Their eyes were wide and they were staggering back toward the front door. Jean lifted her hand and pointed over Weiss' shoulder. "I think we should go now."

Weiss spun around just as the front door slammed shut. His eyes worked furiously over the room until he spotted what Jean was pointing at. In the upper corner of the room, just to the right of the staircase, a zombie was watching them. Its white eyes were almost glowing in the low light of the room as it hung upside down on the roof. Its tongue was working furiously in and out of its mouth as it summed up the intruders.

Weiss took an uneasy step back. "Do you think it sees us?"

The creature let go of the room and fell to the floor. It twisted in mid-air like a cat to land on all fours. The creature lifted its head and issued a loud shriek.

Krista nodded "It sees us, and I think it's calling for its friends."

***

Beta Team, the smallest of the three, was second inside the compound. It consisted of only four members, including Cane, Lydia, one of her coven, a young woman with long, blond hair and blue eyes named Gwen and the last member of the junior OPR team, Django. He was the oldest member of the OPR Fan Club at thirty, but also seemed to have the most life experience. A construction worker by trade, he had told Cane that he'd studied several martial arts and written three published books on the paranormal, one of which Cane had actually read and agreed with the theories posed. He was of medium height, had shoulder length brown hair and ocean green eyes. Extremely well built, Django looked as if he could take on anyone and win. Yet he was very well read and intelligent at the same time. Cane felt very confident with this man at his side.

Cane slipped his walkie-talkie out of his pocket and lifted it to his mouth. "Delta Team, are you in?" He waited for a response. "Delta Team?" No reply. "Bishop?" He turned back to Lydia. "What happened?"

Lydia closed her eyes and took a deep breath. She stretched out with her mind, reaching across the compound. She was almost to Bishop when something intercepted her. It felt as if a hand latched onto her and began to squeeze. Falling back in pain, Lydia's eyes shot open. She let out a soft gasp as she tried to center herself. "I can't see them," she said after a moment. "Something's blocking me."

Kneeling down, Cane placed his hand tenderly on Lydia's forehead. "It's okay. Catch your breath and relax a minute." He lifted the radio again. "Bishop, do you copy?"

"We're here, Cane," Bishop replied. *"The storm must be interfering with our communications."*

"Acknowledged. Are you in?"

"We're entering the second chamber as we speak. I'll report in shortly."

Cane dropped the radio back into his pocket as he helped Lydia off the floor. With his hand on her back, he looked around. Beta Team had entered the building through a side door and was now standing in what was left of the conservatory. The front wall was a continuous sheet of glass that arced back to the roof. It was amazing it was still intact, considering what the rest of the house looked like. Various potted plants littered the few tables throughout the room, while a fern grew large in the corner. The floor was a mess of decaying plants, potting soil and bricks from a nearby wall. Django took the lead and carefully started through the room. Glancing out the window, Cane watched the last sliver of the sun sink down beyond the horizon. The ritual was starting. Pulling his small silver flashlight out of his pocket, he clicked it on and followed Django through the room.

***

Galen stopped just short of the door and turned back to Bishop. "There is evil in there."

"What is it?" Bishop asked.

"I can't tell," Galen said apologetically. "The evil is permeating. I can feel it radiating off the door in waves." He held his tall wooden staff next to his body as a shield.

Bishop nodded. Looking around the small, debris covered room, he let out a sigh. "That seems to be the only choice. The other door is completely blocked."

"We could dig out the door," Hayden suggested.

"That would take too long," Bishop said, shaking his head. "We have to get to the altar room quickly. That's where Lydia said that they would be performing the ritual." He sized up the door in front of him. "We knew we would be putting ourselves in harm's way," he muttered more to himself than anyone else. "Let's go."

Galen stepped forward, his hand hovering just above the door's handle. Taking a deep breath, he wrapped his old fingers around it and twisted. The door suddenly shot open, knocking the old witch away. A howling wind tore through the open door at gale force. Piper was lifted off her feet and sent flailing into the back wall, while Jinx braced herself and leaned into it. Bishop and Hayden latched onto a larger piece of rubble to anchor themselves.

"Black magick," Jinx yelled, barely audible above the howl.

"We have to close that door," Bishop countered. "Can you get to it, Jinx?" Jinx shook her head as her blue sash whipped about her. "It's too

327

strong." Then, just as suddenly as the wind started, it stopped. Everyone fell to the floor. Looking up, Bishop glanced into the open door. A pair of white eyes appeared as a shriek cried out. His heart sank. "Hold on!"

The wind returned, this time, blowing into the door. It lifted the unconscious Piper and Galen and tossed them inside like rag dolls. Jinx tumbled toward the door, but grabbed onto the frame with her fingers. Holding on with every ounce of her strength, she began to feel her hands slipping. "I can't hold on!"

"Fight it!" Bishop yelled, but before the last word was out of his mouth, he watched Jinx slip into the darkness. He snapped his head around to Hayden. "Hold on, buddy!"

Hayden's feet gave out under him and his body was lifted into the air. Clinging to the debris, he yelled for Bishop. Bracing himself against the floor, Bishop let go with one hand and reached for Hayden. The wind around them was deafening. Bishop stretched out his arm to his friend just as one of Hayden's hands broke free. He dangled in the wind, only holding on with the fingers of his left hand.

"Take my hand," Bishop tried to yell above the howl. "Take it!" Hayden's eyes were wide with fear as he reached toward Bishop. His fingers fought through the wind, but he couldn't quite reach. Hayden tried again, this time, making contact, but it was fleeting. His body was growing fatigued. He tried one final time. Reaching out, his fingers connected with the tip of Bishop's hand. Latching on, Bishop held Hayden's hand tightly.

"Don't let go!" Hayden yelled. "I won't."
Bishop nodded.

Hayden snapped his head up to see a large crack forming in the piece of debris he was holding. He watched it arc across the entire piece, weakening it. He swallowed hard just as the piece gave way. His body swung wildly about in the wind and yanked Bishop free of his hold. The two tumbled end over end through the door and into the darkness. The door slammed shut behind them.

***

Horus sat up in her bed. She lifted her arms above her head and stretched her tired muscles. Swinging her legs over the edge, she carefully stood up. She glanced around the room. It was modest, but wonderful. Isis had gone to the trouble of having her servants arrange this for her. Horus' bed sat in the middle of the room next to a window that looked out over the city. A new dress hung on a hangar just to the left of a large mirror. Horus smiled. She wondered how she looked.

Moving to the mirror, she turned to the right, then to the left running her eyes over her new body. Isis' servants had chosen well. This new body was beautiful with its long brown hair and perfect curves. She couldn't have done any better herself. She glanced down at the clothes she was wearing. They were obviously from the previous occupant, as she would never wear anything this conservative. Horus began to pull off the long black leather jacket, but stopped when she felt a bulge in the pocket. Reaching inside, she pulled out a small wallet.

Snapping it open, she rifled through several bills and folded receipts until she came to a photo ID. Lifting it out, she dropped the wallet to the floor. "Well, thank you for your body, Dawn Lassiter." She ran her hands over her hips and smiled. "I will put it to good use."

***

Diving to his right, Weiss narrowly avoided the attack of the creature. The creature landed on its hands and feet just behind the group. Rolling back, it changed directions and leapt into the air again. Sam tried to avoid its claws, but he was too slow. They slashed across his cheek and knocked him to the ground. Cradling his wound, he lifted up and stood back. He didn't want to be hit again. Jean quickly moved to Sam's side and tried to help stop the bleeding.

Lifting to his feet, Weiss watched the creature hit the banister and spring into the air, this time, latching onto the right wall. Moving faster than Weiss could follow, it moved onto the ceiling and dropped toward him. Weiss didn't have time to dodge. He held up his hands to shield his face. After a moment, he looked up to see the creature suspended in mid-air. Taking the opportunity, he backed away toward Sam and Jean. Glancing to his left, he could see Krista and Glimmer standing very still with their eyes closed. They had stopped the creature's fall and given him a chance to move.

He watched the two girls begin to show strain on their faces. Weiss quickly turned to Jean. "Give me your taser."

Jean complied and lifted it out of her bag.

Glancing left again, he saw several beads of sweat forming on the two witch's heads. They were about to lose him. Rushing back toward the creature, Weiss tapped the button on the taser and pressed it hard into the creature's side. A blue arc of electricity flew over the creature's body as it screamed in pain. Pulling back, Weiss hit it again with another charge. He took a step back just as Krista and Glimmer opened their eyes. The creature fell with a thump to the ground, a bit of smoke rising off it. Weiss took the opportunity and zapped the creature again. He watched it flail in pain as the current tore through its body.

Weiss tossed the taser back to Jean as he moved toward the two Witches. "Are you okay?"

Krista nodded. "That took a lot of juice," she breathed. Glimmer nodded as well. "I'm okay."

"Good," Weiss said quickly. "We need to move." He motioned for the others to follow him. He walked carefully past the silent zombie and headed toward the adjoining room. The others were close behind. Weiss led them through what used to be a dining room into another room. He stopped dead in his tracks. There were no other doors or windows in this room. "We need to go back."

Jean, still putting pressure on Sam's face, shook her head as she stared through the still open door. "I don't think so." She watched the zombie pick itself up off the floor and shake its head. It quickly spun around and caught sight of Jean and Sam standing in the doorway. Letting go of Sam, Jean reached for the door and slammed it shut just as the creature hit it. Pressing her back against the door, she looked at the other members of Alpha Team. "I need help!"

Weiss, Krista, Sam and Glimmer hit the door next to Jean. They forced it closed against the superior strength of the zombie. Still holding the door, Weiss looked up at his team. "Now what?"

Chapter Twenty-six

Isis stood in front of the altar and looked down pleasingly at the fourteen full jars on top of it. Across from her were the other two members of the Triad, each wearing black, long sleeved dresses with gold armbands that clung to their upper arms, waiting patiently for her to begin. She had everything she needed to complete the ritual. She looked over at her two companions, both now in human form. "We are ready."

Lifting her hands above her head, Isis sent out a wave of power that reverberated around the room. The numerous candles flickered to life as the dirty red walls melted to white. Two large, black statues of Anubis formed from the floor up on either side of the altar, while a large cartouche appeared on the rear wall bearing the story of Osiris and Seth.

Lifting her staff off the altar, Isis held it in front of her, then brought it powerfully to the ground. Another shockwave of power ran along the floor, folding back into itself as it hit the wall. A long table sprang from the floor next to the altar with the outline of a body on it. "Place the organs at the correct points on the body," Isis instructed. "We will then charge and consecrate each." She smiled and looked at Osiris and Horus, "Let the ritual begin."

***

Bishop and Hayden had slammed hard against the interior wall of this new room. Lifting his head, he glanced around groggily. It was nearly dark, except for a single candle burning in the corner. He saw Hayden and Galen lying lifelessly next to him. Jinx and Piper were nowhere to be seen. Bishop rolled onto his back and took a deep breath. He couldn't tell if anything was broken, but it didn't feel like it. He began to sit up, but stopped. He heard a shuffling sound somewhere in the room. Holding his breath, he waited for the sound again.

Nothing.

Bishop slowly exhaled. Maybe it was just another member of his team coming to. He ran his hand over his face then lifted onto his knees. "Everyone okay?"

Hayden groaned, "Yeah."

In the darkness, he saw the outline of a figure move. "Who's over there?" he asked.

"Piper," she replied. "I need help. I'm bleeding."

Bishop stood and rushed toward the candle. Lifting it into his hand, he moved toward Piper. Dropping down next to her, he stared at the young woman. The hair on the left side of her face was matted with blood. Bishop held the candle close as he brushed her hair out of the way. He spotted a long gash running from the crown of her head to her forehead. It wasn't deep, but it was bleeding profusely. "You're going to be okay," he said as he looked into the young woman's deep blue eyes. "Just keep pressure on it to stop the bleeding."

Piper nodded as she pressed her hand to her head. "Bishop?" she asked slowly.

"Yeah?"

"I'm a big fan," Piper said with a smile. "Are you single?"

Bishop laughed out loud. "If we're both alive when this is all over, we'll talk." He turned his attention to Galen, who still hadn't moved. Squatting down, he placed a hand on the older man's back. "Galen?" He paused, then moved his hand up to his throat and checked for a pulse. "He's alive," he confirmed. Reaching over him, he grabbed Galen's arm and rolled him onto his back. Bishop leaned close to his face and checked for breath. "He's just knocked out. I think he'll be okay."

"What if he has a concussion?" Piper asked. "We need to wake him up."

"Right." Bishop placed his hand on the older man's face and shook gently.

"Galen?"

Galen's eyes slowly opened. "I think I hit the wall a little too hard," he moaned.

Bishop smiled. "Good to have you with us, friend."

Piper walked across the room and stood above Bishop. Turning around, she saw Hayden. Kneeling down, she placed her hand on his chest. "Are you okay?"

Hayden nodded. "I think I landed on my head."

Piper smiled. "Good thing you have a rock for a head."

"Ha, ha," Hayden said sarcastically. Lifting into a sitting position, he ran his hand through his hair. "Is everyone else okay?"

"We can't find Jinx," Bishop said. "Where are we?" Hayden asked.

"I don't know. I haven't even had a chance to look around yet," Bishop admitted. He scanned the

335

darkened room. There appeared to be three doors leading out, one of which was probably the one they entered through. The décor, much like the rest of the compound, consisted of plain brick walls and wood floors. This room was thankfully clear of debris. A single window on the far wall faced outside. Bishop slowly stood. "We need to find Jinx."

Piper moved around the side of the room carefully running her hand along the wall, while Bishop worked around the other. With the candle still in his hand, he held it high to spread the light over the entire room. Stopping just short of a door, he caught sight of a dark form in the corner. "Is that her?"

Piper spun around and quickly moved to the form. Bending down, she placed her hand on the figure's shoulder. As if burned, she ripped her hand away and stumbled back. "It's not Jinx."

"Who is it?" Bishop asked as he ran across the room. Piper immediately spun around and hid behind Bishop with her hands on his shoulders. Bishop slowly lowered the candle toward the form. It was Lexy Weiss in complete zombie mode. "Shit," Bishop muttered. "Get everyone up, we need to move now."

"What happened?"

"I don't know. Maybe the wind that sucked us in grabbed her as well." Piper looked at the creature lying helplessly on the ground. "Should we help it?"

"It will kill you without a second thought," Bishop said, moving away. "Do you really want to wake it up?"

"Good point," Piper said quickly. "I think we should go."

Bishop and Hayden lifted Galen off the floor. The old witch looked at the two men. "What about Jinx?"

"She's not here," Piper said.

"And we need to go," Bishop added eagerly.

"We can't leave without Jinx," Galen protested.

Bishop nodded. "We'll find her. I promise, but right now we *really* need to go." He began to push his team out of the door, his eyes focused on Lexy in the corner. As he turned to leave, his eyes caught something on the other side of the room. He focused through the darkness to see a torn blue sash amidst a jagged pile of rubble. He dropped his head. "Damn."

***

Django stopped. "We're not alone."

Cane took a step forward. "What are you, part Indian tracker too?" Beta Team had moved from the conservatory into the main hall of the compound. In its day, this must've been a stunning room. The ceilings were at least fifteen feet high with old, broken chandeliers hanging from them. The floor was comprised of a white and black checkered tile that seemed to have fared a little better than the rest of the house. Enormous spider webs dominated most of the walls and roof.

"He's right," Lydia agreed. "I can sense another presence in the room." She pushed Gwen behind her defensively.

Snapping his head up, Cane watched two zombies burst from the spider webs and land on the floor just in front of them. It was Allen and Hart.

337

Each rolled back onto the balls of their feet and shrieked at Beta Team. Before he had a chance to yell an order, Django was rushing headlong toward the creatures. "Wait!"

Django stopped just short of Hart and planted both his feet. Rearing back, he sent a vicious spin kick into the creature's face knocking it to the ground. In less than a heartbeat, Allen attacked. He leapt toward Django with claws extended. Without thinking, Django fell to his back and caught Allen squarely in the chest, flipping him over. Kicking up, Django flipped onto his feet and settled into a defensive posture. Hart, now recovered, swept his leg under Django's and dropped him. Hart leapt forward and was on him, his claws poised above Django's head.

Seizing the moment, Cane rushed in and punched Hart in the back of the head twice. The creature swung around and knocked Cane away with the back of his hand. Snapping his hands up, Django caught the creature's wrists and pulled him down. Django slammed his head against the bridge of the creature's nose breaking it instantly. Using all his strength, he rolled the creature off and was back on his feet. Reaching down, he pulled Cane off the floor just as Allen was ready to pounce. Kicking Allen in the head, he rushed Cane back to the group.

"Is there anything you can do?" Cane asked Lydia and Gwen.

Lydia nodded. "We'll try." Reaching down, she took Gwen by the hand amplifying each other's power. Raising her arms, Lydia pointed toward Hart. With one motion, she had lifted him off the ground and flung him across the room. His body hit the brick wall with a sickening crunch. It slid quickly down, leaving a large black streak behind it. Switching her attention to Allen, Lydia balled up her fist. Allen shrieked as he was lifted into the air, twisting end over end, he began to spin faster and faster. She snapped open her hand. The forces pulling on Jax ripped his body limb from limb in one terrible stroke. His head hit the ground and rolled onto Cane's foot.

Cane looked down at the head. The eyes snapped open. "Bloody Hell!

Why won't you just die?" He took a step back and punted the head away from the team. "We need to keep moving. The ritual has probably already started." He pulled his walkie-talkie out of his pocket and hit the talk button. "Bishop, Weiss, what's going on out there?"

"We've got a little problem here," Weiss yelled frantically.

***

"There has to be a way out of here," Weiss yelled while keeping his back firmly to the door. Slipping the radio back into his pocket, he looked across the room at the two witches on his team. "Krista, you and Glimmer start looking." The door rattled behind him as the creature hit it again with his full force. "Now!"

Krista spun around and ran her eyes quickly over the bare room. It wasn't more than ten feet square. Moving to the closest wall, Krista placed her palms against it. She nodded for Glimmer to do the same. The young witch moved timidly at first, but once her hands were on its surface, she understood. Spreading their arms wide, they reached out with their energy. Their powers combined, then swooped in and around the surrounding area. They noticed that the left wall was connected to what looked like a great hall. Stepping away from the walls, they moved into the far corner of the room.

Krista smiled. "I suggest you cover your heads."

"What?" Weiss yelled, barely keeping the door closed.

Before they had a chance to reply, the left wall exploded outward in one mighty blast. Chunks of roof and surrounding wall began to rain down on the group as the structural integrity of the room was quickly degrading. Weiss wrapped his arms behind Jean and Sam and tossed them toward the hole just as a chunk of roof collapsed where they were standing. Moving quickly, he took Krista and Glimmer by the hand and dove out of the hole they created. Behind them, Jax erupted through the door. He dodged left to avoid the collapsing roof, but was caught flat-footed by another piece. Jax threw his head back and shrieked in defiance as the dust, wood and brick rained down about him.

Weiss snapped his head around in time to see the creature smashed to the floor by the debris. Amidst the roar of the collapse, he heard the creature's final cry. Lifting himself off the floor, he dusted himself off and took a step back toward the once standing room. Weiss peered inside, waiting for movement, but saw none. *Nothing could have survived that,* he assured himself, *not even that creature.* He turned and looked over his team. They were all a bit battered, but alive. He and Sam helped everyone up. He stopped in front of Krista and Glimmer. A smirk crossed his face. "Good work but next time, give me a little more warning. Let's get to the altar room."

***

Horus and Osiris stood on each side of the table while Isis retained her position behind the altar. Horus looked down at the table. All the organs had been placed in the correct positions. What looked to her like lime gelatine had oozed up from the table and claimed the organs and was slowly starting to take the shape of a human body. She was now beginning to see the outlines of veins and bones forming. She returned her attention to Isis, who was standing quietly with her hands raised. Every so often, a bolt of electricity would arc over her hands. Horus couldn't even begin to comprehend the power she was channeling. She was growing more powerful by the moment.

"I call on the power of Ra," Isis yelled. "Create this body for me!" Horus and Osiris felt their bodies become rigid suddenly. Their heads snapped back as their arms were forced across their chest. They felt themselves being lifted off the ground. Whipping across the room, they found themselves floating in front of the altar. A sphere of blue energy enveloped each, trapping them in place.

"I offer these two as sacrifices to you, mighty Ra, God of Gods," Isis sneered. "Accept my gift to you so that I might live forever!"

341

Osiris' mouth was forced open by some unseen hand. She gagged as something slithered down her throat. It felt like a snake with its scales and muscles pushing against her esophagus. She felt it burst into her stomach. The snake then reared back and sank its fangs deep into the tough lining. Osiris knew instantly this snake wasn't injecting venom, rather sucking her life force out of her. Her body began to whither under Isis' thrall. She glanced to her left to see Horus enduring a similar procedure.

A thought occurred to her in that instant. Isis had never meant to share the power. They were to be her sacrifices from the beginning. She had given them human form to make this possible. She had used them. Anger welled up inside Osiris. Bearing down, she flexed all her muscles and began to focus her power. She wasn't going down without a fight.

***

Bishop held up his hand to stop his team. Each knew the signal meant "quick, quiet". They pulled back out of sight, leaving only Bishop in the open. Without looking back, Bishop took an uneasy step forward. They had crossed into a large room which could only be described as grand. From their entrance, they had moved easily through the first floor and followed a flight of stairs up until they arrived here. The room was immense. It was obviously created with magick, as a room this size could not exist within the normal structure of the compound. The floor was white marble with several blue veins running through it. A long red carpet ran from the door to an elevated throne in the middle.

Behind it, two open windows showed the storm outside still raging. Several tall torches burned around the room casting a reverent glare. This place felt sacred. Two large, black statues of Anubis on either side of the throne only added to that effect. They looked to be at least twelve feet tall.

Bishop turned to his team and nodded. They quickly moved from their hiding spots to his side. "This is incredible," he breathed to Hayden.

Hayden, poking his head inside the door, agreed. "Looks like we're trying to get an audience with the Pharaoh."

Galen held his staff firmly against his body. "This place reeks of evil," he muttered through his thick beard.

"Yeah, but I think this is the way we have to go," Bishop admitted. He pulled a small hand drawn map out of his pocket and unfolded it. "According to Lydia, the altar room is just through that door," he said, pointing to a single door on the far side of the room. Pushing the paper back into his pocket, he turned to face his team. "Should we wait for the others?"

"To delay might give the Triad enough time to complete the ritual," Piper said, holding a blood-stained cloth to her head.

Hayden nodded. "I agree. If we want to stop this, we need to go now." Bishop turned to Galen. "There are going to be some powerful magicks in that room, can you protect us?"

"I will do my best," the old witch smiled.

"Then it's agreed."

Bishop turned around and took a deep breath. Mustering all his courage, he took a step into the room and looked around. Confidence began to build inside him. He moved up the carpet. A loud crack caught his attention. Twisting his head around, he glanced nervously over the room. There was no one inside but the team. Looking up, he searched the ceiling. No sign of anything. The air in the room became still as everyone stopped and waited.

Bishop turned back to his team. "Did you hear that?"

Hayden nodded. "I...." he stopped. Bishop watched his eyes grow to the size of softballs.

"What?"

Hayden stumbled back.

Bishop felt the hairs on the back of his neck stand up. Turning slowly, he came face to face with an Anubis statue, its staff held at the ready. Without thinking, Bishop dove to the ground and rolled forward just as the dog-headed statue swung down. Its staff hit the marble floor creating a long, jagged crack. The team scattered as Anubis stepped back and sank down into an attack position. Taking the initiative, Hayden leapt forward with taser in hand. Before he could connect, though, Anubis brought his staff around catching him squarely in the midsection. Finishing the swing, Anubis sent Hayden careening into the far wall. Hayden heard a sharp snap as his back hit the wall. He instantly crumbled to the floor.

Lifting up, Bishop found himself directly behind Anubis. Sprinting forward, he leapt up and sprung off the outstretched calf of Anubis. His leap propelled him onto the statue's back. Snapping his arms up, Bishop latched onto Anubis' pointy ears. Anubis squealed as he tried to shake the man loose.

Letting one ear go, Bishop reared back and punched him hard in the back of the head. Letting out a roar, Bishop pulled his hand back completely broken, realizing Anubis was still a statue.

Flipping his staff above his head, Anubis skilfully struck Bishop and knocked him off in one fluid swipe. Bishop hit the floor and skidded back, the wind knocked out of him. As he struggled for breath, he caught sight of Galen approaching. Anubis snapped around to face the old man and produced a low, guttural growl. Standing straight up, his lips peeled back on his muzzle showing his impressive teeth.

Galen was unfazed by the display. Holding his staff in front of him, he slammed it against the ground. "You've been a very bad doggy," he sneered.

Twirling his staff above his head like a samurai, Anubis launched into another attack, the powerful muscles on his body rippling. Still in midstep, he swung the staff down toward Galen. The old man, showing surprising agility, easily sidestepped the attack and countered. He whipped his staff around catching Anubis behind the ankle. Pulling hard, he toppled the mighty beast. The room trembled as Anubis hit the floor. Rolling onto his upper back, the Egyptian warrior kicked his legs and righted his mighty frame. Flipping his staff around his body, he sent another attack at Galen. Snapping his staff up, Galen blocked. Twirling his hands, Galen pushed Anubis' staff to the ground and pressed the attack. Galen vaulted off the floor, his feet hitting Anubis in the chest. The mighty creature stumbled back, but easily recovered.

Landing just left of Anubis, Galen somersaulted forward and was back on his feet just in time to block another attack, but this time, Anubis was ready for him. He dropped down and leapt forward, hitting Galen in the back with his head. The mighty warrior stood over the old man with saliva dripping from the pursed corners of his mouth. Lifting his golden staff, he prepared for the final strike.

Focusing the remainder of his energy, Galen rolled onto his back and pointed his staff at Anubis. Summoning all his power, he released it in one mighty blast.

Anubis howled in horror as the discharge ripped through his midsection and threw him back. Hitting the wall, his legs crumbled beneath him. His torso hit the ground with a thud and became still. Galen lifted himself off the ground and hobbled toward his fallen adversary. Lifting his staff one final time, he brought it down against the back of Anubis' head. The strength of the blow shattered it completely. Shards of black stone skittered across the floor in all directions as Galen fell back in pain.

Piper, standing out of harm's way the whole time, rushed to his side. "Galen, you were magnificent!" She lifted him onto her lap, cradling his head.

"Thank you, my dear," Galen said through his pain, "but I fear it has come at too high a cost."

Bishop, with a battered Hayden in tow, slumped down next to the old witch. "Thank you, my friend," he said, placing a hand on Galen's chest. "You saved us all."

Galen pressed his hand to Bishop's, "That has yet to be seen." With a cough, his head fell back limp.

Piper felt her eyes well up with tears. "No…."

Bishop shook his head. "Don't cry. Witches don't want to be mourned in death. They want their lives to be celebrated." Bishop squeezed Galen's hand. "Thank you." Standing up, he helped Hayden to his feet. "Are you okay?"

Hayden wrapped an arm painfully around his chest. "I think I'm broken," he laughed, but stopped as a burst of pain erupted in his chest. "I hit the wall pretty hard."

"We can't go in there like this," Bishop said as he stared at his broken hand. "We wouldn't last a moment. We don't have a choice. We have to wait for reinforcements." With his good hand, he lifted his walkie-talkie out of his pocket. "This is Delta Team, does anyone copy?"

***

Cane lifted his radio to his mouth. "Good to hear your voice, Bishop. We were beginning to worry."

"Don't stop on our account," Bishop said quickly. *"We just fought a twelve-foot-tall Anubis statue and we've lost two team members."*

Cane hung his head. "Who?"

"Galen and Jinx."

"What happened?" Lydia asked from behind Cane.

"Galen died protecting us from Anubis. We lost Jinx earlier."

347

"Where are you?" Cane asked.

"In the throne room on the second floor. We're right outside the altar room."

"Stay there," Cane instructed. "We've met up with Alpha Team in the great hall and we're on our way. We'll mount the charge together."

"Acknowledged."

Cane turned around to Weiss. "Are you ready for this?" Weiss nodded. "I've been waiting for nothing else."

***

Osiris was in agony. The snake inside her was becoming fat off her life. With each moment, it grew larger and she grew weaker. Looking out the corner of her eye, she watched the body on the table becoming more and more human in appearance. It had almost lost its transparency, but was now covered in a thick layer of slime. The flesh was starting to turn pink. She had to act now before it was too late, before she no longer possessed the strength. She would not let Isis do this to them. Harnessing the last shreds of her strength, she focused them on her stomach. She felt the snake inside wriggling in pain as it tried to fight her. Osiris knew this was the only chance she would have. Isis' power was spread too thinly. She was vulnerable.

Unleashing a blast of power, Osiris annihilated the snake in one quick blow. Ripping her arms away from her chest, she broke free of the magical bonds holding her. She slumped to the ground, her tired frame unable to hold her up. Osiris took a deep breath of Isis' magick and channeled it into her body. Renewed, she stood to face her Queen. Isis was unaware she had broken free. She was still focused on the body and Horus. That alone was enough to complete the ritual. Osiris glanced over at the body. It was almost complete. Lifting her hands, she pointed at Isis and unleashed a powerful burst of energy. The wave hit Isis squarely in the chest, knocking her through the rear wall.

Lifting herself off the ground, Isis snapped her attention to her attacker through the haze of dust. Her eyes pulsed with power. "I knew I couldn't trust you," her voice echoed. It had changed. It sounded as if a cacophony of voices spoke in unison for her.

"I will repay you for your treachery."

Lifting her hand, she tossed Osiris into the air. Osiris quickly countered the attack with another blast of power. Isis fell to the ground amidst a pile of rubble but was easily back on her feet. Stepping through the hole in the wall, she balled up her fists and screamed. Osiris cupped her hands over her ears, but it wasn't enough. She doubled over in pain as she felt a trickle of blood run down her earlobe. Summoning her strength, she raised her hand and lifted Isis off the ground. Swinging her hand to the right, she sent Isis crashing into the wall. Osiris quickly reversed her course and slammed her into the opposite wall. Lifting her hand again, she spun Isis in the middle of the room, finally sending her sailing into one of the statues next to the altar.

Isis let out a moan as she picked herself up. Wiping her hand across her mouth, she saw a smear of blood. "Is that all you've got?"

Snatching her staff off the floor, Isis threw it like a javelin at Osiris. The end of the staff tore through her shoulder and sent her sailing into the wall. The two came to rest pinned almost a foot off the ground. Osiris watched in terror as the gold cobra uncoiled and slithered down the staff. The cobra stopped inches from her face and fluffed its hood.

"With one command, my serpent will strike," warned Isis. "I have injected it with a venom more toxic than any created in the animal kingdom. If it strikes, it will pump my magically charged blood into yours. It will course through your veins destroying everything with which it comes in contact. This will have the unfortunate side effect of death I'm afraid." Isis smiled broadly.

"Go to hell," Osiris gasped in pain. Lifting her hand, she snatched the cobra by the throat and whipped it across the room. Holding up her hand, she threw all her remaining power at Isis. A bolt a blue energy arced off Osiris' fingertips hitting Isis just below her collarbone. A white light enveloped the room, engulfing everything. The force of the blast leveled Isis and everything around her.

***

Alpha and Beta Teams charged into the throne room to find Bishop, Hayden and Piper still gathered around Galen and the broken Anubis statue. Bishop looked up at Lydia, "Galen died bravely."

Lydia nodded. "I know."

Cane glanced over to the far door just as a flash of white light erupted from beneath it. The door stretched and bent, but held to the frame. "What the hell is going on in there?"

Weiss started toward the door. "They're completing the ritual. We need to hurry!"

Lydia reached out and grabbed Weiss by the arm. "Wait," she said evenly.

"That's not what's happening."

"How do you know?" Weiss asked. Lydia winked at him.

"What's going on?" Bishop asked.

"I can't tell for sure," Lydia replied, "but the ritual has failed. Something has interrupted it."

"Should we get in there?" Cane wondered.

"No," Lydia smiled. "Let this play out. Everything's going to be okay."

"We need to move now," Weiss protested. "My daughter could be dying in there."

"No," Lydia shook her head, "she's all right. It is not our battle anymore. We've done our part."

"To hell with that!" Weiss dug his hand into his jacket pocket producing a pistol. Taking a step back from the group, he leveled the weapon. "I'm going in there. If anyone tries to stop me, I swear to God I'll kill them."

The group took an uneasy step back in unison. Cane held up his hands and patted the air. "Hold on, Tom. You need to relax."

"Relax?" An increasingly frantic Weiss yelled. "How the hell do you expect me to do that? Zombies and killer statues have attacked us! I think we should all be a little on edge," he said. "I just want to get my daughter and get out of this godforsaken place."

"Tom," Cane said, taking a step forward.

"Stop right there, Cane," Weiss yelled as he snapped back the hammer on his gun. "I'm not afraid to use this, even on you." He shook the weapon. "I'm going in there!" He momentarily glanced back at the door.

Seizing the opportunity, Cane reached out for the gun. Just as his fingers hit the barrel, Weiss returned his attention.

"No!" Weiss' eyes widened as he pulled the trigger. The bullet erupted from the barrel with a flash.

Lydia quickly raised her hand, her face completely serene. Time froze around her. Walking slowly around Cane she looked disapprovingly at the two former friends. The bullet was hanging motionlessly in the air just inches from Cane's chest. If it had hit, it would have killed him instantly. Reaching over, Lydia plucked the bullet from the air and pointed it toward one of the windows in the room. She knew when she started time again, the bullet would still carry all its momentum. Standing back, she lifted her hand and released her hold.

Cane and Weiss stumbled back, looking at each other as the bullet whizzed out the window. Cane pressed his hands to his chest. He knew he heard the shot, but he was fine. His face grew angry as he looked at Weiss.

"You son of a bitch," Cane growled.

Weiss quickly cocked back the hammer of the gun. "I won't miss again." Lydia angrily stepped between them. "Stop! I will not let you do this!" She pointed her finger at Weiss. The gun crumbled to dust in his hand. "Look at what you are doing to each other. You two were friends once. See what you have been reduced to?"

Each dropped their head in shame. Guilt began to overwhelm them. Whether it was their own, or it was produced by Lydia, it had a profound effect on both.

Lydia turned to Weiss. "Your daughter is not in there," she assured him. Weiss nodded.

She spun to face Cane. "Dawn's future is still uncertain," she admitted, "but you have no bearing on this outcome. We must allow things to play out as they should, we were not meant to be involved in this final conflict. We have done our part, and that is all we can do." Lydia took a deep breath. "We must have faith that everything will turn out as it should."

***

After the smoke cleared, Osiris looked around the room. Everything stood in shambles. The altar, the table and two of the walls had been completely obliterated. Horus and the new body were lying still on the floor. Isis could not be seen. Reaching up, Osiris grabbed the end of Isis' staff and pulled it out of her shoulder. She slumped to the floor in pain. Turning to her left, she saw the golden cobra slithering toward her. Raising the staff, she smashed it down on the creature's head, killing it. Osiris took a deep breath and rested her head on the wall.

353

Glancing to her left, she spotted a hand beneath a pile of rubble. Lifting to her knees, she crawled toward it. Using the last bit of her strength, she began to pull the debris away. Slowly, she uncovered Isis' body. She was bloody, broken and clearly dead. The blast had severed her head from her body and blown a huge hole in her chest. It was over. Osiris fell back on the floor and closed her eyes.

"Is that all you've got?" a voice asked.

Osiris sat up and snapped open her eyes. Twisting her head around, she watched in horror as the new body lifted itself off the floor. The body hadn't properly formed. It looked something like a proto-human with no features. It was still semi-transparent, allowing the veins, bones and organs to be clearly visible. The face was smooth and genderless; it had eyes and a mouth, but lacked a nose. Ooze still dripped off the proto body.

"You transferred in before you died," Osiris gasped.

Isis nodded. "This body may not be perfect, but it will give me the opportunity to try again. And," Isis said with a smile, "it will give me the chance to kill you."

Osiris bowed her head. She had almost nothing left. It wasn't enough to fight.

Isis stood up and faced the other woman. Lifting her hands up, she laughed manically. "I will truly enjoy this." She pushed her hands forward....

Nothing.

A quizzical look crossed Isis' face. She pushed her hands forward again with the same results. "I don't understand."

Osiris tossed back her head and laughed. "You have no powers! In your haste, you didn't let the body develop enough!"

Isis sneered. "I still have the strength to kill you with my bare hands." Osiris shook her head and stood up. Lifting Isis' staff off the ground, she held it firmly in her hands. "I don't think so." Charging forward, she lifted the staff and plunged it into Isis' chest. She watched the golden tip cleave the proto-body's heart.

Isis stumbled back, her hands wrapped around the staff. "If I die, you die as well." As she coughed, blood erupted from her mouth. "It's my magick binding you to that body."

"I know," Osiris smiled.

Isis sunk down to the floor. "Why?"

"I would rather rule in Hell," Osiris smiled. As Isis' body died, her own began to weaken. She slowly sat down next to Isis. "I wanted it all," she admitted. "You were right. This body was everything I wanted. Once I had it, I couldn't stand to give it up."

Isis smiled softly and nodded.

Osiris placed her hands on the staff. "Shall we?"

Isis reached out and placed her hand on Osiris' shoulder. "You were always a good friend."

Osiris smiled. "It would be my pleasure to serve my Queen this one last time."

Isis moved her hands further up the shaft of the staff. She waited as Osiris tightened her grip. Isis nodded. The two plunged the staff through Isis' heart until it broke through her back. The metal tip of the staff hit the wall with a sharp clink. The two women looked at each other one final time as they fell over amidst the rubble.

Chapter Twenty-seven

Bishop pushed open the door and stepped inside. He was met with a scene of total chaos. The room was in shambles. Everything had been destroyed. Four bodies were immediately visible. His eyes widened when he spotted Dawn lying on the floor. Rushing in, he dropped down next to her and brushed away a pile of rubble she was half buried under. Leaning down, he held his ear just above her mouth. A smile grew across his face when he felt her warm breath on his cheek. Pressing his fingers to her throat, he felt a pulse.

Cane was next into the room. He moved to Bishop's side and looked down at Dawn. "Is she...?"

Bishop looked up at Cane with his smile. "She's alive, but she needs a doctor."

Cane signaled to Django, who was standing in the door. "Get help."

Dawn slowly opened her eyes. She let out a soft moan of pain. "Cane...." Cane lifted her hand into his. "It's okay, Dawn. Lie still. Help's on the way." Bishop turned his head and spotted a familiar blond. "Oh my God," he breathed. Standing up, he moved to Kelley's body. Falling to his knees, he paused. Slowly at first, he moved his hand toward her face. With his fingertips, he brushed a strand of her hair away from her face and stopped. She was warm. Leaning over, he lifted her arm and pressed his fingers against her wrist. To his amazement, he found a pulse. "Kelley...."

Leaning over, he pressed his ear to her chest and listened. His eyes widened. She wasn't breathing. Bishop pushed her chin back and opened her mouth. Pinching her nose closed, he exhaled into her. He waited for a moment and repeated. He held his ear near her mouth. His heart skipped. "I'm not losing you again." He breathed into her again and checked her pulse. Nothing. She was fading. "Damn," he said softly and sat back. Dropping his head, he pinched the bridge of his nose as he fought back the tears.

Kelley suddenly lurched forward coughing. Astonished, Bishop rolled her onto her side and began to rub her back. "Kelley?"

Kelley arched her back as she sucked in a deep breath. "Bish," she coughed again.

Joyously, Bishop slipped his arm under and lifted her to his chest. Her arms slowly wrapped around his back. "It's good to have you back," he said softly.

Kelley coughed again, but finally regained some control of her breathing. "Good to be back," she wheezed.

Weiss stepped in and stopped. His tired eyes scanned the room. "Is my daughter in here?"

Cane glanced up from Dawn and shook his head. "I'm sorry, Tom." Bishop looked over at the chairman. He knew where Lexy was, and he knew what Lexy had become. He wondered for a moment if he should tell him, or if that would kill him. He had come out here to prove his daughter's innocence— they all had—only to find out that, in fact, she had been involved in the murders.

A guilt pang hit his stomach. He turned and looked at Kelley, then looked back at Weiss. "Chairman Weiss, Lexy is—"

358

"Daddy?" a weak voice asked from outside the room.

Weiss spun around to see his daughter teetering on weak legs. He immediately wrapped his arms around her for support and in relief. "Lexy," he sighed. The two sunk to the floor together. "Are you okay?"

Lexy nodded. "I just need to rest."

"Once we get out of here, you can sleep as much as you want," Weiss promised his daughter.

She ran her bruised and battered fingers over his cheek. "I knew you would come."

Weiss hugged Lexy. "I'm so glad to have you back."

Lydia and Hayden walked into the room and stood between Bishop and Cane. Lydia knelt down next to Cane and placed her hand on Dawn's forehead. "It will take more than a doctor to treat these two," she admitted. "They have both suffered extremely severe magick related trauma. It will take a skilled psychic healer to mend the wounds completely." Cane started to speak, but Lydia stopped him. "They will stay here with me in Seattle until they are healed. My coven will help them with their recovery."

Cane nodded in approval.

Hayden smiled. "So, another case solved for the Office of Paranormal Research?"

Bishop laughed and extended his hand to Hayden. "We couldn't have done this without you."

Hayden shook his hero's hand. "It was an honor."

"The honor was mine," Bishop said respectfully.

Above them, the full moon broke through the dark clouds and shined down over the city in all its glory. As the teams banded together to help out the wounded, the rain that had been falling for three days finally stopped. Bishop looked up to the sky through a crack in the roof with Kelley still wrapped in his arms. He couldn't help but smile. It was going to be a beautiful night.